Lady
KNIGHT

What Reviewers Say About Bold Strokes Authors

KIM BALDWIN

"'A riveting novel of suspense' seems to be a very overworked phrase. However, it is extremely apt when discussing Kim Baldwin's [*Hunter's Pursuit*]. An exciting page turner [features] Katarzyna Demetrious, a bounty hunter…with a million dollar price on her head. Look for this excellent novel of suspense…" – *MegaScene*

"*Force of Nature* is an exciting and substantial reading experience which will long remain with the reader. Likeable characters with plausible problems and concerns, imaginative settings, engrossing events, and a well-tailored writing style all contribute to an exceptional novel. Baldwin's characterization is acutely and meticulously circumscribed and expansive." – *Midwest Book Review*

RONICA BLACK

"Black juggles the assorted elements of her first book, [*In Too Deep*], with assured pacing and estimable panache…[including]…the relative depth—for genre fiction—of the central characters: Erin, the married-but-separated detective who comes to her lesbian senses; loner Patricia, the policewoman-mentor who finds herself falling for Erin; and sultry club owner Elizabeth, the sexually predatory suspect who discards women like Kleenex…until she meets Erin." – *Book Marks, Q Syndicate, 2005*

"Black's characterization is skillful, and the sexual chemistry surrounding the three major characters is palpable and definitely hot-hot-hot. If you're looking for a more traditional murder mystery, *In Too Deep* might not be entirely your cup of Earl. On the other hand, if you're looking for a solid read with ample amounts of eroticism and a red herring or two, you're sure to find *In Too Deep* a satisfying read." – *L-Word.com Literature*

ROSE BEECHAM

"…her characters seem fully capable of walking away from the particulars of whodunit and engaging the reader in other aspects of their lives." – *Lambda Book Report*

ROSE BEECHAM (CONT)

"When Jennifer Fulton writes mysteries, she writes them as Rose Beecham. And since Jennifer Fulton is a very fine writer, you might expect that Rose Beecham is a fine writer too. You're right… On the way to a remarkable, and thoroughly convincing climax, Beecham creates believable characters in compelling situations, with enough humor to provide effective counterpoint to the work of detecting." – *Bay Area Reporter*

GUN BROOKE

"*Course of Action* is a romance…populated with a host of captivating and amiable characters. The glimpses into the lifestyles of the rich and beautiful people are rather like guilty pleasures…a most satisfying and entertaining reading experience." – *Midwest Book Review*

"*Protector of the Realm* has it all; sabotage, corruption, erotic love and exhilarating space fights. Gun Brooke's second novel is forceful with a winning combination of solid characters and a brilliant plot." – *JustAboutWrite*

JANE FLETCHER

"*The Walls of Westernfort* is not only a highly engaging and fast-paced adventure novel, it provides the reader with an interesting framework for examining the same questions of loyalty, faith, family and love that [the characters] must face." – *Midwest Book Review*

LEE LYNCH

"There's a heady sense of '60s back-to-the-land communal idealism and '70s woman-power feminism (with hints of lesbian separatism) to this spirited novel—even though it's set in contemporary rural Oregon. Partners Donny (she's black and blue-collar) and Chick (she's plus-sized and motherly) are both in their 50s, owners of the dyke-centric Natural Woman Foods store, a homey nexus for *Sweet Creek*'s expansive cast of characters…Lynch, with a dozen novels to her credit dating back to the early days of Naiad Press, has earned her stripes as a writerly elder. She was contributing stories to the lesbian magazine *The Ladder* four decades ago. But this latest is sublimely in tune with the times." – *Book Marks, Q Syndicate, 2005*

Lady
KNIGHT

by

L-J Baker

2007

LADY KNIGHT

ISBN 10: 1-933110-75-9
ISBN 13: 978-1-933110-75-2

This Trade Paperback Is Published By
Bold Strokes Books, Inc.,
New York, USA

First Edition, April 2007

Credits
Editors: Cindy Cresap and J. Barre Greystone
Production Design: J. Barre Greystone
Cover Graphic: Sheri (graphicartist2020@hotmail.com)

By the Author

BROKEN WINGS

Acknowledgments

I cannot thank Cindy enough for her skill, insight, and wickedly funny comment balloons. This is a better book because of her editing—even with *that* scene in it. It has been a pleasure working with her. Thanks to Julie for her diligence, for keeping me adhering to arcane grammar laws, and for kindly providing me with the opportunity to correct a copyeditor's spelling. (Only once: but I shall treasure it.) Without B, I couldn't write a word. Kudos to AndiM for help with the blurb. Sheri, mate, I know the cover for this book was a right royal pain, but you played a blinder. (Yes, that means you did great.)

DEDICATION

In memory of S. T. Baker
(12th April 1939 to 6th October 2006)

No dyke had a better Dad.

You showed me how to catch a cricket ball. We watched rugby tests together. You delighted in calling me Dr Baker. You made my wife welcome as another daughter-in-law. You were so stoked about me writing books and putting my own name on them. I didn't arrive at the hospital in time for you to see my first book, but I held your hand to the end.

You're not here to see it, but I'll always try to make you proud of me.

CHAPTER ONE

R iannon of Gast felt the first pain knifing down her chest as she craned her neck to see the top of the castle keep through the narrow eye slits of her helm. She gritted her teeth on a grunt. She could see no enemy archers or crossbowmen on the roof of the keep. A couple of men dropped rocks from up there. The rocks might crack a few heads of her soldiers breaking down the keep door, but would not prevent the breach. She turned to the knight at her side.

"Get some archers up on the corner tower," she said.

He nodded and hurried away.

Agony stabbed under her skin from right shoulder to left hip. Riannon grimaced as she waited for it to pass again. *Mighty Atuan, lord of battle, that hurt.*

The pains sprang from no wound taken this day, but had they flared while she fought, they could have distracted her with fatal results. Since winter last, the pains had grown stronger and more frequent.

Riannon wished she could slump and remove her heavy iron helm to feel the wind on her sweaty face and to suck in air that did not have to pass through the small holes in the metal, but the fighting was not yet done.

The defenders had foolishly left the stairs up to the first storey keep door intact when they retreated inside. Her men had easy access to batter the door. One of them fell screaming with half his brains dashed out by a dropped rock before bowmen drove the defenders from the keep roof. The end would not be long now.

Riannon stepped over the twisted body of one of the defenders and strode through the smoky haze and noise filling the bailey. The dead of both sides lay in bloody tangles scattered across the courtyard inside the walls. A fire had broken out in the kitchen building. Pigs, which had been herded in to feed the defenders, squealed their fright at the din, smoke, and stink of blood.

Not all the corpses strewn across the hard-packed earth were combatants. Flies crawled across the face of a grey-haired woman sprawled near the entrance to the temple. Women's shrieks added to the last groans of the dying. Frightened villagers had crowded into the castle for safety. Where their lord had retreated into the fastness of the thick-walled keep once the battering ram had bashed down the main gate, those who had sought his protection were left to the mercy of the attackers. Had the fool surrendered, no one need have died here today.

"Sir?" The squire who halted near Riannon had blood spattered up along the mail on his sword arm. The congealing scarlet stained the white stag badge of Roger of Damory. "Lord Damory wishes you to know that a messenger has arrived from his Grace, Count Berenger. His lordship wishes you to attend him, sir. He's in his tent."

A pox on them both. Riannon had no desire to learn in what manner his Grace had changed his mind this time for the conduct of the siege. Whatever these new instructions, they were somewhat late. Nor did it surprise her that Damory was already back in his tent, no doubt quaffing wine and boasting of his cleverness in command. However, since she was currently in service to his Grace, Count Berenger of Tastamont, Riannon could not ignore his will, even when she thought his Grace one of the most addle-pated fools ever born of woman. And one, moreover, whom the gods should never have entrusted with the lordship of a dovecote or midden, let alone one of the largest counties in the Eastern Kingdoms. Nor could she tell his Grace that Damory, his son-in-law, was a lazy, cowardly whoreson.

Before Riannon could speak, she heard a splintering and a cheer. She turned to see the door of the keep staved in. Her men swarmed up the keep steps. Attackers met them with flashing swords.

"Tell his lordship I shall be there presently," she said.

Riannon strode towards the keep. A woman's scream pierced the din. Riannon lifted her bloody sword. She stalked to the temple and stepped past the body of the old woman.

The gloom inside the temple seethed with cringing, sobbing people. Riannon saw three men holding down a wailing young woman, her skirts wadded up past her hips. One man climbed atop her. In two swift strides Riannon was close enough to deliver a stunning blow to the back of his head with the flat of her sword. The man crumpled. His accomplices jerked around. She saw outrage turn to surprise, then fear. They wore white stag badges. She had issued the strongest orders about honouring the sanctity of a holy place, and against rape. Bleakly, she found it no surprise that Damory's men would again prove so ill-disciplined.

"Alan," Riannon said.

Her squire, who had dogged her heels through the fighting, stepped forwards.

"Hang these men," she said.

"Yes, sir."

The woman rose and clutched her torn bodice closed. She gave Riannon a surprise in being neither priestess, servant, nor peasant refugee. Her pale blue gown might have belonged to a lady's maid or gentlewoman.

"My thanks, sir." The woman dropped a practised curtsy.

Under other circumstances, Riannon would have tarried to learn more, but she had a capture still to make and a siege to end. At the door, she ordered two trustworthy men to guard the temple and ensure no further violations took place.

In the keep, the defenders had already been beaten back from their best positions in the constricted entry. Riannon pushed past her own men to gain the main chamber. The fighting blazed savage. Two defending knights in gory mail hauberks stood back to back near a broken overturned chest. Another pair fought a desperate guard on the far door. They must realise they were doomed. Bodies of their fallen comrades and Riannon's men already littered the floor. The knights' diligence and courage were more than their lord deserved. They certainly did not warrant a hopeless death while their master barricaded himself in a chamber above.

"Stop!" Riannon shouldered aside one of her men. "Halt!"

Saer Warin, a stocky Bralland-born knight, bellowed for a cease. Like Riannon, he grabbed a soldier and pulled him back when he might have entered the fray. A quick-thinking pair of squires blocked the door.

A few more blows clanged before the fighting stopped. The four blood-spattered defenders breathed heavily. Their mailed shoulders lifted and fell from their exertions. Two wore the older style helmets with only nasal guards protecting their faces, so their confusion was easy to see. All kept their bloody swords at the ready.

"There's no need for slaughter," Riannon said. "His Grace of Tastamont wishes your lord's submission, not his death. You do him no dishonour by yielding."

The one with a black beard jutting out of his mail coif stared warily up at Riannon's helm as though he tried to read her expression through the metal. His gaze dropped to fix on her chest. He would see the black, eight-pointed star painted on the blood-spattered white linen surcoat she wore over her mail shirt.

"A Knight of the Star," he said. "If you give your word, sir, that our lord isn't to be slain here, we'll ask if we may surrender."

"You have it," she said.

He pounded on the door at his back and called to whoever stood behind it to convey their predicament to his lordship.

One of the wounded groaned and writhed on the floor. Riannon signalled for men to remove him. He screamed as his comrades lifted him. Riannon had seen enough wounds to know that he would not live until dawn, no matter how many healer-priests laboured over him.

As she waited, her old wounds throbbed to unholy life again, though mercifully for but a brief span. When Lord Grammaire finally appeared, Riannon unlaced her helm and removed it as a courtesy to his lordship.

The sleek Grammaire, whose yellow surcoat showed no blemish from the fight, grinned sardonically up at her. "I'd heard rumours of the scar-faced one, but I wouldn't have wagered a groat there was sufficient gold in all the kingdom to induce a Knight of the Star to sully himself in the service of our noble Lord Berenger."

Riannon ignored both his scathingly sarcastic tone and the open criticism of her patron. "Do I have your surrender, my lord?"

"You have my castle," he said. "I doubt me not that my life is worth less than dog's piss, but who'd rather not hang tomorrow than be hacked to death today? Here."

Riannon accepted his sword. Whatever new ideas Count Berenger's messenger had brought, his lordship could not but be pleased to forgo them now that Grammaire had surrendered.

Riannon paused in the bailey to slip her hands free of her mail mittens. She pushed her mail coif, and the linen one beneath it, back from her head and ran her fingers through her sweaty, short-cropped hair. It was a relief to feel the breeze, no matter how warm and smoky, on her head.

Riannon took a wineskin from her ever-resourceful squire. She drank a long pull before resuming her walk towards the broken gate and the delayed meeting with Lord Damory.

Even so peevish and capricious a master as Count Berenger must reward her well for this success. Were he to finally make good his vague offers of the lordship of a manor or two, she would not refuse. Men had served worse masters and kept their personal honour intact. His son, at least, promised to be a lord she would be proud to serve. And what knight would not be happier with his own lands and the prospect of more in the service of a wealthy lord, rather than continue the rootless and uncertain life and rewards to be found at tourneys and wars?

The great wooden mangonels, which had creaked and thudded to hurl boulders to crack against the walls, were silent for the first time in days. The artillerymen celebrated with looted ale and wine. Riannon strode past them across the churned ground to where Damory's gaudy yellow and red tent stood. Doubtless the celebrations in there included a heavy dose of self-congratulation. Ere nightfall, if not sooner, Damory would convince himself that he was solely responsible for the success of the siege and had taken Grammaire's surrender himself.

Pain sliced through Riannon's body. She stopped with a gasp. The whole length of the crosswise scar on her torso felt as though dagger blades jabbed into her flesh. The wineskin dropped from nerveless fingers and she drew her arms protectively against her chest.

"Sir?" Alan stepped in front of her.

Riannon grabbed his shoulder to keep herself from collapsing. Pain first burned with white-hot heat, then seared with cold. *Mighty Atuan, help me!*

"Is it your old wounds, lady?" Alan said.

"Tent," she said.

Riannon grunted as her squire hooked her arm around his neck and supported her to her tent.

Almighty gods, it hurt as badly as her initial wounding, when the strangely singing sword had scythed through the iron rings of her hauberk, sliced the padded gambeson beneath, and carved her flesh. She should have died then. The ghost pain flayed her with such intensity that

Riannon whispered to Alan to fetch a priest. The alacrity with which he bolted from the tent confirmed that she must look as close unto death as she felt.

❖

Two days later, a sore and stiff Riannon rode half a mile to the sprawling basilica complex where Count Berenger lodged with his large retinue. She had been out of her wits still when he suddenly arrived. Her body, aching with every step of her horse, wished she were still abed. His Grace, though always alive to his own comfort and leisure, was not one to feel much sympathy for the weakness of others. Riannon thought it little short of miraculous that he had sent a gift of food and wine to her from his own table. Mayhap it was a sign that he was finally ready to reward her with land.

Riannon suppressed a grunt as she dismounted. Whatever ailed her lingered yet, though the healer-priest had not seen anything other than old scars.

In the main hall, Lord Damory lolled beside his father-in-law. The abbot, wearing what must be his best brown robes, looked incongruously solemn amongst the laughing, drinking men in their bright tunics and hose. Riannon did not see Lord Grammaire. She wondered what the count had done with his defiant vassal.

Saer Warin, the Brallandese knight, detached himself from the noisy group to intercept Riannon. He looked grim.

"It's good to see you about again, Gast," he said. "I didn't know you were injured."

"Not recently," Riannon said. "Wounds three years old are plaguing me. What news?"

Warin glanced to the hearth where the count laughed loudly and slapped a thigh. "He's well pleased. And in an unusually open-handed mood. Wish me well, for I leave to get married. He has granted me a widow with two manors."

Warin sounded more relieved at the prospect of departing than delighted with his good marriage. Riannon was unsurprised when he admitted, quietly, that Damory had taken full credit for the success of the siege and capture of Lord Grammaire. As a hired knight she stood in no position to gainsay the count's son-in-law. Well, let him wear his borrowed glory, as long as she received a more tangible reward. The gods, if not his conscience, would know the truth of the matter.

Lord Damory caught sight of her and beckoned her closer. "Gast! We feared you in a winding sheet when we heard of the leeches hovering about you."

Riannon's chest ached fiercely as she lowered herself to one knee before Count Berenger. He smiled at her over his wine goblet.

"Gast," he said. "Roger has been speaking well of you. He says that you've been a most diligent captain. I'm well pleased to have solved the problem of that snake Grammaire. Here. Take this as a sign of my favour."

Riannon heard murmurs of amazement and envy from the watching men as the count pulled off one of his rings. The chunky gold was warm and weighty in her palm. Her hopes soared. Warin had not been jesting about this lavish dispensing of largesse.

"You may rise. I will, of course, be following that with a goodly purse." His eyes twinkled and he laughed. "What a shame I have no young heir to bestow on you. Or would an heiress be more to your liking, my Lady Riannon?"

The men took their cues from his Grace and joined his laughter. Riannon's fingers tightened on the ring, and she kept her disappointment to herself.

"*Lady?*"

A vaguely familiar man with a jutting black beard pushed indignantly through the ring of men. She remembered him as one of Lord Grammaire's knights.

"A woman?" he said. "But this cannot be! He is a Knight of the Star. If you seek to demean my lord further with this jest, my lord count, I protest though it cost me my head."

Count Berenger smiled. "Knew you not that she is a woman? Though, for certès, it isn't obvious."

The knight's face suffused with fury. "My lord surrendered in good faith on the word of this…this *person*. Now you tell me his trust was for nought? That you played him false by making him swear to a woman?"

Riannon's hand dropped to the hilt of her sword. "You question my honour?"

"Not if you're female," he said. "For you have none and know nought of it. I ask you, my lord count, to account for my lord's safety. Will you swear to me that he's safe in your custody?"

"I pledged you my word," Riannon said.

"Your lord is beyond all possible harm," Count Berenger said.

Damory laughed. It was an ugly sound.

"He rests with the gods," Berenger said.

Riannon frowned at him. Grammaire's knight hissed and reached for a sword that he did not carry.

"Mind your tongue and temper," Berenger said, "or you'll be joining your faithless master. Get this dog out of my sight."

The knight shrugged off the grabbing hands long enough to turn to Riannon and spit at her. "May you rot in the deepest hell for impersonating a man."

Riannon watched as three of Berenger's men dragged him outside. Beyond the ache of her old wounds, she felt a hard, sinking coldness that tasted of gall. It was no less bitter for being familiar.

"He's fortunate that I'm in such a good humour," Berenger said, "or I'd hang him, too. Now, where is that accursed minstrel? Gast, you're not drinking? You there, give her wine."

Riannon ignored the offered cup. "My lord, I pledged my word that you sought not Lord Grammaire's death."

The count waved that aside. "Now that you're walking again, I expect you to accompany me to Destan. I'll hold a tourney there for my son's knighting. I expect you to captain my team."

Riannon should have been elated to be granted such a prestigious position. But she inverted her hand and opened her fingers to let the gold ring fall to the rushes. The soft thud cut off the chatter around them. Damory gaped like a landed carp. Disbelief and anger tightened the count's face.

"With your permission, your Grace," she said, "I'll take my leave. My service to you is ended."

"You dare!" he said. "You'll get not a penny from me."

"I did not expect it," she said.

His face pinched and his lips thinned to pale, compressed lines. "I could have you flogged. Hanged. And where do you think you'll get any other man to take on a...a female who plays the man?"

Riannon wanted to kill him. She kept her thoughts to herself and her hands conspicuously away from the hilts of her sword and dagger.

As she reached the door, she heard a burst of laughter. She did not look back. Another failed opportunity that had glittered as brightly as gold but turned to dross when finally within her grasp. The pattern grew long and dispiritingly predictable.

Alan waited with their horses. His face showed dismay in reaction to what he saw in her expression.

Riannon took her reins from him. "We're leaving."

"Where do we go?" he asked.

Riannon settled in the saddle and put a hand to the ache that mounting had tugged across her stomach. "East."

"The war in southern Kardash that the bard spoke of? Aye, there should be work there aplenty. And good pickings."

Riannon saw the body hanging from the branch of an elm tree. She halted her gelding. Even gently swinging in neck-broken death, Lord Grammaire looked tidy. He would likely have died had he not surrendered to her. But it would have been a better death in defence of his castle. Instead, he died like a common criminal despite her having given her word that no harm would come to him. Would Count Berenger have held her honour at nought had she been a man?

Riannon shrugged. Her muscles stabbed with fresh pain. For several heartbeats, she had to sit with a hand gripping the saddle and her teeth ground down on a groan. When the crisis passed, she licked sweat from her upper lip.

"My lady?" Alan lowered his voice, though only the dead man might overhear them. "Mayhap I should get you back to the tent and fetch the leech-priest."

He always reverted to "lady" when he was worried about her.

Riannon took several uneasy breaths and straightened. "No. We ride. But I'd not object if we found a grove house to pass the night."

The priestess-healers had saved her life once before, when she thought herself beyond healing and hope. Perhaps they could cure her of this recurrent problem with those same wounds. She doubted, though, that she would ever find a cure for the problem of never belonging or being accepted for what she was.

❖

A few hours past noon on the next day, Alan pointed to the low building of a small grove house set on the edge of woods. Riannon's aches had eased enough yesterday that she had refused to stop at the previous groves they had passed. Since before noon, though, her scars had come alive again with their stabbing hot and cold. She doubted her ability to remain in the saddle much longer. The fact that they were now beyond the lands owned by men who owed allegiance to Berenger of Tastamont reinforced her decision to rest beneath a roof.

The dusty track led across a shallow stream and ended in a rough courtyard bounded by several wooden buildings of different sizes. Smoke poured from two of them.

"Shite," Alan said.

Men, horses, and donkeys crammed the tiny compound and spilled into the surrounding trees. Riannon's gaze quickly skipped from men in green tunics to two covered carriages. The entourage was large enough for a countess, but the green cloth of the carriages—which bore no noble symbols—hinted at a very high-ranking priestess.

When Riannon's feet hit the ground, pain jarred her as if someone had sliced her clean through with a sword. She clung to the saddle and bit back an oath. She still fought to recover her breathing when her squire returned.

"We're unfortunate," Alan said. "All these people belong to the escort of no less a person than a naer of the groves. The exalted lady rests here this night. They've no beds nor space to spare for travellers. But I made an offering of coin, and we can camp in a clearing through there. I'll have John take the horses."

Riannon grunted.

"They have a healer priestess," Alan said. "She'll see you if you enter the door that is never closed."

Riannon released the saddle and turned. Pain stabbed deep into her chest. Her knees buckled and she pitched into darkness.

Riannon woke with a cool, damp cloth dabbed against her forehead. She lay on a narrow cot looking up at a thatched roof. The tiny room sported only the cot, a rudimentary shelf, and a wooden symbol of the quartered-circle nailed to the wall. A pretty young woman in a faded green robe of a junior priestess sat beside the cot. She wrung the cloth in a wooden bowl of water and softly hummed what sounded like a fairing song rather than a hymn. She turned to see Riannon watching her and froze.

"Your…your pardon, lady."

"You make a sweet sound," Riannon said. "Pray, continue."

The priestess glanced over her shoulder towards the door. Riannon heard muffled voices. The priestess shot to her feet and spilled some of the water down the front of her robe.

"I…I'm to inform her Eminence, the naer, when you wake," she said.

"A naer?" Riannon asked.

This place appeared too humble to house a priestess of so elevated a rank, and the nervous young sio in her faded robes seemed an unlikely attendant to such an exalted lady of the order.

"We're blessed beyond imagining," the priestess said. "Her Eminence chose our house to break her travels. She's been with us a day and a night. It's been right cramped. We've had to send for ever so much salted fish and goats and grain. More than I've seen before in my whole life. I have to share a pallet with Sio Gwynis in the cookhouse, for there are scores and scores in the naer's escort. It's marvellous. So colourful. And so many horses and donkeys. Men all talking and jesting. Like a yearly market, though without the mummers. I can scarce believe I'd ever see such a high and mighty lady. And she has spoken to me!"

"If you must be gone, sio, I'll not detain you."

The priestess dropped a hasty curtsy and departed. After the door closed, Riannon allowed herself a grin for the priestess's tumbling enthusiasm and awe. The young woman had probably been born of a peasant family not two miles away and pledged at an early age. It wasn't surprising she had seen no such magnificence before as so august a personage as a naer of the groves. Riannon had rarely witnessed it herself.

Riannon sat up and looked around for her clothes to cover her nakedness. She paused as she shoved the thin woollen blanket aside. She did not hurt.

She frowned down at herself and lifted a hand to the puckered, shiny pink scar slashing across her torso. With a finger she traced part of the old wound where it had cut away most of her right breast and sliced down across her ribs. Her flesh felt no more sensitive than normal. The sickeningly intense pain was but a memory.

"Lady of Mercy and Healing, I thank you."

Riannon traced the quartered circle on her bare skin. She must go to the sacred grove to offer thanks and leave a goodly donation for her healing.

She had pulled on her washed and mended linen shirt and was tugging her chamois riding braies up her thighs when she saw the sword hilt beneath the cot. She knotted the waist tie and frowned. The sword was not hers. The hilt looked functionally plain with unusual hand guards. The quillons curved gently down towards the blade rather than projecting straight out to the sides. The simple round pommel bore no inset stone, enamelling, or engraving.

Instead of reaching for a leg of her hose, Riannon crouched to retrieve the sword. The brown leather-covered scabbard looked recently worked with fat, and bore no decorative tool work. Even the protective metal heel on the bottom was plain save for some scratches from use. It was hard to imagine a less likely object for a previous guest to have left without anyone noticing. Riannon's frown deepened. She was likely within the part of the grove house where men were not permitted. She had heard of no other woman like herself who carried a sword.

The door opened. Riannon stood.

The woman in the doorway was tall for her sex, though she had to look up to Riannon. Her dark green robe, the colour of leaves lit by the dying light of an evening, bore deep bands of embroidery around the collar and hem. That and the gold quartered circle symbol hanging at her waist proclaimed her high status. The visiting naer.

The priestess returned Riannon's study with an equally frank one. Her black hair, green eyes, and angular face were familiar to Riannon for they bore close resemblance to the features she saw mirrored in the surface of still water. Colouring and face were formed by family blood, but the arrogant tilt of the chin was the priestess's own. In the four and more years since Riannon had last seen her, her cousin Aveline had changed little.

Aveline pointedly lowered her gaze to take in Riannon's loose shirt and bare legs. Her lips twitched. "Of course, being close kin we needn't stand on ceremony with each other."

Riannon dropped the sword on the cot and reached for her tunic. "You're not here by accident. What do you want with me?"

Aveline closed the door. The room was so tiny that the hem of her robe brushed Riannon's ankle. Riannon caught a whiff of sandalwood incense.

"As blunt as I recall." Aveline watched Riannon pull her tunic on. "What a refreshing change from the diplomatic language of insinuation, hints, and shadows that is my normal tongue."

"In which you were born fluent."

Aveline smiled. "Enough to know that you meant that as no compliment. Only you could insult a naer within a grove house. I marvel afresh at the Goddess whose wisdom plucked you from the solar and deposited your strapping form in the arms yard. You'd not have succeeded at gossiping over the distaff."

Riannon knew herself no match for Aveline's dextrous tongue. She folded her arms across her chest and waited.

"You've grown no more womanly, have you?" Aveline stared at Riannon's face. "What a fierce expression that ugly scar gives you. It's a miracle you did not lose your eye. Did you get the wound at Vahl?"

Riannon's jaw tightened. "I'd thank you to say what you must and leave me to offer my thanks and depart."

"Believe it or not, you are the answer to my prayers." Aveline cast a disapproving glance around the cramped room. "The Goddess showed me that I needed to come here. I could wish our Wise Mother had seen fit to guide our steps to more salubrious surroundings. Two days in this pest hole is verily a penance. You can have no idea how fervently I've prayed for you to regain your wits, so that we may be away."

"I've much to do ere I take my leave," Riannon said. "Mayhap you could get to your point."

"You've already found it." Aveline used a ring-heavy hand to gesture to the cot. "The sword. It's for you. I should've known better than to have despaired of finding a suitable person for this gift from the Goddess. She has provided you."

Riannon frowned down at the weapon. A sword from the Goddess? That would have raised her suspicions even had Aveline not mentioned Vahl. Riannon's scars were souvenirs from that bloody, prolonged siege of the northern Irulandi city by the emperor's army. She should not have been surprised that Aveline, naer of the groves, knew exactly how Riannon had come by her wounds. Aveline could have learned of it from the priestesses where Riannon had endured her protracted healing and convalescence. Nor was it out of character that Aveline use the knowledge to discomfit Riannon. Aveline's reputation for cleverness and cunning had been born in the nursery, and was not likely to have been blunted by the passing years. But why a sword?

"Why do you frown?" Aveline asked.

"I trust you not."

Aveline laughed. "You tatter my expectations of courtly gallantry from the sole paladin of the Order of the Goddess."

Riannon snapped her head around. Aveline smiled up at her.

"Your order is a womanly one," Riannon said. "You have no sworn knights. What need could the Lady of Mercy and Healing have for a paladin?"

"Ordinarily, we'd have no need. But sometimes we must recourse to less gentle means of achieving our ends. Now is one of those times. I must find and invest a holy warrior. That warrior is you."

Despite her bone-deep misgivings, Riannon stared down at the sword.

"Pledge us your service and you'll be a consecrated knight," Aveline said. "None of the other orders would have you, would they? The brothers of the militant Order of Atuan, god of war, welcomed you until they discovered you were female. Then they spurned you as a creature unnatural. At the basilicas of Kamet and the chapels of Naith, you found no better welcome, did you? How many lords have welcomed your service until they discovered what you are? As good as any man, if not better, but always judged in the end as a woman, and found wanting. Well, cousin, I offer you the purpose and place you always sought. As the paladin of the Goddess."

Could Aveline see inside her to read her past? A paladin? Aveline offered her the chance to dedicate her sword, honour, and self to the glory of a deity, not a flawed mortal. There could be no higher calling.

"Can you doubt that so singular a life as yours has been fashioned by our Wise Mother, in her guise as the Lady of Destiny, for a special fate?" Aveline said. "You are the sword I shall wield. Tempered by adversity. Hardened by war and distrust."

Though still clouded with doubt, and aware of Aveline intensely watching, Riannon reached for the sword to satisfy her curiosity. What manner of blade would the female religious order own?

The wire-bound grip of the hilt fit her hand comfortably. She drew the sword out. The yard of steel glittered with oil from the wool lining the inside of the scabbard. The blade tapered to a point with the narrow groove of the fuller running down the centre of each side. The counter weighting from the round pommel balanced it well. This sword would be easy to swing in a cut as well as to thrust.

Riannon could not identify where it might have been forged. Hilt and pommel were too simple for Marchandese tastes, and the blade too straight for a Themalian to carry. Too long to have been smithed in Iruland, and more slender than those swords normally made in Bralland. Beyond any doubt, though, this was no ceremonial weapon fit only for priestesses to dip in blessed waters. The edges looked razor sharp.

"Come," Aveline said. "Oath-taking and blessing are best done beside the sacred pool."

"I've not accepted your offer." Riannon slid the sword back into the scabbard. "If I dedicate myself, what would you have me do?"

"Live."

Riannon turned in surprise.

"The sword is keeping you alive," Aveline said. "Are you not the least curious to wonder how you can be standing there frowning so forbiddingly at me? Do you not remember the pain before you were carried in here?"

Riannon lifted a hand to her chest. "How can a sword have healed me?"

"It's specially blessed. The virtue in it is combating the insidious power left in the wounds you received at Vahl. They were inflicted by no mortal metal."

That last, Riannon had guessed years ago.

"Though your flesh fused again," Aveline said, "seeds of pain were left buried inside you. As the seasons have passed, they've grown. Left unchecked, you would die. By rights, I should be conducting your funeral as we speak. And, I'm afraid, you are not cured. Nor will you be. Healers of the greatest skill could not purge them. You must keep the sword close for the rest of your life."

"How close?"

Aveline shrugged. "I can give you no exact measure to the closest span. You'd be well advised to keep it at your hip, and not let it farther from you than a hundred yards on those occasions when you must remove it. Certainly you'd not want to be miles apart. The blessing on it is powerful, but not infinite. You'll feel when you're too far beyond it."

Riannon read no deceit in Aveline's voice or expression. That left one conclusion. "I have no choice."

"That's not true. You could take the sword without pledging your service."

"What would you gain from that?"

Aveline flashed her a grin. "Truly, cousin, if you assault fortresses and foes in such a forthright manner, it's small wonder that few withstand you. You do not trust to our generosity? But, surely, you've felt it before. Your healing after Vahl was long. You were tended at a grove for the better part of two seasons, were you not?"

Riannon's jaw tightened. Vahl. Aveline had been holding that knife at her throat since she walked into the room. Riannon owed the order her life. Twice over, now.

Riannon bent to scoop up the sword. "I acknowledge my debts. I'll swear your oaths. I'll pledge my body and honour to the service of the Goddess."

Aveline had far too much wit to gloat openly, then or at dawn when she joined Riannon. After a night in vigil beside the sacred pond, Riannon still knew some doubt. But she offered her oath solemnly and without reservation. After all, her service was to the Goddess and her order, not to Aveline personally. Perhaps Aveline was right—Riannon, the only lady knight, had been guided along her unconventional path by the will of the Goddess for this purpose. During the hours of solitary darkness Riannon acknowledged that becoming a consecrated warrior, accepted and acknowledged for who and what she was, satisfied a deep longing she had almost despaired of fulfilling. Now she could build up credit in both this world and the next doing what she did best.

Riannon rose after Aveline's blessing and slid her new sword into its scabbard hanging at her side. She fell in step with Aveline as they strolled back through the trees towards the grove house.

"How glad I am that we can leave this rat hole," Aveline said. "We'll be resting in much better accommodation as we travel north. My men have already gone ahead to arrange it. I do look forward to good white bread that isn't full of grit, and capons that aren't half raw."

Riannon halted. "North?"

"Yes, we go to Tirand." Aveline stopped to smile back at Riannon. "Did I not mention that? I cannot think how it slipped my mind. We go to a wedding. Your brother's."

Riannon's left hand dropped to the hilt of her sword. "You cannot expect me to return?"

"Why ever not? Our fathers—may the gods not judge them too harshly—lie cold in their graves. They were the reason for your self-imposed exile, were they not? My sister rules as queen. To whom, incidentally, you must pay homage for that rat-bite manor of yours at Gast. Surely the news that Tirand has its first woman ruler must have reached you in whichever pigsty you were selling your sword."

Riannon had heard of her cousin's crowning at Count Berenger's court, along with many jests about that unnatural animal, the female king.

"Your bull-witted eldest brother stood behind Mathilda rather than claim the throne himself," Aveline said. "For which we are all profoundly grateful, if somewhat mystified by his lack of ambition. Truly, I suspect Henry must be a changeling. Or a moonling. But the least we can do is thank him with a rich young wife, don't you think? The poor creature who has been selected for him was an aspirant of my order. So, it's fitting that you and I escort the sacrificial virgin to her earthly destiny. What affecting scenes of family reunions await us. But first, I must break my fast. I loathe travelling and absolutely refuse to attempt it on an empty stomach."

Riannon did not follow when Aveline walked away. Her fingers gripped her sword hilt. What else had Aveline not told her?

CHAPTER TWO

Eleanor of Barrowmere heard a shout and looked out the front flap of her travelling carriage. At last. Not a quarter mile ahead, she saw the pale stone walls, so unexpected around a grove of the Goddess.

Eleanor shifted in her chair and put a hand to her belly. Padding and cushions could not ease those rusty aches from the last days of her monthly flux. Had she been able to travel directly to Sadiston, she could have delayed her journey and ridden rather than be cooped up in the stuffy, swaying carriage. Still, a grove house was the ideal place to find a remedy against a woman's discomfort. And, in truth, a few cramps that would pass soon enough were but a minor trouble compared to what faced her niece.

The swaying carriage rolled to a halt in a wide courtyard. By the time Eleanor's men had brought a stool and helped her alight, the green-robed high priestess waited for her.

"Lady Barrowmere." The priestess inclined her head and traced the quartered-circle in the air between them. "Be welcome at our humble house."

Eleanor smiled, returned the greeting affably, and accepted the privilege of kissing the high priestess's offered ring. Humble would not have been how Eleanor would describe the sprawling complex.

The wall bounded at least five acres of buildings, most of which were themselves constructed from expensive stone. Beyond that stretched hundreds of acres of woods, containing the sacred groves and waters, and probably twice as much fertile land accumulated through two hundred years of bequests and gifts. Founded by a king for his daughter who desired the religious life, the Highford Grove was where nobly born women like Eleanor's niece came to take the robe—if their families could afford a suitable endowment.

Eleanor knew how much her late brother-in-law had paid for his daughter's place. Money spent for nought, as it happened, now that the girl was to put aside her robe and wed. Not that Eleanor believed her brother-in-law would have been disappointed to see Cicely as wife of the Earl Marshal, cousin to the new queen and now the most powerful man in the realm.

What Cicely thought of her abrupt change in destiny, Eleanor would shortly discover. She had received a letter four months ago from her niece at the time of the death of Cicely's cousin, the Earl of Havelock. The conventionally polite and pious expressions about the young man's untimely death had revealed little of Cicely's feelings at so unexpectedly becoming one of the most eligible heiresses in the kingdom. It would be gross impiety to pray that Cicely's had not been a true vocation, but all the same, Eleanor fervently hoped, for her niece's sake, that it had not been.

Eleanor accompanied the high priestess across the busy courtyard and into a two-storey building with freshly swept wooden floors. These spacious guest accommodations even had windows of glass. Definitely not humble. Eleanor smiled.

"Truly," Eleanor said, "this was a house built to exalt the glory of the Goddess."

The high priestess beamed. "We are most fortunate in being the recipients of many pious offerings."

Eleanor had heard more subtle shakes of the begging bowl, but she let the hint pass. "How fares my niece?"

"Lady Cicely has been praying much for the soul of her recently departed cousin," the high priestess said. "I've sent someone to inform her of your arrival."

The high priestess ushered Eleanor into her private chamber. Sweet herbs mingled with fresh rushes on the floor. Eleanor would not have been surprised to see the uncommon luxury of a piece of carpet. Servants had brought in platters of sweet wafers and good wine by the time Cicely appeared. Eleanor's heart sank. Cicely looked pale and wore her drab aspirant's robe of green and brown.

"Aunt Eleanor." Cicely dropped a curtsy. "I hope your journey was free of mishap."

Eleanor suppressed the flippant reply that sprang to her lips.

Neither the priestess nor her downcast niece were a suitable audience for merrymaking.

Eleanor offered the priestess what court gossip she knew while she waited for the healer-priestess to bring her the brew against flux pains. As soon after that as she decently could, she took her leave of the high priestess and guided Cicely towards the guest quarters. Eleanor's servants still swarmed with luggage, putting her linens on the bed, and carrying food through to the private kitchens. No chance of any privacy there. Eleanor dismissed her waiting women and asked Cicely to walk with her in the gardens.

The carefully tended physic garden blended with an orchard. Aromatic herbs had released their fragrances under a hot sun for most of the day. Rather than disperse the scents, the faintest of breezes merely wafted them all together into a heady mélange of lavender, thyme, and mint.

Eleanor paused near a wooden bench and, under the guise of admiring the garden, checked that they would not be overheard by a meditating priestess or servant about her weeding.

"I thank you for coming to escort me, aunt." Cicely broke off a sprig of rosemary and absently plucked the green spiky leaves from it.

"We go to the queen's own castle of Sadiston," Eleanor said. "Where, though I hear she keeps a menagerie containing fearsome beasts from the world over, it is not precisely a lions' den."

Cicely glanced up from under her brows. Eleanor saw a hint of amusement amongst the fear. Good enough.

"You've grown since last I looked on you," Eleanor said. "Passing strange, though, you put me in mind of Hawise more than your mother. You'll not remember your Aunt Hawise. She was my youngest sister. When we were girls together, ere I was first wed, Hawise would steal my prettiest gowns whenever she could. I wouldn't have minded, save she was not pretty and did my clothes no credit. To one as fair as you, I yield your choice right willingly."

A ghost of a smile reluctantly surfaced again in Cicely's expression. And, Eleanor thought, a flicker of interest. With any skill, she should be able to get Cicely willingly out of those dour robes and clothed as befitted a countess ere they departed the grove.

"Being such a vain and frivolous creature, I've enough finery to weigh me down to the deepest hell," Eleanor said. "And would be in your debt if you relieved me of some of it."

Cicely looked both amused and scandalised.

"Though, not the scarlet overtunic shot with gold threads," Eleanor said. "I'm willing to endure a little torment in the afterlife for a garment that becomes me so excessively well."

Cicely bit her lip but couldn't fully suppress a giggle. "Do you truly have so many clothes, aunt?"

"My dear, when you reach my great age, you'll realise that no penny spent on cloth that draws the eye from the sagging, wrinkling skin beneath it is wasted."

"You cannot be more than thirty years," Cicely said. "Yet to hear you, you might be as old as Sio Ela."

"Is she much afflicted with years?"

Cicely giggled. "Mary says that Sio Ela might verily have been born from one of the nuts that dropped from the First Tree."

Eleanor smiled and linked her arm with Cicely. As she drew the girl in a meandering stroll through the gardens, she coaxed her to talk. By the time they went inside to sup, Eleanor felt well pleased with herself. Her flux cramps had eased and Cicely had loosened up delightfully. But when Enid, one of Eleanor's waiting women, congratulated Cicely on the magnificence of her forthcoming wedding, the girl paled and her haunted, hunted fawn look returned.

Eleanor would continue her work on Cicely on the morrow. Not that Eleanor could truly fault her niece. She remembered too well being faced with the same prospect of marriage to a man she had not met before they stood at the altar together. Was there any young woman who felt no fears at being given to a stranger—to be his to use as he pleased?

As a widow, Eleanor enjoyed the freedoms of controlling her own finances, actions, and body in a manner that maidens and wives could only dream of. The one drawback was that it could be a lonely course. She had more than once discreetly indulged her need for intimate companionship, but the abandon of sexual pleasure was not always easy to achieve with the spectres of illegitimate children, diseases, and social censure clinging to the bed canopy. On balance, she preferred to continue as her own mistress. While at these wedding celebrations, Eleanor would seek an interview with her liege lady, the queen, for the purpose of negotiating the amount of the fine Eleanor would pay to be allowed to continue for another year as a widow.

❖

When Eleanor returned from her morning ride, she used the dustiness of her tunic as an excuse to change her clothes. She and her women drew Cicely into an examination of the two crammed coffers of clothes that Eleanor had brought largely for her niece's benefit. Some had been hastily made for the girl. Once the news of the betrothal had reached Eleanor, she had written for the girl's size and colouring from the high priestess.

To Eleanor's relief, Cicely proved as susceptible to finery as any young woman. She looked covetous as she ran her hands over the soft wool of a sleeveless surcote dyed the most expensive and deepest of blues. She gasped with unfeigned delight when Eleanor told her the garment had been made for her. Cicely softly admitted that she was pleased with the effect of it worn over a new yellow tunic with long, tight sleeves embroidered with small blue flowers. As well she might, considering their cost.

At Eleanor's signal, Agnes, her senior waiting woman, lifted Cicely's aspirant's gown. "I'll take this away now, shall I, my lady?"

Cicely bit her lip. Eleanor put a reassuring hand on Cicely's rigid back.

"I'm sure the garment will be useful for someone," Eleanor said. "And should be given to the house. Do you not think so, sweeting?"

Cicely's pale lashes shaded her downcast eyes, but Eleanor needed no special skill in divination to understand that her niece looked on this exchange of clothes as symbolic of the change in her circumstances. Cicely gulped. Eleanor waited. Finally, Cicely gave a curt nod. Eleanor gently squeezed her arm and bestowed a smile of approval. Cicely watched Agnes carry the robe out until the door shut behind her.

When they attended the services in the grove, Eleanor saw Cicely's longing looks to her friends amongst the aspirants and young priestesses. She resigned herself to Cicely requesting they delay their departure for another day.

The congregation had knelt to begin singing the final hymn when a commotion of "halloos" carried through the trees. At the end of the second verse, a breathless servant bolted into the clearing. Eleanor watched the woman unceremoniously push through the worshippers and priestesses to throw herself to her knees before the high priestess. What she whispered caused the priestess's head to snap up in surprise.

Cicely shot Eleanor a sidelong glance. Eleanor shrugged.

To Eleanor's amusement, the high priestess signalled to the officiating priestess an unmistakeable gesture of impatience. The singing increased in tempo and the hymn concluded with indecent, if not comical, haste. The high priestess hurried from the head of the sacred pool and barely paused to incline her head to Eleanor and Cicely as she passed.

"A naer has arrived, my lady," one of the older priestesses explained to Eleanor before scurrying away herself.

"Has the exalted lady come because of me?" Cicely asked.

"I know not, sweeting," Eleanor said. "Perhaps she has business with the house. Or she might merely be breaking her journey here."

Eleanor wondered, though, at the priestesses' reaction. A naer was virtually a princess of the order, but so large and prestigious a grove house as Highford would have seen more than its share of naers. Kings had lodged here for a night of their travels.

The noisy shouts and donkey brays grew louder as Eleanor and Cicely approached the courtyard bounded by the guest quarters. They stepped into the cool shade of the long, arched walkway when Cicely put a hand on Eleanor's sleeve. She looked corpse pale.

"May...may we walk the gardens, aunt?" she asked.

Whatever Cicely thought she had to fear from a visiting naer was best asked in private. Eleanor signalled to Agnes and her women to continue. She and Cicely turned to follow the walkway towards the main herb garden. Eleanor noted with approval that even the vines winding around the columns of the walkway were heavy with fruit that the priestesses could eat and preserve. None of the gods' bounty was wasted even in so splendid a house.

"You needn't quail at the prospect of meeting a naer," Eleanor said. "You must remember that you are a countess now. One of the highest ranking ladies in the realm."

Cicely frowned. "I'm not in the habit of thinking so."

"You'll grow accustomed to it," Eleanor said. "There's little in this life that we cannot adapt to, however difficult it might seem at first."

Cicely looked sharply at her.

"Ah, sweeting," Eleanor said. "You don't think that you're the first to feel as you do?"

"What is he like? Lord Henry?"

Prepared for such questions, Eleanor had already mentally ransacked her impressions of the brusque Earl Marshal to find something suitable.

"He's a man of the highest honour," Eleanor said. "There are few who, finding themselves in his position, would not have tried to claim the throne. His actions also bespeak his high regard for his sense of the dues of blood and family. Like his father before him, Lord Henry enjoys the reputation of a man who treats women with the greatest courtesy."

Cicely nodded. "His first wife died many years ago, did she not? He has a son older than me?"

Eleanor signalled for Cicely to precede her through the gate into the fragrant garden. "His eldest son, Lord Richard, has just wed a daughter of the Count of Vahl, one of the leading vassals of King Fulk of Iruland. She is of an age with you. I doubt me not that you and she will—Oh."

Eleanor halted in surprise. A few yards away, standing at the edge of one of the fish ponds, she saw a familiar tall, strongly-built figure. He wore neither hat nor coif, so she could see his short, warrior-cropped black hair.

"What's wrong?" Cicely said.

Eleanor smiled. "There's nought amiss. Quite the opposite. We're in for a merry time, indeed, if he's to accompany us to Sadiston. Come, I'll introduce you to one of the Earl Marshal's younger brothers. There are no men better company than Lord Guy."

Eleanor mentally thanked all the gods for whatever reason brought Guy to the grove house at this time. She had yet to meet any woman, be she shrinking maiden or ageing matron, who stood proof against Guy's charm. Several days of mild and perfectly harmless flirtation would do Cicely the power of good.

Eleanor only noticed the unusual fact that his profile was clean shaven as she neared him.

"My lord," she said, "you converse with the carp? Do they exercise your wit to—"

He turned. He was not Guy.

A badly healed scar carved through the right side of his face from hairline to jaw. Otherwise, though, he was so similar to Guy that he might have been a copy made by a mortal sculptor from the original crafted by the gods. His angular features made for a face handsome with character rather than comely prettiness. Dark brows nearly met above the bridge of his nose. Strong chin. He even possessed the same sensuous mouth that looked out of place on a warrior's face. But the green eyes were darker. More intense. He stared without Guy's ready, boyishly infectious smile.

For the first time in many a year, Eleanor felt the heat of embarrassment rising to her cheeks. "Your pardon, sir. I mistook you for someone else."

He continued to stare openly. The blatant admiration in his gaze, and his complete lack of attempt to conceal it, robbed his attention of all rudeness. Eleanor's sense of humour reasserted itself and she smiled.

"I thought you Lord Guy, cousin to the queen," Eleanor said. "I suspect that I'm not too far in error. You, sir, must be one of his brothers?"

Where Guy would have replied with an easy remark, the man before her looked as though he struggled to find words.

"I have a brother called Guy," he said. "But I'm not his brother. By your leave, lady."

He bowed and stalked away. His long legs swiftly carried him to the gate and out of the garden. A peripheral part of Eleanor's mind noted that his voice was not as deep as Guy's, and that he had barely noticed her beautiful niece. Most of Eleanor's attention, though, wrestled the conundrum of his apparently contradictory statements.

"Did we offend him?" Cicely asked.

"Any offence was of my offering," Eleanor said. "Though I cannot think what it might be. Perhaps he did not appreciate my levity in reference to the carp."

Cicely looked uncertain. "How could he be brother and yet not brother to Lord Guy?"

"That, I confess, has me at a loss. With any man other than the late Earl Marshal, I would surmise he meant that he was a base-born son. But it is said of the late Earl Marshal that he loved his first wife so well that he not only did not remarry, but took solace in no woman's arms after her death. Which is so extraordinary, and contrary to every normal behaviour of men, that there must be truth to it."

Eleanor shook her head. "It seems unlikely that the late Earl Marshal populated the countryside with by-blows. For certès, though, that man looked the image of Lord Guy, and only a handful of years younger."

Cicely cast a frown at the gate. "Does the Earl Marshal resemble him?"

"No. Lord Henry is not, I fancy, quite as tall, but is a much broader man. More powerfully built. He looks strong enough to wrestle a bear."

She did not add that, at four and forty years old, Henry was a good decade and a half older than the man who just departed, with more grey than black in his hair and beard.

"Is the Earl Marshal more handsome than his brother?" Cicely asked. "Still, he must be."

Eleanor's eyebrow arched. Her niece had not considered him good-looking?

"The Earl Marshal isn't horribly scarred, too, is he?" Cicely shuddered. "I cannot imagine looking often upon that disfigurement."

Eleanor compared her memories of the two similar faces—of Guy and his tongue-tied brother—and, in fairness, had to concede that the better looking was without the scar. Though, perhaps, not the more intriguing.

❖

Eleanor dispatched a servant with an invitation for Naer Aveline to sup at her table. She would have offered her hospitality to any other fellow traveller, but this was not only a naer, she was sister to the queen as well. Her appearance at Highford at this time could be no accident. Eleanor thus offered her niece the opportunity to share the position of hostess rather than wait for an inevitable summons to present herself to the naer.

It also occurred to Eleanor that Guy's brother must be travelling with the naer, and this would be her opportunity to satisfy her curiosity about him, too.

Naer Aveline entered the guest hall with the air of ownership. Eleanor smiled as she dipped in a curtsy.

"Lady Barrowmere." Aveline traced a blessing in the air between them. "Your hospitality is most welcome after long hours on a dusty road. I confess that I'd forgotten your intimate connection with the late earl. Your husband is kin to the Earl of Lismore, is he not?"

"He was, Eminence," Eleanor said. "He died some three years past."

"Oh. You're a widow?" Aveline smiled before turning to Cicely. "And this must be the Lady of Havelock."

Eleanor was unsurprised to see her niece on her knees in a submission more appropriate to an aspirant than a countess. The adjustment would take a little time.

"You're most fair," Aveline said. "My cousin will be well pleased with his new bride."

Cicely's pallid cheeks developed flaming spots of colour. Eleanor brushed aside a fleeting worry. Any woman who had attained the rank of naer before her fortieth birthday would have the wit not to enquire what the bride thought of her forthcoming marriage. Aveline did not ask.

Guy's enigmatic copy entered and joined them. The scar gave him a stern and remote air that did not invite conversation. Perhaps because she was accustomed to Guy's easy and affable manners, Eleanor speculated that his outward reserve could be a façade that concealed a similarly attractive personality. She wondered how long it might take her to breach those defences and find out. She remembered his admiring look, and thought, perhaps, it would not take so very long.

"Cousin, you'll not have met our hostess," Aveline said. "Lady Eleanor of Barrowmere. She is aunt to Lady Cicely, Countess of Havelock, who is to become your sister by marriage."

By rights, Cicely should have taken precedence in acknowledging him, but sensing her hesitation, Eleanor curtsied and offered her hand. He took it in warm fingers and bowed stiffly.

Eleanor smiled. "You're most welcome at my table, sir."

"I thank you, lady." He turned to offer Cicely another of his formal bows.

Eleanor noted but could not understand Aveline's evident amusement as she watched her cousin and Cicely. Cicely again sank in a too-submissive curtsy. His impassive expression betrayed neither disapproval nor amusement at her gaucherie.

"It...it gives me pleasure to meet a...a relative of my betrothed." Cicely spoke so softly that Eleanor barely heard her.

"The pleasure is mine, my lady," he said.

"My cousin has been living in foreign lands for the better part of the last decade," Aveline said. "We have our Wise Mother to thank that she has returned to help us celebrate this most illustrious of weddings. Is that not so, Lady Riannon?"

She? Eleanor's gaze shot up to the scarred face. Lady Riannon? *A woman?*

Cicely gasped and tugged her hand free of Riannon's fingers. She stared with open horror. Eleanor mentally cursed whoever had taught the girl her manners, wished she could give her niece a slap, and quickly stepped into the awkward moment.

"Lady Riannon, I have the satisfaction of not having been wholly astray in seeing a strong likeness to your brother, Lord Guy," Eleanor said. "Which is such a balm to my vanity. The boards are set and the cloths laid. Mayhap we should take our places to eat? Your Eminence?"

Eleanor gave her niece a discreet push to get her to escort the naer around to the place of honour. Riannon must have been offended at Cicely's reaction, but Eleanor could read nothing in her expression. Her face was as unrevealing as a knight's helm with the visor pulled down.

At table, Riannon sat on Eleanor's right, which presented her unscarred profile for Eleanor's study. Closer, her features seemed finer than a man's, though not noticeably feminine.

Riannon briefly met Eleanor's gaze when she rinsed her hands in the rose-perfumed water, but did not speak. Eleanor swiftly balanced the desire to gloss over Cicely's discourtesy with the greater good in acknowledging the mistake and apologising.

"My niece was pledged at a young age to the robe," Eleanor said. "She's not yet accustomed to moving fully in society. She's somewhat ill at ease with the sudden change in her fortunes. She meant no disrespect."

Riannon nodded.

Eleanor only half listened to the prayer as she worried the problem of Cicely having truly offended Riannon. That would be an ill-omened start to her entry into her new family. Although, now that she thought on it, Eleanor remembered some dark edge of scandal surrounding

Riannon. Aveline mentioned a long absence from the kingdom. In the years that Eleanor had been on easy terms with Guy, he had not mentioned a younger sister.

Eleanor reached for the salt cellar. With impeccable courtesy, Riannon picked it up and set it close to her. That errant part of Eleanor's mind, which oft times took on a life all its own, noted that Riannon had unexpectedly beautiful hands. They were long and tapered.

"You do not strike me, lady, as one given to vanity," Riannon said.

Eleanor nearly dropped the salt off the end of her knife in surprise. Riannon's expression still looked remote, but her tone might have been teasing. Eleanor hurriedly ran back through their conversation to discover what might have prompted the comment. It was her remark about having not been mistaken in seeing a relationship between Guy and Riannon, and her pride in being correct.

"Though it is a mortification to be forced to admit weakness of personality," Eleanor said, "I'm afraid that, sadly, it's true my vanity is easily pricked. I cannot abide being incorrect. So, you see, I'm doubly damned. Once for being vain, and a second time for my vice taking the highly unfeminine character of an intellectual nature rather than the more acceptable frivolous obsession with my looks."

"No one could think you unwomanly." Riannon politely moved the jugs of wine and water closer to Eleanor. "Nor that your looks excite false vanity."

Eleanor found herself in the unusual position of having no ready reply. How did Riannon mean that? Oblique criticism? Eleanor stared at the angular profile as Riannon bent her attention on a dish of venison and frumenty.

That night, as she lay in her bed with Cicely softly snoring beside her, Eleanor frowned at the dark hangings. Her supper guests both put her on her mettle. Naer Aveline struck Eleanor as a woman who watched and weighed everything and calculated to a hair-splitting nicety. Still, even the daughter of a king would not have risen so high in her order so swiftly without some talent of mind and ambition. Her cousin, on the other hand, presented altogether different difficulties. Eleanor had been seriously caught off her guard with her assumptions from the garden. Riannon was a woman, and yet unlike any other. Where Guy would have teased, Riannon responded with formal courtesy so stiff that it bordered on the daunting.

Eleanor wriggled onto her side. Agnes, another who shared Eleanor's bed, mumbled to herself in her sleep.

Eleanor scratched her memory for events of eight or nine years ago. Having seen Riannon of Gast, the greatest dullard could guess the nature of the scandal surrounding her. That a daughter of the late Earl Marshal should take to dressing as a man would be cause enough for gossip. If Eleanor was not mistaken, though, that elaborately decorated dagger Riannon wore at her right hip was a symbol of membership of a chivalric order. Riannon used a second, plain knife, for eating. Eleanor's eyes narrowed as she relived the scene in the garden. Yes, Riannon had worn a sword. Could she be a lady knight? Eleanor had not heard of one before.

Eleanor also remembered Riannon's look of open admiration. Her frown deepened. She had received enough such looks to recognise sexual appreciation. Yet, Riannon was a woman.

Eleanor's last memory before finally slipping into sleep, though, was of a different pair of green eyes and the sharp interest on Aveline's face when Eleanor admitted her widowhood.

CHAPTER THREE

R iannon nodded to Lady Barrowmere's marshal and turned to stride through the noisy chaos of saddle horses, laden sumpter horses, carts, grooms, esquires, and pages. With Aveline deciding to travel with Lady Barrowmere, their combined entourages resembled a small army and proved only slightly less difficult to manage. Finally, though, they were ready to move. Servants and grooms had gone ahead to secure lodging for the night and purchase provisions. That much, at least, the two marshals—each jealous of his office and the prerogatives of his mistress—had been able to cooperate on when Riannon stood over them.

Aveline emerged from the main grove hall with the high priestess her anxious shadow. Riannon kept well clear of them. Aveline, who disliked riding, headed for her cumbersome covered wagon. Lady Barrowmere's luxurious travelling carriage would be no faster, though the five horses pulling it looked in better condition than the naer's. Their swollen train would be lucky to cover twenty miles a day.

Alan waited with Riannon's horse. "It was less of a headache going to war."

Riannon did not disagree. She took the reins from him and swung up into the saddle.

"But at least one of the ladies is uncommonly easy on the eye," Alan said.

"Which no one could ever say about my Lord Damory," Riannon said.

Alan laughed. "A pity it is that she's taken to the travelling carriage."

Riannon knew he did not mean Aveline. To her surprise, she soon saw Lady Eleanor mount a fine grey palfrey. It had not occurred to her that Alan referred to the lady's niece rather than herself. Beside the handsome aunt, the niece paled to a nervous nonentity who excited compassion rather than admiration.

The cavalcade finally began to move. Lady Eleanor rode at the head, away from the dust. One of her mounted escort included a minstrel. The lady intended to convey her niece to her wedding in fitting style. Riannon thought it a great shame that the Lady Cicely possessed none of her aunt's wit or spirit. Still, a livelier woman might suffer more being married to her eldest brother, if he were anything like her memories of her blustering, bullying, boorish sire. Riannon would have wagered her teeth that Aveline felt no qualms for the match she had designed even now that she had met poor Cicely. After all, Cicely's personal inadequacies diminished the value of her inheritance by not a single acre or knight's fee.

They had gone less than two miles before an esquire rode back to invite her to join the Lady Eleanor. Riannon urged her horse forwards.

Eleanor wore a snowy white wimple framing her face, as befitted a widow, beneath the broad-brimmed straw hat that shielded her from the sun. Her long overtunic was a highly expensive shade of crimson, which looked all the more striking against the pale grey of her mare. Even the loose ends of her girdle glittered with decorative gold work. Nothing about the lady did not catch the eye, though a woman with so fair a face and figure would have drawn Riannon's gaze even had she worn an undyed woollen mantle about her shoulders and stood up to her knees in mud outside a peasant's hovel. Conscious of not wanting to stare, Riannon risked only the most fleeting of glances at the lady's face before fixing her attention beyond her horse's ears.

"In such weather, we should make good time today," Eleanor said. "Do you not think, Lady Riannon?"

"Yes, lady," Riannon said.

After a pause, Eleanor said, "And the road is in an excellent state of repair. Let us hope that more than half my pottery survives this leg."

"Yes, lady."

"Entertainment is an excellent way to pass a long and tedious ride, do you not agree? And what could be more agreeable than rich conversation?"

"Yes, lady."

For the next mile, Riannon responded to Eleanor's bland remarks about the weather, the countryside, the state of crops, and all manner of commonplaces. The road wound through a checkerboard of arable land thick with ripening oats and vetch, and forests resplendent in greenery. In places, the hedges and undergrowth needed severe cutting back where they encroached on the road and could provide plentiful cover for brigands. Not that so large a party as theirs need fear ambush or attack.

Happily, the ford their horses splashed across proved well-maintained and would be no major obstacle to the carts and carriages. Riannon had asked the marshals about the state of the bridges ahead and received reassurances that they need not divert for want of a safe river crossing. The years of her exile left her ignorant of all but the vaguest idea of the route they would travel north to the central royal stronghold and city at Sadiston. What memories she retained were coloured by her angry, violent rejection by her father and her desperate flight away from the lands of her birth. She should have expected such unpleasant thoughts would intrude as she neared the location of those scenes.

"I've previously believed myself fortunate never to have experienced a siege," Eleanor said. "But I find myself now regretting the knowledge I might have gleaned."

Surprised, and unsure she had heard right, Riannon turned to the lady. Eleanor looked thoughtful, as if she worried a problem of gravest importance. Riannon belatedly realised that the lady's escort had fallen back. She and Eleanor rode side by side out of anyone else's hearing. The arrangement could not be accidental and should not have been one she had been unaware of whilst lost in her gloomy past. Riannon caught Eleanor watching her.

"I've never had the privilege of meeting a lady knight before," Eleanor said. "I suppose that you know much about siege craft."

"Somewhat, lady."

"Pray be so good as to tell me, then, which is the more effective, the frontal assault or encirclement?"

Riannon cast a searching look at Eleanor and encountered only an expression of quizzical interest.

"The approach to any siege depends on many factors," Riannon said. "The size of your army. Morale. The quality and number of the opposing garrison. Their stores. If there is a weakness in the defences that you can exploit. These are but some of the considerations that weigh in your decision. Surely, lady, you do not plan to go to war?"

"Not a war. A single campaign. My army is small but, I flatter myself, not without valour and determination. Though the defences I face are truly formidable."

Riannon glanced sidelong. The lady's eyes shone with amused challenge. Riannon suspected she was being outflanked.

"I suppose I could concentrate my artillery on the walls," Eleanor said. "That is an accepted method for battering down defences, is it not?"

"Yes, lady. Have you ballistas or mangonels?"

"Which is the more powerful? My weaponry is of no mean calibre."

Riannon grinned.

"I shan't accept defeat," Eleanor said.

"Perhaps, then, lady, you should offer to parley."

"Oh, I wish for more than just a brief discussion under flags of truce. My aim is a breach in those defences and a lasting, amicable accord to follow."

Confident that she now understood, Riannon tugged off a glove and offered it to Eleanor. "My surrender, lady."

Eleanor laughed and accepted the glove. "To your virtue of courtliness, I must add great forbearance. You take my sporting in good part, and I'm greatly in your debt for it. I must warn you, though, Lady Riannon, that my threadbare stock of good qualities does not include gallantry. You see, I'll tuck this glove in my girdle rather than promptly return it, because I wish to take shameful advantage of our détente."

Riannon retained her amusement, though she braced herself for questions about her scar or the circumstances of her knighting.

"You must have travelled widely," Eleanor said. "I envy you that. Tell me about some of the fabulous places you've seen. I once heard a merchant tell of a land where men have faces as dark as mid-winter mummers with soot smeared over their skins."

Riannon gave Eleanor a long look. "Yes, lady, I've been to where it is never cold. Not even when it should be the deep of winter. Men there have dark skins."

"Do they wear the same clothes? If they suffer no winter, they'd have no need for fur-lined mantles. Do their crops grow all year around if the ground does not freeze at any time?"

Riannon frowned as she cast her mind back to the half a year she spent broiling in the employment of a Themalian prince. Eleanor asked probing, intelligent questions quite unlike any Riannon expected from a woman who mocked herself as frivolous and light-minded. In doing so, Eleanor betrayed an already large store of information about foreign lands and people.

"I correspond with all manner of folk," Eleanor said. "I'm not above pestering anyone with letters and demanding like in return. You see, another of my besetting sins is gluttony."

With the benefit of several hours' acquaintance, Riannon knew the lady did not speak literally in referring to a weakness for food. A single glance at her shapely figure would have dispelled any such notion.

"My greed is for knowledge," Eleanor said. "I am insatiable. No merchant or traveller is safe from my snares. I hunger for stories, fables, adventures, for the fantastic. I hoard words from all corners of the world."

"What do you seek?" Riannon asked.

Eleanor's expression dropped all trace of levity. "I wonder that myself, sometimes."

Eleanor smiled again. "Most of the time, of course, I think very little. Life is much easier that way."

Riannon was unsurprised by the lady's deflection. Eleanor used self-mockery as a warrior might a shield. Riannon wondered how frequently Eleanor let her guard down like that. She could not read the significance of the event. Perhaps she might if she knew the lady better. The learning would be no hardship.

❖

Aveline woke with a gasp. She felt as cold as if a shadow curled inside her. Yet, sweat slicked her skin where it touched that of the warm body of her naked bed mate.

Aveline gently kissed a pale shoulder. The young priestess remained lost in soundless sleep as Aveline eased herself out of bed. The curtains around the bed hung loose, though it would have been less stifling had they been tied back. Privacy made it necessary, since the chamber contained four priestesses from Aveline's entourage asleep on pallets around the walls.

Aveline stepped to the open window. Not a breath of breeze stirred the night. She sucked in humid, suffocating air, yet something cold coiled inside her. Mortal warmth could not touch it. Aveline put a hand to her chest and looked out at the engulfing night with awe at feeling, once again, an echo within her of a divine whisper. She groped in the moonlight for her robe. She didn't bother with her linen chemise, but fastened her girdle, with its hanging purse, about her waist.

Her bare feet slapped on the hard-packed floors as she groped along the dark corridor to find an external door in the unfamiliar grove house.

Aveline walked out into a courtyard washed in grey light. A cat bolted away from the door with silent haste. Aveline sucked in air that proved barely less oppressive than in her borrowed bedchamber. The coolness still nestled behind her ribs and cradled her heart.

"I come to obey your summons," she whispered to the night.

The murmur of snores and footfalls of her entourage carried from the main courtyard on the other side of the modest stable block. Most of her servants slept in blankets on the ground for want of better accommodation at this grove house. The Lady of Barrowmere and her large retinue lodged half a mile away at the manor house of one of her dependents.

Lady Eleanor of Barrowmere. Finding her at Highford had been an interesting surprise, and not unwelcome for relieving Aveline of the necessity of holding the bride-to-be's limp hand all the way to the basilica door. Aveline should have known Lady Eleanor's connection to the new countess. It was unlike her, too, to have forgotten that the lady's husband had died. Wealthy widows made marriage prizes second only to heiresses.

Aveline strode across the courtyard and past the solitary kitchen building wreathed in the stench of rotting food scraps. She paused to take her bearings. The grove must be that way. She headed for the ghostly trees, where she found the well-beaten path and turned to follow it.

Her feet trod the dust stirred by countless priestesses and worshippers. She might be the most important woman called this way by the unspoken will of the Lady of Destiny, but for certès she was neither the first, nor would she be the last.

The first pool looked black. Shadows from the surrounding trees stretched towards it and bled into it. Aveline halted only long enough to sight the way through to the sacred water. Only initiated priestesses trod this path. Aveline pushed a low branch out of the way. In the morning, she would tell the senior priestess that she needed more careful maintenance of the area. That should put the fear of the Goddess into the servile creature.

At this grove, underground springs fed both holy pools. Not even the whisper of trickling water broke the silence. No, not silence. Rustlings of unseen creatures moving across the dry twigs and leaves of the forest litter cracked the night.

Aveline stood listening. On a night like this, cloaked in moonlight and solitude, she felt like parts of her dissolved—as if the sharp edges that set her as a thing apart from the rest of creation blurred, and the outer reaches of herself merged with the greater whole. Not lessened, but more alive to the rest of the Goddess's will. The Goddess called her with divine murmurs and hearing required more than ears.

Aveline knelt at the edge of the sacred pool and muttered the prayer of beginning. She stroked the surface with two fingers. Even the water was tepid this summer's night. She lifted her wet fingers to trace the quartered circle on her forehead and put her fingers to her mouth to touch blessed water to the tip of her tongue. She smelled sex on her hand from her energetic encounter earlier with the nubile young priestess. She smiled. The Goddess would understand.

Aveline opened her purse and found the small bottle by touch. The moonlight drained all colours, so the syrupy liquid inside the precious glass looked dark grey rather than the brown it was under the sun. Aveline settled to a more comfortable cross-legged position before tugging the tiny stopper out and letting a single drop of the bitter syrup fall onto her tongue. She shuddered as she carefully replaced the stopper and bottle. Her tongue curled and her eyes watered. A searing heat burned down towards her stomach but did not touch the chill inside her.

Aveline put a fist against her chest and plunged her other hand into the blessed pool. She shuddered as the bitterness hit her stomach and made it clench. Not for the first time, she doubted that it could be blasphemy to make the mind-freeing syrup taste nice. After all, it was only a tool to allow the priestess to receive the Goddess's message. In no wise did it interfere with the communication. Nor would a little honey.

"Lady of Creation, I am ready to be your vessel," she said. "Wise Mother, reveal to me what you will, knowing that I will hear and obey if you appear to me as the Lady of Destiny or if you turn your dread Dark Face on your servant. I'll try to understand and be worthy of your gift."

Aveline closed her eyes. Bitterness swamped her mouth. Her insides burned. The searing pulsed around the shadow-fist clenched inside her chest. Her heart beat faster. Her neck grew weak, and her head felt as heavy as lead. Aveline let her head sag forwards. Her loose hair brushed her forearm and trailed in the pool around her wrist. The world swayed beneath her. The water tightened around her fist. Squeezed her. Crushing. Sucking her down.

Aveline opened her eyes. She lay on her back. The stars swirled above her in a frenzied dance. With practiced discipline, she resisted the natural urge to struggle to focus and fight against a world gone awry. Instead, Aveline let it wash over her and through her. She was part of the All. After this ritual, she would understand another fragment of it. The sickening lurches, the way the trees seemed to bend down to stab their branches at her, and the bucking of the grassy ground beneath her body were the birth pangs of knowledge beyond most mortal comprehension.

Aveline's body spasmed as the whole of creation tore through her. She heard her own cry dying on her lips.

Aveline woke with a gasp. Her every sinew ached. Her mouth tasted of vomit. She resisted the pulls of the mundane world as her trained mind clutched at the elusive bubble that floated on the periphery of understanding.

Death. She saw death. Blood. A limp hand. A shining sword blade.

Aveline squeezed her eyes shut as she strove to snatch hold of slippery meaning.

The sword. The hilt. It was the gift sword. The one she had given to Riannon.

Aveline opened her eyes. What did this mean? What did the Lady of Destiny try to tell her?

Aveline groaned as she rolled onto her side and levered herself to her knees. Sour bile stained her shoulder from where she had vomited. She offered a prayer of thanks before scooping up a handful of water to rinse her mouth. She was careful to spit on the grass and let no drop taint the pool.

"You honour me, Wise Mother." Aveline traced a blessing over the ground and made sure her precious glass bottle sat securely in her purse. "I could wish you had bestowed powers of mind on me with a more liberal hand. Then I might have been better able to grasp your meaning."

Aveline stumbled back on trembling legs to her guest chamber. She loosened the lacing on her robe and let it fall to the floor. The priestess murmured and stirred when Aveline climbed into bed. Aveline gently disengaged the arm that snaked across her stomach. Too warm. The young priestess relaxed back into sleep.

Aveline lay awake trying to recapture fragments of vision. She had heard cheers. A victory? A battle won? Could the Goddess, in her guise as the Lady of Destiny, be showing Aveline something of her crusade? Might this be another divine blessing for her far-reaching plans to sweep the infidels from the captured land of Evriat? Believers must reclaim and re-consecrate the lost holy places, especially the Cave of the Pool in Limeon in northern Evriat. Then priestesses could again draw power from the holiest of waters formed in the depression where the Goddess once slept on earth. With that magical power at its command, the order could unleash on those accursed unbelievers the full wrath of the Lady of Creation. The glory of the Goddess would shine bright amongst the gods, and her mortal daughters might gain respect for more than their skills at midwifery and making charms and philtres. Men valued might. Women, who alone could receive the Goddess's gift of magic, must wield it to the fullness of its power and without flinching. That end, Aveline believed, she had been divinely called to bring about.

Or, had Aveline been vouchsafed, through the vision, some assurance that her shorter-term plans would come to fruition? Riannon using the gift sword for the Goddess's cause in Sadiston, perchance? The Lady of Destiny had already sanctioned that when she guided Aveline and Riannon to that miserable, remote grove house when Aveline sought a recipient for the gift sword. Aveline also suspected that divine purpose ran even deeper. A female knight was a creature nearly as rare as a mythical horse with a horn. Yet Aveline shared cousinly blood with one. That could not be the result of a chance alignment of stars. She also harboured the strongest conviction how Riannon had acquired the hideous wounds that had required such lengthy healing after the siege of Vahl. Riannon, she believed, was that mysterious hero thought to have died after performing the acts of valour which earned "him" the soubriquet Vahldomne. The Goddess could have created no more perfect instrument for Aveline to use to start a new war than the hero of that last epic siege.

Aveline frowned. Whose death had she felt? Had the limp hand been Riannon's? Aveline would have to make a study of that part of her cousin's anatomy on the morrow.

"You were gone." The young priestess wriggled closer. "I woke, Eminence, and you were gone."

"I'm here now," Aveline said.

Aveline trailed her fingers up the young woman's chest to her throat. The girl sucked in a deep breath and expelled a hot sigh against Aveline's shoulder. She pressed her smooth young body close.

"Eminence..."

Aveline captured the hand sliding over her belly. "It's too hot. In the morning. Before the dawn devotion. We'll have our own celebration of the life of a new day."

Aveline kissed the offered lips, but discouraged the young woman from snuggling against her. She listened to the priestess's breathing relax back into the oblivion of sleep. The pretty young creature was unlikely ever to strive for any goal greater than an orgasm. To the end of her days, in this meagre grove house, the girl would cherish the memory of the night she spent in the bed of a naer. Really, though, given her origins, her life could hold no higher accomplishment than that. Still, not all those with birth and breeding had the drive or clear-sightedness necessary to serve themselves or the gods to their best. Aveline's eldest sister, Mathilda, for one. She had needed Aveline's help shoring up the support of the religious orders and the most powerful lords to claim her throne.

Aveline turned to settle more comfortably on her side. Her last waking thoughts were not of sex or of the queen, but of a coming death.

CHAPTER FOUR

Eleanor shook her head when Agnes approached with a veil. "It'll be more comfortable to wear a cover-chief beneath my hat. The sun would've baked me yesterday without that protection."

"You could ride in the carriage, Aunt Eleanor," Cicely said.

"I cannot abide being enclosed and jolted," Eleanor said. "I never willingly forgo riding. Perhaps it'd do you good to take to horseback rather than shutting yourself in with a couple of my older women."

Cicely frowned down at the litter of scent bottles, combs, scissors, and tweezers on Eleanor's dressing table. Her restless fingers toyed with a bracelet in Eleanor's carved ivory jewellery casket. Eleanor noticed that Cicely had at least taken up her offer to wear whatever took her fancy, though those earrings would not have been her first choice to suit her niece.

"Mayhap you need some fresh air, sweeting," Eleanor said. "I'd value your company. Why do you not let me send instructions to Hugh to have a horse saddled for you?"

Cicely found the single, undecorated chamois glove lying on the chest near the table. She picked it up and turned it in her hands. "This cannot be yours."

"I must return that today," Eleanor said. "It belongs to Lady Riannon. She'll not remain in good charity with me if I keep her possessions."

Cicely could not have dropped the glove faster had it been a hot coal. Eleanor had prayed for some animation from the girl but felt only irritation at this. She dismissed her women with an impatient gesture.

"I know this is an uneasy time for you," Eleanor said, "which is all the more reason to practice good manners. Lady Riannon is to be your sister. It honours neither your natal family nor the family of your betrothed husband if you make no effort to be amiable."

Cicely paled.

Eleanor found herself again torn between putting her arm around the girl and giving her a good shake. She rose and took a cool hand between hers.

"I know you've spent the last five years believing your destiny bounded by a grove," Eleanor said. "And this has been a wrench for you. But, sweeting, you were born and bred to be a noble lady. The gods had their reason for diverting you to a life of devotion for a time, but you're not unprepared or unequipped for what you are to become."

Cicely bit her lip and nodded.

"Your mother must have taught you the way a lady comports herself," Eleanor said. "You're expected to behave in certain ways to people of all stations. No matter how we shrink from a leper, you'd not give alms meant for him to a more appealing beggar, would you?"

"No!"

Eleanor nodded. "You're not only bound by conventions, sweeting, you can use them to your advantage."

Cicely frowned. "How?"

"Courtesy can be your mask and your protection. Give each their due, but keep your private feelings and thoughts to yourself. Good manners cost nought but a little effort and will reward you well with high and low alike."

Cicely chewed her lip and nodded. "Now I understand how you can seem to be so easy with her."

Eleanor cocked her head to the side. "What do you mean?"

"Lady Riannon. I couldn't imagine how you could do it. Laughing and jesting with her."

"Lady Riannon is not, I grant you, the easiest person to talk with. She's no leaky pot spilling words whether you would hear them or no. But the rewards amply repay the attempt. She's one of the most interesting people I've met. She might be overly strong on reserve, but none could fault her courtesy. Nor is her intellect deficient. I'd not have you deceive yourself into thinking that she does not notice how you avoid her. It's greatly to her credit, not yours, that she takes no offence. Remember, she is to be your kin."

Cicely lowered her gaze. "I'll try."

"I'll have Hugh saddle your mare, then. You'll ride with me and enlarge your acquaintance with the woman who'll shortly be your sister."

Cicely cast her a desperate look. "I…I'll remember the leper."

Eleanor paused as she reached for Riannon's glove and cast a frown at her niece.

"Her hideous scar," Cicely said. "And…and how unnatural a creature she is. Not a proper woman. Yet not a man. I'll remember what you said about pitying the leper no less for how he looks."

Eleanor snatched up the glove and rounded on her niece. "I cannot be hearing you liken Lady Riannon to a monster?"

Cicely shrank back and clutched the prayer beads hanging from her girdle. "She…she scares me."

Eleanor's flash of temper died as quickly as it had flared. It occurred to her that the person least needing any champion to defend her was Riannon of Gast. Nor would giving Cicely a sharp slap encourage the girl to grow a backbone.

"I grant you that she can be daunting," Eleanor said. "But, betwixt ourselves, I believe that she does not look so grim purposely to frighten. Lady Riannon's façade of politesse is simply so much more formidable a rampart than most of us employ."

Cicely raised her gaze and her eyes widened. "She cannot be regarding *me* as…as someone from whom she must conceal feelings of revulsion? Like…like a leper?"

"I count it one of the gods' most compassionate blessings that none of us sees ourselves as others do."

Cicely looked deeply uncomfortable. Truly, the girl should have been left in her robe at a grove house. Still, no one was immune from the sovereign's will—least of all an orphaned ward of the Crown who had inherited an earldom. As someone who had been given into one marriage with a stranger, then pressured into a second, Eleanor could sympathise. What baffled her, though, was how Cicely so lacked the grace to accept what she could not change and the resilience to make the best of what life served her. Every female child learned that through watching her mother, sisters, cousins, and aunts.

Eleanor knew that to get what she wanted a woman must pay for it. She had remained unmarried for the last three years because of the hundred pounds of silver she gave yearly to the old king for the privilege. She had no illusions that the new queen's sex would render her any more sympathetic or less greedy. If anything, this queen, new to her throne, had even more pressing needs to buy the loyalty of her leading barons. Cicely was a case in point.

Eleanor knew the outcome of her own forthcoming negotiations with the Crown depended solely on whether the size of the bribe she was willing to surrender would be able to counterbalance any benefit the queen might gain from using Eleanor's lands for political patronage. It was a simple, pragmatic calculation that Eleanor judged her niece utterly incapable of making. Nor could she see herself being able to teach her in the next fourteennight. The best she could hope for was some measure of compliant acceptance.

Eleanor strode to the door. "You'll need to wear a cover-chief or veil to shade you from the sun on horseback unless you wish to burn and peel and be as brown as a peasant on your wedding day."

Cicely offered no demur.

Eleanor nodded and swept out. She still held Riannon's glove. There had been times, yesterday, when she had provoked a fleeting grin from Riannon. How different she looked when relaxed and amused. Eleanor wondered what Riannon would look like smiling. Never one to shy from even a stiff challenge, she determined to find out before the end of this day's ride.

❖

Riannon stepped into the chamber and stopped. Aveline stood beside the bed and had her hand inside the bodice of the robe of a young priestess.

Riannon heard voices from the corridor behind her and quickly shoved the door shut. Aveline straightened and turned to look at Riannon. The young priestess flushed scarlet and made an abortive move to straighten her clothes.

"You wished me to tell you ere we were ready to depart," Riannon said.

Aveline smiled. "My thanks. Run along."

The young priestess dropped a deep curtsy to Aveline, sidled warily past Riannon, and bolted out the door Riannon held open. Her bare feet pattered away down the corridor. Riannon moved to leave.

"Not to your taste?" Aveline said. "Too young? Too pale?"

"Too indiscreet."

Aveline laughed. "You have such deadly skill with rebukes. Let us hope, for her sake, that you feel no need to offer any to your future sister. The poor creature is like to faint dead away under the burden of your disapproval."

Riannon let that pass.

Aveline strolled past her. "Although, to be fair to you, the insipid creature looks too fragile to bear the weight of anyone's frowns. The gods help her when she meets your dear brother."

Riannon's memories of Henry were scant. He had been a man full-grown and knighted the year before her birth. Her impression—which was less than a clear recollection—was of a younger version of their sire, down to a bristling beard and a scowl.

The grove house courtyard overflowed with the naer's retinue readying to move. The senior priestess waited beside Aveline's travelling carriage. She was flanked by most of her underlings, except Aveline's erstwhile bed mate. Off to the side, Alan and John, Riannon's groom, waited with her horses. Her destrier, bred and trained for war, looked restive. Riannon knew how the stallion felt.

"Did Lady Barrowmere claim your other glove, too?" Aveline glanced pointedly at Riannon's bare hands.

"What need have you for me?" Riannon said. "You've men at arms in plenty. Especially combined with Lady Eleanor's escort."

"I've a special task that only you can perform. Not some hired ruffian with a spear."

"What is this task?"

"I'm but the conduit, not the origin, of our Wise Mother's will," Aveline said. "As you're her sworn paladin. We all serve in our different ways."

"I'd feel easier if my way was not blind."

"All will be revealed in good time."

Aveline walked away. The seething throng of servants, men, and horses opened a path for her.

"Why do I feel as though the time is of your choosing and not the Goddess's?" Riannon said.

Aveline halted a few yards away. "Did you know that one of the wedding guests is an ambassador of his Imperial Highness, the Lion Emperor?"

The men who heard her turned to stare. One muttered an oath and spat on the ground. Riannon knew they would not be alone in their unhappy surprise at finding themselves in the presence of infidels. Her own thoughts flew back to Vahl, the last bloody siege before the truce. Her hand dropped to the hilt of her sword.

Aveline smiled. "What merrymaking we shall have, shan't we?"

Riannon frowned as she watched Aveline stroll to where she received the obeisances and farewells from the local priestesses. Aveline had not just learned that piece of news. She had probably known it before she met Riannon in that remote grove house. Aveline knew Riannon's wounds incurred at Vahl had been inflicted by a magical blade wielded by an infidel champion. Putting that in close proximity to Aveline's mention of a special quest resulted in no pleasant conclusion.

Riannon stalked away to her waiting squire.

Lady Barrowmere's retinue already threw up a cloud of red-brown dust on the road ahead. Riannon urged her horse past the trail of carts, sumpter horses, unwieldy carriages, walking servants, and men at arms. The lady, today wearing blue, was a sapphire set on the silver of her mare. Riannon guided her horse in beside the grey palfrey.

Lady Eleanor smiled at her. "Good morning."

"Lady." Riannon nodded a bow.

"Good morning, Lady Riannon," Cicely said.

Riannon suppressed her surprise. She had failed to notice Eleanor's niece riding on the other side of her.

"You look out of temper." Eleanor stretched her arm out. "I hope this has no part in its cause."

Surprised at being so easily read, Riannon offered bland thanks as she accepted her glove back.

"Perhaps I was overly hasty in returning it," Eleanor said. "If the portcullis has been lowered and the drawbridge raised against me."

Riannon couldn't help a fleeting grin. "No, lady, I'm mindful of my surrender. My thoughts were elsewhere."

"Hmm. I wonder if I can count that as one? Mayhap I should, as my challenge seems even more formidable now with your sombre mood. Although, a more scrupulous soul wouldn't lower herself to admitting a grin to be quite the same accomplishment as a true smile."

Riannon knew full well she was being teased. She was not deceived by the seriously thoughtful expression on Eleanor's lovely face.

"On the other hand," Eleanor said, "a more amenable person would hardly make me work so hard. For certès, your brother Guy would have me victorious ere we reach the top of yonder rise. And give me a laugh or two into the bargain."

"You know him well?" Riannon said.

Guy was her senior by three or four years, her youngest brother to survive to adulthood. Unlike their eldest brother, whom Riannon had met once or twice after her sister Joan had taken Riannon into her own household, Riannon had no memories of Guy. Riannon had not lived in her widowed father's masculine household even before Guy had been sent, at seven years old, to begin a man's education as a page to one of their father's important vassals. By the time she had fled Joan's well-intentioned interference and their father's wrath, Guy had been a young knight far away in the service of a Brallandese prince. Given his friendship with the Lady Eleanor, though, Riannon set the unknown Guy considerably higher in her estimation than their eldest brother.

"I have the privilege and great pleasure of numbering him amongst my friends," Eleanor said. "You and he are most alike. In looks, that is. So much that I mistook you for him. But you two are so opposite otherwise. He is light-humoured and ready with his tongue. Easy and charming."

"I am not that," Riannon said.

"No," Eleanor agreed. "But, with the greatest respect for your brother, one cannot always live on a dish of comfits. Perfumed sugar and candied ginger make excellent special treats, but they are less satisfying than a dish of fine spiced venison."

"Does that make me a piece of grilled meat or the hunted deer?"

"Neither! You are the spice, of course. Exotic, rare, and imported."

Riannon smiled.

"One!" Eleanor said.

"If my brother has twice the wit I have," Riannon said, "he must yet be hard-pressed to keep apace with you, lady."

"Whereas I wish that most people had half the wit they think they do. We'd all get much better conversation that way."

Riannon smiled again.

"Two," Eleanor said.

"Two?" Riannon said. "What do you count?"

"Your smiles. I've set myself the challenge of making you smile half a dozen times ere we stop at noon to dine."

"I hope you do not forfeit much if you fail," Riannon said.

"Fail? The possibility had not occurred to me."

Riannon laughed and gave the lady her count of three. Four, five, and six rapidly followed.

The morning passed so swiftly that Riannon was surprised when they came upon the tent set up at the roadside by Eleanor's servants for their noon meal and rest.

Riannon dismounted and helped Eleanor from the saddle. The lady smiled as she dropped to the ground. Riannon lost her smile and went rigid.

"My thanks," Eleanor said.

Riannon nodded stiffly and didn't follow when Eleanor linked arms with her niece and walked to the shade of the gaily-coloured tent. That brief, fleeting, impersonal contact—the first time she had touched Eleanor—jarred every sinew with a shock that was painful because of the pleasure it afforded her. *Shite.*

"Something ails you, cousin?" Aveline asked.

Riannon stared down at Aveline. With a certainty that Riannon would stake her soul on, she did not want Aveline to guess that she felt attracted to Eleanor.

"No," Riannon said. "Nought ails me. Save the old complaint. Which I'll never be free of, shall I?"

❖

Eleanor walked into the crowded hall and immediately spied Riannon. She talked with her squire. The Lady of Gast stood tall even amongst men.

Their hostess, who seemed overwhelmed if not overjoyed at such a large party descending on her hospitality for a night, perched on a bench near the hearth. The addition of a chimney to the high end of the hall must be of recent doing, if the soot coating the rafters and underside of the roof was any indication. Household servants eased their way through the crowd of guests. They respectfully moved aside to allow Eleanor to pass. The dogs needed more of a prodding to get out of the way.

She caught a glimpse of Cicely beside their hostess. Naer Aveline's presence ensured that Cicely tried to shrink into the shadows. Still, Eleanor could not completely fault her niece's wariness of the queen's sister. Her reputation as one to whisper from behind the throne demanded caution.

Eleanor halted near Riannon and couldn't help a smile at her fierce look even though Riannon discussed nothing more vexing than a horse that needed shoeing.

"Have John remain with the smith if needs be," Riannon said. "He can bring the horse to join us tomorrow."

"Yes, sir," Alan said. He nodded to Eleanor. "My lady."

Eleanor smiled at him, then turned her look up at Riannon. Riannon fell in step with Eleanor as she continued her unhurried progress across the hall. Riannon walked the same way as she rode, on Eleanor's right. Eleanor had noticed that, when given a choice, Riannon stood to the right side of anyone. This put her unscarred side closest to whomever she conversed with. Eleanor had not expected such self-consciousness in Riannon. She wished to tell her that the scar made no difference, but she guessed that Riannon would be sensitive about the subject being broached openly. Eleanor would have to pick her moment.

"I assume that your squire, of all men, knows that you're a woman?" Eleanor said.

"Yes, lady."

"Yet he calls you sir. Is that the normal mode of address for any knight, irrespective of sex?"

"I do not deceive."

"I didn't think you would. But do you undeceive?"

Riannon frowned. "I could waste much breath in correcting all who assume I am what I am not."

"I can understand that would become tiresome. Yet, would not your squire calling you sir add to the misconceptions about you? Or, mayhap, you find it more convenient to let others believe you a man?"

"There are men who'd follow the person they know as the knight of Gast up a scaling ladder or through a hail of arrows. Those men would not follow the Lady Riannon into a brothel."

Eleanor didn't pretend to be shocked, but, seeing they were now within earshot of the group at the hearth, she restrained herself from an amused enquiry into Riannon's familiarity with whorehouses. That was definitely not something for her niece's ears.

A page boy told Riannon that the naer's marshal wished to confer with her.

"A most timely intervention," Eleanor said.

Riannon signalled her understanding of the threat of Eleanor's shameless curiosity by grinning before she strode away.

Eleanor smiled as she took a seat on the bench beside her niece. While she devoted half her attention to sustaining a part in the conversation about the price of different cloths at certain fairs, she watched Riannon. She was the most intriguing person. The tales of her travels that Eleanor had thus far managed to coax from her would assure her of a firm place in Eleanor's favour. But there was much more to her than that. And that, Eleanor acknowledged to herself, was a goodly part of the fascination. She had to work to get to know Riannon. The digging was like burrowing through an old coffer of clothes to find a layer of forgotten gold brooches, silks, and ermine. Eleanor guessed that most people would be deterred by Riannon's remote manner, forbidding mien, and austere formality. Few would have any idea that it was a crust overlaying an appealing sense of humour and modesty.

Eleanor wondered, too, if the confusion over gender played no small part in people's aversion to, and discomfort with, Riannon. People might not know how to deal with her once they knew she was a woman and not a man. She had experienced some lack of balance herself when Aveline had revealed the truth.

Riannon nodded occasionally as she listened to the marshal. Seeing Riannon beside a man, it was still not obvious that she was a woman. The lack of beard, though uncommon, was not in itself sufficient to determine her a female. On closer scrutiny, Riannon's build—though large and muscular—was not truly that of a man, but few would see in her a woman at a casual glance. Eleanor wished she could see Riannon stand beside her brother, Guy. The comparison would be a revealing one. For certès, Guy dressed more flamboyantly. Riannon's drab tunic and overtunic only reached her knees and showed sombre hose. Even the brooch that had fastened the mantle she wore earlier was plain. Function, rather than style, dominated her attire. It accurately reflected her character—substance rather than surface.

"You could be forgiven for thinking Robert imparted gravest news to my cousin of Gast," Aveline said. "Looking at her, one might think our way barred on the morrow by flood, brigands, dragons, or war."

"I'd wager that even were such terrors in store, madam," Eleanor said, "the Lady Riannon would remain undaunted."

"You probably have the right of it." Aveline smiled. "It seems, though, that, unlike yourself, my marshal hasn't the secret of making my grim cousin smile."

"Sir Robert doesn't seem the sort to have a light tongue," Eleanor said, "nor the inclinations to amusing, inconsequential chatter."

"I had not thought my cousin had, either," Aveline said. "I've been wondering about her preferences. It seems I need to be more observant."

Eleanor returned a polite smile and wondered what Aveline's real meaning was. When, a little later, Eleanor rose to join Riannon sitting at a window seat, she was conscious of Aveline watching her.

Riannon would have risen, but Eleanor waved her down. Eleanor sat and took the chessboard and box of pieces from the page. She began setting the game up on the seat between them.

"It is the duty of a knight, is it not, to protect the weak," Eleanor said, "and rescue defenceless widows from boredom?"

Riannon smiled. "I must have dozed through that part of the oath. And, lady, you're the last person who'd need my help in conversation."

"How ungallant of you to ruin my attempt to be meek and submissive. Especially since you'll have noted that it's not something that comes naturally to me." Eleanor flashed her a smile as she set the last queen in place. "You do play?"

"Poorly," Riannon said.

"Good. I love winning."

Riannon laughed.

As they played, Eleanor garnered more of Riannon's smiles and infrequent laughter.

At one point, Eleanor reached across to straighten one of her men on the board just as Riannon moved to lift one of her pieces. Riannon ended up holding Eleanor's hand.

"Do you suspect me of trying to capture your knight when you weren't looking?" Eleanor said.

"You already have it," Riannon said.

That errant part of Eleanor's mind, which occasionally delighted in making irrelevant observations at inappropriate times, noted how pleasant Riannon's touch felt. It was only several moves later, when she captured one of Riannon's knights, that she realised both of Riannon's chessmen had been on the board when she claimed her knight already taken.

Eleanor was not long in discovering that Riannon had been truthful in her assessment as an indifferent chess player. Her inattention did not aid her game, for she kept staring at the closed shutter as if she could see outside to the steadily falling rain and beyond. Certainly, it was not intake of wine which dulled her skills, for Eleanor noticed that she drank sparingly and that little was heavily watered.

Eleanor captured Riannon's castle and set the ivory piece back in the box. "I could've removed half your men and you not noticed."

"Your pardon, lady. I did warn you that I'd be an unworthy opponent."

"We're not likely to meet with footpads or brigands on the morrow, are we? I ask because you seem to be contemplating something of little pleasure."

"I'm trying to recall the name of a weed."

"A weed?" Eleanor said. "A particular one or would any specimen serve? I could name you any number if it would help."

"It's a plant that grows in warmer lands. You put me in the mind of it."

"A weed?" Eleanor was too astonished to smother her reaction. "Roses, lilies, violets, and daisies even. I've lost count of the number and types of flowers that my person, or parts thereof, have been likened to. So, I'm somewhat jaded to such comparisons. But a weed?"

"Forgive me," Riannon said.

Her guarded demeanour slammed back into place. Eleanor didn't understand the abrupt mood shift, but decided to try to jest Riannon back into smiling.

"I'll have you know," Eleanor said, "that the more ingenious of my flatterers have scavenged the air for birds of magnificent plumage or sweet voices which might bear unfavourable comparison to myself."

Riannon stared down into her wine cup.

"Once," Eleanor said, "I featured in a song in which my body parts put into the shade a type of tree. I cannot recall which variety, but it'll have been one with particularly pleasing foliage."

Riannon's lips twitched in a grin.

"And the amount of fruit that I have found myself in company with!" Eleanor said. "Cartloads."

Riannon smiled and glanced sidelong. "Fruit?"

"No dish of cherries can hold its head up high anywhere near my lips," Eleanor said. "Surely I didn't have to tell you that? Nor any peach take pride in its skin compared to my complexion. Then, of course, there was the fish."

Riannon turned a genuine look of amusement on her. "Fish, lady?"

"It's not every woman who so fires the imagination of susceptible young men that she's showered with poetical allegories in which she becomes a fish."

"I would hope it was a remarkably fine fish?" Riannon said.

"A haddock, I think," Eleanor said. "No! It was a cod. It's easier to rhyme."

Riannon burst out laughing.

"He was very young," Eleanor said. "And so terribly earnest. But for all his callow rawness, he did not liken me to a common weed."

Riannon sobered and looked like she debated with herself before speaking. "Not a common weed. It only grows in land never touched by ice or snow. Men chew the seeds, which are intoxicating. The virtue in them is such that any who taste them need to taste them again. But each time, he must chew more seeds for longer to satisfy himself."

Eleanor cocked her head to the side as she considered this.

"I...I have seen the seeds for sale in a Kardaki marketplace," Riannon said.

"I've heard that in such places spices are more common than grass," Eleanor said. "I imagine an exotic fair with brightly coloured tents, voices speaking strange languages, and warm air heavy with cinnamon, nutmeg, and cloves."

"They reek of dung, rotting refuse, urine, and sweat," Riannon said.

Eleanor shook her head. "What a sadly unromantic creature you are. I suppose I shouldn't be in the least surprised at the weed."

Riannon's expression closed again. She murmured something about needing to check with her squire and strode away across the hall. Eleanor leaned back against the cool stone of the wall and frowned.

CHAPTER FIVE

Riannon lay awake long after dark on her pallet in the place of honour at the high end of the hall. Snores, snuffling, and groans of sleeping men carried past the screen to her. Earlier, she had been an unwilling listener to the imperfectly muffled sounds of one of the men copulating with a village girl. That did anything but ease Riannon's struggles against the growing problem of Lady Eleanor.

With her eyes open, or against the dark inside her lids, Riannon could see Eleanor with cruelly beautiful clarity. The way her lips stretched when she smiled. That utterly charming playful look when she teased. And tonight, Riannon had sat spellbound when Eleanor played her lute. Her voice had raised the hair on the back of Riannon's neck. Riannon watched her fingers move on the strings and imagined them touching herself. She knew what Eleanor's lips looked like when wet with wine. Today on the ride, Eleanor had forsaken her veil and instead wore a golden fillet about her brows and her hair restrained in a decorated net at the back of her neck. Her hair was a darker shade of brown than Riannon had imagined, with a coppery hint of chestnut in the plaited coils. Riannon's fingers itched to touch it. To feel it against her face. To inhale the lady's scent from it.

Riannon rolled onto her stomach to stifle a groan in the pillow. It had been nigh on four years since she had last lain with anyone. Since before Vahl. Before the disfiguring wounds. She had never taken to bed any woman who had not stirred something more than just need for release, but in all the years since lust first kindled its biting flame within her, she had not been so badly consumed as this. She had spoken no less than the truth when she had clumsily likened Eleanor to an addiction. Every glimpse of Eleanor was a unique balm that soothed and yet also inflamed Riannon's longing.

She need only endure until they reached Sadiston. Eleanor owned a house in the town. Aveline would find accommodation in the castle with the queen. Riannon guessed she would sleep there or in the guest house at the grove. She and the lady need not meet again. The lady was a widow. Well-born. She was not the type for a casual tumble. Intelligent. Lively. Eleanor was a woman whose honour Riannon should safeguard, not tarnish.

And there was Aveline. Riannon had caught Aveline watching her and Eleanor. Only the gods knew what cunning wove through her cousin's brain.

Riannon shifted restlessly. Her thoughts returned to Eleanor. Eleanor's laugh. The way her overtunic fitted snugly across her bodice and emphasised the roundness of her bosom. The look in her eye as she riposted with one of her jesting remarks.

Riannon twisted her face into the pillow and slid a hand down between her thighs.

In the morning, Riannon dressed before Alan dragged himself from his pallet. She kicked John, her groom, awake and ordered him to saddle and ready the horses.

Riannon was belting on her sword when Aveline emerged from the shrine.

"I didn't realise we were in such haste," Aveline said. "I would've prayed faster."

"I ride ahead," Riannon said. "Gast is not thirty miles from here. I would visit it."

"Saying hello to both serfs and the pig sty? Don't tarry, for it'd be a passing shame if you were to miss a single moment of the festivities. A wedding and a ten-day tourney to celebrate the happy occasion in providing the opportunity for hundreds of men to dash each other's brains out and steal each other's horses. Truly, my sister honours your brother beyond all men."

Riannon took her hooded mantle from Alan and settled it about her shoulders. "Are you going to tell me what purpose you have for me in Sadiston?"

"You're the sworn warrior of the Goddess. Your holy mission is to champion her against all who oppose her. There'll be noblemen and merchants from half a dozen countries come to guzzle Mathilda's wine and line their pockets with profits from all and sundry. Who knows what might crop up that'll need your splendid skills?"

Aveline smiled and stepped away. "Oh. Shall I pass on your temporary farewell to Lady Barrowmere? Or does the fair widow already know your intentions?"

Riannon frowned at Aveline's retreating back. The gods could see into hearts and minds. Could priests and priestesses? Riannon traced the quartered circle on her breast and silently prayed that Aveline, for one, could not.

Riannon rode with her hood up against a drizzling rain that swept across the thickly wooded countryside in cool bands throughout the early part of the morning. Alan and John rode behind her. For all that she had been careful to spend most of her adult life attached to the household of some lord, she did enjoy being free and alone occasionally. Not that she truly was free. Aveline now held the reins.

Irksome though it was to deal with her conniving cousin, Riannon would not have revoked her oath if given the choice. Not just because of the sword keeping her alive. Not just because of the debt she owed the order for her healing. She served the greatest mistress, the Goddess herself, and there could be no higher reward than a guaranteed place of honour in the afterlife. Not to mention the more mundane consideration that Aveline had issued Riannon with a writ that would ensure regular payment of a good salary and the right to food and healing at any grove house. Riannon need not again worry about feeding and providing livery and wages for her squire and groom. Plus, Aveline had dropped hints about grants of land that could be held from the order.

A herd of cattle blocked the road. Riannon let her horse slow. One impatient merchant, whose laden wagon was surrounded by a sea of slow-moving cattle, bellowed full-bodied abuse at the herder and his boy. All stopped to turn and stare at Riannon's approach. The herder shouted and cracked his stick over the back of the nearest cow.

Riannon's horse shouldered through the incurious cattle. The herder and merchant removed their hats and bowed. Their boys stared wide-eyed. Considering the traffic on the roads, all heading to Sadiston for the fair and tourney, Riannon wondered that any should be so awed at the sight of one nondescript knight and her squire.

All morning, they passed slower moving traffic. Carts, wagons, livestock, and the escort of a nobleman with a dozen servants and companions. Near noon, they came to the town of Brackenswell. It was scarce five miles from Gast.

Riannon looked at the jumble of houses with the eyes of a stranger. How many years had it been since she had last stolen away from Gast to come here for a fair? What a grand gathering she had considered it. How small and dirty the town looked to one who had prayed beneath the gilded turrets on the Temple of the Sun in Themalia, and walked the noisy, massive spring market at Restouin where the road from the sea to the sea crossed the mighty Ypen River.

Riannon dismounted and tossed her reins to John. Alan strode off whistling like a page boy in search of a bakehouse. The early rain had dampened the summer dust but left the air thick and humid. She looked around the square in the centre of the town. She heard the clanging of a smith hard at work and a hoarse-voiced hawker selling hot sausage. People paused to stare at her. Riannon ignored them. She spied the small stone temple off to her left and strode towards it.

The inside was gloomy and deserted. Neither candle nor lamp burned above the anvil altar, though the metal bore a creditable shine. Riannon's leather boots made no sound on the earthen floor as she strode to the front of the temple. She drew her sword and hesitated. Her weapon was a gift from the Goddess and blessed for her service. Had she the right to lay it on the altar of the god of war?

Riannon tugged from her belt sheath the dagger which symbolised her membership of the Knights of the Grand Order of the Star and set that on the metal altar. She knelt and laid her sword on the ground.

"To you, Mighty Atuan, lord of battles, father of warriors, wellspring of honour, and giver of victory, I offer myself again as your meanest servant who hopes to prove herself worthy. By my blood, and by my intent, I renew my oath to serve and honour."

Riannon lifted her dagger and pricked her thumb. She smeared the bead of blood on the side of the anvil and bowed.

As she strode out into the sun, Riannon felt eased of a care she had not been fully aware of bearing. Had she feared that Atuan would send some sign that he spurned her because she had dedicated herself to the Goddess? Too fanciful. Many men served more than one master and swore homage to more than one lord.

Riannon strode back to where Alan waited for her. He wiped

grease from his chin and handed her a large chunk of bread and hot sausage.

"Are we truly heading for your estate, sir?" Alan said. "I'm right eager to see it at last."

"Don't let your hopes rise. It gives me a name, not riches or dignity."

Riannon spat out a chunk of gristle as she cast a glance over the dreary street. If Brackenswell looked so small and grubby, Gast must shrink to little better than a hovel in a field.

After an enquiry for directions, Riannon took the road northwest rather than continue along the Great North Road. She searched for familiar landmarks from a memory eight years old. This road, which was in a much poorer state of repair, wound and dipped between forested hills. The undergrowth encroached thickly on both sides.

A man screamed.

Riannon drew her sword and urged her horse forwards. She rounded the bend to see two men grabbing for the reins of three laden sumpter horses. A woman lay on the ground with a man standing over her. Another man huddled in the road with his arms protecting his head from the club blows of two more attackers.

Riannon rode towards the closest clubman and swung at him. Her sword cleaved into flesh and bone. Blood sprayed over her leg and horse. The second clubman looked frozen in astonishment. Riannon flicked a backhanded blow at him. Too late, he tried to fend off the strike. A foot of bloody steel carved through his forearm and took off the top of his skull. He died before he could scream.

A part of Riannon's mind registered that something unusual was happening, but the woman's scream kept her focussed on the fight. Alan's horse cantered past as he bore down on the men who now abandoned the pack horses and fled for the cover of the forest.

The would-be rapist foolishly and desperately tugged at his braies as he tried to scramble into the undergrowth. The dense bushes impeded him. Riannon leaned across to her right and swung her sword in a fluid downward arc. Her blade sliced through the back of the robber's filthy lambskin jerkin. He collapsed with a piercing scream. He looked like he fell in two pieces with blood gushing from both parts.

Riannon halted her horse and turned it about. The sumpter horses had taken fright and trotted down the road. John gave chase to them.

Alan had pressed through the undergrowth and rode into the forest. Riannon knew no fear on his account. The merchant, still huddled on the ground, watched her warily with a bloody face. The woman, who looked about forty, scrambled to her feet and raced across to him. He straightened to take her in his arms and draw her away from the corpses closest to him. She burst into noisy weeping.

Riannon looked down. The erstwhile rapist did lie in two unequal halves. She stared at what she could not believe.

Riannon frowned and dropped to the ground. She left her horse in the road and strode back to the corpse. Blood from the body soaked the grass, shrubs, and dirt. The rapist's left arm, head, neck, and shoulder lay some inches from the main part of the body. Riannon could see the unnatural whiteness of bone from his spine and dark, bloody chunks of his innards.

She frowned at her sword. Blood oozed along the groove of the fuller and dripped from the oiled steel. Only Mighty Atuan should have been powerful enough to have delivered a single-handed blow that butchered a man into two pieces.

Riannon frowned across at the other bodies. She strode to where they lay. One strike had cleanly cut the man's arm in two and sliced his head apart. His severed hand still gripped his wooden club. The top of his skull lay in the road like a hairy dish holding white and grey brains. Her second blow had hacked a mortal gouge through the sinews, bone, and organs of the other robber's torso to all but divide the body in two.

"Thank you, my lord." The merchant, still holding his weeping wife, dropped to his knees and drew her down with him. "Thank you, sir. You saved our lives. I...I thought we were dead. They came from nowhere. Killed our valet. Thank you, my lord."

Riannon absently nodded and turned to look again at the rapist's corpse. She had seen, and inflicted, wounds beyond counting. Bodies battered, hacked, and mutilated by clubs, swords, axes, maces, and spears. She had no illusions about the damage a yard and more of razor sharp steel could do to a man. But the blows she had delivered should not have carved as deep as they had. The impact she had felt in her wrist and arm when her blade hit the bodies had been as slight as if she cut down through the surface of a river.

Riannon lifted her sword. When she had practised with it, to accustom herself to its weight and balance, she had not tested the edge against anything.

"Sir!" Alan guided his horse towards her. "Two got away. I thought it not worthwhile to chase them."

Riannon nodded without taking her gaze from the gift sword. Men had relics and charms put in the hilts of swords, or even forged into the tangs, in the hope of protecting themselves against surprise attacks or to ameliorate wounds. In bard's tales, villains and monsters who used magics to gain unfair advantage over their opponents invariably suffered for their evil at the hands of a hero. Real life was not that just.

"Vahl," Riannon said.

That imperial bastard who killed so many men at Vahl, and who dealt Prince Roland his fatal wounds, had used no mortal weapon. Riannon had almost died because of such vile powers—and lived under sentence of death from those same wounds. A sentence that only this sword held in abeyance.

"You are unhurt, sir?" Alan said. "John has the horses."

"Get the heads," Riannon said. "We must take them to the local lord to explain how the men died."

"Sir, my lord," the merchant said, "let me give you the pick of my wares in gratitude. Please—"

Riannon strode across the road and pushed through the undergrowth. She found a tree as thick as her thigh. Using a two-handed grip, she scythed the sword in a horizontal arc. The blade slowed as it bit into the wood but emerged on the other side. She might have been cutting through a wax bier candle. The tree toppled to the side with a splintering crash of breaking branches. Riannon stared with disgust at her sword.

"You bitch," she said. "You didn't tell me about this."

Riannon jammed the sword's point into the fresh stump and removed her belt. The scabbard must have some enchantment on it, too, or the sword would have cut clean through it.

When Riannon shoved back onto the road, the merchant and his wife were still thanking Alan.

"Give me my other sword," Riannon said to her squire. "We must hasten to find the lord before we regain the road north."

Alan frowned. "North? But I thought your estate lay along this road, sir."

"It does and will remain so, even though we do not visit it this day," she said. "I have pressing need to talk with Naer Aveline."

❖

Aveline inhaled deeply. From the earliest time she could remember, that pungent, rich, humid smell of a forest represented power. Her grandfather and father had been kings. They had ruled over men. Their power was of gold, blood, oaths, and land. Not an insubstantial thing, the rule of kings. But a man claimed kingship by right from the gods, no matter how much blood he spilled nor how many bribes he paid to claw his way onto a throne. His grip on the hem of the robe of divinity held him in place.

The true power, the one that smelled of rot and yet also the freshness of a world renewed every day, belonged to the divine. Theirs was the power to unmake mountains. To sink islands into the seas. To rain fire from the sky. It was old and deep and eternal. And it, too, ran in Aveline's veins, inextricably mingled with the blood she inherited from a long line of mortal kings. She took no small pride in being called to be a priestess. She would offer every drop of her royal blood, strain every sinew, and use every ounce of will in proving herself worthy of divine trust.

Aveline lifted her arms in a final supplication before turning to the kneeling worshippers behind her. Most were the green-robed priestesses and aspirants of the grove house. Lady Havelock and Lady Barrowmere, and their household, knelt on the left side, farthest from the blessed stream. Aveline intoned a blessing and signed the quartered circle in the air.

The senior priestess, having hosted Aveline on many previous occasions, arranged a comfortably appointed chamber for the naer. The excellent supper she provided for the enormous combined retinue did the order credit.

A messenger arrived as Aveline retired from the table. The dusty young man knelt and dug a thick packet of parchment from inside his tunic. The black wax seal bore the impression of a woman in clerical robes wearing a chaplet of leaves and holding in one hand a staff with the head of a quartered circle and in the other hand a ewer from which she poured water. The seal belonged to the matriarch of the Order of the Goddess. Aveline accepted the packet herself.

"You've come from Matriarch Melisande?" Aveline said.

"Yes, Eminence," he said. "Her Holiness instructed me to make all speed and surrender this to your hands only."

Aveline dismissed him to the care of one of the local priestesses. Aware of the avid interest of the senior priestess, she strolled away to the chamber prepared for her. She dispensed with the services of her clerks after one had lit lamps for her. Alone, she opened the packet. She found a letter to her sister, the queen. Aveline set that aside and unfolded the other sheet of parchment covered with close lines of neat script in the handwriting of professional scribes.

She read through the usual greetings. In light of the recent accession of Aveline's sister to the throne, the matriarch expressed her understanding of the need for Aveline to remain in Tirand. In such an unsettled time, it was important for the new queen to have access to all possible spiritual counsel and advice. None could be better suited to deliver that than her own sister, who—though she might not enjoy a place on the queen's privy council—would be able to make the voice, and needs, of the order heard through less formal channels. Accordingly, the matriarch saw no need for Aveline to travel to Rhân for the convocation. To further free her to concentrate her efforts in her sister's realm, the matriarch relieved Aveline of her special legatine powers to the court of King Fulk of Iruland.

Bitterly disappointed, Aveline stood to pace. In keeping her from attending the convocation of mother-naers, the matriarch sought to exclude her from the highest level of the order. At that gathering, Aveline could meet and attempt to persuade the mother-naers who debated and voted on matters of policy and doctrine. Their decisions would in turn influence the stance the matriarch of the Goddess would take when the highest representatives of all four religious orders met in the Quatorum Council. One of those issues should be a call for a holy war. Aveline must do all in her power to ensure that it would be. That was the Goddess's will.

She wondered if the matriarch suspected her intentions. Since her elevation to the highest office, Melisande had hidden her passivity and timidity behind the false posture of feminine nurturing. Small wonder the Goddess's servants were held in such slight esteem amongst the other orders. Yes, the Goddess was Wise Mother and Lady of Mercy and Healing, but she was also the powerful primeval female half of Creation. She had a Dark Face she turned implacably to her enemies. Women were vessels filled with all virtues, not just soft ones. Who could be stronger, more tenacious, or fiercer to protect than mothers? Aveline had no patience for the matriarch cravenly shying from this truth. The convocation must be made to acknowledge the source of the strength of their order. They must see that the ultimate goal rested in the Cave of the Pool and the power lying dormant there. They must rid the world of heretics and unbelievers. Consecrated women must raise their voices to call for holy war.

Could the old woman, or one of her supporters, have seen any hint of what Aveline planned? Did the matriarch feel threatened by the prospect of being prodded into action? But this crude stratagem would not stop Aveline. She had a divine mission to see this come to pass.

Aveline tapped the parchment. King Fulk of Iruland, whose vassals' domains abutted the territories most recently swallowed by the last resurgence of the Empire, was naturally most eager to end the truce and wage war on the infidel enemy. The idea of having an army recruited for his aid from all over the Eastern Kingdoms, and sanctioned by the four gods, could not fail to appeal to any monarch. Fulk, who was a cousin of her late father's, had already responded positively to her overtures about a possible holy war. The matriarch acted too late if she sought to keep Aveline from him. The representative the Irulandi king would send as his official observer to the Quatorum Council would be primed to lobby for crusade.

Aveline sat and reread the message. On balance, she was inclined to believe the rescinding of her special authority had no stronger root than the old woman clipping her wings. It was a demonstration of power and a notification that Aveline had been noticed. So be it.

Aveline sat back and frowned at a lamp flame. Mathilda's coronation had probably come as a nasty shock to Matriarch Melisande. Few had believed that men would accept a woman sovereign. Well, they had reckoned without Aveline. There were always means and methods around human problems. It was merely a question of finding the right lever, the right price.

Aveline needed to attend the convocation. She must persuade

one of the mother-naers who would accompany the matriarch to the Quatorum Council to include Aveline in her entourage. If Aveline was present at the Quatorum Council, she would be in a position to stiffen the resolve of members of her own order. She could also communicate directly with her peers in the orders of Atuan, Naith, and Kamet. The Patriarch of the Order of Atuan, god of war, would need no persuading to put forth a call for a crusade. The followers of the other two gods might require more convincing. How much easier they would be to sway if they could be shamed with the taint of cowardice and weakness if the women of the Goddess spoke with a determination to rid the world of unbelievers. Male pride could be a weapon used against them for the good of all.

Once the Quatorum Council published a call for holy war, men would flock to take the vow. Be they freeborn peasant, knight, lord, or king, men would fight knowing their deaths on crusade would guarantee direct entry into Paradise. Their act of dedicating themselves to the gods' will absolved them of their sins. Killing infidels served the cause of righteousness. Some, admittedly, would have one eye on the loot and land to be gained from the reconquest of Evriat. That the rewards could be both spiritual and temporal only added to the incentive. Aveline did not see why avarice could not be used as a means to coax sinners to noble purposes.

The Quatorum Council only met every fourth year. The next meeting was but a handful of months hence in late autumn. She did not want to have to wait another four years for the next opportunity.

Aveline drummed her fingers on the table. There must be someone who would, in return for a gift of land or gold from her sister the queen, arrange for Aveline to attend. She mentally ran through the list of the score of mother-naers on the convocation. Which one had relations amongst Mathilda's vassals who might be grateful that her family enjoyed the financial goodwill of their liege lady?

Aveline remained preoccupied with this when she returned to the main hall. The sound of singing and a lute greeted her. She paused to see Lady Eleanor playing to a rapt audience. The song, Aveline noted as she strolled to join them, lacked the lady's usual vivacity. At the conclusion, the senior priestess offered highly flattering remarks.

"My father told me that I could've earned my meat as a minstrel," Eleanor said.

Her audience greeted this playful idea—of a noblewoman earning wages as a performer—with a prudish horror that Aveline found amusing.

"Fortunately, Lady Barrowmere," Aveline said, "your riches are not limited to musical talents."

"That's true, madam," Eleanor said. "I'm fortunate enough to be able to set aside my amateur efforts and call upon a true artist to entertain us."

Eleanor signalled to her minstrel. He bowed and launched into a long song. Lady Cicely and most of the younger priestesses closely followed the romantic tale of improbable deeds. They sighed often, and murmured dismay at the slightest faltering of the hero. Some of the older priestesses looked scarcely less susceptible. Aveline preferred Eleanor's performance. Perhaps it was the soprano voice. Or perhaps it had been that hint of sadness.

"My mother warned me strictly against unseemly public display," Eleanor said to Aveline. "I'd not considered myself in danger in a grove house."

Aveline smiled. "It'd be a pity if you were to restrict your play to the confines of your home and the ears of a husband."

"Sadly, madam, it has been my experience that not all husbands appreciate music," Eleanor said. "For certès, no more than the sound of their own hunting tales."

"Perhaps it's merely a question of acquiring the right husband."

Eleanor's expression didn't noticeably change, but Aveline detected a wariness.

"Like yourself, madam," Eleanor said, "there are those who prefer to remain without husbands. As your late lord father also graciously accepted."

Aveline nodded. She understood perfectly well what Eleanor implied about wishing to pay to continue her widowhood. She would have to make enquiries about just how extensive Lady Barrowmere's land holdings were.

"Not all are suited to marriage, just as some find no solace in being alone." Aveline rose. "You sing prettily, Lady Barrowmere. Your melody was less melancholy, though, when my cousin of Gast was with us."

The surprise on Eleanor's face lacked any artifice of concealment or disguise. Aveline wondered about that as she retired to her chamber.

CHAPTER SIX

Riannon slowed her horse when she saw the clutter of horses, servants, wagons, and Eleanor's bright tent pitched in a fallow field on the west side of the Great North Road. The day's delay needed to track down the under-sheriff to render her tale of the robbers had done little to sweeten her temper. She dropped to the ground and yanked loose the ties that held the gift sword on the back of her saddle. She stalked across to where Eleanor, Aveline, Cicely, and their principal attendants sat partaking of a picnic dinner.

Eleanor smiled. Riannon nodded to her but immediately turned her attention on her cousin.

"I take it that you found even less than you expected at Gast to entertain you," Aveline said.

"We must talk," Riannon said.

Aveline cocked an eyebrow and looked poised to make a pointed observation.

"Now," Riannon said. "You'll excuse us, lady."

Aveline's amusement appeared to deepen as she passed her trencher to a servant and rose. Eleanor watched with a quizzical frown.

"Did you lose your courtesy somewhere on the roadside?" Aveline said.

Riannon put a hand on Aveline's elbow and propelled her clear of the ears of those around the tent.

"No. I left bodies. Bodies in parts." Riannon released Aveline and dropped the gift sword on the grass at her cousin's feet. "You lied to me."

"Lied? What can you be accusing me of?"

"I cut men in two with that. I've cleaved with it a tree which should have taken a half a dozen axe blows to fell. It is no blade of mortal steel. What other magical properties does this sword have that you kept from me?"

"I made no secret of it being blessed," Aveline said. "A gift from the Goddess. You didn't expect it to be something plucked from any old smithy? Or bought for a few shillings at a small town fair? It's the weapon worthy of being wielded in the service of the Goddess. As for special properties, you know it keeps you alive. You seem to have no qualms about benefiting from that."

"You'd have me inflict such wounds on another. I will not do it."

Aveline lifted a hand to Riannon's face. Riannon caught her wrist and stopped her fingers short of touching her scar.

"You're hurting me," Aveline said.

"Choose another for whatever you design. I cannot and will not use that sword."

"What of your oath?"

"It was given in ignorance," Riannon said. "You deliberately withheld from me the true nature of what you gave me. Such an oath is not binding."

"You've taken to study of the law? You do surprise me. I did not think you knew your letters."

Riannon wrenched Aveline's wrist down. Aveline winced and lost all pretence at amusement.

"You've been granted one of the Goddess's rare gifts," Aveline said. "It'll help you against her enemies. Most would fall over themselves to get some advantage over their opponents. You have it. You'll need it."

Riannon released her as if she found herself holding a serpent. "My honour is not for sale. No matter what else you coerce from me, you mistake the matter entirely if you think you have that bought and paid for."

Aveline rubbed her wrist, though she kept her gaze up on Riannon's face. "How is it honourable to let someone kill you when you have the means at hand of killing him first?"

"I do not expect you, of all people, to understand."

"I know you mean that as an insult, yet I take it otherwise when you talk of such illogical ideas that are against all good sense. So, it's probably for the best that you are what you are, cousin, and I am a creature entirely different. Tell me, does this mean that you forswear your oath of service? What of the debt you owe?"

That was the crux of her dilemma. Her obligation went well beyond merely swinging a particular weapon. Her commitment had been to serve the Goddess against her enemies. Despite her burning sense of betrayal by Aveline, Riannon had given her vow to the Goddess, not the priestess. She scowled down at the sword.

"I'll not use that," Riannon said.

Aveline bent to pick up the sheathed sword. She offered it back to Riannon. "There will be a time when you will need it."

"No."

Aveline shrugged. "You need to carry it. You cannot leave it in this field."

There was the burr under the saddle. Riannon snatched the sword from Aveline's hands.

"You know nought of honour," Riannon said. "But your divine mistress must. It's in that I place my trust. Not you."

❖

Later that afternoon, Eleanor slipped out of the noisy hall as soon as she politely could. Lord and Lady Woodfort entertained the queen's sister. Eleanor knew them little. Her retinue found welcome at their castle because of the naer. Normally she would have considered that all the greater obligation to make herself agreeable and entertaining, and to acquire new acquaintance. Today she needed to find Riannon.

A servant moved aside as Eleanor stepped out of the side door and into a passage that led to the tower chambers and the solar. Which way might Riannon have gone?

Eleanor had been delighted with Riannon's unexpected return at noon, but whatever passed between Riannon and her cousin left her stony and uncommunicative all afternoon. The most number of words she had strung together had been to apologise for being poor company.

Eleanor pushed another door open and emerged into the bustling bailey. With no breath of wind this summer evening, smoke from the busy kitchen building hung thickly between the castle walls. Riannon would have a pallet in the hall to sleep on, so there was no chamber in the keep, gatehouse, or towers she might have retired to.

Eleanor caught sight of Hugh, her marshal. He informed her that he had seen Riannon go into the shrine chamber in the gatehouse. Eleanor picked her way across the bailey and up a narrow set of stone steps. By the light of a lamp above the gilded scales of Kamet, Eleanor saw Riannon kneeling on a prayer mat.

Eleanor stepped inside and shut the door. Riannon looked around.

"I'll leave if I intrude," Eleanor said.

Riannon shook her head.

Eleanor made her obeisance to all four niches. "To Atuan, lord of gods. To Kamet, giver of law. To Naith, bestower of bounty. To our Wise Mother. I humbly present myself and beg your blessing." She traced the quartered circle on her breast and kissed her fingers.

Riannon offered no protest when Eleanor lowered herself to the mat beside her. Her naked sword lay on the tiled floor. Eleanor arranged her skirts as comfortably as she could under her knees, for the thin mat provided scant cushioning.

"If there is aught I can do to help with what troubles you," Eleanor said, "I will."

Riannon sighed and frowned down at her sword. "It's all of my own doing."

"That would certainly make it more uncomfortable," Eleanor said. "But no less susceptible to aid."

Riannon grinned fleetingly. "Are you ever uncertain about anything, lady?"

"All too frequently. Something has made you doubt yourself?"

Riannon's gaze flicked up from her sword to the anvil altar of Atuan, then across to the wilted green boughs in the niche of the Goddess.

"I feel as though I've been given a prize that I've long coveted," Riannon said. "Only to find a crack in it."

"Many things can still function though flawed. Imperfections can be mended. They need not render something unusable or valueless. Do you believe the crack is within yourself?"

"I have flaws beyond counting. You're right to remind me that nothing is without imperfection. I do still value what I've been given. And know there is truth and purpose in my oath. No matter that it is tarnished."

Eleanor wondered about the oath. "Where in that does the fault lie with you? To me, it sounds like you've found yourself in a situation not of your making. Which is all too familiar to anyone who has lived past the age of weaning. But it's not sound grounds for upsetting the surety you have in yourself. Rather, you should be doubting the source of your problem."

Riannon shook her head. "I'm accountable for what I do, no one else. After death, when I stand before the gods, they'll look into my heart, and mine alone, to judge the worth of what I've done and the life I've lived. The task of safeguarding my honour is mine. It's childish of me to wish this should be easy to do throughout the course of a life."

"If so, then I've never met a mature person. Myself included. Though I've the strongest suspicion that most of us select far easier paths through life's problems than you do, my friend."

Eleanor put a hand on Riannon's forearm. Riannon's muscles tensed under her fingers.

"I flatter myself that I can number you amongst my friends," Eleanor said. "Which seems presumptuous after so short an acquaintance. But I have rarely, if ever, known someone with whom I've fallen into such an enjoyable and interesting companionship."

Riannon looked down at where Eleanor's hand rested on her arm. The muscles under Eleanor's fingers remained taut.

"Have I misspoken?" Eleanor said. "Or presumed too much?"

Riannon shook her head. She set her free hand over Eleanor's, to hold it in place on her arm. Her inner turbulence worked close enough beneath her protective surface that Eleanor could all but feel it. How the matter Riannon had just alluded to connected with Naer Aveline and Riannon's fraught encounter with her at midday, Eleanor could not begin to guess.

"I missed you yesterday." Eleanor gently squeezed Riannon's forearm. "I'm loath to admit such a thing about my blood kin, but Cicely makes for a poor companion compared to you."

"And I missed you."

Riannon stroked the back of Eleanor's hand with her thumb, then lifted Eleanor's hand to press a kiss to her fingers. Eleanor smiled, but before she could make a teasing remark about the courtly gesture, Riannon released her, turned away, and scooped up her sword. Riannon stood swiftly to slide the sword into its scabbard.

"I must leave," Riannon said. "For Sadiston."

"Now? You are aware that it's close to dark and with much cloud to hide the moon tonight?"

Riannon's jaw worked as she considered this. She looked for all the world like a troubadour's hero impetuously wishing herself away on a fast steed. Had Riannon been in a better humour, Eleanor would have mock chided her for giving the impression of wanting to flee. Instead, Eleanor held up her hands. Riannon took them and helped her rise.

"I'll not pry," Eleanor said as she shook out her skirts. "Well, no more than I have already. But I hope you feel that you can trust to my discretion."

Eleanor gave Riannon's hand a squeeze and headed for the door.

"Lady? May I visit you?"

Eleanor turned back with a smile. "I expect it. Where will you be staying in the city? With your family?"

Riannon frowned. "I'm unsure. I have no expectation of a welcome with them. Perhaps I'll find lodging at an inn. I cannot guest at the grove house."

The last, at least, came as no surprise.

"I'd be honoured to have you as my guest," Eleanor said.

Riannon accepted the offer with a shy smile. But it was a smile, and Eleanor was content with that. She had little doubt that before the evening was done she could coax Riannon into a lighter mood. Riannon opened the door for her.

"Lady, I thank you," Riannon said.

"I have a name, you know," Eleanor said.

"Yes, lady."

Eleanor laughed and threaded her arm through Riannon's for the walk back across the bailey. Her sojourn in the city, which Eleanor had not been anticipating with unbridled pleasure, now promised much enjoyment.

❖

Eleanor sighed, contented as a cat, as Agnes brushed her hair. One of her earliest memories was of her nurse combing her hair. Although, the nurse had often muttered about Eleanor's unfashionable colouring and tried for years to lighten the chestnut brown with lemon rinses. For all the worries and insecurity that the woman had successfully instilled in young Eleanor about her appearance, Eleanor had not lacked for compliments.

Once Agnes eliminated the few tangles, Eleanor closed her eyes and surrendered to a physical pleasure that was sensual but innocent. She could have sat all night and all day to the comforting rhythm of the long strokes.

"Aunt?"

Eleanor stifled a sigh and turned to see Cicely with her long blond hair already neatly plaited for the night. Cicely's pale complexion, fair hair, and slender neck comprised exactly those attributes most prized in song. Eleanor's childhood nurse would not have tutted sadly over her.

"Aunt, the love between men and women is different, is it not, to the love we have for the gods? And the love I had for my puppy?"

Had the questioner been anyone else, Eleanor would have been hard-pressed not to laugh. Cicely looked in earnest. Eleanor signalled to Agnes to hurry.

"Yes, sweeting," Eleanor said. "Love comes in many forms. In my experience, which is not, I admit, so very broad, the love I feel for different people is in no two cases the same."

Cicely considered this with a grave expression. Agnes's deft fingers finished their hasty plaiting. Eleanor rose, picked up a candle, and drew Cicely behind the screen to their sleeping pallets. None of the women followed them. Cicely sat beside Eleanor. Her fingers, with the nails chewed to nothing, twined together in her lap.

"What worries you?" Eleanor said. "Is it that you feel you're somehow less deserving of the Goddess's love because you've put aside your dedication to her? Sweeting, I don't think she regards a woman inferior for being a wife rather than priestess."

Cicely bit her lip. Eleanor stroked the girl's rigid back and patiently waited.

"How...how can I learn to love?" Cicely blushed darkly. "I...I love the Goddess. And I loved my mother. I must've loved my father, though I was only young when he died and don't remember him. I loved the high priestess, and Sio Margaret and Sio Blanche and...and all of the priestesses. But...."

Cicely slumped and directed a miserable look at the floor.

"No one expects you to love the Lord Henry," Eleanor said.

Cicely straightened with surprise. "He is to be my husband."

"Yes, but the marriage vows say nought of love. Nor should they. That would be wholly unrealistic, sweeting. You and the Lord Henry are strangers. How could you possibly love him?" Eleanor patted Cicely's hand. "I'm sure you'll have no trouble finding much to honour in him, and he in you. Your beauty will be no hindrance to that."

"Did...did you love your husbands?"

Eleanor looked away as if searching the shadows for the past. Perhaps it was Cicely's presence which thrust Eleanor's memories back beyond the usual one that sprang to her mind when she thought of her first husband. Instead of Lionel racked with mortal wounds, she saw him through the eyes of the trembling young bride she had been on her wedding day. A stocky stranger, as old as her father, whose breath smelled of onions and rotting teeth. And his black fingernails. She would always remember his hands—dirty, caked with filth, smearing her pale skin when he clutched her breasts and mounted her. At least William, her second husband, had been clean.

Eleanor shuddered and returned to the present to see Cicely watching her. She forced a smile.

"Like yourself, I knew neither of my husbands ere we wed," Eleanor said. "Though I had met William once or twice, since his father and mine were known to each other. From respect, affection can grow betwixt man and wife."

"Respect? Affection? But are we not to be devoured by passion? The songs...."

"The bards sing of lands where trees bear fruits of gold and no one ever knows hunger or infirmity. They're entertainment, not reality. And who would have it otherwise? For certès, I'd much rather hear about handsome dragon-slaying heroes risking life and limb for but a kind word from a comely woman, than some dreary tale about a man crippled with the gout whiling away an evening in discussion with his steward about the falling price of wool."

Cicely giggled. "That would be a very strange song."

Later, when they lay in their pallets in the dark with their women sleeping around them, Eleanor heard Cicely whisper her name.

"I'm not asleep," Eleanor whispered. "What troubles you?"

"Does no one ever feel love as the minstrels sing? Is it not real? Like golden fruit and handsome heroes?"

Eleanor's thoughts flew past two husbands to a summer during her first widowhood when she'd dallied with a local knight's son. She had believed, at the time, that love burned incandescent within her. Certainly she received a revelation about physical love from him, and without a fresh dose of the pox. She wept at his leaving. But her tears had quickly dried and at no point had she wilted dangerously on the edge of expiring out of grief for her loss.

"I've no doubt that love can burn as brightly and hotly as the troubadours sing," Eleanor whispered to Cicely. "But I also believe that it mercifully afflicts few. Most of us have everyday loves and affection."

"Afflict? You made love sound like a disease."

"Can you imagine how burdensome it must be to lose yourself in another and live only for him?" Eleanor said. "And how hard it must be to breathe normally betwixt all those sighs?"

In the dark, Eleanor did not know if Cicely smiled or looked shocked at her romantic apostasy. How had the girl acquired such unrealistic notions about love and life in a grove house? Did Eleanor now do right in trying to set the girl's feet more firmly on the ground, or should she have left her with a thread of shining hope that might sustain her through the realities of marriage?

Sleep eluded Eleanor long after Cicely fell silent. Her thoughts turned to the arrangements for the wedding. Thank all the gods that the Earl Marshal and the queen shouldered the major burden of the festivities—and the cost. Eleanor would have to have mortgaged fully half the acres she owned to have afforded the planned feasts and tourney. Not that she would have sponsored a tournament even had she a bottomless purse.

Her thoughts drifted from guest lists and account rolls to love. She had told Cicely the truth as she experienced it—that love came in many forms, and none of them the all-consuming passion extolled by bards. Certainly none of the five men with whom she had shared a bed ignited such exaggerated feelings in her. The most enduring relationships were those with friends. Friendship was an altogether different species of love that rarely fired the imagination, though arguably the most valuable, enduring, and rewarding. The newest of which, with Riannon, promised to be a special example.

Very special. Eleanor smiled and turned to get more comfortable. When she and Riannon parted this evening, she left Riannon in a much better humour. She reviewed their conversation in the shrine chamber. There was much to wonder about in what Riannon had left unsaid. That some tie beyond blood bound Riannon and Naer Aveline had grown increasingly obvious. Days ago, Eleanor had discarded coincidence as the reason for the cousins travelling together. Riannon admitted that she did not relish the reunion with her family. What other reason could there be for her travelling to Sadiston?

Eleanor pushed the bedding down to leave only the linen sheet covering herself. It was no wonder she had trouble sleeping on such a close night. Perhaps, too, thinking of those she had bedded had warmed her blood. Yet, the touch which leaped to her recall was not that of any man. Her body remembered the ghostly pleasure of Riannon's hand over hers in the shrine chamber, and the way Riannon's thumb stroked the back of her wrist. She could easily picture the look Riannon had given her after kissing her hand. When she remembered Riannon admitting that she had missed her company for a day, Eleanor felt pleasure that she had not been conscious of at the time.

Eleanor frowned at the night. Riannon was a woman. A friend. Yet, she couldn't help wondering if a part of her mind still mistakenly identified Riannon as the man Eleanor had first thought her. Or, perhaps more correctly, Eleanor's body retained the error about Riannon's sex. Had Riannon truly been a man, Eleanor realised that she might be now diagnosing herself as in danger of falling in love with him. Where did friendship end and passionate love begin? At least with another woman, the question could remain safely abstract.

❖

Aveline stepped from the travelling carriage and offered a silent prayer of thanks to the Lady of Mercy and Healing that their journey ended in Sadiston on the morrow. She had been too many days on the road.

Her attention slipped beyond the approach of the welcoming group of the grove house. Riannon had helped Lady Eleanor and her niece from the saddle and now escorted them through the noisy press of horses and men towards the main doors. Some subtle difference in their physical closeness and the way Riannon looked at Eleanor—signs that others not accustomed to noticing women with women might not detect—wrote a message loud and clear in a language Aveline knew well how to read.

Her own tastes ran to a different type of female, but she could see how Eleanor might appeal to men and women alike—not least because of her wealth. Aveline would not grudge her cousin Riannon any bed sport, save that which might interfere with Aveline's plans for the greater good of the order.

While Aveline received the effusive greetings of the senior priestess, she mentally reviewed the nubile priestesses at the Sadiston grove house. There had to be one she could encourage Riannon into a light, meaningless dalliance with if she needed to work off some lust. Although, given Lady Eleanor's age, perhaps a more mature woman would be to her cousin's liking.

After the twilight service, Aveline dismissed all thoughts of Riannon, Eleanor, and pretty young women, and signalled to her ever-present attendants her need to be alone.

Two torches burned in metal stands driven into the ground near the blessed pool. Their flames writhed to the unseen breath of the grove. Aveline, too, was a flame, alive with an inner power that could be either beneficent or dangerous.

Aveline closed her eyes and inhaled deeply. She was an instrument of the Goddess. This was what she had been born for. Hers was a destiny to fulfil the will of the Lady of Creation. Not by grinding herbs and applying poultices, or attending women in bloody, painful childbed. Not even by managing a grove and increasing its prosperity. The hand of the Goddess had caused her to be third born daughter of a king, so her way did not end in throne and crown. Her path ran less straight and more troublesome. More interesting. Not pawn. Not queen. Not knight. Aveline was not a game piece for others to move. Hers must be the shadowy hand to move others and rearrange them for the glory of the Goddess.

Aveline heard a scuff and whirled around. A pale figure stood with one hand on a tree trunk. Lady Cicely made a peculiarly timorous ghost. Aveline relaxed.

"Have you lost your way, Lady Havelock?" Aveline said.

She thought Cicely might bolt at the sound of her voice.

"I...I did not mean to disturb you, Eminence," Cicely said.

"You do not," Aveline lied. "Do you seek me or the solace of the pool?"

Cicely glanced around as if fearing they might be overheard. "I... I wished to talk with you, exalted madam."

"Come closer." Aveline held out a hand. "Then we need not shout at each other."

The promise of greater confidentiality drew Cicely from the trees. In the wavering light, the girl looked half scared out of her wits. She had not previously screwed up the courage to address Aveline save in response to a greeting or question. Aveline itched with curiosity to know what had spurred her to this encounter, for her imagination failed her.

"How may a servant of the Goddess help you?" Aveline said. "Or is it the sister of the queen with whom you wish to talk?"

Cicely lowered her gaze. Her fingers worked against each other. "Madam, I—You are the most powerful priestess."

"Mayhap I shall be one day," Aveline said. "I take it that a naer will serve your purpose this evening?"

Cicely bit her lip and frowned. On an impulse, Aveline put a hand on Cicely's arm and urged her towards the path through to the sacred pond. Cicely stiffened and might have baulked, but Aveline kept a firm grip on her.

"We'll not be disturbed in here," Aveline said.

Cicely relaxed fractionally and looked around with frank curiosity at a place where only the initiated should tread. She would probably be disappointed, for there was little to see in the grey moonlight save a clearing, a dark stream, and darker trees.

"Now, what has disturbed your peace?" Aveline said.

Cicely looked up sharply, then just as quickly looked away. Her bosom heaved with a deep breath. She gulped in some courage and words tumbled out. "I need a charm. Before I'm married. You can make me one. Please, Eminence. You're so important and powerful. I must have something. I'm so afraid that he won't like me. I want him to love me. Our Wise Mother must understand. I'm so scared. Please help me. Please."

Aveline's left eyebrow lifted. "You wish for a love charm?"

"For my future husband. We will be legally man and wife. That... that cannot be wrong, can it?"

"It was not the morality but the novelty of the request that surprised me."

Cicely chewed her lip. She looked for all the world like a girl half her age braced for a whipping.

Aveline lifted the girl's chin and forced her to return her gaze. "I can help. But you need to have the utmost care in what blessing you ask for. Do you understand?"

"Y-yes, Eminence."

"Are you bleeding with your flux?"

"Y-yes, Eminence. This is my second day. I waited for it before I came to you."

Aveline nodded. Timid the girl might be, but she had lived for several years in a grove house.

Aveline drew her to the stream and motioned for her to kneel. Cicely nearly fell into the water in her haste to obey. She looked horrified as she snatched the hem of her kirtle out of the water. Aveline knelt close and took the wad of dripping cloth in her fingers. She wrung it out. Cool water dribbled over her hand and down her wrist.

"You know that the mind and souls of us mortals are insufficient to understand the will and ways of the divine," Aveline said. "You need to be clear and precise in your mind and heart about what you ask for. Do you understand?"

Cicely nodded.

Aveline closed her eyes, pressed her left hand to the grass, and breathed deeply. She smelled Cicely's perfume. Floral. Intrusive. Aveline concentrated to reach out to the true scents of this place. Humus. Sap. Decay. Crushed grass. Her wet hand tingled as if a shadow from the heart of the woods slid beneath her skin. She spoke a blessing and traced the quartered circle on Cicely's brow with a wet finger.

"What is it you want?" Aveline asked. "How do you wish the Goddess to specially bless you?"

"I...I want him to love me. The Lord Henry. My betrothed husband."

"Remove your brooch."

Cicely fumbled as she removed the gold brooch that pinned closed the neck of her kirtle. Her fingers shook as she offered the brooch to Aveline.

Aveline took it in her left palm.

"I need some of your blood," Aveline said.

Cicely hitched her overtunic, kirtle, and chemise to reach between her legs. She offered Aveline two fingers smeared with blood.

"Are you sure this is what you want?" Aveline asked.

For the first time, Cicely looked directly at her. "Oh, yes, Eminence. Please. I don't know what I'll do else. Please. I'm so scared that he won't like me."

Aveline closed her wet fingers around Cicely's bloody ones and pressed them down on the brooch.

"Put your left hand in the water," Aveline said.

Cicely's eyes widened and she hesitated, then tentatively slipped her hand into the stream.

Aveline closed her eyes. She could hear Cicely's breathing and feel the girl's hand trembling in her grasp, but concentrated on the chilliness within her hand and arm, and the firmness of the ground beneath her legs. She reached out to the primeval power flowing around and through the grove and world. She opened herself to it. She invited it to coalesce within her. The edges of herself blurred and the coldness crept down her arm and spread into her chest. Something cool clutched her heart. Aveline gasped, but didn't let it break her concentration. She had felt this touch of the Goddess before. The ground beneath her rippled as if giant roots burrowed beneath the grass.

Cicely shrieked and jerked. Aveline held the girl's hand clamped between hers. A jolt hammered up from the ground and a searing iciness pulled at Aveline through the contact with Cicely. The shadow in Aveline's chest thrust outwards to meld with the rest of creation. Her body spasmed. Her head was flung back. Cicely's scream came from afar. The shadow swallowed Aveline's senses.

When Aveline grew aware of herself again, she sat slumped with her chin on her chest. She panted. But she was whole and fully within her own body. She heard whimpering.

Aveline's body ached as she straightened and lifted her head. Cicely looked terrified. Aveline's hands, locked in a claw-like rictus, still held the girl and the brooch.

"You can remove your hand from the water," Aveline said.

Cicely yanked her hand out.

Aveline forced her fingers to move. She peeled her hands apart. Cicely snatched her hand away and protectively clutched it to her bosom. Aveline looked down at the brooch she held. The pin had driven into her palm. She gritted her teeth and tugged it loose. Blood welled from the puncture.

"Here." Aveline offered the brooch. "Keep it safe and wrapped in silk. Do not wear it again until you are alone with your husband."

Cicely looked more scared than ever she might at the prospect of defloration by a stranger. She stared wide-eyed at the brooch, seeming unsure whether to regard it as precious or venomous.

"You have what you asked for," Aveline said. "Now, you must leave me."

"Th-thank you, Eminence. I don't know how to repay you. Should...should I promise the Lady of Mercy and Healing that I'll pledge my second-born daughter to her service?"

Aveline suppressed a weary smile. "Let us agree, for now, that you owe. We can determine an appropriate payment later."

CHAPTER SEVEN

R iannon guided her horse through the press of grooms, squires, clerks, women, and horses. Barely a square foot of the ground of the enormous expanse of the bailey of Sadiston Castle stood bare of a person or animal. Half of the wooden buildings inside the grey stone walls looked of recent erection, and they further limited the space. Riannon's memory was of a space vast enough to hold jousts. Today, people had to squeeze out of the path of her mount.

Riannon looked up at the tall round tower at the northeastern corner of the walls. This was where Aveline said Lord and Lady Northmarch lodged. Riannon dismounted, passed her reins to Alan and told him to wait. She ignored his surprise at being left behind. Had Riannon her way, she would have no witness to her meeting with her sister.

Riannon ignored the second looks and stares as she stepped inside the tower and worked her way through a crowd of messengers, clerks, petitioners, and hangers-on. One man wearing the green and black livery of the Earl of Northmarch broke off a conversation at her approach. His gaze held no recognition. She had lived barely a year in her sister's household before her father disowned Riannon and she had escaped. No doubt, though, the servants still circulated gossip about the countess's sister. But it might be that this man simply reacted to the distinctive height and colouring which marked so many of her family.

"A good day to you, sir," he said. "I'm one of lady Northmarch's clerks. How may I help you?"

"I would see the lady," Riannon said.

He bowed. "I'll send a message to her. What name shall I give?"

"Riannon of Gast." She heard herself hesitate before she claimed a relationship that she did not know if Joan still acknowledged. "I'm her sister."

His eyes widened as he stared up at her. She saw the familiar disbelief not completely dissolve into astonishment. She also grew aware of a sudden hush and watchfulness in the chamber.

The clerk quickly regained possession of himself and dispatched a page boy at a run. He himself escorted Riannon up the curving stairs to a quieter and luxuriously appointed upper chamber. The half dozen people in the chamber broke off their conversations to stare. Riannon ignored them. She refused the clerk's offer of wine.

Hangings covered the walls and the rushes strewn on the floor were fresh. The chests and bench bore cushions. As Riannon turned, her fingers found the hilt of her sword and curled around it for unthinking reassurance. She strode to the window. Woods stretched away from the base of the castle hill to the north and west. The river curved through it. Part of the land belonged to the huge grove house on the northern fringe of the city.

She tried to remember her sister on an occasion before that last time. She failed. Her cheek all but stung with the memory of Joan's slap. She had every right to be angry and disappointed with Riannon. And to feel betrayed. Joan had tried to shield Riannon and return her to a more conventional path, one that their father would find acceptable. Joan was not to blame for what Riannon had done or had become. Yet their father had cast out Joan as well. Riannon did not know how to atone for that.

"Dear gods. Nonnie?"

Riannon turned. The well-dressed woman in the doorway should have looked magisterial save she still held her skirts from hurrying down stairs. Riannon looked past the greying hair and more well-fleshed frame to see the sister of her memories. With recognition, Riannon knew a stab of fear. Not for the negligible hurt of another slap to the face, but for the repudiation it enacted.

"It *is* you," Joan said. "I do not think even now I believe it, though I look upon you."

Joan started across the chamber. Riannon knelt.

"Please rise," Joan said. "I would look at you."

"There is a matter betwixt us that I would settle," Riannon said. "Name your penance."

Riannon heard an intake of breath and muttering from the side of the room.

"Leave us," Joan said.

Feet scuffed the rushes and a door shut.

"I must be in my dotage," Joan said, "for my wits deserted me utterly when Walter said you waited upon me. I should've had you brought upstairs rather than hurtle down here. Nonnie, you owe me nothing. Save, perhaps, the chance to look at you properly. Please rise."

Riannon reluctantly stood. "I betrayed your trust."

"That you did. I cannot pretend that I wasn't hurt and angry. But that was the better part of ten years ago. I've long since concluded that it was not nearly good enough cause for me to lose my only sister."

Joan lifted a hand to Riannon's face. Riannon fought the urge to turn her scarred cheek out of reach.

"Was it worth it, Nonnie?"

"I am what I am."

Joan nodded and let her hand fall. "I didn't understand that. Nor do I think I truly do now."

Riannon stood for Joan's open scrutiny. Part of her could not believe in her reprieve. Part of her did not want to be forgiven so lightly.

"It was my fault that our father disinherited you," Riannon said.

"You know that he died the winter before last? He spent the last months of his life in great pain and unable to walk. He sent for me and asked my forgiveness."

Riannon did not ask if he had extended his deathbed remorse to herself. He had declared her dead to him eight years ago.

Joan took one of Riannon's hands and clasped it to her bosom. "I'm still having trouble crediting the evidence of my eyes and hands. I've lost count of the skirts I've worn thin at the knees praying that you were well and would come home. Or that you'd send me some message. I've been waiting for word of you for years. How is it that you come now? I confess that Henry's wedding seems an unlikely event. I do not complain if it is so, though you must have changed greatly if you now have a taste for such grand festivities."

Riannon answered Joan's smile with a grin. She received a shock when she noticed the lines on her sister's face. Joan must now be older than their mother had been when she died giving birth to Riannon.

"What does bring you back?" Joan said.

"I travelled with cousin Aveline."

Joan didn't hide her surprise. "By choice?"

"I'm bound in service to the Order of the Goddess."

"In truth? I've not heard of such a thing. Though, if any knight were to serve the order, who more fitting could there be than you?"

The door opened. The man who walked in was a familiar looking stranger standing eye to eye with Riannon. He returned her stare with open and amused surprise. He wore a jaunty cap over short-cropped black hair. A neatly trimmed black beard framed his smile. His blue overtunic formed a fashionably gaudy contrast to a green tunic and red hose.

"Brother Aymer?" he said. "No, you cannot be him, for he is as fat as a farrowing sow and as dour as his prayer books. But, unless my eyes deceive me, you must be one of the brood. I offer my commiserations."

Joan cast an indulgent smile at him. "Nonnie, you may not remember this lad o' light and peacock. Guy, meet our sister Riannon."

"Sister?" He offered Riannon his hand. "They call me the family jester. You must be the family skeleton. Though, by the look of you, I'd rather meet any number of spectres on a dark night than cross you."

Riannon clasped his hand and detected not the faintest reserve in his welcome. She looked pointedly at his brightly coloured clothes. "I'd prefer to have met you at night."

Guy laughed. "I'd be wounded, save you so obviously lack the least knowledge about what you speak. Well, little Nonnie, I think you and I are going to deal well together. I do so prefer my sisters to my brothers."

Joan smiled. "Nonnie, where do you lodge? I've room here for you and would welcome your company."

"My thanks, but I stay at the house of Lady Barrowmere."

"The lovely Lady Eleanor?" Guy said. "You know her? You may have no taste in clothes, but no one could fault you for choosing the charming widow's company. Passing strange that she has never said aught about knowing you."

"Our friendship is of recent making," Riannon said.

"Henry's bride's aunt." Joan nodded. "You said that you travelled with Aveline?"

"Thank Atuan's toes," Guy said, "that the lovely lady herself was not wasted on our beef-witted brother. She deserves a better, more handsome man than Henry. Someone lively and pleasant."

"Yourself, you mean?" Joan said.

Guy spread his hands. "It'd sadden me to disappoint all those poor creatures who have set their hopes on me and who thrust their favours so pathetically at me in the hopes that I'll carry theirs in the tourney. Alas, only one can prevail. I'm not above an act of charity for a lonely widow."

Riannon could not tell how deeply his jesting ran.

"This self-sacrifice has nought to do with the lady's abundant charms, fairness of face, and the length of her rent-roll?" Joan turned to Riannon. "I'll believe he is serious about marriage when the priest tells him he may kiss his bride, and not a moment before."

Guy put a hand to his chest and assumed a look of deepest hurt. "You wound me with your lack of faith. Are you not the loudest in telling me that I must hasten to marry and establish my poor self in the world ere I fade into miserable destitution? Surely you'd not disapprove of the charming Lady Eleanor?"

"Nothing would give me greater pleasure than to see you wed her," Joan said. "Had you shown more resolution, you could have had the niece and an earldom. If you're serious about Lady Barrowmere, you'll need to exert yourself a little. Take a few hours away from your tourneying and carousing to ask the queen for her permission. I can see no reason why she'd not look with favour upon the match."

Riannon's hands clenched into fists at her sides. Her brother was to marry Eleanor? Could the gods have played a more cruel jest on her?

❖

Eleanor cast another glance around the cavernous great hall at Sadiston Castle but failed to locate the queen amongst the knots of colourful courtiers. Lord Deerfield, the chamberlain, assured her that this morning would be propitious for approaching the queen about her continuing widowhood. She returned her attention to Lady Overwood to hear her tone change from delight at relating scandal to outright condemnation.

"So wholly unnatural," Lady Overwood said. "My lord husband spoke rightly when he said that he'd confine to chains any daughter of his who shamed his blood in such a way. Aye, and whip her daily until he beat the error out of her."

Eleanor made a distracted response as she saw the queen and her sister, the naer, stride into the chamber. The queen stood two or three inches shorter than her sister, though that still constituted a goodly height for a female. Combined with her fuller-bodied figure and a dress sense with a sharp eye for conveying magnificence, the sovereign lady possessed a presence that none could overlook. Still, no woman who faded into the tapestries would ever have stood her ground and claimed the throne. It helped, too, that Mathilda had two promising, healthy sons. Though, again, it was a testament to her strength of character that it was the mother who gained the crown in her own right, rather than be appointed regent for her elder son.

Lady Overwood put her hand on Eleanor's arm and leaned closer to continue her gossip about Riannon. "The old Earl Marshal tried to keep her locked away. She was raised alone under the care of a priestess. Not even at a grove house or basilica. They say it was at a hunting lodge. It's no wonder she turned out unnatural. Her mother died at her birth."

Eleanor wasted no breath on pointing out that Riannon's mother was neither the first nor last woman to die in childbed. Her attention again strayed beyond Lady Overwood.

Queen Mathilda was the only woman able to put into the shade the naer, her sister. Having travelled for several days in Aveline's company, Eleanor wondered at the reality behind such an impression. Eleanor had not met a person with ambition if that flame did not burn hot within Aveline. How many would get blistered by her? Eleanor feared for Riannon; Aveline clearly wanted something from her and exercised some hold over her, though Eleanor could not begin to imagine what it might be. As much a knight errant as any younger son, Riannon owned little and carried no political weight. As so unusual a female, Riannon would hardly be useful as a marriage pawn. But what other role could there be for a woman who was not already bound to the grove, a throne, or a man?

Eleanor imagined Riannon standing with her cousins. What a curious trio those women would make—queen, priestess, and warrior.

"She dressed in men's clothes." Lady Overwood shook her head in disbelief. "And acted like a man. By I know not what trickery, she fooled the late king himself into knighting her!"

Eleanor might have encouraged Lady Overwood to elaborate on that interesting point, save the queen paused to exchange a word with Lord Deerfield. The queen briefly glanced in Eleanor's direction, nodded to him, and continued towards the doors.

Eleanor excused herself from Lady Overwood. There would be plenty of other opportunities for her to learn more about Riannon. First, she must deal with her own nearest concern. Lord Deerfield met her halfway across the hall.

"Her Grace will be happy to have you as part of her audience on the morrow before dinner," he said.

"My deepest thanks," Eleanor said. "I hope Lady Deerfield will be pleased with that blue silk brocade. The colour will become her well."

He nodded and moved away. Eleanor sighed with relief. One hurdle cleared at the cost of a small bribe. The queen, of course, would want far more than a length of silk, but Eleanor was willing to pay much for her continued widowhood.

Eleanor exchanged words with a few acquaintances as she worked her way out of the hall. Her groom waited with the horses for her and her women.

One of the men of her escort cleared a path for their retinue through the busy bailey and out of the gatehouse. Eleanor pointedly did not look across to the tents and tourney field. More interesting to her far ranging curiosity was the less gaudy sprawl of the stalls and booths of the hundreds of merchants come with wares from all over the Eastern Kingdoms. Eleanor wondered what it would be like to walk amongst the noisy, sweaty press. To hear a dozen languages.

"Is that not Lady Riannon?" Agnes said.

Riannon sat on her horse near the fringe of tents surrounding the tourney field. Eleanor should not have been surprised that Riannon would enter the lists. She was, after all, a knight. Although, if Lady Overwood's story held water, Riannon's honour had been gained by deceit. Eleanor doubted that. No one who knew Riannon would conceive of her lying about a matter of honour. One glance at Riannon's scarred face was enough to show her familiar with the sinews of war. Her current interest probably meant she intended to participate in the contests. She possessed the qualification of good birth necessary for entering the tourney. Eleanor could not help that sour twist inside that always accompanied any thoughts of fighting. And that charnel whiff of death.

Alan said something that made Riannon turn. The moment she

saw Eleanor her frown dissolved in a grin. Eleanor smiled. She stopped her horse and waited for Riannon to join her.

"I've done my gossiping for the day," Eleanor said. "I'm on my way to the basilica. You've been looking for comrades?"

Riannon shook her head. "I was watching my brother Guy. He rides a practice course."

"Guy? He'll have so many spectators and well-wishers that he'd not grudge me one. If, that is, you'd not find my company too tedious."

"I've not the breadth of wit to imagine you less than interesting, lady."

Eleanor smiled as Riannon guided her horse alongside Eleanor's mare.

Had Eleanor not met Riannon, the idea of a woman acting as a man might have excited both her curiosity and revulsion. Yet, the person riding beside her seemed anything but unnatural. Had Riannon appeared a woman masquerading as a man, that would indeed have been grotesque. But Eleanor could not imagine Riannon as other than exactly as she was.

They rode at a walking pace past the busy edge of the swollen market. Smells of cooking and smoke drifted across the reek of refuse and over-ripe bodies.

"There." Riannon nodded past Eleanor.

Eleanor turned and saw a man with skin as dusky brown as her mare's coat. Disappointingly, he wore normal tunic and hose. "Where would he come from?"

"Perhaps northern Themalia," Riannon said. "Or the seacoast of southern Rhân."

"Do the women look as dark?"

"Yes. They can be very beautiful."

"You do not subscribe to the acme of beauty in fairness?" Eleanor said.

"No," Riannon said.

Riannon signalled to a man carrying a tray of food. Instead of letting her squire deal with him, she dismounted herself. The man nearly let his wares slip to the ground when he dropped to his knees. Riannon purchased one of the pastries and broke off a part to taste. Satisfied, she offered the rest to Eleanor.

"This is a spiced cheese pie," Riannon said. "A specialty of the Windward Isles, off the western coast of Iruland."

Eleanor accepted the pastry. The tangy taste appealed for its novelty, though she would not be instructing her cook to seek out the recipe.

Their party generated considerable interest from vendors and shoppers alike who stopped to gawk at the riders. Few dared approach Riannon unbidden. The more enterprising tried to accost Agnes or Alan. Eleanor looked beyond them to the uneven rows of stalls. Some merchants operated from the back of wagons. Others set up trestle tables spread with their goods. Most simply arrayed their wares on blankets spread on the ground.

"Is there something you wish me to fetch you, lady?" Riannon said.

"I was remembering," Eleanor said. "As a young girl, I once escaped from my nurse and walked two miles to a fair. I had heard of such places but had never been allowed to visit one for myself. They sounded irresistibly interesting. Of course, I was soon found and returned home. And whipped. But it was worth it. I bought myself a set of ribbons. I hid them, for fear that they'd be taken from me. They were woefully poor quality, but I kept them for years. They were green."

Riannon lifted her arms. "I cannot promise that you'll find anything of interest at this fair, but I swear no one will dare chastise you."

Eleanor smiled and let Riannon help her to the ground.

The merchants goggled at the pair of them strolling down the dusty, refuse-strewn road. The shoes, straw hats, mouse traps, wooden spoons, and cloths were all of such inferior quality that Eleanor felt no temptation to buy anything, and the stink was stronger and less pleasant at ground level, but she enjoyed herself every bit as much as that long-ago little girl had when she slipped loose of the restraints for a few hours.

They saw another dark-skinned man. Riannon beckoned to him. He, too, wore normal clothes, but he bowed in a strange manner with his hand to his forehead. Eleanor listened in amazement as Riannon spoke a few words in a guttural language. The man's eyes grew wide and he offered her the wooden box he carried. Riannon gave him some coins and dismissed him.

"You speak their tongue?" Eleanor said.

"A few words," Riannon said. "Sufficient to get my horse groomed, myself fed, and to be able to tell someone that I think his parentage dubious."

Eleanor laughed. She needed no coaxing to try one of the strange candied lumps in the box that Riannon offered. To her surprise, the inside was a sticky, gooey liquid that tasted of lemons and roses.

"These are a great delicacy," Riannon said. "The chieftains of some of the wandering tribes in the warm lands have more than one wife. They keep them locked away from other men. The women must get bored. They spend their days making themselves beautiful and eating sweets such as these."

"I don't think I'd like such a life." Eleanor licked sticky sugar from her fingers.

"It would be a sin to lock you away."

"I suspect my father would've liked to restrain me more closely. And I wager most men would be nothing loath to have tighter control of their womenfolk."

"I am not a man."

"No," Eleanor agreed. "If you were, you'd likely not be indulging me this way."

Eleanor threaded her hand through Riannon's arm. When next they paused, Riannon gently brushed some sugar grains from Eleanor's chin. The contact produced a tingling in her skin out of all proportion to the soft, casual touch. Eleanor could not help then being aware of her hand on Riannon's arm and the proximity of their bodies. Not as two friends should be. Not as Eleanor had ever felt with her waiting women. Comfortable, yet unsettling.

To Eleanor's disappointment, Riannon did not remain once she had escorted Eleanor past the market to the basilica area. Though, perhaps, an hour at prayer in the basilica of Kamet would not be to everyone's taste. Had Eleanor not needed all the divine help she could recruit for the success of her negotiation over her widowhood with the queen, she might have foregone the pleasure herself.

The lord priest's principal secretary received Lady Barrowmere himself at the basilica door. Her generous donations over the years, principally in thanks for successful commercial and financial ventures, ensured her a warm welcome. The secretary escorted Eleanor to the luxuriously decorated alcove where royalty came to pray. A carved and brightly painted wooden screen wall shielded this part of the basilica from rude eyes while affording a full view of the giant gold scales suspended at the front of the basilica.

The secretary solicitously conducted Eleanor to a padded prayer cushion. Her retinue remained behind her and had to cope with mats. As Eleanor prepared to kneel, she heard a familiar voice. Riannon strode through a side door. Eleanor smiled. The priest trailing Riannon looked anything but amused.

"The Lady Riannon is my companion," Eleanor explained to the secretary.

After a hurried exchange between the priests, Riannon unbuckled her sword belt and handed it to her squire.

Riannon's long stride carried her quickly to Eleanor's side. "Your pardon, lady. It took longer than I expected to find these."

Riannon opened her hand to reveal two green silken ribbons.

"Oh!" Eleanor smiled but felt as though she could weep. "Thank you."

As she looked up at Riannon's grin, Eleanor realised that if Riannon had been a man, it would be easy to fall in love with her. When she should have been clearing her mind for her religious devotions, she instead glanced sidelong at Riannon kneeling beside her.

Eleanor forced herself to intone the prayer of presentation. The sunlight angled in the glass windows and glinted off the brightly polished gold of the scales. She inhaled the cloying incense and tried to clear her mind of all thoughts save the contract she must negotiate with the queen. She wished Kamet, the divine arbiter, god of balance, and lord of justice to favour her cause. She asked no great boon, for she was willing to pay for what she wanted. She must strike a balance between her needs and the queen's. They must find that point where the value of Eleanor's worth to the queen as a reward for a man who had done her a service weighed equally against the amount of silver Eleanor offered.

Eleanor felt no guilt, as she knew she transgressed the will of no gods in her request. Twice married, twice widowed, she had fulfilled the purpose of a daughter, and of a wife. That her womb had proven slow to take seed and too quick to give it up could not be held a fault against her. She had undertaken half a dozen pilgrimages to various shrines in her quest for a pregnancy that she could carry to term. Her prayers had remained unanswered for no reasons Eleanor could understand.

That she had no appetite for subjecting herself to a third marriage could be held as no mark against her. Even the queen had no will for a new husband.

Eleanor opened her eyes to look at her two wedding rings. On her second marriage, she had moved her first ring to her left hand. Green ribbons dangled down the back of her hands from between her fingers. She smiled and cast a glance at Riannon. Riannon had her head bowed and her eyes closed in deep concentration.

Eleanor forced her errant mind back to her purpose. Widowhood. Imploring the god's help in securing her desired future.

While there were some women who required the prop of a husband, the only part of being married Eleanor missed was not being alone. Although, both of her husbands had spent much of their time apart from her. Lionel had devoted his days to hunting and whoring. William had gone twice to war against the empire. Nor, truth be told, had either proven satisfying on those occasions when they shared her bed. Lionel had been a man with peculiar carnal needs, though as a young innocent she had been in no position to know that his demands were strange. William dutifully attempted to get an heir on her once a month during those times he was not away fighting. His sexual interests, though, had been in other men, not his wife.

Even if given the choice of every male vassal of the queen, Eleanor could not point to one she desired as a husband. Like poor Cicely, she had heard many a troubadour's tale of heroism and romance. Unlike her niece, though, she never suffered any disillusionment, for she had not truly believed all-consuming passion to be any more common than dragons. Over the years, Eleanor's requirements in her ideal husband had refined along pragmatic lines.

Lord of Justice, I desire not another husband, she prayed. *But if it be your will that I marry again, he must be strong of mind and spirit, but I'd take ill to being crushed of all occupation and usefulness. A man who is well-travelled, yet one who hails from these lands that I may understand him. A man of well-formed parts, but not of vanity. Pious, but not to the exclusion of enjoying life. A man who sees me as more than breasts, womb, and rent-roll. He must be able to sustain my levity with good part. Finally, he must be able to defend us, our properties, and rights, yet not be so personally devoted to endangering himself that he is likely to leave me a widow for a third time.*

Eleanor opened her eyes and smiled at the shining golden scales.

You see, Lord God, what a hopeless matter it is. Such a man does not exist. It's best if I remain—

Eleanor squinted at a sudden dazzle of the sun setting the polished holy balance ablaze. She averted her face and blinked the afterglow of spots from her eyes. She found herself staring at Riannon's unscarred profile.

Riannon.

In every respect, Riannon fitted Eleanor's criteria for her ideal mate. Save one. She was not a man.

Eleanor frowned at the ribbons hanging between her fingers. Had Riannon been a man…The mental exercise of substituting a masculine Riannon in her thoughts proved facile. More difficult, because it required stark honesty about herself, was the task of examining her likely responses to that male version of Riannon.

Eleanor lifted her astonished gaze to the giant scales.

Lord of balance, you have graced me with an answer that is not at all what I expected. My ideal man is a woman. And I am in love with her.

CHAPTER EIGHT

Aveline watched her young nephew leave the chamber with his nurse. Gilbert was a sturdy boy whose ruddy complexion and pudginess owed more to his father than his mother. She hoped, for all their sake's, that both Gilbert and his elder brother, Edward, had inherited their mother's mind and temperament rather than their sire's. Bardolf had been a braggart whose brains hung between his legs. The gods alone knew why Mathilda mourned the death of that womanising carouser. Thank all the divine powers that the worms had feasted on Bardolf before he had an opportunity to ruin Mathilda's claim to the throne. No brother-in-law had met a more timely end.

"I'll be sad when I must surrender Gilbert completely to tutors," Mathilda said. "Still, it's better than parting with a daughter as a child to some foreign court. I'm glad I have sons."

"A few daughters would have been useful." Aveline poured herself more wine. "As, indeed, would more sons."

"I'll not marry again." Mathilda shook her head and held out her goblet.

Since they were alone in the queen's private chamber, Aveline poured for her sister.

"I'd be the last to counsel you to such a step," Aveline said.

"It's bad enough to have to bury one husband," Mathilda said.

"I rather think a live husband the greater problem. How could a queen obey her husband and yet rule other men?"

Mathilda shrugged. "I miss him sometimes. At night. Not that I expect you to understand."

Aveline sat on a padded chest beneath one of the windows. "Why should I not?"

"You've never been married. You don't know what you're missing."

One of Aveline's eyebrows lifted. Mathilda's eyes widened and she turned away, but not before Aveline saw her blush. Aveline smiled.

"You should never ask questions, even unspoken ones, that you don't really want the answers to," Aveline said. "None of my vows was chastity."

"But—" Mathilda made a vague gesture with her goblet. "What if you'd had children?"

"Would you not foster them for me? And claim kinship?"

Mathilda looked so comically shocked that Aveline was more amused than disgusted with her prudishness.

"They'd be bastards," Mathilda said.

"And every bit as useful as daughters of yours would be as marriage pawns for building alliances. I suppose we could always betroth Gilbert to a Rhânish princess."

"Do we really want him to marry there? Is it wise of us to commit him so young?"

"I said nothing of commitment," Aveline said. "There are many ways out of betrothals. We just need the southeastern border quietened for a year or two."

Mathilda frowned and dropped onto her padded chair. "Henry thinks we should fortify the castles in the southeast and threaten King Renauld into taking his unruly vassals in hand himself."

Aveline sighed. "Cousin Henry might have a fine understanding of which end of a sword to hold, but if he had to use his wits to shave with he'd not need to fear cutting his own throat."

Mathilda laughed.

"Promises are more versatile and useful coin than threats," Aveline said. "And far less expensive than fortifying castles. One need only keep promises bright and shiny and tempting, but never deliver them. The last thing we need is to get sucked into a wholly unnecessary war of Henry's making."

Any troubles Mathilda feared in the southeast lands could—must—wait. Aveline needed every last man available to ride to the northwest once the Quatorum Council published its call for holy war. Then the Earl Marshal could have his glut of blood and plunder for the glory of the gods and earn his passage to paradise by trampling infidel bodies underfoot.

"Henry should be thinking more of his girl bride," Mathilda said. "Has he met her yet?"

"I believe he sent a betrothal token rather than visit in person. Which I think is wise. It'd not do to scare the poor creature witless ere she speaks the vows."

Mathilda looked torn between shock and amusement. "Is she that timid? Still, her mother was not a spirited woman. I hope Henry did not send Guy to his bride. That man could charm the hose off any woman."

"And does so regularly."

Mathilda laughed. "I was thinking it high time cousin Guy respectably settled. There must be some heiress we can marry him to."

Aveline toyed with the possibility of Guy marrying one of the many Rhânish princesses. That might solve two problems.

"How about Lady Barrowmere?" Mathilda said. "Henry's bride's aunt. She's a wealthy woman. Guy has a partiality for her."

"How rich is she?" Aveline asked.

"She was a co-heiress with her two sisters of their father's estates. Plus she has dowers from two husbands. Her first was Lionel of Torhill. A third of the honour of Torhill alone would make her a prize for any man." Mathilda nodded. "She's to see me tomorrow. I suspect it's about her widowhood. She paid our father well for the privilege. But I think giving her to Guy would be a far better idea. Do you agree?"

Aveline stroked the side of her goblet. "I think we ought not be too hasty. There's no pressing need for Guy to marry. There might be better uses we can put Lady Barrowmere to. Why don't you leave her for me to think on?"

"What about my audience with her on the morrow?" Mathilda said.

Aveline shrugged. "Dissemble. Delay. Are you not also our father's daughter?"

Mathilda again looked torn between laughter and dutiful disapproval. Amusement won.

Aveline rose. "I must take my leave. I have to visit the grove house."

"Is it true?"

Aveline paused with a hand on the door. "Is this the beginning of a philosophical discussion on the nature of truth and perception? If so, might it wait until the morrow?"

"I heard a rumour about Riannon. Our cousin Riannon. You remember her. The outcast. Gossip has it that she's here in Sadiston. And that Joan has received her. You know everything. Is there truth in it? Has she dared return?"

Aveline smiled. "Not so much dared, as came on the end of a leash."

Mathilda frowned.

"Riannon of Gast is alive, well, and in the city," Aveline said. "She lodges with Lady Barrowmere. She'll be visiting you shortly to perform homage to you."

"Ought I outlaw her?"

"For what reason?"

Mathilda shrugged. "Her father disowned her. Our father wanted her confined in a cell."

"They're both dead. Riannon is here because I want her here."

"In truth? For what reason? Do you plan something devious?"

"Speaking of devious, what make you of the imperial ambassador?"

Mathilda made an exasperated noise in accompaniment to an irritated gesture. "I wish to the gods you had not advised me to accept the emperor's offer of a visit from his representatives. Every man from Henry to the pimply stable boy wishes to cut them into strips. I can see nought of any good coming from this. If he or any of his men gain a scratch, it'll bring war. I do not want to go to war with the empire. Aveline, you must help me."

"If I have anything to do with it, no harm will come to any representative of the empire whilst under the protection of your safe-conduct." Aveline lifted the door latch. "Nor will anyone declare war on you."

Aveline had quite different ideas for those imperial ambassadors, which required one of them voluntarily relinquishing the protection of Mathilda's sworn guarantee of safety. Plans that required Riannon. Now, too, she had the disposal of Lady Barrowmere to consider.

❖

Eleanor had never wanted visitors less than that afternoon. She encouraged Cicely to shoulder her share of the burden of hostess. To Eleanor's relief, her niece had finally developed signs of acceptance for marriage in two days time. Even if it gave her something of the air of one approaching martyrdom, that seemed preferable to shrinking timidity.

Eleanor moved away from the boisterous group at the hearth. For a woman who revelled in company and conversation, she felt uniquely anxious to be alone. She stroked the green ribbon tied around her girdle. Would Riannon notice? But what if she did?

Eleanor took a moment to marvel at herself. Indecisive. Hesitant. Anxious. She had no grounds to chastise Cicely for exhibiting those same traits.

When Eleanor had fancied herself in love before, the follow-up with a man had been straightforward compared to what she now faced. Had Riannon been male, Eleanor could have reasonably expected that he'd have some carnal interest in women. But how was Eleanor to test whether another woman shared her surprising attraction to one of her own sex?

A familiar man's laugh drew Eleanor's attention across the hall. For a heartbeat, she thought she saw double. Two dark-haired, tall, strongly built men walked towards her. The illusion broke with one being brightly attired and bearded and the other clean-shaven and drab. Guy and Riannon. Brother and sister. Eleanor's gaze flicked eagerly between them as the pair neared her. Her memory had not played tricks, for they were every bit as alike as she believed. They could be the male and female version of the same person, though not the contrast of masculine against feminine.

Riannon returned Eleanor's smile with a guarded look and nod.

Guy smiled. He offered her an exaggerated bow in the manner of an actor's comic parody of an oily Marchionese courtier. "Lady Barrowmere."

Eleanor retaliated with a prim curtsy. "My Lord Guy, you honour my humble house."

Guy laughed. "It's safer breaking lances with a hundred knights than entering the lists with you, fair lady. I always come away bruised. But I have reinforcements now. Though, whether my little sister would side with me or you is probably best not tested."

Eleanor smiled. Guy, for one, had clearly accepted his unconventional sister in his stride. Eleanor happily surrendered her hand for him to kiss.

Eleanor steered them both towards the tables that had been set up for eating. She performed a rapid review of her guests. Strictly, they should be seated according to precedence. Eleanor was not sure where that might put Riannon. Erring on the side of inclination, she guided the queen's cousins to places on either side of her own.

"Do I compete with you, strange sister mine," Guy asked as he rinsed his hands, "for the honour of carrying this charming lady's favour in the tourney?"

Before Eleanor could remind him that she offered her favours to no one, nor attended any tournaments, Riannon said that she had no intention of competing.

"I could assure you a place on the lists," Guy said. "If you lack introduction to the heralds and marshal."

"I thank you," Riannon said. "But I've no great need of coin."

Eleanor turned in surprise. "You do not compete merely for the gratification of breaking men's heads? Then, most assuredly, you must indeed be a female knight."

"Or her purse is plumper than mine," Guy said. "I can never have too many ransoms."

Eleanor turned a mock look of shock on him. "My lord, should you not, rather, have spoken of winning honour and glory?"

"I would," he said, "save you've never before believed that I risk my adorable self solely to prove myself worthy of your most grudging smile."

"True," Eleanor said, "but that should be no disincentive to continued effort on your part. Unless you wish me to think you inconstant and fickle."

Guy chuckled.

Throughout the meal, Eleanor shamelessly encouraged him to turn the largest share of his good humour and charm on Cicely sitting on his right side. Eleanor turned to Riannon.

With Riannon on her left, this presented her scarred profile to Eleanor. The disfigurement was not easy to look at. The badly healed flesh looked as though it must still hurt. The slash gave her more than a passing resemblance to those cautionary murals on temple walls that showed demons raking talons across sinners' faces. Unlike those terrified, shrieking figures, though, Riannon sat silent and remote. Eleanor wanted to make her smile. And she wanted to touch her.

Eleanor shifted in her chair. "It was most unwise of you to confess no interest in the tourney."

"Why is that, lady?"

"Because it encourages me to encroach on your goodwill. You see, though I enjoy the bustle of a city, I like to take rides. But I often lack an escort."

"I am at your service."

Eleanor smiled. "You should've driven a hard bargain with me. Asked for something in return."

"I'll be getting the reward I want."

Eleanor paused as she reached for a platter of goose. Was that simply Riannon's formal manners? Had a man said that, how would Eleanor have interpreted it?

Riannon stabbed a slice of goose breast with her eating knife and offered it to Eleanor. Eleanor looked up as she slipped a bite between her lips. When her gaze met Riannon's eyes, the contact jarred her as if it had been a physical contact. Riannon quickly looked away.

Eleanor wondered. Her body had no mistake about her own response. She remembered the first time Riannon looked at her, back in the garden at the Highford grove house. Naked admiration. Ironically, Eleanor had interpreted it without any cloud of doubt because she had believed Riannon a man.

But what of Riannon's interpretations? She had more cause for caution and doubt than Eleanor, for she knew Eleanor had been married twice. No reasonable mind could deduce from that evidence that Eleanor would harbour an interest in one of her own sex. The onus was on Eleanor, then, to convey the correct impression to Riannon.

Eleanor smiled to herself as she reached for her cup. How ironical, after her confusions and mental contortions of thinking of Riannon as male, that it must fall to herself to perform the masculine role of declaring her interest in a woman.

L-J BAKER

CHAPTER NINE

Riannon helped Eleanor dismount in the inner bailey of the castle. She secretly gloried in even the impersonal touches of the lady. Eleanor graced her with a warm smile and let her hand linger on Riannon's arm. Riannon would have bartered much for the opportunity to ride away with the lady, but Eleanor went to meet the queen, and Riannon had pledged her own company to her sister Joan. So, she parted from the lady with the promise to wait for her.

When Riannon entered the tower where Joan lodged, there were plenty of looks again, but no delay in ushering her through to the Countess of Northmarch.

Joan received her with a smile and kiss on the cheek. "I feared that you'd not come."

Riannon followed Joan through a chamber filled with men who bore the unmistakeable air of retainers waiting for their masters. There were too many of them to belong only to her sister and brother-in-law. The men subjected her to professionally measuring looks rather than the morbid fascination of those who knew they looked upon a woman.

A servant opened a door for Joan. Riannon stepped after her sister and stopped. Half a dozen men in lordly finery stood or sat near the empty hearth. The only one to turn at Joan's entrance was her husband, Humphrey, Earl of Northmarch. He had grown even thinner and lost more hair in Riannon's absence. With a grey beard, he looked as gaunt and dour as a tomb effigy. He regarded Riannon with hooded eyes that showed neither surprise nor warmth of welcome.

"They want us to surrender him to them?" A middle-aged man standing near the hearth shook his head. "You cannot be serious."

Riannon's hand wanted to reach protectively for her sword hilt. She recognised the speaker. In her eldest brother, Henry, she might be looking at her father come to life again, down to the thrust of his chin, his bullish build running to fat, and a faint, incongruous lisp. The likeness triggered memories of which he had no part, but which stirred not one whit less of a trace of unease in her. She did not want to be in this chamber. Joan had not warned her this would be a family gathering.

"You expect no less from the imperial dogs, surely?" This speaker's grey-streaked black hair and green eyes marked him as another brother, but Riannon did not know him. He dressed more neatly and richly than any of the others, and had a slickness about his manner. "You did not think this ambassador came merely to congratulate us on having a new queen?"

"Mayhap they came for the wine, women, and good company, like the rest of us." Guy, who lounged on the window seat across the room, lifted his goblet and smiled at Riannon.

No one paid him much heed.

Riannon had no taste for remaining, and guessed few of her brothers would welcome her presence, but Joan silently urged her to take a seat beside Guy. Riannon complied with the reluctance of obligation. Guy offered Riannon his wine. She shook her head.

"Was the Vahldomne—the hero of Vahl—not Irulandi?" a young man asked.

Vahldomne? Riannon snapped her attention to the speaker. Surely none of her family could know that she was the reluctant possessor of that soubriquet?

"That is our nephew Richard," Guy whispered to Riannon. "The apple of brother Henry's eye—and his own."

Riannon fleetingly grinned. Guy softly identified the well-dressed, older man as their second-eldest brother Thomas.

"Is the Vahldomne not dead?" Thomas said. "Is he not supposed to have died of his wounds within hours of Prince Roland's death? Do the imperial dogs wish us to dig him up and give his bones to them?"

Riannon frowned. The imperial ambassador wanted her?

"This must be some insult," Humphrey said. "They cannot expect us to surrender the man to them, be he dead or alive. He's a hero precisely because he killed their damned emperor's son."

Riannon's frown deepened to a scowl. The man she'd killed at Vahl had been a son of the Lion Emperor?

"Would they have handed over their precious princeling to us if he'd survived after killing Prince Roland?" Richard said. "I think not!"

"Well, I care not what they want," Henry said. "I'd as soon give this Vahldomne, whoever he is, the pick of my daughters than tamely turn him over to them."

Guy leaned close to Riannon to whisper. "I've seen our nieces. You'd need a hero's courage to accept any of them."

Riannon grinned.

"Mayhap the emperor has been encouraged to think us ready to surrender things of value that fall within our grasp," Thomas said.

Henry glowered.

Even Riannon, stranger to her family and politics, understood that barb at Henry's not claiming the throne for himself. Against expectations, she felt some sympathy and respect for him. Not another man in a thousand who found themselves in his position would have resisted the temptation to grab a crown. Thomas clearly numbered amongst the nine hundred and ninety-nine.

"That one would not let a clipped penny loose from his grasp," Guy whispered. "Unless, by doing so, he could gain two shining new ones in its place."

"I wish that tattooed imperial bastard entered his name on the tourney list," Richard said. "What I'd not give to break lances against his fat hide and see him eat grass."

"You and every able-bodied man in the kingdom," Humphrey said.

"Just you and your young hotspur friends remember that the ambassador and his men have safe-conducts," Henry said to his son. "You'll not break our liege lady's sworn word."

Richard's pugnacious scowl looked a young mirror of his father's. "You needn't lesson me in honour, father."

"What honour is there in feasting and supping with our enemies, I wonder?" Thomas said.

Henry, his face darkening with anger, turned on his brother.

"Perhaps there is more pleasure to be had in the company of enemies than family," Guy said.

Henry barked out a laugh. Thomas didn't bother throwing even a contemptuous glance Guy's way.

"Let us not forget," Joan said, "that we're here to celebrate Henry's wedding, not start a fresh war."

Henry's gaze flicked from Guy to Riannon. "Atuan's beard! Aymer. I knew not that you were in Sadiston, little brother. What happened to you? Lost your prayer books and half your weight, by the look of you."

"You would've been better advised to remain at your devotions, if that scar is a mark of your skill with a sword," Thomas said.

Riannon glared at him.

"One of these days," Henry said to Thomas, "I'm going to hear that someone has ripped that poisoned tongue out of your head. My only question will be to ask if they had the good sense to make you eat it."

Richard laughed. No one else did.

"This is not Aymer," Joan said. "Many of you will not have met our sister Riannon."

"*Sister?*" Henry swung his fierce frown from Joan to Riannon.

Riannon stood. "I am Riannon of Gast, your Grace."

"The girl who would be a man," Thomas said. "A fine addition to the family, eh, Henry?"

"You're no family of ours," Henry said to Riannon. "Our father disavowed all connection with you. I remember how you shamed our lord king, and our father. You're a disgrace. And still masquerading as what you are not."

Riannon strode towards the door. Joan intercepted her and put a restraining hand on Riannon's arm.

"You needn't leave," Joan said.

"I've no place here," Riannon said.

"A pity you didn't remember that before you intruded on us," Henry said. "Your presence is a mockery."

"If I'm nothing to you," Riannon said, "I can hardly dishonour you."

"What do you know of honour?" Henry said. "No woman understands it."

"Can you be sure you talk to a woman?" Thomas said.

"You're a living falsehood," Henry said to Riannon. "An unnatural creature that shares no blood of mine. Your mannish garb condemns you for all to see."

Riannon exerted her self-control to the utmost to stop her hand from reaching for her sword hilt. "You might wear your honour on your skin, your Grace. I do not."

Henry's face purpled and he all but snarled at Riannon.

Joan stepped between them. "Harry. Nonnie. For the love of the gods, stop this."

Henry visibly reined in his temper. Riannon remained taut and returned his stare.

"You've the right to welcome any to your own hearth," Henry said to Joan, "but I'd thank you to keep that *thing* away from me. Or I'll be forced to end what our sire began."

Riannon's hand dropped to her sword, but she turned and strode to the door.

"Wait!" Henry called. "By the gods, you have a nerve! I'll have you in chains and flogged if you do not remove that sword. You might choose to degrade yourself, but, by Atuan's fist, I'll not let you flaunt a false knighthood."

Riannon's restraints trembled. She remembered her father's fury, so like Henry's. She remembered his fists. Being whipped and locked in a chamber with the promise of more punishments to come. Unlike the youngster she had been, she had years of hard-won experience and adversity to help keep her fear and temper in check.

"You know not of what you speak, your Grace," she said.

"By the gods!" Henry jabbed a finger at her. "As the head of this family, I demand you remove that sword and stop this insult! Or must I take it from you?"

Riannon's chest tightened in anticipation. Unformed violence bristled in the air she breathed. Henry's son Richard and Guy had both risen to their feet.

"Harry!" Joan said.

Humphrey held his wife's arms to prevent her intervening.

"Only the three and twenty men of the order that conferred this honour upon me can deny me my right of knighthood." Riannon slowly reached down to tug her dagger from her belt. She held it up by the blade between her and Henry so that he could see the ornate red enamel decoration on the hilt. "You are not one of them, your Grace."

Henry glanced at the dagger. Some of his anger bled into disbelief. "Curse it! Where did you get that?"

"What is it?" Thomas asked.

"A Knight of the Star?" Richard said. "Atuan's legs!"

Riannon slid her dagger back into its sheath. "I'm not answerable to you as knight, vassal, servant, nor sister—since you cannot claim back what our father denied. Good day, your Grace."

No one tried to prevent Riannon leaving. She resisted the urge to slam the door behind her.

Riannon strode outside and paused to look for where the grooms waited with hers and Lady Eleanor's horses.

"Riannon!"

Riannon turned to see Guy following her.

"As fine a piece of bear-baiting as ever I've watched," he said. "I've not seen brother Henry's face turn so purple since his swaggering son broke the leg of his favourite horse."

"He'd value any horse above me," she said.

"If it's any consolation, I probably rank no more than a straw or two above the stables myself."

"You seem not to take any of it to heart."

"I must make myself amiable. I'm the youngest. Guy Lack-land. Dependant on the charity of my family." Guy lost his grin. "To give big brother his due, he does take blood ties and being head of the family seriously. Not even his bitterest enemy could accuse him of neglect."

"I'd be satisfied with complete disregard."

Guy smiled. "It pains me to be the one to have to point this out to you, strange sister mine, but you're hardly a person who passes unnoticed through any chamber."

Riannon grinned.

Guy put a comradely hand on her shoulder. "A word from one who has spent a lifetime needing the goodwill of others. I can perfectly comprehend the temptation to raise Henry's bristles for the pleasure of seeing him rage and foam at the mouth, but have a care. Remember that he is the queen's mailed fist. He commands her armies."

"I doubt I'll ever be called to serve with him."

Riannon saw John bringing her horse.

"Do you return to the lovely Lady Eleanor's?" Guy said. "I'll accompany you."

He was the last person she wished to see with Eleanor, if he truly intended to marry her, but Riannon could hardly forbid him the lady's hospitality.

"I'm not returning directly to her house," Riannon said. "She is meeting with the queen this morn."

"Then why do you not come with me to the tourney field? They have practice courses. You can let me boast of my sister belonging to the Grand Order of the Star. And let me take my chance in besting you in riding."

"Mayhap another time."

He nodded amiably and clapped her on the back. "Later, then. Oh. There was one thing I meant to ask you. Were you at Vahl?"

Riannon felt a chill which seemed to snake down the scar across her body. "Why do you ask?"

"Several times, I've had men ask me if I was there during the siege," Guy said. "I was not. It has just occurred to me that mayhap people mistook me for memories of you. It seems likely that you might have deeds I'd be happy to claim as my own."

"I wish I could feel certain in returning the compliment."

Guy threw back his head to laugh. "Not unless you wish a reputation like none other with the ladies. Drink with me one afternoon, strange sister mine, and we can swap stories."

Riannon watched him stride jauntily away. Her youngest brother was a difficult man to dislike, even if he did plan to marry Eleanor.

❖

Eleanor emerged into the busy bailey and saw Riannon waiting with the horses. She lifted the hem of her skirts clear of the dung and dust, and crossed to her. Riannon looked as distracted in unhappy thoughts as Eleanor felt.

"Your audience went well?" Riannon said.

"Possibly for someone," Eleanor said, "though whom, I'm unsure, save it was not me."

Riannon helped her mount. "The queen refused your request?"

"Not refused, but nor did she accept. I must speak with her again in a few days. She is considering the matter. I feel a pressing need to escape before returning to the wretched wedding preparations. Will you abet me?"

"Willingly," Riannon said.

When Eleanor dismissed all her escort save one waiting woman and a groom, Riannon offered no objection.

Eleanor guided her mare along the road from the gatehouse and across the stone bridge. She turned north, away from the city, and along the cleared strip parallel with the river. As soon as the ground permitted, she urged her mare to a canter. Riannon easily kept abreast and made no attempt to discourage her pace. Eleanor kicked her mare to a gallop.

The powerful thudding of the horse's hooves beat in time with Eleanor's soaring heart rate as she sought to outrun her unsatisfactory meeting with the queen. Her horse sped along the riverside. Trees loomed ahead as the forest closed on the bank. Eleanor spied a path she remembered and headed for it. A glance over her shoulder showed Riannon faithfully following, though not regaining the ground lost to the surprise of Eleanor's sudden gallop.

Eleanor let her mare slow to follow a cleared path between well-spaced trees. Riannon drew level with her. She glanced behind and remarked on the lead they had on the groom and maid.

"They know my wild ways," Eleanor said. "And will not be long in catching us."

"I'm unsure if I should be complimenting you on your riding skill," Riannon said, "or marvelling at your recklessness. Do you never fall?"

"Often. But I endeavour to overcome such setbacks without allowing them to curb my normal impulses. My pride is such, you see, that I cannot bear to allow the world to know me as a weak, poor-spirited creature."

Riannon smiled. "No one who ever met you, lady, would mistake you for fainthearted."

"Which, alas, is not universally considered a virtue in a woman."

Riannon lost her good humour and directed a frown beyond her horse's ears. Eleanor wondered what had happened in Riannon's meeting with her sister.

Not far ahead, the path crossed a narrow stream. It would feed into the river, though they were far enough within the woods that neither the towpath nor river were visible. Off to the right, a blackened circle showed where someone had recently camped in the clearing. For now it was ideally private.

"Would you mind if we halted and walked?" Eleanor said.

Riannon helped her dismount and surrendered the reins to the groom. He and Eleanor's waiting woman remained a discreet distance away. Eleanor slipped a hand through Riannon's arm. They strolled towards the stream.

"I was gladdened to see how you and Guy have so quickly struck up amiable terms," Eleanor said. "With the welcome you received from your sister, you must be gratified that your homecoming has been better than you feared."

Riannon scowled.

"Have I misspoken?" Eleanor said.

"No. But it would be best if I did not accompany you to the wedding festivities."

"Why ever not?"

"The Earl Marshal would not welcome my presence. There, or anywhere." Riannon shook her head. "I should not have returned."

"Am I allowed to most vigorously dissent? I'm proud and pleased to be numbered amongst your friends. To have this chance to know you. And I hope this is but the beginning."

Riannon fleetingly smiled. "You'd think, would you not, that after a lifetime of being something apart, I'd not expect to be treated in any other way? And feel no discomfiture from it."

They had reached the stream and halted.

"Lady, will you grant me your pardon?" Riannon said. "I'm dull company today."

"You're never that. And owe me no apology. I'd have you no other way."

Riannon shot her a guarded look. "I wish I had the easy tongue and manner of my brother. He makes you laugh. I burden you with my frowns." She scowled across the stream. "Are you to marry him?"

"Guy?" Eleanor made no attempt to hide her surprise. "Your brother is, indeed, one of the most charming men of my acquaintance. I enjoy his company above most people's. But I've never seriously considered him as a husband. You see, I have a fancy for a companion who will grow old with me and expire quietly in my bed. Guy is like to die in any one of a hundred women's beds."

Riannon grinned. She offered Eleanor her hand to steady her as she stepped across the stream. The physical contact roused Eleanor's awareness of Riannon's proximity. She slipped her hand again through Riannon's arm as they resumed their meandering stroll.

The forest breathed a calm that was at the same time vitalising. Relaxing, and yet heightening her senses. The green ferns looked as though they had been freshly painted by the gods that morning. The air smelled rich with sap and life. With each breath and step, Eleanor lost her annoyance at her inconclusive interview with the queen and the insecurity it introduced to her future, and she set aside the myriad vexations due to the wedding.

Her relaxation to the physical world allowed a growing awareness of her body and of Riannon. The reawakening of her own capacity to love gratified her, even as she experienced its edgy shadow in which coalesced all her doubt and uncertainty that her feelings might be reciprocated. She heard again that sibilant voice inside that told her she loved alone and in vain, and which, at its darkest root, whispered the corrosive message that she did not deserve to be loved.

She looked up at Riannon. She, too, had lost her frown. Eleanor's gaze traced Riannon's profile. She paused on Riannon's lips. Not framed by a beard. They might be the only soft part of Riannon. Eleanor knew an urge to touch them. To trace them and to test their pliancy.

Riannon glanced down at her. Eleanor's rush of warmth sprang from far more than a blush of embarrassment. She felt the muscles of Riannon's arm tense beneath her hand. Riannon put her free hand over Eleanor's. Just as quickly, though, Riannon removed her hand, as if thinking the gesture might be unwelcome. Eleanor wanted Riannon's touch and Riannon's kiss.

"I hope you'll reconsider attending the wedding festivities," Eleanor said. "I'd miss your presence greatly."

Riannon halted and looked down at her. Eleanor reached across to take hold of Riannon's free hand and return it to cover hers. For the length of several heartbeats that might have lasted as long as forever, they stared at each other. Riannon regarded her with desire so obvious that even the greatest act of wilful self-deception could not have misconstrued it. In that brief eternity, Eleanor felt herself fall towards Riannon though she physically did not move beyond a laboured intake of breath.

Riannon looked away and let her hand slip free again. "Um. We... we had better return to our horses. We've walked beyond sight of them."

"It is my desire never to sit out any dance for want of a partner," Eleanor said.

The *non sequitur* surprised Riannon into turning back to her. "I cannot imagine you'd ever find yourself in need. My brother Guy, for one, would be pleased to oblige you, I'm sure."

"It is not Guy I wish to give my hand to," Eleanor said. "Would you honour me?"

Eleanor believed she saw, for the first time, Riannon's defences knocked flat. Riannon looked fearful, disbelieving, and hopeful. Her vulnerability could not have been a starker contrast to her war-scarred face.

"Me?" Riannon said.

"Yes. If you want me."

Eleanor offered her hand. Riannon's throat worked. After a hesitation, Riannon's fingers closed around Eleanor's hand. Eleanor smiled.

With a tender deliberation that made Eleanor's heart race, Riannon gently peeled Eleanor's glove off. Riannon flicked a look at Eleanor's face as if checking that her attentions were truly welcome. While keeping eye contact, Riannon lifted Eleanor's naked hand to her face. Eleanor felt breath hot on her skin before Riannon kissed her fingers. Eleanor's own breathing grew heavier. Riannon pressed her lips to Eleanor's palm, wetter and hotter than the kiss on her fingers. Eleanor swallowed down a tightening throat and watched Riannon put her mouth to the inside of Eleanor's wrist. Without breaking contact with Riannon's lips, Eleanor pressed her hand against Riannon's cheek. The skin was smooth. No coarse hairs of a beard nor prickliness of stubble.

"Oh, lady," Riannon whispered warmly against Eleanor's skin.

Eleanor ran her thumb across Riannon's lips. They were soft. Not framed in moustache and beard. Just smooth skin. Not a man. But an object of desire—aching desire— all the same. Eleanor wanted to touch her. To be touched.

Eleanor slid her hand up Riannon's cheek and around into short hair. She pulled Riannon's head down so that their lips met. Eleanor's eyes closed as they kissed. She inhaled breath from close to Riannon's skin as Riannon tenderly sucked Eleanor's bottom lip. The thrill arrowed down to Eleanor's breasts and blossomed hotly between her thighs. Her fingers curled against the back of Riannon's neck, her nails scraping skin.

Riannon slipped her arms around Eleanor. She pulled her into a tight embrace against a firm, muscular body and kissed her hard. She sucked hungrily at Eleanor's lips as ardently as any man ever had. Eleanor clutched the back of Riannon's tunic and clung to her as desire both inflamed and weakened her. Riannon's tongue parted her lips. Eleanor moaned into Riannon's mouth and met tongue with tongue. Her whole body yearned for contact. Her breasts, sensitive and heavy, craved a firm touch to cup and fondle them. Her hips pressed against Riannon. They found no ridge of an erection to rub. Eleanor didn't care. She pulsed with melting arousal. She wanted sexual fulfilment. She wanted Riannon.

"By the gods," Riannon whispered.

"I'm ready to burst into flames."

"There are few things I'd not sacrifice for you." Riannon drew a ragged breath and straightened without releasing Eleanor. "Your honour is one of them. I'll not tumble you on the ground like a serving wench."

Eleanor reluctantly looked to the side and remembered where they were. Riannon was correct. Glorious though that blinding rush of passion was, bedding in the dirt would not do. With more self-control than relish, Eleanor released Riannon and took a step backwards.

"Tonight," Eleanor said. "I'll make sure I'm alone in my bedchamber. Will you come to me?"

Riannon nodded. She bent to retrieve the glove she had dropped and returned it to Eleanor. She touched Eleanor's face as softly as she might something precious and fragile, and kissed her with a tender reverence inhumanly restrained from the passionate force of just moments before. Eleanor's own heart and breathing had yet to calm.

"This day will be the longest of my life," Riannon said.

Eleanor agreed.

CHAPTER TEN

A veline watched her host, the Archbishop of Sadiston, select a piece of crystallised ginger with fastidious care. He offered it to her.

"It's refreshing to find a woman who understands the necessities for war," he said. "Mistake me not, for I'd have the natural order no other way than yours as the softer and gentler sex. Where would we be without the nurturing hand of our mothers?"

Aveline popped the lump of confectionary in her mouth. It was sickly sweet, yet also carried a fiery sting.

"But we cannot deal with unbelievers as we would naughty children." His expansive gesture drew attention to the many rings biting into his pale, podgy flesh. "If they cannot see the error of their ways in this life, then it's our duty to send them to the gods where they will be punished for their recalcitrance."

"There's no stomach for attempting the conversion of our imperial visitors," Aveline said.

The archbishop's hesitation was telling, though he masked it in another of his searches for exactly the right piece of candied violet from the comfits arrayed on the silver platter in front of him. He was far too clever a man and astute a politician to make the mistake of thinking of her only as a naer and not also the queen's sister. Whatever his private feelings about Mathilda's wisdom in accepting the Lion Emperor's embassy, Aveline knew he would speak no word of criticism about the queen.

"Their presence is providential." He popped a sweet into his mouth. "A goad. They remind men of what has been lost to the infidels. Of Evriat shamefully conquered and writhing beneath the lash of unbelievers. Its holy places and altars defiled. We can use this to our advantage."

Neither his candour nor his including her in the gain to be had out of the situation escaped Aveline. Fat and hedonistic he might be, but she had not misjudged his brain. What he failed to grasp was that Aveline walked three paces ahead of him. He clearly had not the slightest idea how she planned to use the situation of the imperial embassy and the seething animosity towards it. Aveline had no intention of enlightening him. She did not need his help with that. She cultivated him, rather, for his influence on the Quatorum Council. Not that the priests of Atuan, god of war, needed much prodding when it came to glutting their lord god's appetite through a call to crusade.

"The infidels are a provocation," Aveline said. "One need not cup one's ear to doors to hear whispers and muttering about reclaiming lost Evriat. And how unjust is the twenty year truce. It's like a drying summer wind across a mown field. Before long, the merest spark will prove incendiary."

He stroked his fussily combed beard and nodded. "You'll be present at the council meeting?"

There was the crux of the matter. In the face of the matriarch's moves to block Aveline from the highest circle of her order, Aveline harboured few illusions that Matriarch Melisande would not also try to have her excluded from their deputation to the Quatorum Council. She needed to get one of the mother-naers who would attend to take her as part of her staff. The obvious candidate was Katherine of Fourport, the only mother-naer born in Tirand, and whose family were Queen Mathilda's vassals. But Aveline had yet to find a point of leverage.

"I suppose, since you've been absent recently," the archbishop said, "that you're unaware of the death of the wife of Sir Ralph of Howe."

Aveline frowned as she tried to remember who Sir Ralph Howe's wife had been and why her death might be important. "She was a daughter of your brother-in-law, Hubert, was she not?"

"Yes. A pretty young thing. Died before she could give Ralph an heir. He—"

"Sir Geoffrey of Howe," Aveline said. "He is Ralph's father. Geoffrey's first wife was the sister of Katherine Fourport. So, Ralph is Mother-Naer Katherine's nephew."

The archbishop smiled as he wiped his fingers on an embroidered napkin. Aveline lifted her cup of hippocras to salute him. She had an ally. He had given her the means of ingratiating herself with the mother-naer. A man with no heirs needed a wife. Giving him a rich bride would please him and, far more importantly, please his aunt.

Aveline knew exactly how she was going to buy her way to the convocation and the Quatorum Council meeting.

❖

Riannon outwardly watched Guy's sublime display of horse-manship as he raced his mount through a tortuous course of poles and obstacles. Inwardly, she could think only of Eleanor.

Though it smacked of blasphemy, Riannon regarded that moment in the woods this morning, when Eleanor offered her hand, as how she imagined a holy revelation would feel. So unexpected, though fervently desired. Heavy with meaning, yet making Riannon light-headed. To her dying breath, Riannon would have that scene etched on her memory more distinctly than any mural on a chapel wall. The earthy smells. The precise blue of the sleeve of Eleanor's outstretched arm. That thrilling and terrifying moment when she realised Eleanor's meaning. The feel of Eleanor's body in her arms. Eleanor's kiss...

Riannon drew an unsteady breath. The sun had never crept through the western half of the sky more slowly. A pox on Henry and his wedding. Had Eleanor not needed to attend to Cicely and the preparations for the morrow's ceremony and festivities, she and Riannon could even now be in bed.

Henry's bristling bellicosity might have belonged to their sire. She fleetingly appreciated the irony of his willingness, albeit unknowingly, to offer her—as the Vahldomne—the pick of his daughters. She would wager much that he would loudly denounce her as unnaturally playing a man if he caught any hint of her proclivities. Had he known it, he'd be self-righteously satisfied that his accursed wedding kept Riannon from Eleanor's arms.

Riannon wished Joan had not exposed her to the rest of their family. Though this morning's meeting had gone more or less as Riannon expected, that did not make it more palatable. She remained as outcast as when her father disowned her. At least now, though, she belonged in two places.

When she had presented herself to them as the person to whom the dying Prince Roland of Iruland had passed his dagger of membership, the Knights of the Grand Order of the Star had been shocked to learn that their exclusive fraternity had been invaded by a woman. After much heated discussion, they reluctantly accepted her because she was Prince Roland's choice and the intertwined fact that she was the one on whom the bardic epithet of the Vahldomne had been bestowed. She should not have flaunted her dagger, though, when Henry confronted her.

Her other membership was to an even more exclusive sorority, paladins of the Order of the Goddess. Quite what Aveline wanted from her in Sadiston, Riannon still could not guess. Aveline had not contacted her. Riannon was not sorry for that—especially now. As a woman who loved women, Aveline would detect Riannon's full-bodied interest in Eleanor. That was not knowledge she trusted her cousin with, for her sake or Eleanor's.

A cheer drew Riannon's attention back to the field. Guy triumphantly held aloft a red cloth. Spectators clapped and cheered him. Even those workers putting the last touches to the newly erected stands for the coming tourney had turned to watch Guy.

Riannon noticed a knot of riders near the covered stand built for the queen. Some of the men wore the blue and yellow livery of the Earl Marshal. Henry's brawny figure sat astride a large bay horse. The equally bulky rider on the horse beside him wore a strange brown cap. Riannon would not have known him for one of the imperial representatives, save for the dark tattoo covering the left half of his face. They were not close enough for her to make out the pattern. Her memory filled in the details. It looked like the dark imprint of a dragon's claws against the side of his face, as if their reptilian godling had clamped its talons around his head. Claiming him as it marked him. Just like that man she had killed at the siege of Vahl, who had been the son of the Lion Emperor. The man whose killer the emperor wished turned over to him.

No, Riannon did not think the emperor or ambassadors naïve enough to believe their request would be taken seriously. It must be a pretext. But for what?

"Little Nonnie!" Guy halted his horse near her and dropped to the ground.

For all his jesting, Guy took at least one activity seriously. He rode as one born in a saddle. Riannon guessed her brother would prove as skilful with sword and lance as with words.

"Did you see?" He accepted a cup of wine from a squire while another took his horse. "That braggart Morechester fell on the—Oh. I see big brother consorts with the enemy again. Harry looks as delighted about it as a virgin escorting her elderly groom to bed, does he not?"

Riannon grinned. "Too close to the bone."

Guy laughed. "Yes. I'd forgotten poor Cicely. I'd not exchange being born the last son for the first daughter, not for the largest inheritance in the world."

"Especially not for that," she said.

"You have the right of it. Lack of money can be a monstrous handicap to a man, but possession of it an even greater one to a woman." Guy drained his wine. "What think you the emperor schemes at with this embassy?"

Riannon shook her head. "I know not. But I doubt it's to our benefit. Mayhap you should ask Aveline."

Guy turned his frown from the now retreating entourage of their brother to Riannon. "Aveline? Our cousin the naer? I'd thought it fitting that the gods endowed women with the ability to conjure philtres and charms, since they lack our strength of body and mind. But if there is any woman I'd not trust with magical power, it's her."

Riannon wondered if she should reveal her connection with Aveline and the order.

"Men might grumble in their beards about having a queen," Guy said, "but they should thank all the mighty gods that Mathilda is the elder and not Aveline. If that one wore the crown, no one would be safe. Whenever she opens her mouth, I expect her to hiss."

Riannon felt she ought to defend Aveline, but could not fault Guy's assessment.

He clapped a hand on her shoulder and leaned close. "It's not surprising that she looks to women to bed rather than men. Women tolerate much more than ever we would in an intimate companion."

Riannon frowned at his back as he strolled into his arming tent.

❖

Riannon watched Eleanor talking with the people who had come to share supper with the Lady of Barrowmere. Normally a light meal eaten with household and intimates, the large gathering of nobility in

Sadiston for the Earl Marshal's wedding provided many who attended Eleanor as kin, friends, place seekers, and entertainers. Eleanor seemed to know everyone, and her lively conversation and generous table drew even more about her. Riannon wished them all a thousand miles away. Her fingers ached to touch Eleanor's smile, to kiss her, and to feel again that supple warmth of Eleanor leaning against her.

Sitting beside Eleanor at table proved the most delicious torment. They were so close, but only able to indulge in seemingly accidental touches. Riannon's gaze wanted to devour Eleanor. Her pale throat. The way her bodice drew tight across her bosom. The flicker of pink tongue as she licked her lips. Riannon shifted in her chair. Had she been made of wood, Eleanor's look from under her brows would have caused her to burst alight. Instead, Riannon grew wet.

Normally, Riannon revelled in Eleanor's every word, but that long, long evening she remembered little of what was spoken. Eleanor and she communicated in a silent, private language that excluded everyone else.

The guests lingered. Their noisy chatter tapped at Riannon's nerves. She imagined bodily ejecting them one at a time. Eleanor finally escorted the last to the door and bade him a good night. Riannon waited for her at the inner doorway out of the hall. Waiting women trailed Eleanor.

Eleanor paused as she passed Riannon. She whispered, "An hour. I'll be alone."

Riannon nodded. She watched Eleanor mount the stairs and cast her a burning look before disappearing out of sight.

In her chamber, Riannon unbuckled her belt with fingers surprisingly steady. Alan stripped off his tunic and shirt and talked about some men he'd watched practising for the tourney. Riannon ignored him and poured some wine into a cup and added a generous splash of water. The candle flame burned steadily but with excruciating slowness down to the hour mark. That she would soon be entering Eleanor's bedchamber, and be able to hold and kiss Eleanor again, seemed as unreal as a dream.

She set her cup aside untasted and began to pace.

She had believed, until she heard that teasing voice in the grove house garden and turned to see Eleanor, that the wounds she'd received at Vahl had killed part of her. For four years she'd accepted that she sacrificed any chance for intimacy. Her knighthood had been bought at the cost of her strange sort of womanhood. The scars that carved through her body, and which yet marked her with the dormant potency of death delayed, had been a peculiar form of gelding. She had erred.

What she had not expected was to find a woman who would care to look deeper than disfigured skin. Even after their ardent embrace this morning, Riannon could not quite rid herself of all doubt that any woman, let alone one as magnificent as Eleanor of Barrowmere, had truly invited her to her bedchamber.

Riannon fiddled with her discarded belt. Since less than thirty paces separated this room from Eleanor's chamber, she could safely leave her sword here for an hour or two. Good. Eleanor would have had something to say had Riannon turned up to make love with a sword in hand. Riannon grinned and trailed her fingers to the sheath of her knife. The ornate gold and red enamel pattern on her dagger of the Order of the Star glinted in the candlelight. Thank the gods that Eleanor was a widow, not a maiden or married woman. Riannon did not know how her scruples would have withstood the temptation of an assignation forbidden by every courtly precept.

Eleanor.

"Yes, sir?" Alan said.

Riannon did not realise she had spoken aloud. "Go to sleep. You want to be fresh and at your best for the wedding tomorrow."

"For certès, there'll be pretty women aplenty to dance with. And they say that wine will flow in the streets."

"Then let us hope, for the Lady Cicely's sake, that no heads get broken."

"Do you need me to aid you with aught?" he said.

Riannon shook her head and cast another glance at the candle.

Alan climbed into his pallet at the foot of her bed, hastily mumbled his prayers, then settled to watch her with a curious frown. Riannon could not stop nervously pacing. Her squire had not known her to visit a lover. Though she had sent him on his way to sport himself in brothels, she found herself unable to admit why she prowled the chamber rather than retire to sleep. He was not unintelligent. Long before the candle finally began to melt the hour mark, Alan's imperfectly suppressed smile signalled that he had guessed what she was about—if not who with.

The house lay quiet and dark, though the sun would not yet be fully set outside on this unbearably long summer night. Riannon shielded the candle as she made her way to the lady's chamber door. Her leather soles made no noise.

Riannon paused. She felt that tightness twisting her entrails familiar from facing a battle. She was scared. What of? Not a beautiful woman who wished to make love with her? Riannon drew on every ounce of experience of war to open the door and step into the chamber.

Eleanor stood partway between a richly hung bed and a table littered with cosmetics. The flame from a single oil lamp caressed her with a soft yellow light. She wore only her linen chemise. Her recently brushed hair fell loose about her shoulders. Long and dark with coppery highlights. Riannon had never seen anything more breathtakingly beautiful. Awe added to fear and held her immobile.

❖

Eleanor stared at Riannon standing just inside the door. Riannon's physical largeness struck her. Her lover stood taller than most men, and she radiated muscular power and the strength of a warrior. The wavering light from the candle in her hand cast a huge, looming shadow on the wall behind her. Her scar seemed to writhe like an unquiet serpent. Yet it was Riannon's stillness that unnerved Eleanor. Had she changed her mind?

"It passes my understanding," Eleanor said, "why the men of religion regard with utmost suspicion assignations such as these. I cannot recall ever praying so much as this afternoon. Not, I grant you, that my sudden excess of piety was for enlightenment. But, rather, for the dark of night."

Riannon grinned. Eleanor exhaled a knot of nerves that had begun to gather beneath her breastbone. Riannon crossed the chamber in four long strides and set the candle on Eleanor's dressing table. The look she turned on Eleanor banished any doubts that she wished to draw back. Riannon stared at her as if she were trying to commit every curve to memory. She touched Eleanor's hair and lifted a lock to her lips.

The gesture might have been an act of worship. Eleanor did not want to be treated as a wooden icon. Her blood coursed warm, barely contained beneath her skin. Ignorant she might be of the exact nature of what they would do in bed with each other, but passion and Eleanor were old friends. The fire spread along familiar paths to burn in her breasts and low in her belly. Eleanor knew what she wanted. She wanted Riannon to give it to her.

"Love me," Eleanor said.

She slid her arms up around Riannon's neck, stood on tiptoe, and kissed her. Devoured her lips. Invaded her mouth with her tongue. Riannon clamped strong arms around her and pulled her close. Eleanor pressed against a hard body. Her own body melted and yearned for Riannon, heedless of unusual contours. Riannon's strong grip on her buttock drew a moan from her that cared nought for the sex of the fingers squeezing her desire to the surface.

Eleanor tugged at Riannon's overtunic. "Take this off."

Riannon impatiently pulled the garment off and dropped it. Her tunic followed quickly. Eleanor drew her towards the bed. She stripped off her own chemise and let it fall to the rushes.

"By the gods, you're beautiful." Riannon cupped one of Eleanor's breasts. "Perfect."

Eleanor inhaled sharply at the contact and looked down to see her pale flesh firmly captured by one of those big, beautiful hands. Her nipple stiffened against Riannon's finger. Oh, gods, she wanted this. It felt as though Riannon's touch brought boiling to the surface every moment of every day of every month of Eleanor's unwanted celibacy, and exquisitely concentrated all her unsatisfied needs where skin met skin. The blistering heat flooding through Eleanor threatened to melt her knees and between her legs. Beyond caring how wantonly she acted, she reached under Riannon's shirt for the laces holding up her hose.

"Please," Eleanor said.

Riannon yanked up her shirt. No engorged penis tented the linen of her underwear. But the urgency with which her fingers fumbled her points, and the breathy voice she used to mutter an oath as she tugged off hose and braies, just as surely signalled her arousal.

Without waiting for Riannon to strip off her shirt, Eleanor pulled her through the hangings and down onto the bed with her. Out of habit, Eleanor urged Riannon on top. It made no difference whether the weight of a lover's body pressing her down into the mattress was male or female.

Riannon's hot mouth worked down from Eleanor's mouth to her

throat, then to her breast. Eleanor's body responded beyond her control as it lifted and strained into Riannon's touches. As Riannon's dextrous tongue teased Eleanor's nipples, her hand slipped between their bodies. Eleanor's hips tilted into the contact. She was wet and ready. Riannon's fingers found her clitoris. Eleanor groaned, arched her back, and dug her fingers into Riannon's shoulders. With her eyes closed, and lost to everything but the sensations roaring through her flesh, she clung to Riannon's solidly muscled body. Desire pushed her upwards. Riannon's firm, knowing, rhythmic strokes drove her to that unbearable tension. Eleanor cried aloud when she came with two of Riannon's fingers inside her and her nipple squeezed between Riannon's lips.

Eleanor didn't have to tell Riannon not to leave her. She enjoyed the softening glow of her relaxing body with Riannon's weight pressing agreeably on her and with Riannon's head against her chest, her warm breath softly caressing Eleanor's skin.

When Eleanor had command of her limbs again, she ran her fingers through Riannon's short, bristly hair. That part of her might have been male. Eleanor opened her eyes. No, her lover was not a man. And no man who had shared Eleanor's bed had done for her what Riannon had just done. Yes, Eleanor had occasionally achieved climaxes, but her pleasure had never been the sole aim of their lovemaking. Her male partners, even David who had initiated her in many of the mysteries of physical love, had not left themselves unsatisfied in deference to her need and enjoyment.

It was a truth, too, that she had not climaxed so rapidly before. It ought to be something she found embarrassing. Immodest. Hoydenish. Sinful, even. Eleanor smiled at Riannon and sighed contentedly. She did not feel in need of penitence or absolution. She felt wonderful.

"Religious theory holds women as failed men," Eleanor said. "The next time any man tries to tell me that, I'll inform him in no uncertain terms that he has not the faintest idea what he's talking about."

Riannon smiled, kissed the side of Eleanor's breast, and eased herself off to lie beside her. Her gaze, nearly as heavy as a touch, travelled Eleanor's naked body and she captured a strand of hair to wind around her fingers. She kissed it.

"There is nought of failure or imperfection in you," Riannon said.

Eleanor wriggled onto her side and tugged at the collar of Riannon's shirt. "Take this off. I would see you. And touch you. You must teach me how I am to make you writhe and cry out with such pleasure."

Riannon put her hand over Eleanor's hand and held it still. "Let me love you again."

"Oh, you didn't think there's much chance you'd leave this bed without doing that, did you?" Eleanor sat up to look down at Riannon. "But first, I must see you."

Riannon pulled Eleanor on top of her and held her with strong arms. Eleanor couldn't help but kiss the mouth so close to her own. Riannon's hands began stroking and exploring Eleanor's back. Eleanor's skin leaped to life beneath Riannon's touch. Eleanor found her will crumbling and her desire reviving as fast as embers blown back to flames.

With lips, tongue, and hands, Riannon played Eleanor with more skill than any minstrel did his harp. When Riannon slid her thigh between Eleanor's legs, Eleanor moaned and pushed against firm muscle. She would need little of that to tumble her over the edge, but Riannon proved she had a mind to spin out an epic saga on Eleanor's body, not a quick ditty.

Judging to a fiendish nicety the line between excitement and frustration, Riannon aroused Eleanor to a prolonged pitch where she lost herself completely to sensation beyond the power of thought. She writhed. Her fingers knotted the sheets. Her legs twitched and her heels drummed the mattress. Riannon's tongue flicking inside her threatened to drive her out of her wits for all time. Her gasps, moans, whimpers, and begging were the music Riannon drew out of her. When her climax finally burst, it ripped at the very roots of her as if, for the first time in her life, sexual pleasure engulfed even her immortal soul.

❖

Eleanor lay spent. Vaguely aware of sweating and panting, she slowly drifted back to her body. She sprawled in wanton abandon across the middle of the bed. Riannon lay close on her side, propped up on an elbow, watching and softly stroking her fingertips along Eleanor's arm. She looked smug. Eleanor sighed and reached a languid hand up to put her fingers to Riannon's smile.

"I know not why you look so pleased," Eleanor said. "The joy was all mine."

"Not so, lady."

Eleanor tapped her finger against Riannon's lips. "I have a name. I would hear it from your mouth."

Riannon kissed Eleanor's finger. "Eleanor."

"How strong you make me sound."

Riannon smiled and leaned to kiss her tenderly on the lips. Eleanor slid her arms around Riannon for the simple pleasure of holding her lover and feeling her. A new body for her to get to know that was solid and real and exciting. But Riannon still wore her linen shirt. Eleanor tugged at it. Riannon again gently but firmly captured her hand and kissed her. Eleanor yielded to the renewed exploration of Riannon's mouth but did not forget her purpose.

"I would see you," Eleanor said. "I would feel you. All of you."

Riannon sat up. "I'd best not tarry. Your servants will gossip enough as it is without me falling asleep here and being found in the morning."

She was right, but Eleanor was neither so easily deflected nor inclined to end their evening just yet. Eleanor levered herself up and wriggled around to sit astride Riannon's legs. The imperfect light angling in through the gap in the bed hangings illuminated Riannon's guarded look. Eleanor wondered what Riannon's shirt concealed. What would possibly be so bad that Riannon denied herself the sexual pleasure Eleanor was clearly so willing to offer her?

Instead of again reaching for Riannon's shirt, Eleanor looped her wrists around the back of Riannon's neck and smiled.

"I could get the idea," Eleanor said, "that you are no stranger to ladies' bedrooms. Which reminds me of something I've been meaning to ask since this morn. Pray tell, just how many serving wenches have you tumbled in the woods?"

Riannon smiled.

"Do you know that it's my particular conceit," Eleanor said, "that I'm one of the few people who can make you smile?"

Riannon put one hand, hot and heavy, on Eleanor's thigh and captured some of her hair with the other. "How could I not be happy with you naked sitting on me?"

"Though it sore wounds my vanity to acknowledge it, the world is stuffed with people who would remain utterly unmoved by the situation. Now, let me fetch us wine so that I can be comfortable while you tell me how intoxicated my beauty makes you. Though, given your dismaying habit of likening me to a weed, perhaps I should settle for the simple drunkenness of the grape."

Riannon laughed.

Eleanor slipped off the bed. She found the wine jug and a cup. She had not asked for two cups to be left. When she returned, Riannon had rearranged the pillows and sat propped against one. Eleanor handed her the wine and fetched the candle to set in the niche in the bed head.

Eleanor settled against Riannon with Riannon's arm around her. Their bare legs pressed together. Riannon's long limbs were strongly muscled with sparse black hair only around her shins. Her shirt had ridden up to the top of her thighs, but still concealed the whole of her torso and hips. An old white scar, so unlike the one torn through her face, angled across the meat of her thigh. Eleanor traced it with a fingertip. Shirt or no shirt between them, Eleanor felt again the wonder of physical closeness to a desired other. This time, though, she knew herself desired in return. She need only look up into Riannon's face to see the miracle of her feelings reflected.

They passed the cup of wine between them. Eleanor had to continually explore Riannon's body as if needing constant reassurance of her physical reality. To touch her hand. Kiss her fingers. Rub her foot against Riannon's calf. She wanted that shirt off her, to run her hand across Riannon's firm torso. To feel the muscles. To put her face to Riannon's strong shoulder and taste the skin there. To smell Riannon. To test her novel fascination with another woman's breasts.

Eleanor set the cup aside and drew Riannon's face down for a kiss that tasted of wine and passion. Eleanor put her hand to the side of Riannon's neck to anchor herself. Riannon's pulse thudded under her fingers just as hard as her own raced. Riannon stared at her with an exhilarating intensity more sincerely flattering than any words.

"How fierce you look and yet how tender you are." Eleanor's fingers slipped over Riannon's jaw and across her cheek. The scar felt no different to Riannon's unmarked flesh.

Riannon jerked back and snatched Eleanor's hand down from her face. Her fingers gripped Eleanor's wrist tight enough to hurt. Her guarded look slammed back into place.

The speed and vehemence of her reaction caught Eleanor by surprise. After a couple of heartbeats, Riannon released her and climbed off the bed.

"I must leave," Riannon said.

Eleanor scrambled across to catch Riannon's arm as she straightened from scooping her clothes from the floor. "Riannon?"

"I'll leave you now to sleep," Riannon said. "You've much to do with the wedding on the morrow."

In Riannon's not looking at her, Eleanor understood where she had erred. But understanding did not present her with a simple solution. She wondered what grotesque continuation of the disfiguring scar marred Riannon's body beneath her shirt. She slipped her arms around Riannon's waist and rested her cheek against Riannon's chest.

"You will come back to me tomorrow?" Eleanor asked. "My lover."

"Do you want me to?"

"If you do not, I'll be forced to throw myself at you where everyone can see us, like one of your countless serving wenches."

Eleanor felt Riannon relax and looked up to see Riannon's grin returned.

"I'll be a long time living that down," Riannon said.

"Even longer, if I have aught to do with it."

Riannon smiled.

Eleanor lifted her face in invitation. Riannon obliged without hesitation. Improbably, that kiss stirred what Eleanor had believed well sated. Riannon's hands kneaded and stroked her desire back to life. Eleanor moaned and sagged against Riannon.

"How can you keep doing this to me?" Eleanor whispered.

"Would you like me to stop?"

"No. Yes. Please. Don't. Oh, merciful lady..."

When Riannon lifted her onto the bed and climbed on top of her, Eleanor's arousal soared and pulsed between her legs. She ached to be filled. Her thighs parted and she locked her legs around Riannon's hips to hold her in place. A small, rational voice, squeezed almost to oblivion at the back of her mind, reminded her that Riannon did not have the erection her body craved. It didn't matter. Eleanor's fingers dug into Riannon's back as she came with Riannon's groin rubbing hers. She called Riannon's name.

Eleanor sleepily let Riannon pull the sheet up over her. Riannon retrieved her candle, then bestowed a lingering kiss warm with the promise of unfinished business. Eleanor sighed happily and listened for the door to softly shut after Riannon's departure.

Tomorrow, she would think of some way to deal with those scars and giving Riannon some taste of the pleasure she had given. Tonight, she stretched contentedly and let her eyes sag closed. She drifted into sleep smiling.

CHAPTER ELEVEN

R iannon hardly saw Eleanor the next morning, busy as the Lady of Barrowmere was with helping her niece ready herself for the day's festivities. The ceremony would take place at noon in the basilica of Kamet, lord of justice, giver of law.

Riannon escaped the bustle of the busy household by stepping into the house shrine chamber. After laying her dagger on the miniature anvil of Atuan, she sat on Eleanor's padded stool. Her thoughts raced back to Eleanor's bedchamber. She smiled, though still partly dazed by the wonder of what had unfolded. More than just the joys of flesh, Riannon had discovered a part of herself she had not suspected. Deeper than memories. It had lain curled up inside the core of her, protected from every day bitterness and disappointments, to emerge fresh but fully-grown and powerful like the god Naith from the chest of Atuan, his father. Yet the part of her that Eleanor had released last night owed nothing to any male.

The door shut. Riannon turned. Eleanor walked towards her. The look in her eyes banished any doubt that last night had been an imagined fancy—or that the lady would wake full of regrets. Riannon rose to envelop her in an embrace. Their mouths met hungrily. Eleanor's fist knotted Riannon's overtunic.

"I needed that," Eleanor said. "I needed to touch you. I was beginning to think last night a dream."

"It may have been a shared dream."

"Then I never wish to wake. At least until this accursed wedding is over."

Riannon smiled. "How is Lady Cicely?"

"As well as I could hope for, but not as well as I might wish, for her sake. I've explained to her the physical side of marriage. And shown her the traditional charm against the pain of defloration that I'll put on her when it comes time for the bedding. It seemed to frighten her more than comfort her. Which is not wholly surprising."

Riannon kissed her. Eleanor sighed, leaned against Riannon, and slid her arms up Riannon's back.

"All the while I talked with her," Eleanor said, "my brain plagued me with the most wickedly wonderful thoughts of coupling that contained only pleasure. How merciful the gods are not to allow others access to our thoughts. I know not how I kept my countenance when poor Cicely remarked that I seemed to be fairly glowing. A truly good aunt would have sought to reassure her that she, too, will know that sudden confidence in whatever little beauty you have when you know yourself desired."

"You are most truly desired."

After a long, deepening kiss, which they had to break for air, Eleanor put a hand on Riannon's chest. Her face was charmingly flushed and wholly desirable, yet she frowned instead of resuming their kiss.

"Much as I'd like to tarry," Eleanor said, "I'd best leave. This afternoon is like to be torture. All those hours at table and not being beside you. A plague on this wedding. Promise me that you'll dance with me."

Riannon had not intended attending the ceremony or celebration feast.

"You did take my hand," Eleanor said.

Despite her misgivings, Riannon let Eleanor's smile persuade her. "Yes, lady."

❖

At the grandly decorated basilica, where the air hung thick with expensive incense, Riannon found Guy talking with a young woman and her sharp-eyed mother. He used Riannon's approach as an excuse to extricate himself. They moved closer to where their family gathered.

"It's sad," he said. "The poor creature cannot help making eyes at me. Being handsome is a terrible burden that few truly understand."

Riannon grinned. "She is very rich?"

"Thousands of acres," Guy said. "Manors all over the realm. In truth, little Nonnie, she'll need every last blade of grass. As insipid as watered milk. There's not a woman who can compare with our dear Eleanor. Ah, here comes the radiant bride. Outshone by her aunt."

Riannon wholeheartedly, if silently, agreed. Eleanor looked magnificently alive and colourful in her gold-shot scarlet kirtle. By contrast, Cicely faded to a pale shadow that the deep blue of her clothes unfortunately threw into greater relief. From their vantage against the wall, Riannon and Guy watched their brother marry the richest heiress in the realm. Riannon wondered how she would feel if Henry had instead wanted a rich widow—if she stood and watched Eleanor marry. She could not do it.

The man most likely to be Eleanor's groom clapped a hand on Riannon's shoulder.

"Let us hope that our cousin the queen has dipped deeply into her purse for some good wine," Guy said. "Someone ought to enjoy this wedding. Why should it not be us?"

The great hall of Sadiston Castle must have taken hundreds of servants three days to decorate with flowers and green boughs. Even the floor, with its uncounted years of accumulated dirt, food scraps, and rotted rushes, had been swept, the tiles scrubbed, and fresh rushes strewn across it. The dogs prowled as if searching for their familiar scents and muck.

"How are you enjoying the happy occasion?"

Riannon turned to see Aveline smiling at her.

"Unless I miss my mark," Aveline said, "we're in for an unsurpassed afternoon of merrymaking. We and our imperial guests."

Riannon frowned. "What do you plan?"

"To enjoy myself."

Aveline strolled away to join her sister. Riannon turned her frown from the naer's back to the imperial ambassador and his brawny companion. The man's dark tattoo made half his face look dead and rotting. She wondered if that was how people saw her scarred face. Save, miraculously, Eleanor.

By insisting that his sister sit beside him at the high table, Guy all but gave the steward a palsy. Riannon would have been more comfortable at a lower table, but Guy smiled, jested, and got his way. Riannon could look along the line of diners to Eleanor but could hear none of her conversation, let alone exchange any words.

Servants swarmed around the tables carrying dishes without

number. Pies, meat, stews, fish, and even swans with gilded beaks and their feathers stuck back in place. Guy ate with gusto and kept his and Riannon's wine topped up. Hers needed little in the way of replenishment. His drinking lubricated a near continuous stream of comments about most of the marriageable age women in the hall. The earls, barons, and knights from all over the realm, and their womenfolk all dressed in their best finery, provided Guy with plenty of meat for his monologue.

Riannon let his chatter flow past her. Her thoughts tended to return to Eleanor's bedchamber. No holy vision could be more marvellous than the sight of Eleanor, naked, abandoned to sexual pleasure. Riannon could remember the taste of her skin. The satin softness of the inside of her thigh. The smell of her arousal. The sound of Eleanor calling her name at the breaking pinnacle of her excitement. The joy of simply holding Eleanor in her arms.

"You're not drinking?" Guy said.

Riannon blinked at him and quickly reeled her attention back.

"You've not taken some peculiar vow?" he said. "I've heard members of those exalted knightly orders do such things. Like priests. I'm all for abstinence and piety, but in its place. And as long as someone else does it who is more suited than I."

"I've no great taste for wine," she said.

"You've a distaste for conversation, too? I swear you've barely opened your mouth."

"You say enough for us both."

Guy laughed.

The minstrels who had been entertaining between courses played a fanfare to herald the arrival of the subtlety. Three men had to wheel it in on a trolley. The pastry confection was shaped like a castle, complete with surrounding grass dyed green with parsley juice, and miniature banners flying from the towers. The model did not resemble Sadiston Castle, but if the portrayal were halfway accurate, it represented a fortress that would prove formidable to assault. Cheers, claps, and whistles greeted it.

"At the marriage I attended of a Marchionese countess," Guy said, "they made a subtlety shaped like a woman in childbed."

Riannon stared at him. "You jest!"

"On my oath," he said. "Not exactly appetising, but an honest acknowledgement of what the whole business is for. Although, Henry getting his hands on Havelock Castle is equally as blunt."

After the next course, when even the guests at the lower tables were looking mellowed from eating and drinking their fill, the dancers and tumblers gave way to a thin, extremely handsome man of middle years. A servant carried a stool for him and set it facing the high table. Another servant followed carrying the man's lute.

"Oh ho," Guy said. "Now we're in for a treat. Have you ever heard Raoul de Nuon?"

Riannon had heard of him. Who had not? His reputation stretched from the snowy mountains of Bralland to the scorching sands of Themalia. Someone had paid good coin for this performance. She looked down the table and saw Eleanor's delighted expression as she watched the troubadour bow. Aveline shifted and intercepted Riannon's glance. She smiled at Riannon and settled back in her chair. Riannon frowned.

The troubadour sat and took his instrument. His strong, deep voice sounded both mellow and virile as he sang the traditional many-versed wedding song. Even Cicely smiled and clapped.

"Wait there, Master Nuon," Henry called, though the bard had made no attempt to depart. "Another song. To honour my bride. Here."

Henry pulled a ring from his finger and tossed it to the troubadour. The extravagantly generous gesture brought another round of clapping and cheering, and even drew a smile from his wife's pale face. Riannon had to credit Henry for that.

Master Nuon's first chords brought a hush to the hall. Riannon wiped her fingers on a crust and settled back to listen. The strings filled the air with an unexpectedly melancholy sound. The troubadour's voice began soft and haunting. People leaned forwards to hear about a beautiful young woman's lament for her husband and brother, whom she feared dead. Master Nuon's artistry all but conjured the woman as a presence in their midst. His clever words gradually unfolded around the woman a city under siege. His music filled the hall with notes of rising desperation.

"Who would save doomed Vahl?"

Riannon went cold.

With a dramatic strum, Master Nuon recited the taunting challenge of the commander of the besieging imperial army.

Riannon was not alone in glancing across the hall to where the ambassador and his small entourage sat. This was not a diplomatic song to be singing in their presence.

The song continued, sweeping through the death of man after man who ventured forth to fight the imperial general. The woman wept when her brother cowardly refused his turn to take up the challenge, and then wept again when he died at the hands of the imperial general in the killing field beyond the city walls.

Master Nuon's dancing fingers produced a lordly melody to introduce valiant Prince Roland to the song. He spoke against the loss of good men one at a time and called for those who would sally forth with him. It was suicide. And the song, composed for the exultation of glory, passed silently over the sufferings of hunger and disease of those trapped in the city. Over the pretty words and melodic chords Riannon's memories slotted in the stink of unburied bodies. The pinched face of a starving child. The relentless crash of boulders shattering against the walls and crushing houses. The perpetual fear.

The bard's music conjured the heartbeat of horses' hooves on that desperate ride. The song wove heroically high and tensely low, as men fought blow for blow.

Riannon's memory of Vahl did not fit the tune. It was a hard, jagged set of images of blood and desperation. Screams. Thrusting swords. Prince Roland confronting the imperial general. A glint of sunlight off his sword as he lifted it in salute to his foe. The prince toppling from the saddle with agonising slowness as if time itself tried to stop in an effort to stave off the terrible moment of his hitting the ground. The prince's horse rearing.

The music throbbed with the prince's peril. Not only a single, lordly man lay at the enemy's feet, the whole city and all the people in it faced merciless annihilation.

"He came, the hero, on a horse with flying mane."

Riannon dropped from the saddle and fought her way to the prince's body. His face was mangled and bleeding. His helm carved in two. But his blue eyes were still open and seeing. Riannon stood over him. The imperial general's tattoo twitched as he shouted and sliced his sword down in front of her. Not touching her. But carving her open with pain so searing that it numbed. That momentary gap between act and comprehension. She was already moving. Lifting her sword. Throwing herself at him. He could not swing his unnatural blade, but it sliced into her all the same as she shoved the edge of her sword up across the side of his unprotected neck. His warm blood fountained over them both. She crumpled. Someone carried her back to the city.

"Foe felled and sent to his powerless gods," the troubadour sang. "The city saved by the single stroke of a hero."

Prince Roland leaned over her, his gallant blood staining the bandages swathing his face. Men had to hold him upright. He gripped her shoulder feebly. "Be thou a knight." He had no strength to buffet her. An anonymous anguished gasp sounded from behind the failing prince when Roland set on her chest his own dagger of membership of the Order of the Star. He knew he was going to Atuan, god of heroes, and would have no more need of mortal symbols. "Be true. Be just."

The lute strummed a final chord. "Vahldomne!"

Riannon shuddered back to the present. One of her hands pressed her chest as she had when the wounds were fresh. The hall throbbed with silence.

"Vahldomne!" a woman said.

Riannon twisted around to see Aveline holding her gold-rimmed mazer up in salute.

"Vahldomne!"

The roar from hundreds of throats battered Riannon and threatened to lift the roof off its rafters. Men leaped to their feet to shout the name again. Even Guy rose and lifted his goblet. Master Nuon remained seated and smiled as if the acclaim was solely his.

Riannon looked across to the men of the empire. They sat pale, tight, and unmistakeably alive to the meaning of the song. With poetic exaggeration and embellishment, Master Nuon glorified the last act of the war between the empire and the Eastern Kingdoms. Their emperor's son had been portrayed as a villain blacker and more evil than any monster from the depths of the sea. Now they sat and heard the shouts and cheers for his killer. This was not well done. Whoever had paid for this performance had not acted with honour.

Riannon looked along the table. Henry had thrown his ring and requested a song. Everyone would think the Earl Marshal responsible, but he had not chosen the subject. Someone paid the most renowned troubadour in the Eastern Kingdoms to come here and all but openly insult the representatives of the Lion Emperor. Who? To what end?

❖

Eleanor could have wished that Master Nuon had turned his magnificent talents to a more fitting song for a wedding. The shouts and cheers celebrated a dead hero rather than a marriage freshly born. The bride, though, looked flushed with excitement at the long tale.

One of the handful of people in the hall beside Eleanor not infected with fervour for the heroic was Riannon. Her lover wore that guarded look she retreated behind whenever troubled. Eleanor followed her gaze to the small group of imperial visitors. She was unsurprised when they took their leave as soon as the queen rose and servants dismantled the tables and removed the boards.

Henry and Cicely led the first dance. Henry's eldest son Richard solicited Eleanor's hand and used the length of the music to practise callow gallantries on her. She nearly made herself laugh aloud in imagining his reaction had she informed him that he wasted his breath, for she shared a bed with his aunt.

Guy, whose gallantries were well practised and smoother than Rhânish silk, purposely made Eleanor laugh while they danced.

When Eleanor set in search of claiming the dance Riannon had promised, a thickset man of about her own age intercepted her. Out of politeness, she accepted his hand for a pavane. She spent the first half of the stately dance ransacking her memory for his name. Ralph, son and heir of Lord Howe, contrived to give her the impression that he conferred some great favour on her by partnering her. Eleanor politely refrained from comment and moved briskly away once the end of the music freed her.

A lively but generally older group of revellers, including the queen and the newlyweds, debated the advantages or disadvantages of conjugal love. Normally, Eleanor thrived on such disputation. This afternoon, she found herself impatient when she heard the chamberlain lugubriously expound his belief that love followed marriage because people chose who they loved—as though passion was a meek child of duty. Perhaps that was a man's experience of love, but it was not hers.

Eleanor had been married to two men she had not loved, however much she had wanted to. She looked around the hall at the faces of men and women, familiar and strangers. Could she fall in love with any and all simply by wanting to? Her every fibre said no.

Eleanor remembered last night with Riannon and knew she would not have the patience to reduce passion to cold, pallid logic. She walked away to find her lover.

She paused every few paces to exchange pleasantries with individuals or groups and accepted their congratulations on her niece's elevated wedding. She finally spied Riannon and Guy near the low end of the hall.

Brother and sister stood close, talking, at ease in each other's company. Eleanor had noticed, to her dismay, that Riannon's other brothers avoided or ignored her. Not that many people sought out Riannon. The scar and her serious expression lent her an unapproachable air. How different was Eleanor's experience of a smiling, tender lover. As Eleanor watched the pair, Riannon said something to make Guy throw back his head and laugh. Eleanor smiled and threaded her way determinedly towards them.

Both greeted her—Riannon with a discreet but warm reserve, Guy with a witty remark. The three of them sat on a bench, Eleanor in the middle.

Eleanor looked from left to right, from Guy to Riannon. He was a handsome man. Those same facial features would not have made a beautiful woman even without the disfiguring scar. He exuded charm, knew how to please a woman, and took an easy part in any company. Though the Riannon behind her defences proved a delightful surprise, the rigidly formal manners she held between herself and most people discouraged intimacy and conversation. Yet it was the sister and not the brother who set Eleanor's passion smouldering fit to blaze.

For the whole course of her life the idea of her own sex as objects of desire had simply not occurred to her, whereas she could readily see the potential attraction in a man's handsome face, a kind smile, or a broad pair of shoulders. No bosom or woman's beauty excited her. Since her birth, she had shared a bed with other females: nurse, sisters, friends, maids, waiting women. To the best of her recollection—and surely she would remember such a thing—not once had her blood quickened with lust towards one of them. Now there was Riannon.

Less dramatically than her realisation in the basilica, Eleanor experienced another of those profound revelations. She was attracted to a person, not a sex. The fact that her fancy had previously only fallen on males had disguised that with a false pattern.

She wondered if she were the only one to realise this. Or were there many in the hall who had this self-knowledge before her? Was she just slow to discover this? Why had her mother breathed no word about this when she had explained marriage and coupling and a wife's duties? Why did none of the religious teachings expose and espouse the idea? What conspiracy kept troubadours' tongues still about the subject? Was it a knowledge to be kept hidden—like some power too fearful to be unleashed rather than a joy to be cherished? Could it be, like magic, a power accessible only to women?

Eleanor looked up at Riannon and smiled.

❖

With the wine flowing freely, talk grew noisier and more boisterous and, inevitably, bawdy. Eleanor kept an eye on Cicely. She remembered vividly her own first wedding day. She had been a virgin bride, embarrassed and nervous, listening to the comments and jests about bedding and coupling. What she had seen today of the Earl Marshal's courtesy for his young bride had forced Eleanor to favourably revise her opinion of him. She hoped, for Cicely's sake, that his presence proved sufficiently quelling to avoid the worst excesses of bedding revels.

Guy had moved away some time before and, by way of a succession of pretty women, found himself on the fringes of the lively group at the main hearth. Curiously, it was not he who drew out Cicely's shy smiles, but Richard, Cicely's new stepson.

Eleanor heard raucous male laughter from a group of young men across the hall and judged it time to act.

"I had best go and be an aunt," Eleanor said.

Riannon nodded and lightly brushed Eleanor's hand in a subtle gesture that produced most unsubtle effects in Eleanor. Tonight she would take her own pleasure. First, she must ensure that the nuptial chamber was prepared and ready for the bedding of bride and groom.

The scent of roses and sweet basil greeted Eleanor as she entered the chamber. They had been strewn with a liberal hand amongst the fresh rushes on the floor. Wine waited beside the bed. The rich bed hangings were truly beautiful and would be proof against any draughts. In the swans, unicorns, and lilies, the pattern married the Earl Marshal's emblem with that of Cicely's father and her late cousin, the earl. They were the Earl Marshal's bridal gift.

Eleanor caught a faint hint of rosemary. That carried her straight back half a lifetime to a similar chamber, though not as grand. Not that she had savoured it in peace like this. She had been fearful and flinching. The morning after, when she had leisure to appreciate her surroundings, the world had become a place more bewildering and alien.

"Is all in readiness, Lady Barrowmere?"

Eleanor's eyes snapped open and she turned to see Joan, Riannon's sister, in the doorway. "Yes, madam. Your brother has done my niece proud."

Eleanor accompanied Joan back towards the hall. In lieu of sisters and mother, Cicely had chosen to be attended by her aunt, her new sister-in-law, and a couple of young women she had befriended in the last few days.

When they stepped back into the hall, Eleanor immediately felt the tension. Riannon stood rigid, returning her brother Henry's glare. Eleanor did not hear what he said that made Riannon turn and stalk away. As she began to follow, Joan hurried past her to intercept Riannon. Eleanor stopped. She heard muttering and saw disapproving looks from those who had been close enough to have heard what passed between brother and sister.

Joan detained Riannon just inside the door. Much as she wanted to go to Riannon, Eleanor moved instead towards her niece. She owed this last service to Cicely—to ease her away from any tension that would add to that she would already be feeling.

Cicely lost all but the borrowed blush of rouge from her cheeks when Eleanor took her hand to lead her away. Some of the men could not resist a few coarse remarks about mares and mounting. Eleanor clasped Cicely's cold hand and drew her from the hall.

Eleanor and the other women helped Cicely undress. She sat, her skin as pale as her chemise, to have her hair brushed. Eleanor could not help remembering when she had sat like that, trembling but resigned. By the look of one or two of the others, she was not alone in her reminiscences. Eleanor rallied herself to a smile in the here and now.

"Now, let me act as mother to you," Eleanor said.

Eleanor reached into the purse hanging from her girdle and

extracted a necklace with a teardrop-shaped piece of cloudy green onyx hanging from it.

"This has been blessed in the waters of the sacred pond of the grove house." Eleanor fastened it around her niece's neck. "And we women all offer our own blessing to you. So that you may know no pain, but only the blessing of children from your marriage bed."

Eleanor could not help her mind silently remarking that pleasure in plenty could be had in a bed, though with a lover rather than a husband. That was the sort of wisdom an aunt might pass on in a few years, perhaps, but not on a wedding day.

Each of the women touched the stone and kissed Cicely's cheek. A cheer carried from the hall.

"Now, sweeting." Eleanor encouraged Cicely to rise. She smiled reassuringly and pulled her niece into an embrace. "All will be well."

Cicely bit her lip and nodded.

How young and frightened she looked when she huddled naked in the big bed with the sheet clutched up over her breasts. She flinched when the door burst open. Men spilled into the room, loud and lewd. The groom took one look at his bride and turned to assert himself. The chamber cleared quickly, though not without more crude jests tossed back over departing shoulders. Eleanor gratefully offered the Earl Marshal a curtsy. He nodded to her and the other women.

Eleanor's last glance in the room, as she shut the door behind her, was of Cicely's desperate look at her. Eleanor leaned against the door and bit her lip. She knew what it felt like to wait for a hairy stranger. And to know, but yet not know, what he would do with her.

Eleanor shuddered and strode away. She felt a spurt of disappointment when she could not see Riannon. She worked her way down the hall, absently acknowledging greetings, but searching for her lover. She finally found Riannon standing as rigid as a sword near the far wall, her expression as closed as a castle under siege. Eleanor would have to enquire what had happened with the Earl Marshal, but later, when they were private and her own nerves were not so raw.

"I had feared you'd left," Eleanor said.

"I would have done so," Riannon said, "save I had to wait for you."

"Thank you. Nonnie, take me home now, please. Take me away from here."

In her own bed and in Riannon's arms, Eleanor made new memories to displace those triggered by her niece's bedding. She snuggled against a warm, loving body. She had only to twist her head to look at Riannon's face and see herself valued for who she was, not what she owned or how many children she might bear. Perhaps that was the secret of the pleasure of a lover—they both voluntarily came together. She had not been compelled to subject herself to Riannon's embrace nor become a piece of property passed from one man to another.

"What's amiss?" Riannon asked. "You shudder."

Eleanor slid her arm across Riannon's ribs and pressed herself close. Riannon still wore her shirt, but Eleanor did not care. First things first.

"Haunted by yesterdays," Eleanor said. "Unlike you, who had an unhappy today."

Riannon kissed the top of Eleanor's head. "It's of no consequence."

"Is that your way of saying that you wish not to talk about it? Because I cannot imagine you, Lady Riannon, my knight errant, would perjure yourself so easily. And not to your lover."

Eleanor felt Riannon's grin in a fractional relaxation of the arms around her.

"Guy is a braver man than I've ever met before," Riannon said. "To dare to battle wits with you. It would be a surer victory to face a dragon."

Eleanor smiled.

"A good, modest woman would not take that as a compliment," Riannon said.

Eleanor jabbed a finger into Riannon's side and initiated a tickling match. Neither unhappily nor surprisingly, Riannon won. Eleanor lay beneath her with Riannon's hands pinning her wrists to the mattress.

"I wager any good, modest woman would do this." Eleanor lifted her knee up between Riannon's legs and under the tail of her shirt. She pressed her thigh against Riannon's groin.

Riannon grunted. Her seeming involuntary hip movement against Eleanor's thigh excited Eleanor.

"Um. No, lady," Riannon said. "Not modest. But most assuredly good."

Eleanor laughed. She kept up a steady rhythm with her leg.

Riannon grunted and shifted to release Eleanor's wrists and take her weight on her own hands.

When Riannon closed her eyes, Eleanor put her hands to Riannon's breasts. Whatever the shirt hid on the right side was much smaller than the left. Riannon's reaction was as swift as when Eleanor touched her face. Her fingers clamped around Eleanor's wrist and pulled her left hand away. Riannon stared down at her, her expression closed, but she didn't roll away or otherwise try to disengage.

While keeping eye contact with Riannon, Eleanor let her free hand continue exploring Riannon's left breast. Her fingers found a hard nipple beneath the linen. Intrigued and thrilled at this evidence of Riannon's excitement, she gently squeezed.

"Oh, gods." Riannon groaned and, needing the support of both arms again, released Eleanor's wrist.

Eleanor deliberately set her hand to Riannon's side and made no attempt to touch her right breast again. To her delight, Riannon's physical response strengthened and she did not remove Eleanor's hand from her left breast.

Eleanor craved to touch Riannon's skin, but contented herself with continuing her stimulation. Riannon's hips worked against Eleanor's thigh. Eleanor wanted to see and kiss where her hand squeezed. She could feel Riannon's hairs, heat, and wetness against her leg. So different to holding and rubbing an erect penis. Though she lay beneath Riannon, Eleanor felt strangely powerful as Riannon tensed and moaned. Riannon's veins corded in her neck. Eleanor caused it. Controlled it. She had no feeling that Riannon's closed eyes meant that she thought of another woman while she moved against Eleanor. When Riannon came, her back arched and she grunted as though her orgasm were being squeezed from the marrow of her bones.

Panting, Riannon sagged onto her elbows and let her head drop onto Eleanor's pillow. Eleanor slipped her arms around Riannon and held her. She overflowed with an intense sense of satisfaction. She kissed Riannon's sweaty temple.

"Oh, lady." Riannon rolled off Eleanor to sprawl on her back.

Eleanor settled comfortably on her side to watch the result of her handiwork. Now she understood Riannon's smugness. She softly stroked the side of Riannon's neck with her fingertips. Riannon's pulse thudded hard. Eleanor couldn't stop herself kissing the beating vein.

Riannon sighed and opened her eyes.

"Methinks I just earned my spurs in womanly bed sport," Eleanor said.

"Spurs, sword, and cloak," Riannon said.

Eleanor laughed and clambered out of bed to fetch wine and a platter of sweet wafers. She fed them to Riannon as they shared the cup of wine. Riannon looked as relaxed as Eleanor had ever seen her.

"I wish to know why you looked insulted by your brother," Eleanor said. "So, the decision you must make is how hard you want to make me strive. Now, considering that you've just called my name in the height of passion, it would be churlish, do you not think, to expect me to exert myself again so soon?"

Riannon failed to suppress a grin. "Naturally, the thought of discretion did not occur to you?"

"Naturally not."

Riannon kissed Eleanor's hand. "It was as I expected. My father outcast me. My brothers have neither will nor inclination to claim me back. I'm intimate with lack of welcome. Sooner or later, men discover my sex. I'm accustomed to moving on because I am other than what people expect. But my brother Henry would have me be less than I am."

Eleanor drew Riannon's hand into her lap. "I hope you do not plan to leave the realm soon."

"I have little to detain me. Gast is scarce more than a farm and a village. It's assessed at but a fraction of a knight's fee. The place gives me a name and not much else."

"How did you keep it, if your father disowned you?"

"There was a provision in our mother's marriage portion, which set aside some property to be divided between her daughters. I suppose it was my grandfather's way of ensuring that we had a minimal dowry. My father could not take it from me, though he did administer it with severity, so my sister tells me."

"That's a shame," Eleanor said. "But properties can be restored."

"In truth, I've little will to do it. Nor much coin."

"Then you'll have to do as all knights errant must do—marry well."

"Men do not wish me to remain in the same county as them once they realise my sex." Riannon reached for the last wafer. "Even were I so inclined, none would want to marry me."

The idea of Riannon submitting herself to a man—in or out of bed—defied Eleanor's imagination. Not that she wished to think of her new lover with anyone but herself for any reasons, however pragmatic.

"Come and visit me," Eleanor said. "Be my guest. When the celebrations end, I go from here to Waterbury, one of my larger manors in the Eastmarch. In my own homes, we needn't hide. I could show you some good hunting. I have rights in several forests."

"You tempt me."

Eleanor set the wine cup aside and tossed the empty plate to the end of the bed. "You clearly have little idea how tempting I can be."

Riannon was smiling when Eleanor kissed her.

CHAPTER TWELVE

Riannon regretted the necessity of retiring to her own chamber to sleep. In the morning, though, she and Eleanor rode out with only a maid and groom to trail them. They heard the roars of the crowd from the tourney field, but Eleanor urged her horse in the opposite direction.

While their sweaty horses walked side by side, Eleanor flirted, laughed, teased, and entertained Riannon. Riannon's arms ached to sweep the lady from the saddle and hold her. Other parts of Riannon's body throbbed and tightened with more serious longings. Mercifully, Eleanor curtailed their ride and they headed back to the city.

Before returning to Eleanor's house, and Eleanor's bedchamber, they took a necessary detour to the grove house. The priestess in the chamber behind the ever-open door eyed Riannon with naked suspicion. She politely but firmly refused to allow Riannon into the holy grove while wearing the sword that had been a gift from the Goddess. Riannon was more amused than inconvenienced. Not one person, since she had vowed her service, had recognised in her a paladin of the Order of the Goddess. Whatever plans Aveline had for a warrior were not generally known even within the priestesshood.

Eleanor prayed and left an offering for the success and fruitfulness of her niece's married life. It was all Riannon could do to keep her hands off Eleanor whilst they knelt beside the holy pool. Eleanor flashed her a burningly provocative look.

Before noon, Eleanor and Riannon sported in Eleanor's bed. Agnes, Eleanor's principal waiting woman, had given Riannon a knowing look when Riannon stepped into Eleanor's chamber. It had been a strangely neutral expression—not encouraging, but neither condemning. Riannon did not find it surprising that Eleanor inspired uncommon loyalty in her household.

Riannon drifted off into a sated doze with her arm possessively around Eleanor. When she woke, Eleanor lay propped on an elbow watching her. Caught in that twilight moment between sleep and full wakefulness, the sight of Eleanor—creamy skin, soft expression on her face, her hair tumbling around her shoulders—gave Riannon a vivid insight into the afterworld paradise that men said awaited those chosen few favoured of Atuan, god of war and lord of heroes.

"You look different when you sleep," Eleanor said. "I was going to say younger, but that's not quite right. Less used, perhaps. Less battered by life."

"You have a unique way with flattery."

Eleanor's eyebrows lifted. "I was attempting nothing of the kind. I'm the one who should be wooed and flattered by you. Though it pains me to point out that you're woefully deficient in that regard. Not a single poem have I had from you. Not even a rash promise of some wildly improbable deed that I could dissuade you from performing."

"I beg your pardon, lady, but you must've missed my poem while you were otherwise occupied with your climax."

Eleanor giggled. "I'll have to concede you that one, won't I?"

"Mayhap I ought to try again now that you're quieter. Pray tell, what rhymes with haddock?"

Eleanor grabbed a pillow and beat Riannon with it. Riannon laughed and reached for her. Eleanor shrieked, evaded her, and brandished her pillow harder. Inevitably, the pillow burst. Down filled the air inside the bed hangings like warm, giant snowflakes. Riannon and Eleanor collapsed together laughing.

"Say you'll come for a visit," Eleanor said.

"Yes. Aveline does not need me now. I cannot see that she would miss me for a few weeks."

Eleanor sobered. "Aveline? Your cousin the naer?"

Riannon plucked feathers from Eleanor's hair. "I'm here at her will. I owe service to her order. Did the lover who likened you to a fish ever have the good sense to remark on how comely you are with feathers resting here and there on your naked body?"

"This might surprise you, but telling me that I resemble a sea creature is not the key to admission to my bed." Eleanor sat up and prodded a finger against Riannon's stomach. "How many lovers do you think I've had?"

Riannon trailed a feather down Eleanor's throat and across a breast. Eleanor shivered and her nipple hardened to greet the delicate touch.

"I think you could've had as many lovers as you wished," Riannon said. "I'm fortunate beyond words that your choice fell to me."

Eleanor smiled. "I've not the slightest doubt about your prowess on a battlefield. You have the uncanny ability to disarm at will. You're a hard person to pretend to remain annoyed with."

"As faults go, I cannot be unhappy to have that one laid at my feet."

Riannon could not help thinking, though, that many people found it too easy to find her existence and appearance provoking. The blackest irony lay in the contrast between the barely concealed hostility she'd seen in faces turned to her in the hall at the wedding, with the shouts and cheers of those same people on their feet as they toasted the Vahldomne.

Riannon forced those thoughts from her mind and looked outward, to the beautiful woman beside her. She reached for Eleanor and saw a genuine welcome for her touch. Riannon lost herself in a world kinder and more loving than she had ever known, and tried hard to banish the knowledge that it would end.

❖

Eleanor would have preferred to have remained in bed with Riannon but bowed to the necessity of being present as hostess during the dinner for her niece and her new husband.

"I'll find a meal elsewhere," Riannon said.

Eleanor bit back her protest. She knew if she asked, Riannon would change her mind. That would please her but make Riannon highly uncomfortable in the company of her brothers. As with Riannon's compulsion to keep herself hidden in her shirt, Eleanor forced herself to accept this choice. If she had learned anything in two marriages, it was to exercise care in selecting when she took a stand, and when to let go. Not all battles could—or should—be won.

Cicely greeted her aunt as warmly as a boon companion she had not seen for years. She looked well enough, though Eleanor noticed that

L-J BAKER

she frequently shot glances at her husband with the air of one expecting
a reproof. Eleanor did see her niece laughing, though, when Cicely sat
with her new stepson, Lord Richard. He was two or three years Cicely's
senior.

"You must be gratified, Lady Barrowmere, to see your family
united so closely to that of our queen."

Eleanor, whose thoughts had actually strayed to her own more
intimate relationship with a cousin of the queen, stared at the white-
haired speaker for several heartbeats before she recalled his name.

"For certès, my Lord Geoffrey," she said. "And my niece looks well
pleased with her new family. I fear, though, I must offer condolences on
the recent loss of your daughter-in-law."

He nodded. "Katherine died in childbed. And her child with her.
May the gods have welcomed them into paradise. But my son is young
yet and has plenty of time to sire an heir. I was older than he is now at
his birth. So, I do not despair on that account. But I'll miss Kate. She
was a lively young thing who brought some spring back to my life."

"You make it sound as if you are in your dotage," Eleanor said.

"I feel it," he said. "The only creaking my son hears from his
body is the leather straps when he dons his armour. My joints plague
me every morning and night. I'm an old man. I remember drinking and
hunting with your father when we were younger than my son."

"If you keep on thus," she said, "you'll have me buying the russet
for my mourning weeds for you. I wager, though, there's life enough
yet for you to dance with me. Or should I escort you to a bench and
press a restorative plaster against your brow?"

He chuckled. "There's every ounce of your father's liveliness in
you. Did he ever tell you about the time we went with the old Earl
Marshal into Iruland to challenge Prince Fulk and his followers on the
tourney field?"

Eleanor dutifully counterfeited an interest in his tale of past glory
while they danced. Most of her mind wondered where Riannon was,
and how soon she could be rid of her guests.

When the dance ended, Geoffrey's son, Ralph, strode towards
them.

"At your age, father, you ought to be sitting with the dowagers,"
Ralph said.

"I've yet the strength to take the hand of a pretty lady," Geoffrey said. "And legs enough to sustain me for the length of one dance."

"Yes, but not wind enough for two." Ralph smiled at Eleanor, clearly believing she would share his ill-mannered amusement. "Now, my lady, let us show my father how a dance should be performed, not shuffled."

"I'm afraid I must decline the pleasure," she said. "I'm promised to Lord Guy."

Ralph had the ill-grace to frown in Guy's direction. "I ought to count myself fortunate that I'm refused for him rather than that creature who claims to be sister to him. It pleases me, for your sake, Lady Eleanor, that the mannish creature has not intruded herself here and soiled your gathering."

His rudeness and staggeringly impolitic remarks left Eleanor speechless as he stalked away.

"My son is a man of action and strong passions," Geoffrey said.

Those were not the words Eleanor would have used. Her opinion ran much closer to Guy's.

"Ralph Howe is a braggart and a page-beating bully," Guy said. "His father is a man of honour."

Eleanor agreed. "Save he is not honoured by his son."

Guy lost interest in the Howes. "You're looking remarkably pretty this day."

"Do I not always seem fair to you?"

Guy smiled. "I pity any callow or maladroit young man who has been left flat-footed by that attack. I, on the other hand, can simply kiss your fingers and change the subject. Where's Nonnie? I'd hoped to persuade her to join me one morning at the tourney."

"She preferred to dine elsewhere."

Guy shook his head. "Henry is a fool. If Nonnie were our brother, he'd welcome her back with open arms. If only he'd heard half the things about her that I have in the last few days. But all Henry sees is that she's not as he believes a sister should be. It's not as though Nonnie has asked him to find her a husband."

Eleanor guided him away from the other dancing couples and towards the relative privacy of a bench against the wall. "What have you heard about her?"

"Fragments here and there. The sort of talk that you lend no credence to unless you know for certès that a female member of the Order of the Star exists. Then you listen with interest to snippets that get spoken over wine. It seems my sister has been all over the Eastern Kingdoms. When you shake aside the chaff about females who act as men, the wheat left behind convinces me that Nonnie has much skill as a captain."

Eleanor found nothing to surprise her in that. "Know you how she gained the scar to her face?"

Guy shook his head. "I've not asked. And she has not told me."

Eleanor saw the dark green robes of Aveline moving towards Lord Geoffrey Howe. "Do you think your cousin Aveline might know?"

"The naer? It seems unlikely Nonnie would have confided in her."

Eleanor had intended to probe what he knew of the link between Riannon and Aveline, but now discarded the question.

"Your niece seems to be taking quickly to the duties of being a stepmother," Guy said.

Eleanor turned to look through the intervening people to see Cicely dancing with Richard. Her niece's colour was unusually heightened.

"Brother Henry looks like a cream-fed cat," Guy said. "Think you he's besotted with his bride? Or is that fatuous expression merely a sign of indigestion?"

Surprised, Eleanor studied the Earl Marshal. He watched Cicely and Richard dancing. However unlikely it seemed, there appeared to be truth in Guy's observation of Henry's visible affection for his bride. Eleanor sat astounded at Cicely having inspired that in but two days of marriage—especially since Cicely bestowed more attention on the son than the father.

Eleanor wondered if she shared the Earl Marshal's vague and misty look. No, her feelings for Riannon were not hazy and nebulous. Her feelings and the responses of her body pulsed strong and definite. She was, she realised, well on the way to falling more deeply in love with Riannon of Gast than she had ever imagined herself capable of. She would have laughed that possibility away had anyone suggested it to her scant weeks ago. But, back then she had known Riannon not at all and herself not nearly as well as she did now.

Riannon had agreed to accompany her when she departed Sadiston, so their idyll could extend to weeks or even months. The thought put

Eleanor back in charity with the world and permitted her to endure, with some semblance of complaisance, the next hours until Riannon's return.

❖

Aveline watched blood flowing towards her like a scarlet tide. Shouts bludgeoned the air. Men yelled the names of the gods. Screams. Horses' hooves thundered all around the darkness as if Atuan's hall of dead heroes burst asunder and men of legend charged forth. The blood poured over her feet. The thick fluid was cold. The screams beat against her. They hit her and hurt her like blows. Aveline tried to lift her arms to ward them off. The din thickened and solidified. It pinned her arms to her sides. She could not even raise them to implore her Goddess for help.

A new cry sounded. Triumph raked with the pain of others ripped towards her. She couldn't move. The blood surged up past her waist. She was going to drown in pain, in screams, in blood.

Aveline jolted awake.

A tentative hand touched her arm. "Madam?"

Aveline stared at the girl. She still saw blood. Her ears rang with the inseparable echoes of victory and despair and death.

A young face, a stranger to war, stared at her. Pale in the dark, but with large, caring, trusting eyes. "You called out in your sleep, madam. I knew not if I should wake you."

"Did you?"

The head shook. Aveline felt the tendrils of loose, long hair against her arm. "No, madam. You might've been having a true dream."

Aveline hoped not. "Fetch wine."

The girl scrambled out of bed and slipped through the gap in the hangings. Aveline took a deep breath to try to steady herself.

Had it been Sight delivered to her as she slept? Such a phenomenon had been known to occur rarely to chosen individuals. Aveline bent her concentration on remembering. War. Unsubtle imagery. Much as she would like to interpret the nightmare as a sign from the Dark-Faced One that her crusade was coming, Aveline judged it a bad dream. She felt none of the chill shadow inside which signalled the whisper of the Goddess. More likely the cause of her nightmare was the rich dish of lampreys she had eaten for supper.

When the girl returned, there was a moment, as she passed back through the hangings, when moonlight lit her from behind and limned her in an unearthly beauty. Aveline reached for her and drew the warm body close. The hot young mouth responded eagerly to her kiss. Resilient flesh moved into the touch of her hand. The novice's moans and cries formed a fresh, gentle, living barrier against the fading screams of Aveline's nightmare. Instead of blood, the warmly pungent juices of sex oozed onto her. Aveline drifted into heavy, dreamless sleep.

The next morning, Aveline lingered beside the sacred pool after the conclusion of dawn devotions. She remembered the dream of war, and frowned down at her reflection. No, it had not felt like the Lady of Destiny had murmured to her in her sleep, much as she would have liked to be the recipient of more divine messages. She was favoured more than most.

"I do your will," Aveline said. "To the best of my ability, sparing none—myself included. I shall endeavour to let no mortal obstacles block your wishes."

She lifted her hand to trace a blessing. Her mirror-self in the pool held a tall staff with a symbol of the quartered circle on the top. Aveline froze and stared. Her image on the pool surface wore a chaplet of flowers. An indistinct figure stood close behind her reflection. She could make out no features, merely an impression of great size and power. Between one blink and the next, the illusion vanished. Her reflected self was simply a faithful copy of her surprise. She whirled around. No one else stood in the clearing.

Aveline put a hand to the quartered-circle symbol hanging against her front. Her fingers gripped the gold. She had seen herself wearing the trappings of the matriarch, the first mother of the Order of the Goddess.

I shall endeavour to let no mortal obstacles block your wishes.

Matriarch Melisande. She attempted to bar Aveline from following the path of the Goddess's will. She could not be removed, save by death. That might not be long in coming, for Matriarch Melisande was an old woman. The new matriarch would be elected from one of the twenty mother-naers. Aveline needed to become one of them. Yes, she was young, but she was able, and acting for the good of the order. Her rise to the leadership of the order was clearly the Lady of Creation's will. The Goddess had bidden her to chew that bitterest and sweetest and most addictive meat called ambition.

"So be it," Aveline said.

She strode out of the grove with heightened purpose and strengthened conviction. Her only doubt lay in the identification of the large indistinct figure who had stood behind her matriarch self. Had it been an avatar of the Goddess? Or had it been Riannon?

Aveline set that aside for later contemplation. One strand of her efforts to bring about the crusade hovered on the brink of success. The tinder neared readiness for her to strike the spark that would start the conflagration.

After the wedding feast, Mathilda had raged about the insolence and idiocy of Master Nuon the troubadour. Aveline had listened calmly as her sister threatened to have him hanged from the gatehouse. Unmoved by her sister's temper, Aveline remembered the bristling of the hairs on the back of her neck when her toast of "Vahldomne" had been shouted back at her from hundreds of throats. *Oh, Lady of Destiny, yes!* They called the name of their hero who would lead them in a new holy war. From the look on Riannon's face, Aveline had guessed truly who that hero was. How the imperial ambassador's face had pinched with an insult barely tolerated. Did he also hear the roar of a war cry coming?

The ambassador had looked no happier yesterday in the tourney stands when a pair of dwarf fools from the entertaining troupe had re-enacted the climactic duel at the siege of Vahl. The dwarf representing the emperor's son wore a pig's head. The dwarf in the part of the Vahldomne beat him with a leg of red hose stuffed with straw and made to resemble a penis. Crude, and vastly ironical to one who knew the Vahldomne to be a woman, but it had served its purpose. The imperial ambassador retreated from the stands amidst raucous laughter and hoots of derision. Aveline judged him on the brink and needing but a gentle shove to push him into incaution.

This morning, she must turn her attention to another strand of her plans—her need to ingratiate herself with Mother-Naer Katherine of Fourport. She would not only be useful in taking Aveline to the Quatorum Council, but was also just the woman to nominate Aveline for the next vacancy amongst the mother-naers. In light of her gift image in the pool, this took on additional importance. The greater good of the order depended on Aveline's success.

Aveline did not rise from her chair when her attendant ushered in Geoffrey of Howe and his son, Ralph. The son openly looked around and bristled an arrogance whose wellspring Aveline could not begin to imagine. He was a dull, boastful boor with no achievement in life to show for his thirty-odd years unless, perhaps, he prided himself on winning some drinking contest in a whorehouse.

"Your invitation to an audience does us great honour, your Eminence," Geoffrey said.

Aveline indicated that he might take a seat. The son stood, feet planted apart, and stared down at her. Ill-mannered pig. What a pity this arrangement would benefit him.

"If we can be of service," Geoffrey said, "to yourself or our queen, its discharge would be a privilege, madam."

"Yes," Ralph said. "We stand ready to serve."

"I was saddened to hear of your recent bereavement," Aveline said.

"You're most kind, madam," Geoffrey said. "My daughter-in-law was young and in good health. But, alas, as is lamentably common, childbirth proved stronger than she."

"The babe died with her," Ralph said. "A man child, it was. The damned midwife should've been whipped and hanged for her incompetence."

Aveline stared at him. A fool without the wit of a sheep as well as boorish. Did he not recall that midwives were trained by, if not initiates of, her order? Still, neither brains nor good sense were necessary requirements for undertaking a marriage.

Aveline addressed the father. "He has no heir, has he?"

After a couple of heartbeats to digest the remark, the old man's eyes widened fractionally with realisation. However imbecilic the son, his dull wits were not inherited from his sire.

"I need a new wife," Ralph said.

"We've made no firm choice yet," Geoffrey said. "We will, of course, consult our liege lady before any settlement. Is that not right, Ralph?"

Ralph grunted agreement.

Aveline smiled. "Have you heard, lately, from your sister-in-law?"

"Mother-Naer Katherine is in good health, Eminence," Geoffrey said. "She continues vigorous at Wermouth. Are you acquainted with her, madam?"

"Not as well as I wish to be," she said.

Aveline watched comprehension creep across the father's features with avarice as its shadow. He couldn't suppress a toothless smile.

"I'm sure she'd be honoured and delighted in your interest, madam."

"My sister, the queen, has in her power of gift the marriage of a widow who might suit your son," Aveline said.

"Who?" Ralph said.

"I'm sure our family would all feel the truest and deepest gratitude for any favour from our sovereign lady, madam," Geoffrey said.

"Is she wealthy?" Ralph asked.

"The woman is Eleanor of Barrowmere," Aveline said.

"Oh ho!" Ralph clapped his hands together. "Rich and beddable."

Geoffrey beamed and looked indulgently at his son. "She is, indeed, quite a notable prize, madam. Extensive lands. She holds a third of the honour of Torhill, does she not?"

"Aye, money is important," Ralph said. "But my sap has not dried, father, like yours. I value a woman for her body as well as her other attractions. I'd find no hardship in getting sons on Lady Eleanor. When may we wed?"

"Perhaps you ought to leave the dull matter of settlements to me," Geoffrey said. "Have you not a tourney challenge this day?"

Ralph looked torn. "I do. We'll talk again ere we approach the lady's lawyers and men of business about settlements, father. You'll need me to ensure we get what we can."

Aveline watched with concealed contempt as Ralph kissed her ring and strode out. Geoffrey sat absorbed in thought and appeared to take no offence from his son's overbearing rudeness.

"My son has the right of it in saying that the Lady Eleanor is comely and vivacious." Geoffrey tugged his white beard. "Is it not true, though, that she is barren? She must be nigh on thirty years. Possibly more, though not a whit less handsome for her maturity."

Aveline wondered where this was headed. Surely he would not turn down the lady's wealth? "She has no living child. Any children your son got on her would be her heirs as well as his."

"My son needs an heir," Geoffrey said. "Mayhap it would be

best if he found a younger wife to bear his sons. I could marry Lady Eleanor."

Aveline made no attempt to conceal her surprised smile.

"After all," he said, "my sister-in-law will be just as gratified with a new sister as she would a niece."

After he left, Aveline fleetingly wondered how his son would take the news that his "beddable" bride would be going to his father's bed. Still, that was their problem, not hers.

She went in search of Mathilda. It was time to tell her how they were going to dispose of Lady Barrowmere. Best not delay the wedding, not the way Riannon was hanging so closely on Lady Eleanor's sleeve. Aveline needed Riannon free of entanglements when the imperial ambassador snapped. And that should happen any day now.

❖

Eleanor sighed and turned a lazy smile across the pillow to Riannon. She was in love. Passionately. Deeply. Dizzyingly. Just like the love she had told Cicely so rarely afflicted people outside bards' songs. Her body responded to Riannon's touch, her presence—a look, even—as if the gods had given her a sixth sense that had lain dormant until it collided with Riannon. Now it leaped to life at the slightest stimulus. Even the thought of her could set it singing. Eleanor had stigmatised love as a sickness or madness. She had been right. But, oh, what a glorious madness.

She studied Riannon's profile. Riannon dozed. Her enviably long, dark lashes curved upwards. This was the unscarred side, of course. Even in bed, Riannon remained conscious of her disfigurement. Her left side was not without battle mark, though, for a faint white souvenir of a cut angled across her cheek from just below her ear. Even Riannon's blemishes were precious and fascinating.

Eleanor smiled at her own folly. Definitely madness.

Riannon sighed and her eyelids fluttered, though she did not open her eyes. Eleanor levered herself up on an elbow so that she could lean across to lightly kiss Riannon's lips. Her hair fell around her shoulders and stroked Riannon's face.

"How your fair hair shines gold in the sun," Riannon said, "dearest Margaret."

Eleanor's mouth dropped open. Riannon opened her eyes and grinned.

"You!" Eleanor grabbed a pillow.

Riannon surged up to hold her. Laughing did little to hamper her reflexes and strength. She quickly overpowered Eleanor and held her pinned to the bed.

"Wretch!" Eleanor said.

"You should have seen your face," Riannon said.

"Oh! I did not suspect, until this moment, how easy it would be to dislike you."

"Passing strange, for I adore you."

Eleanor felt herself soften and smile. "So much for chivalry and fairness. You use the most underhanded stratagems. How could I possibly feign anger when you tell me that you adore me?"

Riannon released her and sagged to the side, chuckling to herself. She did not notice that her shirt had pulled up. Eleanor could see Riannon's hips, with the wedge of black hair marking her groin, and up to the bottom of Riannon's ribs. A scar as puckered, shiny, and angry pink as that cloven into her face ran down from beneath the shirt to Riannon's left hip. From the angle, Eleanor could imagine it cutting across Riannon's right breast. She remembered the difference in the feel of Riannon's breasts, and how much smaller the right was than the left. Even the lie of the linen against Riannon's chest showed the disparity. The weapon that had sliced through Riannon's face and body had cut most of her breast away. Eleanor winced at the idea. Was that what Riannon hid?

Riannon lifted Eleanor's hand to kiss.

Eleanor drew her gaze up to Riannon's face again. As much as she wanted to know what had happened, and what Riannon concealed, she did not want to think about Riannon wounded. Lying bleeding and taut with pain, as Lionel had when he died.

"You shiver," Riannon said. "If you're cold, come here and let me warm you."

Eleanor gladly clung to Riannon. She felt warm, hard muscles and a strong heartbeat.

"How I long to ride with you along the shore of Burn Lake," Eleanor said. "And watch a fiery orange sunset from the top of the keep at Barrowmere with your arms around me. And to have you return home from hunting. Flushed with victory, and possibly wine, but boisterous and happy. And knowing that you come to me."

"You do not hunt? Not even with hawks?"

"I know I must lower myself in your eyes, but promise me that you'll try to hide it. You see, I've the strongest aversion to witnessing slaughter. Even a broken bird with but a few bloody feathers sets my nerves on the raw."

Riannon's arm gently tightened around her. "I feel only the urge to protect you."

"It was my husbands. They both died of wounds. Unnecessary ones. From tourneys, both of them, if you can believe."

"I've seen many men killed and maimed at such."

Eleanor closed her eyes against the past, but that did not stop her from remembering the stench. "William lingered in agony. His foot began to rot. The flesh was black. The stink…the stink was beyond sickening. I can still hear his screams when they cut his leg off. And the scrape of a saw through the bone."

"Hush. There's no need to torment yourself this way."

"I had to be there. It's a wife's duty. Though William did not know me at the end. He did not know his mother. The rot, they said, had crept up through his entrails and into his brain."

Eleanor gripped Riannon though her mind saw that pain-racked travesty of a man. The horror of changing his foetid bandages. Vomiting hot bile until she thought her stomach would erupt from her throat.

Riannon kissed the top of her head. "That is past."

Eleanor shuddered and struggled to banish her spectres. "You'd be well-advised not to take poorly near me, else you'll discover what a weak and craven creature I truly am. For I could not tend you."

Riannon reached the wine cup down from the ledge and offered it to Eleanor. Eleanor wriggled upright and accepted the drink with trembling hands. Riannon put one of her larger hands over Eleanor's to hold the cup steady.

"I wept like a child after I killed my first man," Riannon said. "And was greensick. Is this why you avoid tourneys?"

"Foolish, I know." Eleanor tried to rally her lighter spirits. "I tell most people that I have no relish for giving away my sleeves or gloves. I'd much rather people believe me aloof and stingy than that I fall queasy at the sight of blood."

"I hope that you can leave folk with the correct impression of your generosity, love, for you can say that your favour is claimed. I'll bear whatever you care to grant me, though it might gain no more glory than watching our bed sport."

Eleanor finally managed a smile. She leaned back against her pillows with Riannon's arm around her shoulders. "It surpasses my understanding how I did not realise long ago that my perfect knight would be quite other than what everyone else expects. Although, I wish you not to bloat with overweening pride from that admission. There are still areas where you sorely fall short of—Oh."

"What's amiss?"

Eleanor stared up at Riannon. "You called me love."

Riannon nodded. "It would not surprise me. For I do love you."

To her own dismay, Eleanor burst into tears. Riannon took the wine cup from her and gathered her close. Eleanor used Riannon's shirt to mop her face.

"Oh, this is wretched." Eleanor sniffed. "How like me to be so happy that I weep. Nonnie, do not laugh at me. We're supposed to be solemn and ardent and poetically earnest when we declare ourselves in love."

"I've not noticed a strong tendency in you to do as you ought."

"Which is all the more reason I should do one thing properly."

Riannon smiled. "You're being foolish, love."

"That's because my wits have deserted me. I told Cicely that love is an affliction. I knew not how truly I spoke. I can think of nothing but you—even in those rare moments we're out of bed."

"If it is a disease, love, then I have a full dose, too."

"Do you think any other couple would reduce love to a divine pox?"

Riannon laughed.

After a long kiss, Eleanor snuggled against Riannon with Riannon's arms around her. She rested her head on Riannon's shoulder.

"I've never been in love and loved in return before," Eleanor said. "I much prefer it to loving alone."

"Yes."

Eleanor frowned, but set that aside as something she would probe later. "Let me tell you about my favourite places. And where I wish to take you. The homes I wish to be with you in. You see, I am woefully conventional in many respects. I'm prideful about what I own, and I would show it off to you to further gain your approval, and set myself higher in your valuing of me."

"A few acres of land and some flocks of sheep or their lack will not affect my feelings for you."

"A few acres? I'll have you know that I have estates all over the realm. I administer them so efficiently that my revenues are steadily increasing, despite the recent decline in wool prices. Yes, I have sheep. A fair few flocks, in truth. Though I'll not bore you with fretting over the depredations of the murrain, nor my opinions about the tax the queen wishes to levy on wool sales."

Riannon grinned and twined a lock of Eleanor's hair around her fingers. "I'm undomesticated, love. But I'll not tire of hearing you boast, for I love the sound of your voice even if I have no understanding of the words."

"Now that is a surer proof of love than slaying dragons." Eleanor smiled as she snuggled more comfortably against Riannon. "Let me tell you all the delights I have to offer you. I promise I'll not tax your patience unduly with talk of bailiffs, tally sticks, mining rights, and my new mills."

CHAPTER THIRTEEN

Riannon nodded to the red-cheeked page for him to deliver his message.

"Sir—Lady, I come from her Eminence, the Naer Aveline," he said. "She wishes you most particularly to attend her at the Earl Marshal's feast."

Riannon frowned as she tossed the boy a coin and dismissed him. Aveline? Why would the naer wish her to attend yet another feast? Riannon stood on the verge of persuading Eleanor to forgo the invitation in favour of returning to bed.

Eleanor, who had reluctantly risen from their scandalously long interlude in her chamber to receive the visit of her principal man of business, strode across the hall. Lover and beloved. The strength of her own feelings did not surprise Riannon, for Eleanor was a woman whom bards should sing about rather than the wilting, insipid, passive creatures they favoured as their subjects. What had taken her unawares was Eleanor's professed reciprocation of feelings. To Riannon, that seemed little short of a miracle. Even more perplexing, she could not understand why men did not fight each other for the privilege of the lady's attention. Or why Guy lingered a single moment before declaring his interest in her—though, Riannon knew she would find it impossible to watch if her brother prosecuted a more active suit of Eleanor. Thank all the gods that Eleanor had the wealth to pay for her continuing widowhood.

Eleanor smiled up at Riannon with a wicked warmth that dragged most of Riannon's mind along wanton paths all leading to Eleanor's bed.

"I'm happy to say that I can afford to entertain you in good style," Eleanor said. "Though I'll not bore you with talk of pennies. Most timely, too, was this accounting, for I received a summons to talk with her Grace. I assume she has set a price for my fine. How glad I am that she does not know that my love has added greatly to my desire to remain unwed. She'd be astounded to learn how much she could screw out of my purse for the privilege. Now, I suppose we'd best not tarry in getting to the Earl Marshal's feast."

Riannon resigned herself to biting her tongue and struggling not to ram Henry's teeth down his throat.

Soon after they arrived in the crowded hall, Riannon left Eleanor talking with an acquaintance and sought out Aveline.

"I'm here," Riannon said. "For what reason did you wish my presence?"

"I've barely seen you since we came to the city," Aveline said. "You're much in Lady Eleanor's company, I hear?"

"I am the lady's guest."

"You're sworn to the Goddess. Forget that not."

Riannon frowned. "I do not forget oaths. Does this mean you have something I must do?"

"If all goes well, yes." Aveline smiled in the direction of the ambassador. "I have every reason to believe that all will go very well."

Riannon directed her frown at the small group of the Lion Emperor's men. The beefy one with the tattoo glared at everyone and looked like he wished he had his sword in hand. Although, given the general reaction to them at the wedding, she could scarce fault him.

"If you wish me to protect them," Riannon said, "you'd be better reminding others that they have our liege lady's safe-conduct."

Aveline's eyebrow cocked. "Protect them? Oh, no, fear not that I'd foist so unpleasant a task on you."

When it came time to take places at the tables, Riannon sat beside Eleanor. In carving and passing the choicest morsels to Eleanor, Riannon indulged in an understated but determined flirtation. Eleanor responded with masterly skill. She could make sipping soup from a spoon sexual. Before servants cleared away the second course, Riannon wished food, her family, and everyone else a hundred miles away and herself in bed with Eleanor. Eleanor's hand on her thigh under the cover of the tablecloth played havoc with Riannon's ability to skewer pieces of food.

After servants removed cloths and boards, Eleanor had to linger at the queen's pleasure, for Mathilda seemed in no hurry to talk with Eleanor about her widowhood. Riannon listened with half an ear to Guy's humorous account of the ongoing tourney. She kept checking the whereabouts of Aveline and the imperial ambassador. When she heard raised voices from across the hall, she was unsurprised to see the tense tableau centred about that pair.

The ambassador leaped to his feet. Though Riannon could not hear what Aveline said, her smile looked to be a blatant taunt. The ambassador's bulky companion bristled. Henry stepped forwards to put a hand on Aveline's arm. The ambassador spoke words that apparently needed no translation. Henry stiffened and glared at him. Aveline's reply triggered surprised murmurs from those close enough to hear. The ambassador's face flushed.

A hand touched Riannon's arm. Eleanor frowned at the confrontation.

"Can you hear?" Eleanor said. "What's happening?"

"Aveline baits the ambassador," Riannon said.

"Baits? But why would she—"

The ambassador cracked a slap against Aveline's face. The priestess made no attempt to evade the blow. Henry stepped threateningly towards the ambassador. Aveline grabbed his arm to restrain him. The ambassador's large companion moved to interpose himself between his master and the irate Earl Marshal. A shocked collective intake of breath rippled out from the confrontation, followed quickly by excited chatter.

Riannon understood the mime show. The emphatic gestures of the ambassador and his man accepted a challenge. Aveline, her cheek red, looked far from cowed.

Enraged voices hurried the words "duel" and "champions" through the hall.

Henry offered himself as Aveline's champion. Riannon knew, to the marrow of her bones, the priestess would decline. She alone in Sadiston Castle's great hall stood unsurprised when Aveline named her champion in a ringing, triumphant voice.

"The Vahldomne!" Aveline said.

Hundreds of voices quickly drowned the moment of stunned silence. Eleanor's hand tightened on Riannon's arm. Riannon had her answer as to who had paid the troubadour to sing of Vahl. Anger hardened inside.

"Is not the Vahldomne dead?" Eleanor said.

That looked like the question Henry turned on Aveline. The priestess radiated sublime confidence. The ambassador stalked off. Noisy speculation erupted.

"I might think it a stratagem to diffuse the situation and negate the challenge," Eleanor said. "Save your cousin the naer looks more triumphant than conciliatory. And not at all distressed."

"No," Riannon agreed. "She does not look upset."

The queen strode to her sister. After a short exchange, she, Aveline, and Henry left the hall. Only Aveline appeared unconcerned.

"I need no soothsayer to tell me that I'll not be receiving my audience for some time," Eleanor said.

Guy joined them. "Well, what make you of this latest sport? Methinks our cousin the naer knows something the rest of us do not."

"That the Vahldomne lives?" Eleanor said.

"And who he is," Guy said. "You don't name as champion in a death duel a ghost whom you hope will sally forth from Atuan's hall of heroes to defend your honour."

"Death duel?" Riannon said.

"Holy gods." Eleanor paled. "You're not serious?"

Guy nodded and used a sweeping gesture with his wine cup to indicate most of the people in the hall. "Even if the Vahldomne doesn't show, Aveline shan't want for a replacement. Most have been straining for a chance at the imperial dogs. It just needed him to relinquish his safe-conduct to let the tide loose."

Riannon's anger gained a bitter edge. She glared at the door through which Aveline had departed. That cunning bitch had planned this before she gave Riannon the sword.

"I think your analogy of a tide might prove apt," Eleanor said. "I've heard whispers about crusade. This duel is like breaching a dam and letting the flood loose."

"Atuan's beard," Guy said. "Think you how enraged the Lion Emperor will be if he hears that one of his men was slain by the Vahldomne. We'll not be the only ones baying for revenge and a renewal of holy war."

Riannon's hand dropped to where the hilt of the sword she was not wearing would have been. Was that what Aveline wished a paladin for? To start a holy war for her, commencing with one unbeliever at a time?

"I think the greater cause for concern," Eleanor said, "is how our men will react if the ambassador's man kills the Vahldomne. It would be awful if the hero returned only to die."

❖

Riannon saw a woman approaching and recognised her as one close to the queen. The woman curtsied to Eleanor and informed her that the queen required her presence.

"Is the naer, her sister, with the queen?" Riannon asked.

"No, lady," the woman said. "Her Eminence departed some time ago for the grove house."

Riannon nodded. "Lady, would you excuse me from escorting you home?"

"I'm sure my men will prove adequate for the task," Eleanor said. "Until later, then?"

Riannon pressed a brief kiss to Eleanor's fingers before stalking out of the hall.

The priestess in the room behind the ever-open door stood hastily at Riannon's entrance. "Blessings on you, sir. How may we help you?"

"I must speak with the naer," Riannon said. "Naer Aveline. She's expecting me. I'm Riannon of Gast."

Aveline looked complacent when a priestess guided Riannon into a well-appointed chamber.

"You asked what my purpose for you was," Aveline said. "Now you have one."

"You planned this before you took my oath," Riannon said.

Aveline set her goblet down. "What if I did?"

"What you've done is not honourable. You deceived me. You paid that troubadour to insult the ambassador. I know not what other wiles you used to provoke him, but this whole matter is not well done."

"They're unbelievers. If you don't think they deserve to be slaughtered like the animals they are, you stand alone in the Eastern

Kingdoms. Surely you heard their emperor wants your entrails, Vahldomne?"

"Don't call me that."

"The modest hero. How bardically noble of you. If you—"

"I'll not die for you," Riannon said. "Find another to do this. I will not."

Aveline's eyebrow lifted. "Need I remind you of your oath?"

Riannon's hand dropped to her side. "It was given to the Goddess, not to you. I've told you before that I will not act dishonourably."

Aveline spread her hands. "Is not defending my good name, and that of the Goddess's servants, an act worthy of you? The imperial lump of offal insulted me and dared call our Wise Mother false and whore. You refuse to champion my cause?"

Riannon folded her arms across her chest. "Why is it so important that you begin a war?"

Aveline looked surprised.

"That is what you are working towards, is it not?" Riannon said. "Whether I win or die in this duel, you'll have pushed us closer to war with the empire."

"Can I have underestimated you?" Aveline said. "Or do I hear Lady Eleanor speaking? Yes, that's it. She's no fool, however much she plays at the merry widow ready to flirt with one and all."

"You've not answered me. Why do you want a war?"

"For the same reason as countless other people. There can be no peace while imperial dogs defile the holy places in Evriat. We must reclaim those lost lands. Purify them. Consecrate them again. Turn them back into fit places for the worship of the true gods, and to allow their powers to flow again."

Riannon nodded. "That is a worthy reason. But what is *your* reason?"

Aveline laughed and turned away to reclaim her wine. "Ah, cousin, you waste no words, do you?"

"Whereas you twist and bend them and turn them inside out so that they seem to be what they are not."

"You wish me to be plain. Then let me essay it. I want you to champion the Goddess against that imperial filth. I want you to kill him and prove that his false gods are puny with pretension. Be what you swore to be. That's what I expect of you. You need not fear death. Your life belongs to the Dark-Faced One. You live because of the blessed sword you carry. With that blade, you need fear no trickery from such a foe. You have right on your side, because you are the weapon I wield in the name of the Lady of Destiny. You face an infidel who denies our Wise Mother and would defile her with insults."

Riannon frowned. Aveline spoke truly. Riannon had sworn herself to serve the Goddess. This was the very purpose she had been seeking. Live or die, she would have honoured her oath. She would have given her life in a holy cause. She would be assured of a place in paradise. Yet she did not feel uplifted by the prospect. The problem was that, for the first time, she had something other than her honour to lose—something to live for.

"Well?" Aveline asked.

Slowly, Riannon nodded.

❖

Riannon pushed open the door to Eleanor's bedchamber. Eleanor stopped and turned. It looked as though she had been pacing.

"Nonnie!"

Riannon met Eleanor halfway and pulled her into a firm embrace. Eleanor's arms gripped just as tightly. Could she have guessed the news Riannon carried?

All the way back from the grove house, Riannon had worried the problem of whether to tell Eleanor about the duel. Eleanor had a right to know that they might have only one and a half more days together. But she did so fear violence. Would it be best, for Eleanor's sake, if she remained in ignorance until after the event? It was the only protection Riannon could offer her, but she was unsure that she should.

"Oh, my love." Eleanor pressed her face against Riannon's chest. "Why could we not remain like this for the rest of our lives?"

Riannon's heart sank. Eleanor sounded so melancholy, not at all like her normal self. She must have deduced the truth. Riannon kissed the top of Eleanor's head.

"The worst may not come to pass," Riannon said. "It is as the Goddess wills."

"Give me a short while to surrender to despair in your arms. I'll return to rational thought then. Please, just hold me. Hold me like you'll never let me go."

Riannon mentally cursed. This was what she had dreaded. Eleanor slid her arms in the long slits of the arm holes of Riannon's surcote and clutched the back of Riannon's tunic.

"I know this is an unpleasant surprise," Riannon said.

"Surprise?" Eleanor shook her head. "I should've guessed. I should've seen it coming. I've had the example of poor Cicely under my nose these weeks, have I not?"

"Cicely?" Riannon's frown deepened. "Of what do you speak? Nell?"

Eleanor sighed and slipped her arms out of Riannon's clothes. She looked pale save for redness around her eyes.

"Have you been weeping?" Riannon asked.

"How could I not?" Eleanor clasped one of Riannon's hands and held it against her bosom. "Oh, Nonnie, what are we to do? I have never felt so wretched. I've never more desperately needed clear wits to think, yet my mind keeps stumbling over and over the same words."

"What words?" Riannon said.

Eleanor cast a despairing look up at her. "You don't know. Here I've been so lost in my own misery with no thought for you but having you comfort me."

"I do so willingly. But what has upset you?" Riannon forced her thoughts past her own devastating afternoon. "The queen?"

Eleanor bit her lip and nodded. Her fingers tightened around Riannon's hand.

"How much did she demand from you in fine?" Riannon asked.

"Not a penny. You see, I'm not to remain a widow. It's my liege lady's pleasure that I marry."

Riannon felt as though she had received too many strong blows to the helm. "Marry?"

"With all haste. Even now, my man of law is discussing it with Lord Howe's man."

"Lord Howe?" Riannon said. "But...but what of Guy?"

Eleanor released Riannon and crossed the room to retrieve her silver-rimmed cup. She drank deeply. Riannon stared at her rigid back, not quite able to believe what Eleanor had told her. Yet, the part inside which chilled with horror grew. Eleanor married. To a man. The woman she loved was to be owned by a husband. *No. Shite!*

"How can we avoid it?" Riannon said.

"We cannot."

"There must be a way. There must be something we can do."

"I confess that I haven't been thinking clearly. But I cannot see how it is to be avoided. The queen was adamant. I'm her vassal. I'm subject to her will. Everything I own—everything I am—is mine because I owe fealty to her. It's her right to decide who is to be lord of those lands. I have no choice."

"Could you not offer her more money? I have very little, but it's all yours."

Eleanor flashed her a smile. "Thank you, love, but I did try to buy my way out. With sums I hardly dare think of again. She would have none of it. She has her mind set on this course. Although, why Sir Geoffrey, I cannot imagine. He was not prominent amongst those who supported the queen. He isn't prominent in any way."

Riannon scoured her memory for him. He was a white-haired man of more than sixty years with few of his teeth remaining. The idea of him touching Eleanor soured her bile. And him kissing her. He would want to bed her.

"Shite! No." Riannon's fists clenched. "There must be something we can do."

"Make love to me. Please. Make me forget everything but me and you in this room, now."

Riannon wanted to be gentle, but she could not banish the idea that this might be one of the last times they lay together. In just a few days, she might be dead and Eleanor married to an old man. Desperation shadowed her every touch. She wanted each kiss to convince Eleanor how much she loved her. She clutched possessively. She wished to transmit through her hands, mouth, and legs a whole lifetime of joy and giving condensed into one intense act. Eleanor's fingernails dug into her flesh as if she wanted to gain a hold on Riannon that neither the queen nor fate could break. When Eleanor called out Riannon's name, anxiety stained ecstasy.

❖

Eleanor tugged the bed hangings a few inches apart to let in more of the brightening dawn. She wanted to watch Riannon sleeping. She must etch the memory deep in her mind so that time could not easily erode it. This was the woman she loved. Her lover, but not the person she would live out the rest of her life with. Although, given that Sir Geoffrey was old enough to be her father, his death would likely be the one that ended her sentence.

Eleanor blinked back tears and wriggled closer to Riannon. Riannon sighed but did not wake. Eleanor drew Riannon's arm across her stomach. How could the heaviness and solidity of Riannon's touch be so ephemeral? Passion was supposed to be eternal. But if it was, where would that leave the two of them? A sad travesty of a troubadour's couple made pale by a love reduced to hopeless sighs and unrequited longing.

Eleanor ran her hand up and down Riannon's arm. She wished she could touch Riannon's skin rather than her shirt.

How would she be able to lie with Sir Geoffrey while remembering Riannon, and loving Riannon, and wanting Riannon? She had endured the attentions of two husbands she had felt little physical attraction for. She could do it again. The world was stuffed with women who submitted themselves to their conjugal duties. But she had not had to do it while passionately in love with someone else and knowing that her lover lived and loved her. How could she not think of Riannon while Sir Geoffrey mounted her?

Eleanor shuddered and clutched Riannon's arm. Gods, how could you do this? You brought her to me and you made me see the truth of my love for her when I might have continued blind. Did you open my eyes to make this all the more painful? What lesson could benevolent gods possibly teach in such a callous fashion?

Eleanor wiped away her tears when she felt Riannon stir. She initiated lovemaking not because she wanted an orgasm, but because she needed to be physically intimate. To give herself to Riannon. She wept afterwards in Riannon's arms.

"I simply cannot see a path clear of this," Eleanor said.

"Perhaps we should take each day as it comes."

"I could evade the marriage by taking holy vows."

"Would you want to?"

"No," Eleanor said. "That life holds no appeal. I could not relinquish everything I own without a true vocation."

Riannon stroked Eleanor's hair. "Love, let us pretend, for today, that the rest of creation has ceased to exist. That you and I are the only people alive. And that we can be like this always. Just as you said yesterday."

Eleanor held one of Riannon's large, beautiful hands. It smelled of their sex. She pressed a kiss on the palm. "That is what I needed then. Now, my mind cannot be so easily stilled. I'm accustomed to finding solutions to my problems. If ever there has been something in my life worth fighting for, Nonnie, it's you and I. Do you not feel that, too?"

"Yes. But anything may happen on the morrow. Let us enjoy today, love. Please."

Eleanor heard that flat, distant tone in Riannon's voice that signalled a retreat. Surprised, she turned to see Riannon propped against the pillows frowning at her. The guard was definitely in place.

"You cannot think I want this marriage?" Eleanor said. "That I would prefer him to you? That I had any hand in this?"

Riannon shook her head.

"Then what has you so pale and reserved?" Eleanor put a hand to Riannon's cheek. "Nonnie?"

Riannon put her hand over Eleanor's. "Love, let us enjoy today."

Eleanor let Riannon pull her close. She pillowed her head against Riannon's chest. She tried to step beyond how the catastrophe affected herself to see it from Riannon's eyes. Riannon would have it easier, since she would not be the one submitting herself to Sir Geoffrey's will and surrendering control of her land, her money, and her body. But it would not be easy for her.

Eleanor sat up. "You won't leave the kingdom, will you? I don't think I could bear not seeing you again. Oh, how selfish of me. Holy Mother, help us. You must do what you need to. You've little to tie yourself to this land, have you? I miss you already, and yet I'm here with you."

Riannon gathered her again and held her in strong arms. Eleanor listened to Riannon's heartbeat. Wherever that heart beat, some part of Eleanor would always be there also.

"No matter what happens," Riannon said, "I will love you. Remember that. There is one person who has lived who has loved you beyond all women, who has held you as the most precious person the gods created."

Eleanor blinked, but the tears flowed freely. "Nonnie, don't. You make it sound so final. As though the world was poised to end. I thought we were to pretend. At least for today."

There had to be a way she could keep hold of Riannon for not just this day, but the rest of her life.

❖

Riannon looked up from Eleanor's head in her lap to the gap in the bed curtains. The day died. She must leave soon for the twilight blessing at the holy pool. She stroked Eleanor's hair. Like something alive, the soft chestnut waves covered Eleanor's pale shoulders and spilled across Riannon's lap. She did not want to go. She did not want to say goodbye to Eleanor, because it might be for the last time. Nor did she want to tell Eleanor why she must leave.

Was it cowardice to want to protect the woman she loved? Eleanor's knowing that she was the Vahldomne would bring her nought but sorrow and worry. Yet, could Riannon deceive her about her reasons for being unable to remain tonight? Was it better for Eleanor to suffer anxiety for a night and half a day, but be prepared for the news should Riannon be wounded or slain? Or would it be easier on her to pass the intervening hours in ignorance and learn the truth tomorrow?

The honourable part of Riannon warred with the lover.

Riannon stroked Eleanor's hair. She lifted some to kiss. She wished she could cut off a lock and carry it with her. She would not ask.

"Love, I need to rise," Riannon said.

Eleanor straightened and settled back against the pillows. Riannon gently touched her cheek when she really wanted to pull the two of them together so hard that they fused into one inseparable being. Riannon climbed out of bed and passed through the hangings. Their clothes lay in untidy piles. With a heart heavier than lead, she pulled on her braies.

"You're dressing?" Eleanor poked her head through the hangings. "Where are you going?"

Riannon finished tying the lace from the top of her left hose leg to the waist cord of her braies. "I must leave you for a few hours, love."

Riannon turned from Eleanor's frown to retrieve her tunic.

"When will you be back?" Eleanor said.

"On the morrow."

"The morrow? Where are you going?"

Riannon pulled her tunic over her head and tugged it into place. This was what she dreaded.

"I go to pray," Riannon said.

"It'll soon be dark. Could this not wait until the morning?" Eleanor closed on Riannon and ran her hands up Riannon's arms. "We could go together. I think it would be a good idea, considering the divine aid we need. I do not want to spend the night without you. Every moment is precious."

"I know, love. Believe me, I would remain if I could."

"Then why must you leave now? And pray? What could be so important that—" Eleanor paled and her eyes widened. She stood as still as one turned to stone with a look of horror on her face. When she spoke, it was in a fearful whisper. "No. Nonnie, no. It cannot be."

Riannon's heart sank. She put a hand to Eleanor's cheek. "I'll be back."

"Naer Aveline. Your service to the order." Eleanor gripped Riannon's tunic in her fists. "Holy Mother, tell me it's not true! Tell me that my imagination is overheated. Nonnie?"

"I will return. The Goddess's cause is right and will prevail."

"Oh, gods." Eleanor covered her face with her hands but failed to stifle a sob. "Oh, gods. No. I cannot bear it. I cannot."

Riannon put her arms around Eleanor. Eleanor's sobs were harder to bear than blows. "Love, I'll be back."

"It was hard enough to think of losing you while you yet lived. How could I cope if you are killed?"

"The cause I champion is just."

Eleanor's hands clutched Riannon's tunic. Tears flowed freely down her face. "I can see you bloodied and battered and dying. I've seen it before!"

Riannon held her tight and kissed the top of her head. "Love, please try to be calm."

"I cannot watch. I cannot."

"I know. I don't want you to be there. Let me think of you here and smiling."

Eleanor stifled a sob against Riannon's chest. Her body shook with weeping. Riannon squeezed her eyes shut in a vain attempt to stop her own tears. *Atuan, lord of battle, help me. Give me courage.*

"Nell? Love?"

Eleanor sniffed. Riannon could feel her taking deep breaths and trying to collect herself.

"I shouldn't be doing this." Eleanor straightened and wiped her face. "I've sent a husband off to war. You do not need my tears. You need to know that I can be as strong as you. That I love you and wish you to return."

"I will return. The Goddess's cause is right. Believe that, love."

Eleanor nodded in a brave effort to rally.

"I know you don't give out favours," Riannon said, "but would you give me a lock of your hair that I could carry? It would comfort me greatly to have some pledge from you."

Eleanor drew out a lock of hair, twisted it, and tied the end in a knot. She let Riannon cut the knot off. Eleanor unlocked her jewellery casket and returned with a green silk ribbon. She secured the knot of hair to it and tied the ribbon loosely around Riannon's neck. Riannon tucked it inside her shirt, to be next to her skin, and kissed Eleanor.

"I'll bring it back to you," Riannon said.

Eleanor touched the scarred side of Riannon's face. Riannon flinched but forced herself not to pull away this once.

"Did…did you get these at Vahl?"

"Yes."

"Come back to me."

"I shall."

Riannon walked away from Eleanor believing that she would return. She had to.

CHAPTER FOURTEEN

R iannon took the gift sword from Alan, retrieved her own weapon from the cot, and left him to oil her mail hauberk. She strode from the guest wing of the grove house towards the woods. She stood at the back of the worshippers in the grove for the service. Aveline's notorious challenge had swollen the size of the congregation. Riannon set both sheathed swords on the ground where gnarled tree roots hid them from curious gazes.

The singing aroused in her no special feeling of closeness with the Goddess. The priestess who spoke about the strength of faith probably had the duel in mind. Riannon found nothing in her words that touched her. Her mind proved distressingly apt to return to Eleanor. Pale, red-eyed, but trying to look brave with her glorious hair tousled from their lovemaking.

At the end of the service, Riannon watched the congregation and priestesses file out of the grove. Aveline halted near her and signalled her attendants to continue.

"I began to wonder if you'd come," Aveline said.

"You had my word." Riannon bent to scoop up both swords.

"Just how many weapons do you intend using? The gift of the Goddess will serve you well, and better than any plain steel."

"I told you that I shall not use it. I brought it to this place because it seemed meet that I do so."

"You will need it." Aveline turned and headed across the grove. "Come."

Riannon didn't bother with a second denial and strode after her cousin.

After following a path that looped through several clearings with pools, each of which Riannon might have taken for the holiest of holy ponds, Aveline halted beside a large, teardrop-shaped pool. No visible stream fed it. Though still twilight, the water looked black, as if this was where shadows coalesced until they could creep out into the woods at night.

Aveline lifted her arms at full stretch, letting her robe sleeves fall back to her elbows, and inhaled deeply. Riannon sensed no one in the nearby trees, though she was more aware than normal of the air around her. It felt like that prickling tension before a thunderstorm. The sky overhead burned pink and orange.

Aveline sighed and let her arms fall. "Can you feel it? We stand at the start of something that will shake the world."

"We are but two mortals."

"No. If you were just Riannon of Gast, you'd not have every man in the realm behind you. You're the Vahldomne. More—much more— than just a flesh and blood woman. There is an idea about you, like an aura that reaches out and touches men's imaginations in a way the woman could never do. They do not see you, they see their hero, the stuff of legend that they know and can follow. And I am not just priestess or younger daughter of a king. Naer Aveline is royal and consecrated, and the combination makes her greater than those two simply added together."

Aveline clasped the golden quartered-circle symbol hanging at her chest. She seemed to be looking into and beyond Riannon.

"We are servants of the gods," she said. "They move in us as we give creation a good push for them. Most people, it is true, are born, live, breed, and die without ever tasting anything sweeter, without even knowing there is anything more to life than their futile existence. Perhaps that is why you and I were chosen to abstain from breeding. Our life force must be spent in a different way. Not the screaming, bloody, sweaty toil of squeezing a protesting infant into the world from betwixt our thighs."

"Is not motherhood the holiest purpose for a woman? That is what all four orders teach, is it not?"

Aveline smiled. "But they do not teach that fatherhood is the pinnacle of a man's purpose, do they? Once he has sown his seed, he is encouraged to honour the gods by becoming all he can be, the better to add to their lustre. Why can you and I not be something that is both male and female? We are not made of ordinary stuff. We were not drawn along mundane paths. Our lives, and if necessary our deaths, belong to the Lady of Destiny."

For the first time, Riannon believed she heard Aveline the priestess speaking truly and without a filter of guile. She felt that prickling tension invading her sinews as if she had inhaled Aveline's words. Who did not, in the deepest part of their heart, cherish the idea that they were chosen by the gods for some special fate?

Riannon knelt at Aveline's feet beside the sacred pool. She unsheathed both swords and laid them naked, side by side, on the grass. Aveline intoned a blessing and scooped a handful of the holy water from the pool to sprinkle droplets on the swords. She traced the quartered circle on Riannon's forehead with a wet fingertip and began another chant.

The prickling inside Riannon strengthened. Something in Aveline's prayer drew it from deep within Riannon's entrails to swirl through her veins. She felt—believed—that a power planted in her before her birth now stirred to the call of purpose and need.

"Can you feel it?" Aveline whispered.

"Yes."

"Did you feel it at Vahl?"

The world in front of Riannon ripped apart. Instead of the folds of Aveline's dark green robe, she saw the tattooed man screaming. His brown eyes widened with pain and shock. She could see the whorls of the green-black tattoo engraved in his flesh. Her sword sliced into his neck and liberated a spray of warm blood. The tip of his singing sword sizzled. The blade did not touch her flesh yet it carved her face open.

Riannon snapped her head up. Aveline stared down at her.

"What did you see?" Aveline asked.

"The man I killed at Vahl."

"The Lion Emperor's son."

"The man who nearly killed me, like so many others." Riannon stood. If she heard the quaver in her voice, Aveline must also. "I thank you for your blessing."

"You'll remain here for the all-night vigil?"

"No." Riannon retrieved her swords. "I need to sleep."

❖

Aveline did not sleep. She maintained the fast she had begun the moment the ambassador cracked a slap to her face. The only moisture she sucked all day was the holy water she licked off her hand after blessing Riannon and the swords.

She remained alone in the innermost grove. At nightfall, she rose from her praying at the edge of the pool. Her bare feet touched more than dusty ground; her flesh met the skin of the Lady of Creation. Night looked down on her with countless white eyes. Where Riannon had knelt, Aveline unlaced her robe and let it fall about her ankles. Naked, she stooped to immerse hands and face in the holy water—the tears, the sweat, the juices of the Lady of Destiny.

Anointed, Aveline stood and began to dance. Her sweat dripped to nourish the earth. Her feet thumped her heartbeat into the grass. She was part of creation, and creation ran through her.

Whatever happened tomorrow at noon would be a victory for the cause of crusade. Win or lose, the flames would flare and Aveline would fan them into a conflagration to scorch the earth. The Quatorum Council could not ignore a fire already blazing with righteous zeal.

Her feet bled. Still she danced.

She danced for Riannon. For her triumph. For her life.

❖

Eleanor did not sleep.

She lifted her head. Her fingers still curled around the tiny metal anvil. The shining surface reflected the yellow flame from the oil lamp.

She had been an infrequent worshipper of the god of war. Would he hear her now? One worried, frightened, tearful voice?

Eleanor looked around the shrine room. She had knelt first and longest in prayer to the Lady of Mercy and Healing, who seemed to have turned her merciful face from Riannon. Eleanor had then implored Naith, nurturer of life, and Kamet the arbiter, lord of justice and settler of disputes.

Just yesterday, she felt her world had ripped asunder with the queen's decision that she must marry Lord Howe. But fate had sliced an even deeper wound into that cut. Now, she would marry any man thrice over if it would spare Riannon.

"How can you let this happen?" Eleanor tightened her fingers on the unresponsive metal. "I did not think I could bear to lose her once. Yet you make me face it twice. Have you not hurt her enough?"

She made no attempt to curtail her tears. Her soul bled.

"Take from me what you will. I beg you. Anything. As long as I can love the living Riannon and not spend a lifetime mourning her. Even if I never see her again. Just let her live. Please."

❖

Riannon watched dawn silhouette the woods. The rising light drenched the underbellies of the clouds in livid pink. The colours soon leached away to leave an unremarkable summer morning. She joined the end of the line of green-robed priestesses going to worship.

After she returned, Alan brought food from the kitchens. Riannon ate. Her nerves tightened and twitched before battle, but not to the point where she could not look to the sustenance of her body. She had seen countless men who could not sleep or eat, and who spent the time before arming in pacing or checking equipment and horses. One Irulandi she had known used a whore all night if he could find one—as though he needed the act of creating life to counterbalance the fear of losing his own. He died of a plague he caught from a camp follower.

"It'll be a hot day," Alan said.

Riannon nodded.

"The ground will be firm underfoot," he said. "I didn't know those imperial whoresons didn't fight with lances. You'd have had him on his arse eating dust, sir."

Riannon asked him to go and check her horses. Normally, his nervous prattle washed harmlessly over her. Today, she found it difficult enough to clear her mind in readiness. A living ghost haunted her. Eleanor.

Riannon touched the lock of hair she wore at the base of her throat. Her cause was just. Holy warrior. She fought for the good of the Goddess against an unbeliever. Her sword, her skill, her life had been dedicated to the highest purpose. She stood but hours from the promise of immortal favour. She had striven for this. The strength of the Goddess flowed in her.

Yet, the prospect of earthly and divine glory contained a spot of tarnish, small but persistent, coloured more chestnut than rust red. What a wretched time for her to have discovered a purpose for her life that ran contrary to everything she believed she wanted.

Aveline had stirred her last night. The Dark-Faced One had spoken through the naer to Riannon. That the two of them had been chosen for a special purpose brought something alive within Riannon. But an inconvenient fragment of herself pulsed with longing for the mundane existence she had believed she could never achieve even had she wanted it. Now she yearned for a life settled and fixed, where she hung her sword belt on a peg in Eleanor's bedchamber.

"It was never to be," Riannon whispered. "Even if I see this day's end, she will not be mine."

❖

Riannon tugged the quilted gambeson more comfortably across her shoulders while Alan knelt to pull the mail chausses over her feet and up her legs like metal hose. She again slid a finger inside the neck of her shirt to touch the lock of hair there.

Over her mail hauberk, which hung to mid-thigh, Alan helped her pull into place the long, flowing white linen surcoat. He fastened the cord about her waist. When it came to her sword belt, her squire hesitated. Riannon pointed to her own sword.

"You will carry the other for me," she said.

Riannon strode out to the pool where she would receive her final blessing. Alan followed, carrying her helm. Priestesses stared openly at her. As the only armed knight to ever walk this way, none could mistake who she must be. To Riannon's unease, most dropped to their knees as she passed.

Aveline waited beside one of the less commonly used pools. At her signal, a priestess carried to Riannon her shield newly painted. It bore, on a green background, a gold tree. The blazon was not that of Riannon of Gast, Knight of the Grand Order of the Star, or even of the Vahldomne. This badge marked the paladin of the Order of the Goddess.

Aveline prayed with Riannon, and for her.

"We will prevail," Aveline said. "Their false god might have claws, but it can be no match for the true majesty of divinity. Our cause is right."

Riannon nodded.

"I'd best go and take my place in the stands," Aveline said. "Lest that imperial piece of filth take heart from my absence. You're not wearing the gift of the Goddess. You'll need it."

"I've told you why I shall not use it," Riannon said.

Aveline's eyes narrowed. "You wish your stubborn stupidity to cost your life and forfeit the challenge? That sword is blessed for this purpose!"

"No," Riannon said.

"What amazes me, cousin, isn't that you're so scarred, but that you yet live if you have permitted such hare-brained considerations to guide your actions. How many people are given a divinely favoured gift? Is it arrogance or madness that you practice?"

"Honour."

Aveline's jaw worked and she jabbed her glare at Alan. "Well, at least you'll have it close by when you need it. I'll have the best healers with me."

Riannon watched Aveline stalk away. The naer limped and pulled up at the point where the path turned into the trees.

"I'd prefer it if you did not need their services," Aveline said.

"As would I," Riannon said.

Aveline flashed her a grin in parting.

Riannon looked at her shadow. From its shortness, she judged it about an hour before noon. She muttered a last prayer, traced the quartered circle on her breast, and strode back to where John waited with her horse.

The city streets, normally teeming with people, echoed with an eerie emptiness as Riannon rode through them towards the tourney grounds. She could mark her direction by the muted roar of cheering, like an angry surf pounding a cliff.

The grounds were packed to overflowing. Hawkers and pickpockets must be doing a thriving business. Some of the thousands of spectators looked at Riannon, but most gazes slid away without snagging. She was just another knight amongst many.

At Guy's arming tent, she dismounted. Not surprisingly, her

brother was absent. She dispatched a page to find him. Alan found her some water to drink. Her throat was tight and dry. She sent Alan to inform the marshal that Naer Aveline's champion would present herself at noon.

Another roaring cheer rolled from the crowd. Riannon closed her eyes and pressed her fingertips to the base of her throat. Beneath the linen surcoat she felt the supple but hard mail shirt. Eleanor's lock of hair lay beneath many layers. Riannon knew that it touched her skin, just like this time yesterday when they lay together in Eleanor's bed. She loved and was loved in return—more passionately than any troubadour's song, more simply profound than any blessing.

"You are what I regret," Riannon whispered.

A flurry of commotion preceded Guy bursting into the tent.

"Nonnie! This is a surprise. I'd not thought you eager for the games?"

Riannon signalled for Alan to leave. Guy frowned at her shield. Riannon put a hand on his shoulder.

"Brother, you are the greatest fool the gods created," she said.

Guy grinned. "You're not the first to tell me so. What brings you to this conclusion?"

"Eleanor."

Guy nodded. "She, I believe, was one of the first to tell me that my pate is addled."

Riannon tightened her grip on his shoulder. "Listen to me. The queen has told Nell she must marry."

Guy lost his smile. "Who?"

"Old Lord Howe."

"You jest! Him?"

"I am in earnest," she said. "But it isn't settled yet. You must speak with the queen. You boast that you can get any female to do as you wish. Very well. Put your charm to the test. Convince her to let you wed Eleanor."

A blast of horns cut through the background hubbub. The tent flap twitched. Alan said, "Lady."

"Speak with her," Riannon said to Guy. "Surely you have more claim on her largesse than this old man."

"You seem right eager to get me wed," Guy said. "Why does this concern you so?"

Because if I cannot have her, the next best thing is for you to. Because if she loves me, she might grow to love you and be happy. Because I cannot bear the thought of her with that old man.

The horns sounded again.

"I must go," she said. "Don't waste your last chance."

Guy followed her outside. He frowned as he watched her don her helm and stand for Alan to lace her mail mittens in place.

"Nonnie?" Guy said. "You are to fight? But...Atuan's legs! Nonnie, you're not—?"

Riannon jabbed a mailed hand at his chest. "Eleanor. Forget her not."

She swung up into the saddle. The horns sounded their third call.

"Nonnie!" Guy stepped close to her stirrup. "You are the Vahldomne?"

"I am late," she said.

"Go with the gods!" he said.

Riannon lifted a hand in salute and urged her horse forwards.

Alan and John, on foot, shouted and shoved a path through the tightly packed crowd for her. The curious stares riveted on her now. Riannon looked past and above them through the slit of her helm. She guided her horse to the entrance to the marked off ground. Numerous squires and young knights stood as she passed them. They raised arms in salute.

"Vahldomne!"

The shout rippled around behind her as Riannon urged her horse across the scuffed and beaten turf. The marshal, marked by his man holding a banner behind him, waited in the field. Riannon heard a strange, muted sound like a thousand indrawn breaths. She halted her horse near the marshal. The imperial champion stood a few feet beyond, with a supporter behind him.

The marshal, on foot, frowned up at her. "Sir, you are the Vahldomne?"

Riannon dismounted. By this time Alan had jogged to her and she passed him the reins.

"I offer myself as Naer Aveline's champion," Riannon said. "If she will accept me."

The marshal nodded. Beyond him, her imperial opponent stared stony-faced as if he understood none of their words.

Riannon turned to the stands. The queen sat on her painted chair under a canopy bearing the royal blazon. Her sister sat to one side.

Riannon bowed to the queen before striding closer to the stand. As ritual required, she drew her sword and held it pointing up at Aveline. Aveline removed the gold quartered-circle emblem she wore and tossed it to Riannon.

"Be my champion," Aveline said. "Know that you fight not for me but for the Lady of Creation. Prove her cause to be right and just."

Riannon sheathed her sword and strode back to the marshal. Alan fastened Aveline's symbol to Riannon's sword belt. Riannon fleetingly wondered if this gift also contained some magical property that Aveline saw fit not to warn Riannon about. She settled her shield on her arm and turned to face the marshal and her opponent.

"The challenge was to the death." The marshal looked between the combatants. "But if one of you yields, we'll ask the principals if they'll accept that."

The man behind the imperial warrior spoke in a fluid language to him. The warrior shook his head.

The marshal bowed to the queen and stepped back. "May the gods guide you."

Riannon lifted her sword and concentrated on her opponent.

She was two or three inches taller, but he was of bulkier build. His shoulders were as bullishly thick as her brother Henry's, and his middle thickening to a similar paunch. His unusual armour, of many small metal plates reminiscent of fish scales, was the same as that of the man at Vahl. His open-faced helm showed his tattoo clawing its way up his face out of the confines of his mail coif. The pattern on his shield was a dragon's claw. He flashed his sword upwards in some form of salute, though whether to her or his gods, Riannon did not know.

He stood with his sword raised and muttering. She withheld her attack until he finished his prayer. The hilt of her sword felt familiar in her hand. Her shield hung comfortably on her arm. She could feel her breath inside the helm. She already sweated. In this heat, it would not be a long contest.

The crowd noise had fallen to an expectant murmur. Over it, Riannon heard a strange buzzing like an angry wasp. The warrior's sword scythed down towards her. Riannon lifted her shield to catch it and swung her sword at his shoulder. The blow on her shield cracked the wood with a splintering blow. The weight on her left arm lifted. He deflected her strike easily with his own shield.

Riannon stepped back and looked down. Half her shield hung on her forearm. The rest lay on the grass. The buzzing whipped towards her. Riannon jerked backwards and hastily shrugged off the useless remnant of her shield.

Buzzing. Just like that singing blade at Vahl. Such a weapon could cut without touching. It carved through armour, she remembered, as easily as through sheerest silk. *Shite.*

Riannon switched to a two-handed grip on her sword and aimed a strike at his sword side. He interposed his weapon and buffeted her with his shield. The blow caught her on the upper arm. Riannon staggered back out of reach. He was strong, but clumsy and a fraction slow. Not the sort you would choose as champion in a fair fight. But was this fair? That sword...

He snarled and swung his sword at her in a scything arc at chest height. Riannon lifted her sword to easily parry. The air buzzed. Steel met steel in a clang. Riannon's hilt jolted with the shock, then jumped in her hands. Through the slit in her helm she blinked at what she saw. Her sword ended three finger's width above her left hand. The blade was gone. Snapped. *What the—?*

Buzzing swooped towards her.

Riannon threw herself backwards. The magical sword sliced the air in front of her chest. She heard the moan of the crowd. She lifted the stump of her sword. Not snapped. The blade had been cleanly cut.

Shite.

The warrior stepped towards her, sword raised again.

Riannon retreated. Now she understood why a mediocre swordsman could confidently undertake such a duel. That sword could cut through anything. It needed scant skill to hack an unprotected opponent to death.

He stalked her. The buzzing blade slashed the air. Riannon danced backwards. Pain slammed into her left shoulder. The point of his sword hadn't come within two feet of her. Yet Riannon knew his magic had cut through the many layers of her armour and hit flesh. It had happened before—at Vahl. If the strongly forged steel of her sword could not stop his blade, what could?

He spoke his fluid language again and stepped confidently closer.

Riannon flung her useless stump of sword away, turned around, and saw Alan. She ran to him.

"Lady!" Alan said. "You—"

Riannon grabbed Aveline's gift sword from his hand and yanked it from the scabbard as she turned. The warrior advanced. Riannon ignored the stab of pain from her left arm as she dropped her empty scabbard.

"Right, you whoreson bastard," she said. "Two can play this game."

He swung. The sword buzzed. Riannon lifted her sword to parry. The magical blades met with an ordinary jarring clang of metal and metal. Both blades held. The buzzing turned into a sizzling like fat dripping into a fire. His eyes widened in surprise.

Riannon stepped aside. Her shoulder must be bleeding. It hurt. The real pain would come soon. Riannon aimed a blow to his shield. He lifted it. Her sword cut it in half and bit into his forearm. He bellowed and swung wildly. Riannon flicked her blade up to deflect his blow. Her helm exploded with noise. Sunlight burst in from above her left eye. His magical sword had cut part of the edge of her helm off. Riannon staggered to the side. He made no attempt to follow-up. His shoulders sagged and he held his left arm against his body. Blood dripped from his forearm down the dangling half of his shield.

Riannon aimed a double-handed blow at his right side. He turned awkwardly to interpose his sword. The force of her blow carried his own weapon against his body. That contact did not seem to hurt him. But he had not tried to use his left arm.

Riannon aimed slash after slash at his left side. He stumbled backwards under the onslaught, clumsily but successfully fending her off, though he lost both ground and blood.

Riannon swung and swung. His buzzing blade denied her contact. Steel met steel. Magic warred with magic up and down their blades. Blood dripped from his arm. She saw it in his eyes when he knew he was going to lose.

"Do you yield?" she shouted.

He swung wildly. Riannon caught his blade against hers.

"Do you yield?" she shouted.

He swung. Riannon knocked the clumsy blow aside, and aimed low as she pivoted. The end of her sword caught him a hand's width above his knee. As it had with the tree, the blade sliced through his mail legging, muscles, and bone.

He crumpled with an ear-splitting howl.

Riannon's panting breath sounded too loud inside her helm. His severed left leg lay inches from his body. Blood pumped around the amputated stump. He lay on his back glaring up at her with a look of utter disbelief.

Riannon stepped closer and put the tip of her sword against his chest. "Do you yield?"

He snarled. His sword arm lifted. Riannon thrust her point down into his chest. The tip of her sword pierced the metal plates and sank into his body as if it were warm butter.

His arm flopped back on the grass. The buzzing died as the life faded from his eyes. The infidel had gone to face the true gods, where he would make the terrifying discovery that he had believed in a false god. The real ones would make him suffer for his error until he had absolved himself. Riannon staggered clear of the body. Blood smeared the shining rings covering her left arm and stained her surcoat.

"Lady!"

Riannon turned to see Alan jogging the last few paces towards her.

"You're hurt," he said. "Healers. I'll fetch—"

"Remove my helm," she said.

Alan tugged her laces loose. The air on her face felt like it came straight from the gardens of paradise.

"Atuan's beard," Alan said. "A piece has been cut from your helm! How—"

Riannon stepped past him. The marshal strode towards her. He trailed her as she walked to the stands.

"Vahldomne?" he said. "You need to see a healer. My own tent is at your service. I'll send for—"

"I thank you, but the naer will send her priestess-healers to me."

Riannon halted at the foot of the stands and pushed her mail coif and the linen one beneath it back from her sweaty hair. The marshal stopped beside her and his face dropped as he recognised her.

"I asked him to yield," she said. "He refused. Though, now that I think on it, mayhap he did not understand me."

Riannon turned to look up at Aveline. She lifted her bloody sword in a salute. Aveline smiled triumphantly. A roaring cheer broke out again. The battering ram of sound beat against Riannon.

"Nonnie!"

Guy rose from near the queen's chair, squeezed past the noble spectators on the benches in front of him, and vaulted the railing. He stopped himself from clapping a hand on her injured shoulder.

"I'll need to use your tent," she said.

"You need to do a lot of talking," he said.

"Not while I bleed."

Her legs began to shake as the reaction to her fight set in. Her shoulder burned. Alan hovered behind her with her helm.

"Lady," he said, "should I—"

"Run," Riannon said.

"Lady?"

"Run," she said. "Take my horse. As fast as you can. To Lady Eleanor. Tell her I sent you. Tell her I shall return to her soon. Answer anything she asks, but don't tell her that I have a wound. Go!"

Guy looked strangely at her. He shouted for his squires and fell in step beside her for the walk to his arming tent.

"Did you speak to the queen about Eleanor?" Riannon asked.

"It has barely been an hour," he said.

Riannon knew she should be exasperated with him, but her strongest feeling was an utterly illogical rush of relief. She did not want to think of Eleanor married to anyone, not even Guy.

CHAPTER FIFTEEN

Eleanor halted her pacing and spun around. Agnes stood in the doorway. Eleanor's blood felt as if it stopped in her veins.

"A rider has arrived, my lady," Agnes said.

"Lady Riannon?"

"I know not. As soon as the servant told me that—"

Eleanor already hurried past her woman. She ran to the closest chamber with a window overlooking the courtyard. *Please, gods. Please, merciful gods. Please!*

She gripped the edge of the window opening and took a deep breath before looking down. Her gaze snagged on a sorrel horse held by one of the grooms. Riannon's horse. The rush of relief surged past the tightness in her throat and welled out as tears.

Eleanor sagged against the wall with her eyes squeezed shut. She traced the quartered circle against her chest. *Thank you.*

"My lady?" Agnes said. "You have a visitor."

Eleanor turned with a smile even as she hurriedly wiped her eyes. Her smile froze and shattered. Alan stood in the doorway. Not Riannon. Fresh blood smeared his sleeve. *No...*

Alan bowed. "Lady, I was bid come with all haste. Lady Riannon wished me to tell you that she prevailed. The cause she championed—"

"Prevailed? She—Lady Riannon lives?"

Alan smiled. "Yes, madam. The Vahldomne killed him. She showed that imperial pig."

He said more, but Eleanor's mind clutched fast the fact that her lover lived. At that moment, that was the only thing that mattered in all of creation. *Lady of Mercy and Healing, I thank you. Oh, how I thank you.*

"My lady, have I your permission to withdraw?" Alan said. "My place is with her."

"Where is she?" Eleanor asked.

"Lord Guy's arming tent," he said. "I'm sure his men are good enough, but *I* am her squire."

She understood his desire to return to Riannon. But a thought stopped Eleanor before she nodded a dismissal. Her gaze fixed on the blood stain on his sleeve. It could be anyone's. Riannon had killed a man. He would've bled. Alan came from a tourney field. Such places bred wounds. Torn flesh that led to long, agonised, stinking deaths. Eleanor's hands curled into fists. She clenched so tightly that her nails dug into her palms.

"My lady?" Alan said. "Have I your permission to—"

"How badly is she hurt?" Eleanor asked.

"When I left her, she was walking with Lord Guy."

Eleanor ripped her gaze from the blood stain. Alan wouldn't meet her eyes. She felt as though a hand gripped and twisted her entrails.

"I ought to return to her," Alan said to the floor. "May I—"

"She told you not to tell me," Eleanor said.

Alan shifted and fidgeted with the cap he held in his hands.

"I'll send to the grove for healers," Eleanor said.

"There's no need. Her eminence, the naer, arranged for the senior healers to attend her. They will even now be—" Alan broke off with a wince. "I mean...Do I have your permission to leave, my lady?"

Eleanor remembered Lionel. His bloody bandages and his cries as he writhed his life away. And poor William. His black, rotting foot. The stench. Leaving his room and feeling nothing but guilty relief that her ordeal was over. A lonely corpse.

"No," she said. "She can't be like that."

"My lady?" Alan said.

"Take me to her."

Eleanor ignored the astonished look on her waiting woman's face and sent an order for a horse to be saddled.

Alan escorted her to the tourney ground. Their mounts pushed through a boisterous throng moving in the opposite direction. Every mouth seemed to be crying "Vahldomne." Shouts and cheers erupted as if this were a festival holy day. Eleanor wanted to scream at them all to go away. Riannon was wounded and needed the ministrations of the city's best healer priestesses.

"Make way!" Alan shouted at knots of men standing amongst the arming tents. "Stand aside, there!"

Eleanor looked warily at the gaily coloured tents, the limp pennons, and the crowds. The air of celebration flourished more strongly here, yet how many men lay stretched on cots in those tents with their bodies battered, bruised, and broken?

Nowhere was the gathering of people louder and thicker than around Guy's arming tent. Men in the green and black livery of the Earl of Northmarch held back the tide to prevent it from swallowing the blue tent. Alan had to shout and threaten and enlist the aid of some of the armed men. Eleanor's raw nerves found no balm in the commotion. Guy ordered the guards to let the riders through. Eleanor gratefully slid to the ground with his help.

"This is a surprise," he said. "What brings you to this place?"

Eleanor stared past him to the tent. The canvas did not seep with blood. She heard the talking and laughing and shouts from behind her—and a man singing—but no groans or cries from inside.

"How is she?" Eleanor asked.

"Famous. Heroic. Modest beyond reason." Guy gestured at the uncountable crowd. "And popular."

"I must see her," Eleanor said.

"The healer priestesses are with her. She doesn't want any near her while they work. She evicted even me."

"I must help." Eleanor saw his frown. "She—Nonnie is my guest. I have an obligation to…she will see me."

Eleanor strode to the tent and pushed inside the flap before she could lose her nerve.

She walked into the stink of unwashed bodies, oil, and leather trapped inside the tent and heightened by the heat of the day. Pieces of armour and clothing draped chests and hung from poles. A kneeling young woman in green robes looked up from the potion she stirred in a bowl.

"You must rest, my lady." The speaker was a grey-haired priestess who stood with her back to Eleanor. "We are making a restorative potion, but you must lie and let the blessing work undisturbed."

"I thank you for your advice, sio, and I shall rest," Riannon said. "But not here. I must go elsewhere."

Eleanor's clenched fist rose to her bosom and she gulped a breath of relief. Another middle-aged priestess moved and Eleanor glimpsed Riannon. She sat on a stool in profile. Her scar exaggerated her frown. She wore an embroidered shirt that Eleanor didn't recognise. It must be one of Guy's.

"You have lost blood," the grey-haired priestess said. "The drawing of it is your area of skill, my lady, but mine is the succour of it."

"I've said that I'll take your potion." Riannon stood. "I'll take it with me and drink it willingly. But I have someone to see and cannot tarry."

"Nonnie, sit down," Eleanor said.

Riannon's head snapped around. "Nell?"

Eleanor forced herself to ignore the ripped shirt and bloody rags on the ground. She stepped closer to Riannon. Part of her wished to throw herself at her lover and verify this blessed reality with all of her senses.

"You shouldn't have come," Riannon said. "I told him not to—"

"If you wish to lay blame for me being here, then it must lie with yourself," Eleanor said.

"Myself?" Riannon said.

"Yes. Had you not attempted to keep the whole truth of your condition from me, I would not have concluded that you would make a poor patient. Should you not be resting?"

"She should, my lady," the older priestess said. "And she needs to drink the blood restorative."

"Sios, I thank you for your care," Riannon said. "You must have other business to attend."

"Sit down." Eleanor turned to the senior priestess. "I'll see she drinks."

Riannon subsided onto the stool. Eleanor took the small bowl of potion. The priestesses offered brief blessings and departed.

Riannon put her right hand over one of Eleanor's hands. "You tremble."

"You'd better drink this before I spill it over us both."

Riannon took the bowl in one hand. Her left arm hung at her side and she made no attempt to lift it. The linen of the shirt bulged over bandages swathing Riannon's upper arm and shoulder.

"How badly are you hurt?" Eleanor said.

"Little more than a scratch. But Aveline's healer priestesses brought many bandages and felt compelled to use them."

Eleanor saw a different wound; the one that had Lionel writhing in pain. Gaping. Stinking. Weeping dirty pus.

Riannon set the bowl in her lap and captured Eleanor's hand. She held it firmly with the strength of a living person, not a dying one. "I'm not gravely hurt, love. I swear it. You have my word."

Through the kiss Riannon pressed on the back of Eleanor's fingers, she silently reaffirmed a bond that Eleanor knew death might have sundered but not effaced. Eleanor blinked back tears as she nodded and tore her gaze from Riannon's shoulder.

"You should be drinking," Eleanor said.

Eleanor caught sight of a white surcoat with a bloody stain. She felt the blood drain from her own face and her gorge rise. She steadfastly turned away. Riannon watched her with concern. Eleanor forced herself to rally.

"Drink," Eleanor said. "You'll need to regain your strength if you plan to do aught more energetic in the next few days than kiss my hand."

Riannon grinned and lifted the bowl to drain.

"I know what it cost you to come," Riannon said. "I wanted to see you above all things. I know not how to thank you."

Eleanor had too much to say for words, and she did not want to admit how difficult it was to be here. Love should have made this easy. She kissed Riannon hard.

"I couldn't not come," Eleanor said. "I had to see you."

Riannon touched Eleanor's face. "I did not know it was possible to love this much. If I ever—"

"Sir? May I help you?"

At the sound of Alan's voice, Eleanor straightened and turned. The squire held the flap of the tent partly open, but remained discreetly out of sight.

"I'd best leave," Eleanor said.

"I'll dress and come with you," Riannon said.

"No. The priestess said you must rest to let the potion work on your blood." Eleanor glanced at Riannon's shoulder. "Don't do anything that will upset the healing. Please. I've seen what can happen to wounds that go bad. Don't do that to me, Nonnie. Please."

Riannon nodded, squeezed Eleanor's hand, and kissed it. "Yes, love. I'll rest."

❖

Later that afternoon, Eleanor watched the noisy crush of men pushing through the entry doors to her hall. She stood, impervious to the many people crowding her house, as Riannon returned to her. Eleanor took in Riannon's pallor and her sling. She wished Riannon had rested longer, but Riannon smiled at her. Eleanor thought all her tears of relief shed hours ago, but she blinked away more.

Her servants scurried about with ale and wine. A hundred men jostled each other and talked in several languages. The press surged and separated her from Riannon.

The stout Count of Vahl pushed a man from a bench with his own hands to make space for Riannon to sit. A grandson of the king of Rhân claimed the place on Riannon's right and signalled to a servant to bring her wine. Even Riannon's elder brother, Thomas, stood near her deep in conversation with Guy. The word on every pair of lips was "Vahldomne."

Riannon looked tired but more relaxed than Eleanor felt. Where Eleanor had only ever seen her lover withdrawn in company, or guarded at best, this afternoon Riannon paid close attention to the men about her and offered comments. Men sought her opinion. Eleanor was seeing Riannon recognised for what she was, rather than shunned as an oddity. Eleanor felt a deep sadness. Riannon had had to risk her life in front of them to bring this about.

The Earl Marshal arrived.

"Lady Eleanor," he said. "My wife sends her greetings."

"My thanks, my lord," Eleanor said. "I hope Cicely fares well. Wine?"

Henry took a cup from a servant and gestured towards the group around Riannon. "It's not often we get to host a hero, let alone one come back from the dead. Nor did I ever expect to find myself related by blood to the greatest one of our age! I cannot understand why Riannon did not tell us."

Eleanor could. She chose not to tell him her theory that Riannon would have been proud had he extended his hand to her simply as brother to sister.

"Riannon is nothing if not modest," Eleanor said.

"Ha!" Henry shook his head. "You have a gift for understatement. Anyone would think she'd concealed a mere tournament win. That she is the Vahldomne! Look at them. Every man who is anyone wishes to talk with her. There'll be some profit in this for us all."

Eleanor said nothing to detain him from elbowing his way through the group around Riannon. The wine in her cup tasted sour. She had not seen so much hypocrisy in such a small space before. Did Riannon see it?

When it became clear that some of her guests were determined to make a long evening talking and drinking with the Vahldomne, and that Riannon did not intend retiring early, Eleanor slipped out of the hall. Much as she wished to order Riannon to bed, to sleep, she had not that right.

She sat for Agnes to brush her hair. A long, unhurried session of even this pleasure was no substitute for being with Riannon. But her lover was not just Riannon of Gast any more. Even had Eleanor not been forced to marry Lord Howe, she would have had to resign herself to sharing the Vahldomne with the rest of the world.

The idea that Riannon was a hero, the subject of song, had shocked Eleanor last night. Riannon might die because of it. Eleanor experienced no rush of pride that she supposed the Vahldomne's lover would be expected to feel.

To Eleanor, Riannon's heroism meant she possessed that reckless courage which earned most men an early grave. To win a name she did not use, Riannon had paid a heavy price. Scars disfigured not only her face, they gouged through her confidence in her own body. The hero of Vahl could not bear to expose herself to the woman she loved in the privacy of their bed even at the height of passion. *That* never made it into troubadour's songs.

Agnes finished fastening the end of Eleanor's night plait. She fiddled unnecessarily with the brush and combs before speaking.

"Do you wish me to retire to the back chamber for the night, my lady?"

"There's no need. We'll keep to our usual arrangements."

Riannon would not be fit to join her, even if her newfound boon companions departed ere midnight. Eleanor wondered if she ought to have tried persuading Riannon to retire early. Whatever that bandage concealed needed longer healing than the few hours she slept this afternoon.

Eleanor knelt in private devotion before the portable travelling shrine in the corner of her bedchamber. She again thanked all four gods for Riannon having passed through the duel. The ordeal had not only been Riannon's.

Loving a hero meant more days and nights of hell for Eleanor like those she had just suffered. The waiting. Wanting to scream at her utter impotence while imagining her lover in mortal danger, and knowing that Riannon would throw herself in when more prudent men would hesitate. The constant, unrelenting, harrowing not knowing if the moment that had just passed was the last one Riannon knew before a sword thrust killed her. Living in perpetual expectation of the arrival of news that Riannon was dead—or that she had died days or weeks before and Eleanor had lived on in ignorance of her abrupt loneliness. Or the unspeakable nightmare of racing to Riannon's bedside to find her alive but beyond all mortal aid and lingering in racking agony that Eleanor could do nothing to ease.

She could see bandages crusted with dirty pus. It was too easy to substitute Riannon for memories of poor tortured, dying William. There was nothing heroic in the gut-churning stench of soiled sheets and rotting flesh.

"It didn't happen," Eleanor whispered. She forced her fingers to relax from their white-knuckle grip on the edge of the shrine. "She's safe. Almighty Gods, I thank you. You, who see into all hearts, know how deeply and profoundly grateful I am."

Before rising, Eleanor added a fervent prayer that she could think of some way of averting her marriage to Lord Howe.

Though she had not slept last night, Eleanor lay awake with Agnes softly snoring in the other half of her bed. Since sleeping with Riannon, Eleanor found the commonplace habit of sharing her bed with other women disquieting. She did not desire Agnes. She did not desire any woman other than Riannon. Yet, she now felt a self-consciousness about herself and her proximity to another woman. She imagined she would feel the same wary discomfort if she found herself lying in the same bed as a man. Women had become possible sexual partners.

The house quietened. Eleanor no longer heard male shouts and laughter from the hall below. Riannon's visitors would have departed—

or been carried home by their servants—and Eleanor's household would have retired to pallets on the floor.

Eleanor rose. She groped her way in the dark to the shrine. She found a flint there for lighting the shrine lamp.

She shielded her candle as she walked through the intervening rooms to Riannon's door. She lifted the latch and let herself in. Alan jerked upright on his cot at the foot of the bed.

"My lady!" he said. "What—"

"Ssh." Eleanor put a finger to her lips. She stepped closer to him and whispered, "How is she? Does she sleep?"

"Nell?"

Eleanor's blood quickened at the sound of Riannon's voice. She smiled as she stepped through the gap in the hangings. Riannon looked tired. Eleanor wanted to throw herself at Riannon and hold her. The candlelight showed the bulge of a bandage beneath the left shoulder of Riannon's shirt.

"I feared you were asleep." Riannon tugged the bedding aside in invitation. "But I hoped you'd come."

Eleanor set her candle down and eased herself under the sheet. She made no remark on the unusual arrangement of being on Riannon's right, scarred side. "I want to touch you so badly, but I'm afraid to hurt you."

"You'll not hurt me." Riannon put a gentle hand to Eleanor's cheek. "But I won't be much use to you tonight, love."

"I need the comfort of being with you."

"That I can do."

Eleanor snuggled against Riannon's uninjured side and slid a hand over Riannon's ribs. Riannon kissed Eleanor's temple.

"This is what I've needed more than any healers or cups of wine," Riannon said.

Eleanor turned her head on Riannon's uninjured shoulder to kiss the side of her neck. With her lips feeling Riannon's pulse, her body hugging the warm solidity of her, and inhaling the sweaty, musky scent of Riannon—when every sense confirmed that Riannon had come back to her alive—Eleanor began to weep. She let all her sadness and fears sob out of herself at last. Her tears wet Riannon's shirt. Riannon held her and murmured to her until Eleanor quieted. Then, finally, Eleanor was able to slip into the peace of sleep.

❖

Eleanor stood at the window watching the dawn and waiting for servants to bring up the food tray she had ordered. Alan had tactfully scrambled into his clothes and departed the chamber. Behind her, Riannon slept. This was how Eleanor wished she could always start a day. She might not greet another morning this way.

The queen had directed the chancellor himself to oversee the negotiation of the marriage contract and ensure a speedy settlement. For reasons of her own, which Eleanor did not believe had any connection with the desire to be present at the ceremony herself, the queen wished them married in a hurry. It could be but a matter of days. She ought to consider herself fortunate that the queen insisted they make a contract, for it was not always the case with swift marriages. Eleanor had more to protect than most. She needed to safeguard her own lands so that they reverted to her control on Geoffrey's death, should he sire no children on her. Unscrupulous heirs were not above claiming the widow's lands as their late father's.

She frowned past the shutter at the brightening sky. By the time this day faded into twilight, she might have signed the contract and be betrothed. She suspected Riannon would decline to continue their physical relationship at that point. The knight who did not claim for herself the name of highest renown would not use sophistry and lawyers' arguments to pick apart shades of adultery for her own convenience.

Eleanor would, though.

"Nell?"

"I'm here."

Eleanor strode back through the bed curtains. Riannon looked stiff and unusually awkward as she moved.

"Stay there," Eleanor said. "Servants are bringing food for us to break our night fasts."

Riannon frowned. "This is my chamber, love."

"I know it. And so do my household. You don't think that a single one of them will be ignorant of our intimacy ere this night?"

"Your honour is at stake. Lady—"

Eleanor silenced her with a kiss. "Now, lie back and let me look after you. Like a good, modest woman should."

Riannon grinned. "Would your notions of goodness and modesty require you to join me in this bed?"

Eleanor smiled and propped a pillow behind Riannon. "After the servants have left. Then I'll have you at my mercy."

Riannon gave Eleanor's night braid a playful tweak.

Eleanor doubted Riannon's fitness for any bed sport, but did climb back into bed to share the meal that the servants brought. She derived immense satisfaction from feeding Riannon. All the while, she was conscious of a shadow voice at the back of her mind whispering that this might be the last time.

Eleanor put part of a wafer in her mouth and turned to Riannon. After a moment to understand the invitation, Riannon bent to put her mouth to the wafer. They kissed and bit off the wafer between them. Crumbs fell into the sheets. Eleanor didn't care. She laughed and snuggled closer to Riannon to claim a proper kiss.

"Hmm," Riannon said. "Good, but not quite as tasty as a cheese wafer."

Eleanor hit her good shoulder. "Then I'll leave you to make love to the food."

As she expected, Riannon grabbed her and prevented her leaving the bed. Eleanor, mindful of Riannon's wound, offered only gentle and short-lived resistance before yielding to another long, deepening kiss. Eleanor's blood stirred and heated between her legs, but Riannon sagged unhappily against the pillows.

"I'm sorry, love," Riannon said. "I don't think I could manage it this morning."

"Does it pain you?"

"No. Truly. The discomfort is no more than you'd expect. I swear it."

Eleanor tore her gaze from Riannon's shoulder and nodded. "I'm so eternally grateful that you're alive. I prayed so hard. There was little I didn't offer the gods in return for that."

"I hope you didn't pledge chastity."

Eleanor smiled. "Considering how quickly I've come to your bed, that virtue would have bought me not even the merest sliver of divine favour, would it?"

"It'd be ungallant of me to make any remark to the disparagement of your chastity, would it not?"

"Extremely! Since you are the cause of my incontinence."

L-J BAKER

"For which I'm wholly and utterly unrepentant."

"Thank the gods!" Eleanor said.

Riannon laughed. Eleanor caught herself trying to memorise the sound. The more she tried not to think about it, the more aware she grew of how short a time they had together.

"Now why do you look so sad?" Riannon asked.

Eleanor could not summon a merry remark or rally her spirits. She traced the contours of the unscarred side of Riannon's face.

"Whenever I wake in the night," Eleanor said, "I want to be able to feel your smile."

Riannon frowned. "There must be something we can do."

Eleanor sighed and shook her head. She looked around for the wine cup. "I've been beating my brains. If only you had been a man."

Riannon stiffened and the defences slammed into place. Eleanor put her hand over Riannon's fist.

"I do not mean that I'd love you any more, had you been a man," Eleanor said. "For certès, I've no desire for a cock and balls. You give me intimate pleasure I'd barely dreamed of beneath a man. And I've no fear that you'll leave me with the pustules of some disease that will canker my womb again. No, I'd have you no way other than exactly as you are."

"Then why the regretful remark about a man?"

"Because I might've married you. Clandestinely and quickly. Not even the queen could force me to commit bigamy."

Riannon scowled, but she relaxed her fist and interleaved her fingers with Eleanor's. "We owe fealty to the queen."

"I know. Were we to defy her in such a way, it'd cost us dear. The queen couldn't let us cross her without punishment. Fines, loss of land, mayhap even loss of liberty for a time." Eleanor set her cup aside and turned fully to Riannon. "But we would've been together."

"We could run away. I could take you to some of those foreign lands you yearn to see."

Eleanor leaned her head against Riannon's good shoulder and stared up at the hangings. "You'd throw me across your saddle and we'd ride off together into the sunset? Perhaps Master Nuon would compose a song for us. We could live on that instead of manchet bread."

"I'd not let you starve."

Eleanor hugged Riannon's arm. "I know. But you barely earn

• 220 •

enough to keep your squire and horses fed. How would you fare with a highly expensive lover?"

"I'd find a way. Mayhap a prince would pay well for the services of the Vahldomne, rather than Riannon of Gast."

"You'd do that for me?"

"There is little I'd not do for you."

Eleanor felt awe as a lump in her throat. "Oh, Nonnie, what did I ever do to deserve your love?"

"You are you."

Eleanor smiled and kissed the base of Riannon's throat. Riannon smelled strongly of sweat, but it was not unpleasant. It was a smell that Eleanor would always remember.

"I don't know how I'll bear losing you," Eleanor said, "but knowing that you'll be out there somewhere, alive, is a thousand times more endurable than having only a memory and wishing to be haunted by a beloved ghost."

"Why can we not run away?"

Eleanor smiled sadly. "Because we are not eighteen years old with our heads stuffed full of troubadours' songs. Because you are you, and I am I."

Riannon tensed.

"Beloved," Eleanor said, "you and I can dream, but we're old enough to know ourselves and to know dream from what is and what might be. Could you break your oath of homage to your liege lady? Could you break your sworn word and service to the Order of the Goddess? Running away with me would mean both."

Riannon's jaw worked. Eleanor touched it gently.

"No more than I could ride away from everything I own," Eleanor said. "I hold my responsibilities dear. Running my estates, managing them, making decisions about leasing, renting, buying new properties, investments, the welfare of my retainers, and all the other myriad things I oversee and control. That's a great part of who I am. I enjoy it and derive great satisfaction from it all. I could no more give that up for a tenuous hand-to-mouth existence than you could pick a goose girl and make her queen. And what would become of me if something happened to you? Would you have me begging? Or whoring myself for meals?"

Riannon glared at her. "Never! You cannot believe—"

"No. I do not." Eleanor stroked Riannon's cheek. "Not by choice.

But what if you became injured or ill and couldn't earn our meat? What would become of us then?"

"You want to marry him?"

"No! Oh, gods, no." Eleanor sighed and made a despairing gesture. "But I can think of nothing else to do. Can you? Fancies and wishes I have in surfeit, but of a real solution I cannot even see its footprints across my mind, let alone stand close enough to grasp it. I'm at my wits' end. But I'm not blinded by folly. We cannot eat love."

❖

Aveline watched her sister pacing. Mathilda snatched her cup off a shelf and hurled it against the far wall. The wooden vessel cracked and left a dark stain on the beautiful tapestry hanging.

"I don't want a cursed war!" Mathilda said. "A plague on the emperor! A plague on that ambassador! A plague on our damned cousin Riannon. Why could she not have stuck to spinning and needlecraft like other girls?"

Aveline sipped her wine calmly as the queen strode about the room. "Your lands share no border with the empire."

"Surely you don't think a hundred miles of Iruland will be a barrier to the emperor's legions!" Mathilda emphasised her words with wild gestures with her fists. "I cannot afford a war! Henry and the other idiotic hotspurs are all rattling their swords and frothing at the mouth about the bloody Vahldomne leading them to glory. A pox on men! A pox on glory! We need a good harvest, not a fucking war!"

"Your treasury wouldn't be unduly drained by a war," Aveline said.

"That oily ambassador with his adder's tongue will pour lies into the Lion Emperor's ears about the death of that fat dolt with the tattoo, and the next thing you know there'll be a hundred thousand accursed infidels stomping into my lands, burning and pillaging for vengeance. If only I hadn't agreed to let that poxed ambassador come! I knew no good would come of it." Mathilda jabbed a finger at her sister. "I blame you for this!"

"Yes."

Mathilda stared, nonplussed.

Aveline set her cup aside. "There will be a war. But you'll not have to finance it beyond a grand gesture of support. It'll be a crusade."

Mathilda's expression brightened. "Crusade?"

"All those dangerous hotheads—those landless and feckless young men you find so troublesome—will throw themselves into a holy war for the reclamation of Evriat. They can gorge themselves on glory and loot well away from your lands. And keep the emperor far too busy to bother you."

Mathilda looked thoughtful and began twisting her coronation ring. "If this is to be, then mayhap Henry was right."

"About what?"

"Riannon. He has urged me to grant her a manor or two. To more firmly tie the Vahldomne's allegiance to me, rather than let Fulk of Iruland snap her up as one of his leading vassals. Yes." Mathilda nodded. "Especially if this crusade does win back some of Evriat. You know Fulk will want to claim lordship of it for himself. Greedy whoreson. At least we should keep the Vahldomne as our own."

"It's a sound idea," Aveline said. "But, I warn you, she'll be leaving on crusade. However, I see no trouble with her being a leading member of the Tirandese contingent as well as the representative of my order."

Mathilda nodded and looked around. Aveline offered her own wine cup. Her sister took it and drank.

"Or I could marry her off," Mathilda said. "That'd be even cheaper than using some of those properties I escheated from that prick Greywater. I must have a ward I can use. Though, he'd need to be an unusual lad, do you not think?"

Aveline smiled as she rose. "If you'd wanted to endow her that way, we've already used up the ideal marital candidate. Now, I must be away. I've business at the grove. I'll return to join you after your afternoon ride."

Aveline strolled to the door.

"Who?" Mathilda said.

"For Riannon?" Aveline asked. "Eleanor of Barrowmere."

Mathilda's mouth fell open. "You...you jest!"

"What makes you think that?"

"They're both women. Although, I suppose our cousin might be something in betwixt male and female. For certès, she is not feminine." Mathilda gave an exaggerated shudder. "It makes me feel unclean to think about such unnatural things."

Aveline stared at her. "Why do you think you have no bastard nieces and nephews from me?"

Mathilda scowled at her. The moment of her realising Aveline's meaning was as transparent as if a flame leaped to life behind her eyes and set her brain on fire.

"Just so," Aveline said.

❖

Aveline sat back on her heels and dried her wet hands on the sleeves of her robe.

"Victory on all fronts," she said. "And wheels set in motion for continuing rewards."

She rose and stared down at her reflection in the holiest pool. She saw merely her image, but she remembered herself as matriarch. One day, she would stand thus at the edge of the Cave of the Pool in northern Evriat. The holy site would be recaptured and re-consecrated. Perhaps she might be matriarch then. She could be the one to draw power from the holiest of waters. If only half the tales of the power of the cave pool were true, she would be able to tug on threads of divine magic beyond the imagining of most mortals. She could bathe the world in the might of the Dark-Faced One. And then…let the emperor, and his legions, and his tattooed witch-priest warriors with their puny powers, all tremble before the might of the Goddess.

Aveline's reflection smiled back up at her.

She grew aware of not being alone. She turned to see a junior priestess standing at the entrance to the clearing.

"Yes?" Aveline said.

The priestess curtsied. "Forgive me, Eminence. The Vahldomne waits to speak with you."

Aveline's eyebrow arched. "Escort her to the pool of contemplation."

The priestess hurried off. Aveline cast a frown down at her reflection. Perhaps Riannon needed more healing. If so, it was unlikely she would come here and wish to talk with Aveline.

Riannon paced the clearing. She wore her left arm in a sling and the gift sword at her hip. Aveline thought better of a remark about

Riannon's having recourse to it to win her duel.

"Your legs have suffered no hurt, I see," Aveline said.

Riannon turned a fierce frown on her. "You have what you wanted."

"The duel? True. I daresay the outcome was to your liking, too."

Something behind Riannon's expression hardened. Aveline took note of the warning.

"Not that the Goddess's cause could have failed to emerge victorious," Aveline said. "You served the Goddess well and earned yourself no small reward. Two days ago, any man who spoke of Riannon of Gast did so with revulsion. Today, I only hear admiration and wonder when those same men speak of the Vahldomne. I see that you've even regained your family and Henry has clasped you to his burly bosom. Why the grim look? Is this not what you've always wanted?"

"You have influence with the queen," Riannon said. "If you bear me any gratitude, or if she truly wishes to engage my thanks, have the marriage of Lady Eleanor stopped."

Aveline took a couple of heartbeats to recover from surprise. "Well, cousin, you certainly have a way with frontal assaults."

Riannon stepped closer and looked down at Aveline. "I have bled for you. You can do this thing for me."

"Actually, your service, as you've reminded me more than once, is to the Lady of Creation, not to me."

"Whatever her Grace needs that old man to do, let me do it instead and leave Lady Eleanor alone."

Aveline frowned. "You're smitten with her?"

"The lady wouldn't be happy wed to a man old enough to have whored with her father." Riannon's jaw muscles worked. "Why can the queen not marry her to Guy?"

"Would that be more palatable to you? Imagining your brother with—"

Riannon's large hand clamped around Aveline's throat. Aveline could all but taste the violence her cousin barely contained. She remembered yesterday. Once Riannon had negated the witch-priest's supernatural sword, she had killed him quickly. She might be the perfect weapon that Aveline would wield again for the order, but a sword had two edges. She had spoken more truly than she realised with her casual remark to Mathilda about Riannon and Eleanor.

"You credit me with more power over my sister than I have," Aveline said. "I'm not even on her privy council."

Riannon's hand withdrew. Aveline resisted the urge to massage her throat.

"You could speak with her," Riannon said. "If you chose to."

"I can try," Aveline said. "What would you have me say? That you want Lady Eleanor unwed so that you can bed with her?"

Riannon glared and strode to the pool. Her right hand clenched tightly into a fist.

"Your purpose lies elsewhere," Aveline said. "Holy war is coming. You and I, our kind, have no place in the mundane world of domesticity. Especially not we two. Remember your higher purpose. Your rewards will be the divine favour that many dream of but few earn."

When Riannon turned, her expression was grim and obdurate. She stalked across the clearing and past Aveline like she faced another death duel. She halted three paces beyond Aveline.

"Can our kind marry?" Riannon asked.

"You wish me to persuade my sister to find a husband for you?"

"No. I want to know if I can take a wife."

Aveline was too taken aback to try to conceal it.

"Is marriage betwixt two women or two men forbidden, or just not done?" Riannon asked.

Aveline's mind raced along different paths of possibility simultaneously. She addressed what she thought Riannon intended. "The Lady Eleanor is already pledged to Lord Howe."

Riannon strode away. Her long legs swiftly carried her along the path between the trees.

Aveline frowned. This could be dangerous. She had best hurry to Mathilda. Get that marriage solemnised before Riannon tried anything foolish. And have Riannon feoffed with those manors, if only to make her undergo another ceremony of homage. Riannon needed a reminder that she served the queen's will. The last impediment Aveline's plans needed was her paladin outlawed or imprisoned because of a woman.

CHAPTER SIXTEEN

When Riannon stepped into the garden, Eleanor's posture confirmed her fears about the betrothal. Despite the heat of a summer's day and her shoulder burning with a growing ache, Riannon felt cold. She strode along the neatly clipped path between herb beds. Eleanor turned. She had been weeping.

"Hold me, Nonnie."

Riannon slipped her good arm around Eleanor. Eleanor clung to her. The scintillating blue of the cloudless sky mocked their tiny island of misery. Riannon wanted Fate to appear before her in human form. She would do her damnedest to cut the slippery trickster apart.

"When is it to be?" Riannon asked.

"The sixteenth."

"Shite. So soon."

"Hear me." Eleanor looked up. "Whatever happens is not the choice of either of us. Given the freedom, our immediate futures would be together. Believe me when I tell you that neither he nor anyone will reach that part of me from whence love springs. You are there at the root of it, where it is purest and strongest. Where no one has dwelled before."

"Marry me," Riannon said.

Eleanor's eyes snapped wide.

"You said that if I were a man," Riannon said, "we could marry and prevent this. I am not a man nor ever could be. But why must that stop us marrying?"

Eleanor frowned as she considered this. She shook her head. "Man or woman, we're still vassals of the queen. We'd still be breaking our oaths to her. Could you really do that? And we know not what punishment she would mete out."

"I...Shite. Yes, I want to do this."

"Truly?" Eleanor said. "Just four days ago, you risked your life rather than break your sworn word."

Riannon ground her frustration between her teeth. "I cannot bear the thought of you unhappy."

"Nor I you. And you would be, if you did this thing for me. Not at first, mayhap. But what about later? As the years passed, you'd brood on the stain on your honour. The disgrace would not lessen with time. You'd blame me."

Riannon shook her head. "I've always lived with the consequences of what I do."

"Beloved, I know." Eleanor touched Riannon's face. "But what if those years passed for you in captivity?"

"I'm useful to the queen. As the Vahldomne. She may be lenient because of it."

"That's true. But I'm not particularly useful, aside from as a pawn." Eleanor squeezed Riannon's hand. "You've no idea how tempted I am. A future with you. But my head tells me, while my heart and other bodily parts are lost in their blissful fancy, that we're deluding ourselves. Even if we were to marry—and I'm not at all sure that we could—I'd wager such an unusual ceremony could be quickly annulled. Forget not that the queen has a naer for a sister who'd be capable of discharging that for her most expeditiously. And where would that leave us?"

Riannon scowled down at the path, where Eleanor's hem draped over the toe of her boot. "You sound like you don't wish us to try."

"I'm being realistic, beloved. And you know it."

Riannon did not want to admit it.

She had surrendered before. It was the honourable course in the face of overwhelming force. But she had so much at stake now. There must be a way, while she had strength and breath.

"Come and sit." Eleanor drew Riannon towards a bench. "You need to rest, however much you protest. Let me have Agnes fetch my lute and I'll sing to you. Then you can tell me more tales from outlandish places you've been. This afternoon is ours. We'll enjoy each other's company and forget that life can be other than the two of us together. Tomorrow, and all the tomorrows, can wait."

Riannon obediently sat, though every fibre futilely vibrated with frustrated purpose. This was one problem she could not solve with a sword.

"We'll be like one of those beautiful pages in a breviary," Eleanor said. "The ones which show a couple in a garden under a lapis lazuli blue sky. Whenever I open a book and see such a gorgeous picture, I'll again be here with you, the woman I love."

Riannon lifted Eleanor's hand to kiss. The idea that she would not be able to do so in a few days' time defied all belief. She studied Eleanor's face. Eleanor was dearer to her than even the cherished idea of the woman who had died bearing Riannon—the only person she had believed might have loved her.

Dear, but not dearer than honour. Or was she? Could Riannon cast aside every principle that had sustained her through her contrary life? Could she trample those years of striving and adversity for love? Everything that Riannon had become, through all the struggles that shaped her, was founded upon a bedrock of her belief in her sworn word, her rectitude, and living the truth of the word of the gods. Never had she stained her own honour in her dealings with men or women of any station. No matter what other calumnies men levelled at her, or how they reviled her, none could ever impugn her integrity. Eleanor was right—Riannon had risked death rather than dishonour.

Love, too, was such a fickle emotion. It could afflict strongly one day, then leave after but a few weeks or months, or sicken and wither. Was it a sound basis for building a secure future? Perhaps not, but…

"Does your shoulder pain you?" Eleanor asked.

Riannon shook her head. Caring not who might see, she bent to kiss Eleanor. Eleanor slipped her arms around Riannon's neck. Riannon had often wished she could have been other than she was, but never more acutely than at that moment.

❖

Riannon would rather have been a thousand miles away, but Eleanor had asked her to attend.

Nonnie, please be there. Let me see that, even though I must do this thing, you'll still be with me in some part.

So, Riannon, standing beside Guy and surrounded by her family, watched Eleanor marry Geoffrey of Howe.

Eleanor looked pale but strikingly handsome in her scarlet kirtle. No one looking at her could doubt why anyone would want to marry her. She was beautiful and wealthy, with a reputation for generous hospitality and lively charm. To those attractions Riannon could add many more—facets of Eleanor's character which had unfolded to love and intimacy.

Riannon stood ten feet from the most splendid woman the gods had created and did nothing to stop her from marrying an old man. No sword cut wounded her deeper, or left sharper seeds of misery, than the brief glance Eleanor cast her way when Lord Howe slipped the ring on her finger.

"You were right," Guy said to Riannon. "I'm a fool."

Not nearly as big a fool as me.

Riannon let Guy guide her to the hall decorated for the wedding feast. She numbly acknowledged the greetings of men and women who had ignored her at the last wedding feast she had attended—before they knew her to be the Vahldomne. Even Cicely offered her a meek hello.

Riannon could not stop watching Eleanor. The way she walked. How she gestured with her hands as she spoke. That slight tilt of the head as she considered something. Riannon did not need to see Eleanor's face to know exactly how her lips curved when she smiled, or how her whole face radiated joy when she laughed. Not that Eleanor did much laughing that day.

"Vahldomne, how honoured I am that I can boast of your presence on this happy occasion."

Riannon dragged her attention from the figure in red across the hall to the man before her. Lord Howe smiled up at her.

"When a man marries," he said, "it's a privilege to gain new relations and friends. I'm fortunate beyond most men in that I not only gain a charming bride, but the most illustrious of family connections, and acquaintances that must make me the envy of all."

He spoke courteously and with good humour. Riannon hated him. She loathed him so strongly that it threatened to choke her. She could barely bring herself to offer him a polite nod of acknowledgement. Even more than she despised him, she reviled herself. There must have been something she could have done to prevent this.

One of the entertainments was, again, the famous troubadour, Raoul de Nuon. Riannon sat through his smoothly powerful rendition of the traditional wedding song. Then, just as he had done at Henry's wedding, he sang of Vahl. Riannon frowned down at the table and let it wash over her. The wine in her cup might as well have been sand. At the conclusion, the cheers broke out again. This time they were clearly directed at Riannon. Even the arrogant troubadour himself bowed to her before acknowledging the cheers for his performance. The acclaim, which every young aspirant to knighthood and fame dreamed of, echoed hollowly through the hero.

Riannon watched Eleanor dance with her husband. She bled inside.

Guy danced with Eleanor and made her smile. But even he had never seen that soft, glowing look left on Eleanor's face from the turbulence of her sexual climax.

"They make a handsome couple," Joan said.

Riannon nodded.

"I wish that brother of ours had more resolution," Joan said. "The lady would have been a prize for him. And they are such good friends. It seems a grievous waste that Lady Eleanor go to so old and inactive a man."

Riannon wondered if she would feel any better if Eleanor had married her brother. She would not have wanted to hate Guy as she despised Geoffrey.

The music ended.

"I'm surprised that the lady wasn't given to the son," Joan said. "Though, for the lady's sake, I cannot help being thankful it isn't so."

Riannon did not care about Ralph of Howe. Another dance began to form. She passed her cup to her sister and strode towards Eleanor. People watched her and moved aside for her. Some bowed and curtsied to the Vahldomne.

"This must be my dance, madam," Ralph Howe said to Eleanor. "Since you refused me your hand in—"

"She is promised to me," Riannon said.

Ralph scowled up at her. "You're a woman, so they say. You have no business dancing with my father's wife."

Riannon stared down at the rude whoreson. "They say other things about me, too. Do you wish to test them?"

Eleanor put her hand on Riannon's arm and tugged. "I'm promised to the Vahldomne. Mayhap a later time, Ralph?"

Riannon resisted Eleanor's pull while she returned Ralph's stare. Despite her shoulder, and despite the disgrace it would cause, part of her wanted him to give her an excuse to vent her self-loathing fury on someone.

"Just the man I wished to find." Guy slapped a comradely hand on Ralph's shoulder. "My brother, the Earl Marshal, is talking about horses. Come and tell us what you know."

Ralph wavered. He was clearly flattered, but he looked reluctant to let himself be drawn away from Riannon.

Eleanor dug her fingers into Riannon's forearm. Riannon finally turned and dismissed Ralph from her thoughts. Eleanor looked worried. Riannon awkwardly moved her arm across in her sling to softly touch Eleanor's fingers digging into her forearm. *I love you!* A softening of Eleanor's expression showed she heard the unspoken cry.

Riannon did not care who watched or how many tongues she set wagging by dancing with the bride. Ralph Howe might be fool enough to challenge her to her face, but no one else in that hall was. For as long as pipes, lute, drums, and tabor played the tune, she had Eleanor to herself again.

Through their innocent touches—hand to hand as the dance dictated—they reassured each other that, no matter what drove them apart, there remained a part of themselves that would belong to the other. A piece of Riannon might have shrivelled as she watched Eleanor speak her vow that gave herself to Geoffrey of Howe, but that part was not Riannon's love for Eleanor. Only after the music stopped and people moved between them did Riannon realise that they had spoken not a word to each other during the dance.

From the time when her mother had died giving birth to her, Riannon had largely lived alone. A priestess and wet nurse had raised her in isolated Gast, because her grieving father could not bear the sight of the babe who had killed his cherished wife. Outcast, her adult life had followed a singular path. She knew what it felt like when men who had called her friend, and fought shoulder to shoulder with her, spurned her as a woman and creature unnatural. Never, though, had she felt more searingly lonely than in the middle of a hall loud with merriment, with her name warm on every second pair of lips, as she watched a group of laughing women draw Eleanor away to the nuptial chamber. Eleanor met her eyes for one look of distilled regret.

A raucous cheer heralded the second part of Riannon's torture. In loud, tipsy voices, men encouraged Geoffrey of Howe to join his new wife. They shouted crude suggestions as to what he should do to her.

Riannon wanted to kill. She could not stop herself imagining Eleanor in a bed somewhere close. Naked. Anointed with perfumes by her female attendants. Her glorious hair brushed and loose about her shoulders. Lying in bed, waiting for him.

With a cheer, men lifted Geoffrey on their shoulders. They carried him towards one of the doors.

They would strip him and bundle him into the bed with Eleanor. Her Eleanor. His now. His to do with as he wanted.

Riannon closed her eyes against the pain. "I was wrong. Gods, I've made the biggest mistake of my life."

Too late.

Guy put a hand on her shoulder. He looked as serious and unhappy as Riannon had ever seen him.

"I'm going to get drunk," he said. "Coming?"

"Yes."

CHAPTER SEVENTEEN

Riannon dismounted in the courtyard of Barrowmere House. A few days ago, she had lived here with Eleanor. Now she was a visitor to Lady Howe. Lord Howe had wasted no time in moving into the large and comfortable property he controlled as Eleanor's husband.

Strange servants moved about the hall.

"Vahldomne!" Lord Howe strode towards her. "How pleased I am to welcome you to our home. You honour us greatly. Please, take your ease. Servants! Bring wine! My wife said that you'd be no stranger to us."

He smiled toothlessly through his white beard and gestured for her to take a seat.

Riannon didn't move. "Is Eleanor here?"

"I'll have her fetched." He signalled to a page boy. "She'll be right pleased to welcome you. We'd have been honoured had you remained a guest under our roof. Please, will you not sit?"

As little as she wanted to be anywhere near him, Riannon knew she would be serving herself and Eleanor an ill turn with churlish behaviour. She stepped across to the padded bench. Lord Howe lowered himself with visible effort.

"I hope your wound heals well," he said. "I could scarce believe my eyes when I watched your combat with that imperial dog. In all my years, I've not seen a blow as mighty as the one you delivered to fell him. Cut his leg clean off! Oh ho! I've lost count of the songs I've heard about the Vahldomne's mighty courage and skill, but I confess that I thought most of them the exaggeration of these songsters. Now I know they spoke only the truth. Here is the wine at last. My wife has an excellent supply of Rhânish white."

Riannon accepted a cup, though she had no intention of drinking. She wanted him to go away.

"Your health!" He lifted his cup in salute.

Eleanor walked across the hall. Riannon stood. Colour sprang back into a world leached of all but jealous greys.

"Ah," Geoffrey said. "There you are, my dear."

Riannon gritted her teeth.

Eleanor smiled at her. Riannon ached to hold her, to put her arms around Eleanor and pull her tightly against her chest. Lord Howe reached up to put a hand on Eleanor's arm. Riannon tasted black bile.

"You see we have a most illustrious visitor," he said. "I was about to tell the Vahldomne, my dear, that she is a most welcome guest at any time. And at any of our estates."

"Yes, of course," Eleanor said. "I believe she knows it already."

Eleanor must know that Riannon was unlikely to accept such an invitation.

"Come and sit with us, my dear." He drew Eleanor down onto the bench between himself and Riannon.

Riannon sat. Her calf brushed the skirts of Eleanor's overtunic. But the hand which rested on Eleanor's arm was not hers. Lord Howe's gnarled, callused fingers curled in comfortable possessiveness on Eleanor's sleeve. An old man's hand with wrinkled skin and brown spots. Riannon could easily force him away from Eleanor. She could break his arm. Or cut it off. Aveline's witch-sword would slice the old man into pieces before he had a chance to raise himself on his gouty knees.

"Vahldomne?"

Riannon wrenched her attention up to his smug face. She had not the faintest notion what he asked.

"Are you not supposed to be meeting your son this morn, my lord?" Eleanor said. "Let us not detain you. You'd not wish to keep Ralph waiting. You may trust me to entertain Lady Riannon."

"Oh," he said. "Very well. I'll persuade Ralph to join us at table, my dear. You'll excuse me, Vahldomne. It's always a pleasure to welcome you."

He rose slowly and touched Eleanor's shoulder before walking away. Men of his household swirled out after him.

"It gladdens me to see you," Eleanor said. "I hoped you'd come. It's not to say farewell, is it?"

Riannon studied her. Every curve, every hair, every expression was so precious. And belonged to him.

"Nonnie?" Eleanor put a hand on Riannon's thigh.

"Has he slept here? With you? In your bed where we—"

"Don't!"

Riannon turned away to glare at the rushes on the floor. Eleanor's fingers gently squeezed her thigh.

"Sorting out our households and a new schedule for travelling between our manors will take some time," Eleanor said. "But he is anxious to visit Waterbury, so we'll be departing soon. What are your plans? I heard that the queen has given you lucrative property. It doesn't surprise me. Your services are too valuable to let slip into the hands of a different master. Nonnie? Will you not even look at me? Or let me look at you?"

Riannon turned. Eleanor looked drawn and sad. Gods, how had she let this happen?

"He's not a bad man," Eleanor said. "He treats me with courtesy and kindness."

"Aveline says there is to be a crusade."

Eleanor frowned. "I'd heard rumour of such, but knew not how much substance there was to it. Or if it was wishful thinking spurred by the presence of the emperor's men and your victory. You'll be going to war?"

Riannon stared down at Eleanor's hand still resting on her thigh. She laid her hand over the top. She whispered, "I cannot bear to see him touch you. How can you let him?"

"He's my husband." Eleanor dug her fingers into Riannon's thigh and lowered her voice. "We knew what it would mean. I've told you that it makes no difference to how I feel about you."

"I want to kill him."

"He won't live forever. Remember that. I know you'll do nought rash or ignoble, no matter how strongly you feel. Beloved, this is no easier for me than you."

Riannon nodded. She watched her thumb stroke the back of Eleanor's hand. "I think it'd be best if I went away."

"You'll not forget me?"

"When they cut my heart out for burial, they'll find your name engraved on it."

"I'll pray that this marvel won't be exposed to the world for many, many years."

Riannon heard the tease in Eleanor's voice and looked up to see Eleanor's smile. It was a lover's smile with shared secrets at the corners of her lips. For a couple of heartbeats, time wound back several days. Eleanor was correct—nothing that happened now would change what had been. Riannon grinned and lifted Eleanor's hand to kiss her fingers.

"You'll keep yourself safe?" Eleanor said. "And come back to me?"

"I'll be back, love."

❖

Aveline prepared to climb into the litter when she saw Riannon ride into the grove house courtyard. She stopped to watch. Riannon dismounted and strode across to her. Aveline wondered if Riannon's shoulder wound pained her, for she looked grey and taut.

"I would speak with you," Riannon said.

Aveline signalled her escort to remain and stepped away towards the privacy of the woods. Riannon strode at her side.

"I leave on the morrow to travel to Wermouth to visit the grove house there and the mother-naer," Aveline said. "I assume you'll wish to see your new lands and organise the bailiffs. I'll be travelling to the convocation in Rhân next month, and thence to the Quatorum Council. I expect you to join me and accompany me."

Aveline had already savoured several different scenarios for breaking the news to Matriarch Melisande, and the mother-naers in attendance, that she had secured as the paladin of the order no less a person than the Vahldomne. In combination with Katherine of Fourport's sponsorship, and some judicial bribery, she saw Riannon as the key to her election to the next vacancy amongst the mother-naers. The Goddess's will would be done.

Riannon halted and looked around. They stood alone between the trees.

"I need something," Riannon said.

Aveline waited. Riannon's behaviour in the last several days had given her some dangerous surprises.

"You make charms," Riannon said.

"The Goddess has seen fit to endow her initiated daughters with the ability to channel specific blessings, yes. What do you desire?"

"Something to make a man impotent."

Aveline made no attempt to conceal her astonishment as she grappled with imagining what use such a thing might be to Riannon. After several heartbeats, she conceded defeat. "Why?"

"Does it matter?"

"I suppose that—Howe." Aveline stared at Riannon. "Shite. You want the charm to make Lady Eleanor's husband incapable of coupling with her."

Riannon's expression chilled to frosty bleakness. "I'll go on this crusade for you. I'll do all you wish. Make this thing for me."

Aveline wondered if she should. Such items were common for women who had borne many children and wished no more, or where the health of the woman was not strong enough to bear the burden of pregnancy and childbirth. Neither applied to Lady Eleanor.

"I will do anything," Riannon said.

Aveline needed her paladin. She must bind Riannon, the Vahldomne, close to her and not let her fall under the sway of anyone else in the order. The marriage between the barren Lady Eleanor and an old man was unlikely to be blessed with children. Unexpectedly, Aveline found herself wondering how it would be for a woman—and especially one who loved women—to submit herself in the bed of Lord Howe.

"Come." Aveline led the way through the trees. "I need some of your blood and the water of the holiest pond."

CHAPTER EIGHTEEN

Eleanor watched slanting rain fall as she played her lute. A mild winter had melted into a soggy spring. She wished she looked out from the oriel window in the hall at Barrowmere, but Geoffrey, for his own reasons, insisted they come to Tarby. Instead of beautifully fertile rolling hills, woods, and fields sprouting the green stubble of young crops, she looked across a dismal rocky landscape and a grey lake.

Small wonder the castle felt so damp that the very stones of the walls might be weeping. No amount of wood in the fires defeated the knifing draughts that made her ankles ache and aggravated Geoffrey's joint ague.

She wondered what the land around Gast looked like. Though, the last she had heard, Riannon had not tarried long in Tirand. Eleanor had received a letter written by a paid scribe and delivered by a mendicant priest of Naith. Riannon had been with Aveline, who had attended the Quatorum Council. From that autumn meeting, the call to crusade had unfurled across the Eastern Kingdoms like Atuan's own war banner.

Riannon would have to cross Tirand in travelling west to Iruland. Eleanor had hoped and prayed that Riannon would visit her. She was disappointed, but not wholly surprised, that Riannon had not come. The part of her that wore the charmed ring Riannon had given her understood why Riannon could not bear to see her with her husband. But that did not stop her wanting and craving to see Riannon again. They had sparked a conflagration in those few weeks last summer whose embers yet glowed within Eleanor. Had they dimmed in Riannon?

"That's a plaintive melody," Phillipa said. "We must not succumb to melancholy at the thought of my husband's departure. He isn't gone yet."

Eleanor would not dream of enlightening her new stepdaughter-in-law by informing her that Ralph's imminent departure to join the crusade was the one bright spot on her rainy horizon.

"You're right." Eleanor dragged her attention back into the chamber and began picking out a more lively tune. "I should be merry, especially when the weather isn't."

"And, if my prayers have worked, we have cause for celebration." Phillipa patted her stomach.

Not for the first time, Eleanor faced the question of whether Phillipa hid a thin, sharp claw of spite inside the passive folds of her nature. Since Eleanor had been married half a year longer than Phillipa, without any quickening of her womb, Phillipa's comment might be considered barbed. Eleanor guessed that Ralph lived in fear of her producing sons who might compete with him for his inheritance. She wouldn't even be surprised to learn that he had convinced himself that his wicked young stepmother planned to work on her elderly husband to persuade him to supplant Ralph entirely. Ralph was that stupid, held his father in such contempt, and disliked Eleanor that much.

As it was, Eleanor took no hurt from Phillipa's oblique slight on her womb. Her history had not been fertile, beginning with three early miscarriages in her first marriage. Lionel had been far more successful at giving her doses of the pox than a child. She had no real expectations that Geoffrey's older, weaker seed would take root where that of her two younger husbands had failed. Not that he proved diligent in visiting her bed nor in achieving his ends when he did. Though the charmed ring did not always render him incapable of gaining an erection, it did so often enough to leave his chances of siring a child on her all but non-existent—and to trouble her conscience.

A young page burst into the solar and slammed the door on the chilly breeze that chased him. "Lady, his lordship wants you to know that visitors have arrived. It's the Earl Marshal's brother."

Eleanor set aside her lute and smiled as she hurried to the hall. Men shook out their wet mantles and accepted cups of warmed wine. She spied the tallest with doubly familiar black hair.

Guy took both her hands and kissed her cheek. "The lady worth riding through any bad weather for. Now, seeing you, has spring truly begun for me."

"I think, my lord, that though the rain water has not dampened your spirits, it has wet more than your clothes," she said.

Guy laughed. "Leaked down through the cracks in my poor head, no doubt, to turn my wits soggy. Ah, you are a joy to see again."

The white crossed-circle badge sewn on the breast of his overtunic made clear where he was headed. Eleanor drew him to the main hearth and introduced him to Phillipa. She was amused to see Phillipa coyly smiling and responding to Guy's warm, easy charm. For certès, Phillipa received no such gentle attention from her husband.

"My lord!" Geoffrey limped across the hall. "You are a most welcome visitor. Whatever brings you our way, I'm grateful to it. Sit, sir. Please. Do you bring tidings of the crusade? I know my wife is as hungry as I for news, though she writes and receives letters from members of the Quatorum Council itself. It's to a man's credit that his wife occupy herself in such a way."

"Better that she busy herself so," Ralph said, "than meddling and interfering in a man's business."

Eleanor held her tongue, as she had learned to do, and watched Phillipa shrinking when Ralph dropped down beside her.

"You're the envy of many men," Guy said to Geoffrey. "You have a wife of learning and wit and beauty."

"I'm aware of my good fortune, sir." Geoffrey patted Eleanor's knee.

"A woman's true virtues are chastity, obedience, and the bearing of sons," Ralph said.

Phillipa paled and put a hand to her stomach as if his criticism had been levelled at her rather than Eleanor.

"You flatter us with the ability to work miracles," Eleanor said. "How could any chaste woman grow large with child? Methinks there are not angels enough to go around for the task."

Guy laughed. Ralph glowered.

"You're playful, my dear," Geoffrey said. "A woman's natural place is the hearth. That is indisputable. As a man's world is the governance and lordship of her and their lands. But I, for one, am not sorry for a little liveliness and learning in my wife."

❖

Eleanor stepped inside the gate Guy held open for her. The herb garden looked starkly bedraggled with little yet in the way of green fuzzy traces of returning life. Though the damp wind contained an icy edge, Eleanor was thankful to be outside of smoky chambers and alone with Guy.

"It gladdens my heart to see you comfortable," he said. "Still, I wager you'd make even purgatory seem a pleasant place."

"Not that you are like to test the truth of that, since I doubt me not you're destined for a place other than purgatory. And it'll be your tongue that takes you there."

Guy chuckled. "Aye. And sped on my way by the wishes of some who'd have me flayed in one of the hells. Ralph looks at me as though he's choosing which ribs to thrust his knife betwixt. Tell me how you think such a man as your husband begot such a dullard and boor?"

"I'm glad he leaves soon to join the crusade. Whence, I think, you go, too? Mayhap I should suggest that you travel in company?"

Guy swore. He used Riannon's favourite oath. Eleanor laughed.

"I'd feared that marriage would fetter you," Guy said. "It pleases me beyond words that this isn't the case."

Eleanor had no intentions of discussing her married life and its myriad petty irritations. "Have you news of your sister? The last letter I had from her was nigh on half a year ago. She said she'd be joining the crusade."

Guy nodded. "I go to join her. She's in Iruland. And in high favour with King Fulk and his son, Prince Oliver. You'd expect no less from the Vahldomne. The Irulandis have as many songs about her as the whore of Galston, which is fame indeed."

Eleanor laughed. "I'm sure Nonnie enjoys that."

"More than she'll enjoy the news that our brother, Henry, plans to be but a week or two behind me."

"The Earl Marshal crusades?"

"He expects to lead the crusade," Guy said. "I'll not deny him his skill in battle. If only his way with men was as good as with a lance."

"What of King Fulk?" Eleanor said. "Will he not be the natural leader?"

"For the little that my opinion is worth, we'll have a surfeit of leaders. You will pray for us, will you not?"

She smiled and linked her arm through his. "I've missed your company. Will you take a letter to Nonnie for me?"

"I'll even tell her to send you one in return."

Eleanor squeezed his arm and smiled.

Though he was a breath of fresh air in her stale life, and few men were better company, she could not help wishing he had been his sister. She had heard that whisper from deep inside before. It had not been quiet since the day she married Geoffrey. Every time he interfered with her management or dismissed one of her servants, the voice grew a little louder. Each time her conscience pricked her about wearing the ring that rendered him mostly impotent, the whisper reminded her why she kept it on her finger. As she strolled arm in arm with Guy, she could hear the whisper as clearly as if her longing had lent it to the wind swirling about the garden. *Riannon.*

❖

Aveline strode ahead of the women holding a canopy over her. A few drops of rain would not hurt, and she was impatient to be inside, sitting comfortably in a chair that did not sway and jolt, and sipping good wine. There were times, generally after several days stuck in her travelling carriage, when Aveline understood the lure of becoming a hermit or anchorite.

Still, she could hardly grudge this journey, as she headed towards the consecration of a new grove founded by her sister, Mathilda, at Aveline's suggestion. She would officiate as the principal assistant of Mother-Naer Katherine of Fourport. The revered lady's entourage rolled a mile or two behind Aveline's. Since the Quatorum Council meeting, Mother-Naer Katherine consulted Aveline on all important issues. Eleanor of Barrowmere was proving to be worth every penny of the two thousand marks a year of her income given to Lord Howe.

Aveline accepted the welcome of the senior priestess of the nondescript grove house. The chambers proved draughty and smoky. Although, when she sat down to supper, the food set before her was good. By providence or design, they served her favourite dish of eels.

Aveline relaxed near a warm hearth and enjoyed the performance of a startlingly pretty young priestess playing a cittern and singing. Perhaps this was a well chosen rest stop after all.

The way fortune's wheel turned for her this year, she would not be surprised to learn soon of a vacancy in the ranks of the twenty mother-naers to which her new patroness, Mother-Naer Katherine, could nominate her. It would not be an unusual eventuality, considering that most of the twenty were sixty years old and more. The Goddess's will would be done.

Aveline sipped her wine and contemplated success and an attractive bed mate.

A worried looking priestess interrupted. "Eminence, a messenger has come. He says it's of the utmost importance that he speak with you."

Aveline signalled that he could approach. He knelt before her chair and dripped water from his mantle.

"Exalted lady, Sio Nicola sent me with all haste to bring you tidings of the mother-naer," he said. "The Revered lady has suffered a palsy attack and lies stricken. They have sought shelter at Stonebridge. Sio Nicola says to tell you that she does not believe the Revered lady will live to see the dawn."

Aveline shot to her feet. "Have a horse saddled for me."

After a miserable ride through the deepening dark lashed by bands of stinging rain, Aveline strode behind a hunched priestess carrying a lamp. The light bobbed wildly along the dirty walls of the manor at Stonebridge, which proved little better than a glorified barn. Only direst need could have driven the mother-naer to choose this run down place for the night.

Katherine lay in a crude bed. A fresh candle burned in the niche in the bed head. Her flesh already had the bloodlessly yellowed look of a corpse. Her mouth hung open. Aveline could not hear the old woman breathing.

Sio Nicola, a muscular woman who looked more like a blacksmith than a senior priestess, rose from kneeling at the side of the bed. Rumour named her Katherine's granddaughter. Aveline could believe it. Nicola's lumpy, bovine features concealed the same razor-edged political acumen that had carried Katherine to the top ranks of the order. Nicola shook her head at Aveline.

Aveline gestured the blessing for the recently departed, then let her hands fall and stared at the corpse. There lay her best chance of selection to the convocation. Dead. Aveline had wanted a vacancy in the ranks of the twenty to fill, had she not? Well, there it was.

Shite.

Nicola lifted her hand and opened her fingers to offer what she held in her broad palm. Aveline looked at the silver ring set with chunky emeralds. Katherine's ring of office. Aveline accepted it and turned it in her fingers. It didn't mean anything, of course, because mother-naers didn't designate successors. But it might be a start.

She looked at Nicola, closed her fist around the ring, and nodded. Nicola left the body and followed Aveline out of the room.

❖

Riannon shielded her eyes with her hand as she watched the boulder arc from the cup of the mangonel towards the city wall. She saw the puff of dust and the boulder break before she heard the thud of the impact.

"The tower should fall soon," Prince Oliver said.

Riannon nodded. "Yes, my lord. But let us hope that it lasts until after we have risen from our dinner."

Oliver laughed. Like his eldest brother, the dead Roland, this son of the Irulandi king had an easy laugh and a head of golden hair that looked as though he already wore his father's crown.

Riannon's brother Henry, though, speared her a dark glare before turning his horse. Four days ago, he had fumed and roared and cursed at their having missed the opportunity of a breach in the walls because they had been eating. Before they learned of the chance and scrambled to arm, the defenders had patched the gap with beams and stones. Well, that was war. Henry's blustering and glowering looks would not make it otherwise. Nor did his ill humour endear him to many. Riannon wished he would return to his young wife, of whom she—for one—was heartily sick of hearing. Her brother acted like a lovesick stripling.

"Mayhap we could load Harry in one of the engines," Guy said, "and hurl him over the wall. His departure would raise our spirits and plague the defenders to death. They'd be opening the gates and begging to surrender in no time."

Riannon laughed. Prince Oliver roared even louder.

Guy and Riannon accepted Oliver's invitation to join his company. He lodged in a set of buildings that had once been a house dedicated to monks of Kamet, but which the imperial invaders had converted to a baron's fortified manor. Irulandi crusaders along with their servants, hangers-on, whores, laundresses, and the gods knew who else pitched their tents nearby or rigged up makeshift lean-tos of whatever materials they could scavenge. The fertile land was being picked clean at an alarming rate by foragers and looters.

Riannon lowered herself to a padded stool and accepted a cup of mead. Guy lounged close and engaged in light banter with one of the Irulandi lords. Riannon's gaze curved around the room from man to man. Most were high-born Irulandis, though one or two were Oliver's relations through the marriage of his sisters into the royal families of Marchion and Bralland. Every one of the dozen or so men in the room knew she was a woman. A couple didn't like her, and some betrayed discomfort around her, but in Oliver's presence they accepted her. Good enough.

"Today is the anniversary of my brother Roland's name day," Oliver said to Riannon. "He'd have enjoyed being here and the challenge of this siege."

"He'd have enjoyed this mead," she said.

"Aye! He could drink any two men under the table and still piss without wetting his shoes," Oliver said. "Why do you refuse my father's offer to be warden of Cliffton?"

"It's a generous offer," she said. "But my service is already pledged."

"There are men beyond counting who serve two masters. Take Eustace, there. He holds lands of both my father and his uncle, the king of Bralland."

He lowered his voice confidentially. "Hear me out before you refuse, and think on it. Whatever lands we reclaim in this crusade, my father plans to give to me. He has an understanding with the patriarch and the Quatorum Council. My brother Payn is his heir and will be king in Iruland after our father, so it's only fair that I get part of old Evriat. I'll need men I can trust to hold these lands for me."

"Thank you, my lord," she said. "You honour me beyond my expectation."

Oliver nodded and called to Guy to sing them his witty verses about a middle-aged man besotted with his teenaged bride.

When Guy and Riannon left the gathering, the raised voices of the singing and laughing Irulandi lords followed them. Guy had drunk more than his share and walked unsteadily to where his squire waited with his horse. As they rode back through the countryside scarred by the besieging army, Guy hummed and sang. Her brother was a happy drunk.

Riannon's thoughts centred about the possibility of property in re-conquered Evriat. Though Oliver was lord of only half a dozen castles and a handful of towns that the crusaders had already stormed and captured, the possibilities of pushing back the infidels loomed large. A gratifying number of men from all over the Eastern Kingdoms had answered the call. Every day brought more. Riannon doubted that Fulk would be able to stake his claim to the re-conquered lands without much political opposition and manoeuvring, but the chance of Oliver's kingship was real. The patronage of a friendly and generous king could open up great possibilities for reward. If she were rich…

A shout jolted Riannon back to grubby reality. A barefoot woman bolted from amongst a tangle of tents and wagons. She held her skirts hitched with one hand and a knife clutched in the other. Half a dozen men hurtled after her.

"Thief!"

"Stop her!"

The woman saw the horses and slowed to look for a way around. One of her pursuers lunged and grabbed her loose hair. She shrieked and whirled around with the knife like a cat striking with claws. One man yelled and fell with his hands clamped over his face. Two more panting men threw themselves at the woman. She went down under the bodies.

"Stop!" Riannon called.

The chasing men who had been poised to dive into the fray halted and stared up at her. Alan and Guy's squire dismounted and strode purposefully to the ongoing tussle. Alan, cursing roundly, grabbed one man by the leg and hauled him off. When the men saw Riannon and Guy, they subsided. The woman picked herself up off the dirt and wiped a trickle of blood from her face. Her torn bodice revealed part of a pale breast.

"Whore," someone muttered.

The woman spat at him.

That nearly started the fight again.

"Come here," Riannon said.

The woman strode towards her and openly eyed Riannon. Beneath the dirt and bruises, she looked unafraid to the point of insolence. Even had Riannon not been intrigued, she would not have left the woman to the mercy of the men.

"Bring her along," Riannon said.

Guy grinned as he urged his horse to a walk beside hers. "You shiny knights of the star take being noble too cursed seriously. That hellcat is neither innocent nor defenceless."

Riannon grinned and looked back to see the woman riding behind Alan. Her squire wore a wary expression as if he feared for his purse or his genitals.

"You'll have your hands full there," Guy said as they dismounted outside their shared tent. "Not that I can fault your taste. She'll scrub up nicely. Damned fine pair of legs."

Riannon frowned at him.

"I've been wondering what your taste is like," he said. "We've that in common, too, it seems."

Riannon scowled as she followed Guy inside. He acted as easy as if they were two brothers discussing women. "You—When did you guess?"

"I flatter myself that I'm as needle-witted as the next, but I could lie and say that it was two heartbeats after I met you rather than the three it probably was."

Guy sagged onto their only chest, stretched his long legs, and called for a servant to bring him wine.

"You'd best do something about her," Guy said. "She doesn't seem the type to tamely wait."

"Oh." Riannon cast a look back through the open flap of the tent. "I was going to let her go, not bed her."

"Now I know why I've not heard your cot creaking much these last months. Who'd have wagered on the fearless Vahldomne being bashful?"

"She looks the type who'd prefer your privy parts to mine."

Guy grinned and spread his arms. "Who would not? I'm hung like a bull. Though it is other men I give cuckold's horns to."

Riannon threw her gloves at him and strode out to leave him to his wenching. Though a pretty face or swelling breast might spur her lust, there was only one woman she wanted.

Riannon squinted at the city. Mid-summer heat made the air dance and shimmer as though the walls were melting.

If they could keep beating back the infidels and nibbling away at the territory, Oliver might have his new kingdom. She could be one of his chief barons. So, when Geoffrey of Howe died, she would be in a position to support Eleanor in sufficient style that Eleanor would feel small pangs for the loss if Queen Mathilda confiscated every acre Eleanor and Riannon held in her realm. Perhaps, one day, it would not be a dream, any more than wiping the infidels from Evriat was a dream. When that tower in that city wall fell, both would be one small step closer to reality.

❖

Eleanor strode into her husband's chamber and saw Geoffrey sitting on the bed with his leg bared. A grey-haired priestess from the local grove stopped her ministrations to bow to Eleanor. Eleanor waved her to continue. He must need healing for a return of his joint ague or his pustular abscess. Either way, it was likely to be his own fault for over-taxing himself and drinking too much sweetened wine. Sometimes he acted as though he believed himself closer to her age than his own.

"It gladdens my heart to see your face, my dear," he said. "I've had my fill of Sio Anne's sour looks and strictures."

"Mayhap she wouldn't need to scold," Eleanor said, "if you followed her advice."

Something the priestess did made him wince instead of answer. Eleanor went to stand looking out the window. Her husband could be touchy about his infirmities.

"What can I do for you, my dear?" he said. "Distract me from these ungentle ministrations."

Eleanor passed on some humorous gossip she had heard from her steward about one of their neighbours. She waited until the priestess bowed herself out, and Geoffrey sat on the side of the bed with his leg of hose back on, before she broached the matter that brought her to him.

"My steward tells me a strange tale that I find hard to credit," she said.

"Then it must be a tangled problem indeed, my dear," he said, "if it defeats your understanding."

Geoffrey levered himself to his feet. He limped as he crossed to join her. She let him take her hand to kiss.

"You're frowning, my dear," he said. "What troubles you?"

"Matthew tells me that a man employed by someone called Bland turned him away from the manor at Breakwood. This Bland claims to own my land."

Geoffrey patted her hand, released it, and went in search of something near the bed. "That's correct. Ere he left, Ralph feoffed Bland with the place. The man has served him well and deserves reward. Ralph must be mindful of his reputation for largesse and bind loyal men to him. It's important for a man."

"That was my land," Eleanor said.

"It's such a small place and inconveniently distant from any of our larger estates, my dear." Geoffrey waved vaguely and limped around to the other side of the bed. "I've arranged for some replacement property to be part of your dower in its stead. Really, my dear, it's a matter of no import."

Eleanor bristled, but strove to rein in her indignation. "Ought I not have been consulted?"

"You can have little interest in your dower properties, my dear, until I am dead. Let us hope, considering the pain Sio Anne has inflicted on me this morn in the name of remedy, that is not for some time. Can you see where I left my rabbit's foot? I know I took it out to hold when that wretched woman came in to do her butchery on me."

Eleanor stalked across to snatch the brown furry lump from amongst the rushes and thrust it at him. "The timber on that property was to be sold this year at considerable profit."

"We'll not miss a few coin. But it'll be greatly to Ralph's credit that he gives so generously. Now, my dear, was there aught else? I'm riding over to Longfield chapel to make offerings for my healing and for the coming harvest. You're welcome to join me."

"I have much to do this day."

Geoffrey kissed her cheek. "That new gown becomes you, my dear. I'm the envy of men half my age. In truth, you make me feel half my age."

He cupped her left breast. Eleanor, still simmering, stepped away from his touch.

"I'll not be late in returning home," he said. "Send your women to sleep elsewhere tonight, my dear."

After he limped out, Eleanor folded her arms and glared.

Riannon swung her sword down. The blade cut through a padded jerkin and bit into flesh. The man screamed as he fell. His companion dropped his spear and fled. Riannon watched him running across the plaza. He was not alone. Defenders from the breach in the wall all the way along to the closest gate gave up their resistance and bolted in the direction of the castle. A couple of the young knights who had followed her over the wall took off in pursuit.

Riannon turned to see more fighting amongst the buildings bordering the open space of the plaza. She had to squint through the glare of the morning sun. She did not see the blue surcoat and shield she looked for. She and Guy had fought their way down from the wall and across to the gate together. After they had forced the gate open, the surging tide of the fight parted them.

Riannon blinked sweat from her eyes. She could feel her shirt stuck to her skin beneath the layers of her gambeson and mail hauberk. Her flowing green surcoat, with the golden tree emblem on it, only partly succeeded in keeping her metal armour from broiling her.

"Sir?" Alan offered her a water skin.

Riannon removed her helm and took a long drink. Smoke from inevitable fires drifted in lazy black clouds across the open space. Noise rolled and echoed back from the fronts of the massively impressive buildings planted around the sides of the giant square.

"Sir!" Alan pointed to a group of horsemen. "The prince."

Riannon wiped sweat from her face as she stood waiting their approach. Prince Oliver had the visor of his gold-trimmed helm lifted. He smiled at her.

"I think we'll find some place suitable to eat our dinner inside the walls," he said.

"Yes, sir," she said. "The city is yours. But I fear the garrison might yet need a little persuading."

She signalled in the direction of the castle. Oliver nodded and waved to one of his men.

"I'll get a horse found for you," he said. "My thanks to you and your brother for opening the gates. Where is Guy?"

"He's probably found the city whorehouse," she said.

Oliver laughed. He pointed to the sword hilt protruding over her left shoulder. "You need two swords?"

Riannon had bowed to the necessity of carrying Aveline's witch-sword, though still not reconciled to using it. She wore her own sword at her hip and carried the gift-sword on her back. That kept it out of her way while ensuring that she would not be parted from it.

"I'm loath to miss the opportunity of killing an infidel on the chance that one sword broke," she said.

Oliver smiled and drew his own sword. He gripped it by the blade and offered the gold-decorated hilt to her. The ruby in the pommel flashed like a predator's eye. "This sword was forged by Grandmort in Madusca. It'll not break however many infidels you try it against."

Riannon took the sword with no small sense of awe. "My lord, this is a gift beyond price."

"It was not given lightly," he said. "You might call it a reminder. Not only that I value your services this day, but of what we spoke yesterday."

Riannon nodded.

"And it seems only fair, since my brother gave you a dagger, that I give you a sword," he said. "But I was wondering if you had need of that second sword, since I seem to be without a weapon."

Riannon handed him the sword from her hip scabbard. She saw one or two envious looks from the men who rode off in Oliver's wake.

She lifted her new weapon. The shining steel blade bore the characteristic mark of the best weapon smith in the Eastern Kingdoms— a craftsman of such fame that he only made swords for kings and princes. Legend credited him with quenching the hot metal in buckets of blood.

Oliver had given her treasure. More importantly, it might be the forerunner of even greater rewards. Riannon saw pride and envy in the looks of her squire and the men who had attached themselves to her since she had joined the crusade. She could not yet afford the reality of supporting her own mesne of knights and squires, but, mayhap, the time was not far off when she could. When she owned lands that would earn her a goodly living, she could endow faithful men. And support a wife.

"Lord Guy!"

Riannon turned to see where Alan pointed. A knot of men emerged from a street on the east side of the square. Guy's azure surcoat led them. He had not yet found a mount. Only sporadic knots of grappling men and the bodies of the fallen littered the vast square.

Riannon waved. Guy gave no sign he saw her. Instead, he strode off to the north. In that direction a handful of men looked like they tried to beat down the doors of the largest building with a makeshift battering ram. A dull thud-thud carried across the plaza.

Riannon frowned as she saw the banner flying above the building. A dragon's claw. She studied the building harder. Flanking both sides of the broad fan of steps to the doors stood two large pedestals supporting bronze statues. The right was a lion and the left a dragon. It was a temple to their god.

Without waiting for the prince's man to appear with the promised horse, Riannon strode north across the plaza.

She was about halfway when Guy reached the bottom of the steps. Shouts erupted. The men at the top flew backwards as if a giant invisible hand swept them aside. The doors slammed open. Bodies fell onto the steps like broken dolls. Guy and his men dropped to their knees or fell flat.

Riannon paused, not sure what she was seeing. A single figure swathed in brown stood at the top of the steps. He held a sword aloft. At the same time she heard the whining buzz, she saw Guy leap to his feet and bound up the steps.

"No!" Riannon dropped the prince's sword and hurriedly tugged the baldric off her shoulder. She drew Aveline's witch-blade from the scabbard as she began running. "Guy! *No!*"

Riannon saw the witch-priest scythe his sword down towards her brother, though Guy had not reached the top of the stairs. Her legs pumped as she ran as fast as she could. Guy threw up his shield. He recoiled from a blow, though still beyond the priest's reach.

She felt as though she ran through thick honey rather than air, so slowly did she seem to be moving. She could only watch in despair as the witch-priest's enchanted blade hit Guy's sword. The steel of Guy's severed blade glinted as it tumbled aside. The two men who had followed Guy stood rooted in surprise partway up the stairs.

Riannon's foot planted on the bottom step. The buzzing sword scythed across Guy's front. She watched her brother crumple as she hurled herself up the fan of steps and past the startled men.

The ensorcelled sword swung down at Guy's defenceless body. She flung her sword forwards. The warrior-priest's buzzing blade clanged against it. Where enchantment met blessing, a crackling sizzled the air. The tattooed priest's eyes widened in disbelief. Riannon swung. Surprise slowed him. Her blade carved into his torso before he moved to parry. Blood burst from his chest as Riannon's sword erupted out his back. He fell, all but cloven in two pieces. His sword dropped from lifeless fingers to clatter on the stone.

Riannon whirled and knelt beside Guy. He lay on his back. His surcoat and mail bore a cut angling from breastbone to shoulder. Blood gently oozed from it. Far more blood ran from the top of his left thigh. Deep red already pooled on the pale stone.

Riannon shoved his severed mail out of the way. The enchanted blade had sliced through the tail of Guy's gambeson and his braies.

"The bastard didn't touch me," Guy said through clenched teeth. "I swear it."

Riannon hastily untied the waist cord of her surcoat and threaded it beneath Guy's thigh. She feared some vein in his groin cut open.

"Atuan's balls," he said. "That smarts. My sword broke. It'd better not have cost me—"

He grunted as Riannon pulled the cord tight. She frowned as she watched and silently prayed that the flow staunched. Her brother's blood coated her hands.

"I'll fetch a ladder or cart, Vahldomne, to carry our lord back to the healers," one of Guy's men said.

Riannon nodded. She looked up to see Alan close. "Take the horse that man is bringing for me. Find a healer."

Alan reverently set her new sword and the witch-sword scabbard down beside her before he bounded away.

Riannon eased bloody cloth aside to get a better look at Guy's injury. The cord had slowed the bleeding. The cut looked partly burned, just as her own wounds had been. This would produce an ugly scar that had even nicked and blistered the bottom of his scrotum. Had his genitals been larger and bulged in the way of the strike, he would have lost more than just blood.

"Nonnie?" Pain strained Guy's voice. "I hardly have the courage to ask. The wound…Has it…?"

"It has not gelded you," she said. "All the whores from here to the Themalian desert can breathe easy again. But had you truly been as big as a bull, you'd be a steer."

Guy's grin was more relief than amusement. Riannon was glad to see it.

❖

Riannon walked into the shadowed interior of the vast temple. Space swallowed her soft footfalls. A thousand and more people could stand between the marble walls. Painted dragons curled up and around the thick columns supporting the soaring roof. Fanciful minds might believe the soot patches peppering the walls had been caused by the fiery breath of such lizards rather than torches burning in cressets. She heard a murmured obscenity from behind her. Only a handful of men had followed her inside.

She wandered past the second set of columns when she heard a thin, high-pitched whine. She looked down at the sword she carried. She had confiscated the dead witch-priest's weapon and scabbard, but it was silent. The noise emanated from near her left ear—from Aveline's sword. She set the witch-priest's sword down and tugged at her shoulder baldric until she could draw her blessed blade. All the while, she scanned the temple interior ahead.

"Vahldomne?"

Riannon signalled for the men behind her to stop and stay back. How many witch-priests would a temple like this house?

Riannon held her sword, softly whining, in front of her as she walked warily forwards. She flicked her gaze left and right, into the shadows.

Instead of an altar, the infidel temple had a large raised dais. A massive gilded statue of a man with a dragon's head, claws, wings, and tail, stood on the top. The inhuman figure towered over Riannon when she paused at the foot of the dais. The sword in her hand now hummed. To her bare hands, the hilt seemed warmer than normal.

Doubly alert, Riannon cautiously worked her way around behind the dais. She found only the body of a priest, his throat slit. She heard voices. When Riannon returned to the front of the dais, she saw a dozen men striding towards her. Most wore the distinctive triple bars of blue across their surcoats and shields of the Most Holy Knights of the Order of the Shield Temple. They were the paladins of Atuan, god of war. The slender man, with the grizzled beard poking from the edges of his mail coif, was Grand Master Marbeck. The proud, arrogant man did not look pleased to see Riannon here before him.

"Vahldomne," he said. "We'll have this place cleaned out and re-consecrated. There are none of the filth left?"

"No," she said. "Just one warrior-priest. But there must be more somewhere. Mayhap they retreated into the castle."

"We passed what was left of a body outside," one of the knights said. "Cut near in two."

"Your handiwork?" Marbeck said.

Riannon nodded. The sword in her hand hummed loudly enough that others must hear it.

"Well, you can leave this to us now." Marbeck signalled. "My men will guard the place and stop any more looting. We'll have that abomination pulled down."

Riannon wondered what he would say if she claimed the temple for the Order of the Goddess. The gilding on the giant statue alone would be worth a prince's ransom. She held her tongue, though. Aveline had said nothing about claiming properties. The Quatorum Council could argue the division of spoils amongst themselves.

The grand master strode away. Most of his men followed.

The sword in her hands still hummed. The noise grew louder when she walked away from the dais. She stopped and turned. The gold-skinned giant loomed over her. They worshipped a fearsome and ferocious deity rather than a benign or lordly one.

Riannon mounted the dais steps. The sword's hum strengthened and deepened. Her ears rang as if she stood too close to pealing basilica bells. She frowned as she put the tip of her sword to the back of a colossal gold calf. Green sparks sprayed from the contact. A bone-deep boom rolled over Riannon.

"What was that?" one of the knights shouted.

The grand master and his men halted and turned back to stare.

Riannon swung her sword. The blessed blade bit through gilding and into the idol's wooden leg.

An unseen force smacked into Riannon's front. The impact lifted her off her feet and flung her backwards. Her shoulders slammed against something solid. Riannon crumpled in pain. Before her vision dimmed to black, she saw the gold dragon god toppling.

Eleanor...

CHAPTER NINETEEN

Aveline tried not to show her disappointment and impatience as she looked around the chamber. The afternoon sunlight angling in the windows, like bright spears hurled from the Goddess's own hand, cruelly highlighted the sagging features of the three mother-naers. Sibyl of Hierenne accentuated her wrinkles with a scowl directed squarely back at Aveline.

"This is all very well," Sibyl said, "but our Wise Mother is more familiar with the distaff than the axe. War is men's business, not ours. I've told the matriarch this and have no qualms about repeating it."

She paused to lubricate her scratchy voice with a sip from a cup that held something considerably stronger than watered wine. Inviting the crotchety old bird had been a mistake. Still, the other two looked less obdurate. Aveline had best make haste to ensure that they did not lend too close an ear to Sibyl's anti-war talk.

"The crusade has been launched," Aveline said. "We—"

"To your glee." Sibyl levelled a gnarled finger across the table at Aveline. "I'm not in my winding sheet yet, girl. My body might be decaying, but the rot has yet to touch my wits. I know full well why Katherine cast so unusually sharp a shadow at the Quatorum Council. It was because you walked closely behind her."

Aveline sat back in her chair. "I hardly think, madam, you would be the first person to castigate another for ambition. You and I could count the bodies we have clawed our way over. The tally would not be in my favour."

Sibyl's eyes bored into her. For a taut moment, Aveline thought she had misjudged the old woman yet again, but Sibyl barked out a strange, harsh chuckle.

"It's true," Sibyl said. "You've a ways to go yet, girl, before you could steal any light from me."

Aveline allowed her relief to leak out in a faint smile. "The surest way of safeguarding yourself from my ambition is to render me indebted to you."

Sibyl snorted and signalled for her attendants to pull her chair back. Aveline frowned as she rose to watch Sibyl prepare to leave.

"If I were one of the twenty," Aveline said, "you'd have an ally."

"I have allies." Sibyl shuffled to the side and stood to allow her attendant to settle a mantle about her bony shoulders. "Even if I did sponsor your candidature, I could not count on you for support save when it suited you."

Aveline discarded the idea of a denial.

"I know you better than you imagine," Sibyl said. "I know you almost as well as I know myself, for I see myself in you. I've less doubt about your becoming one of the twenty than I do about the sun rising in the morn. But I also know to the marrow of my bones that it'd be a mistake for it to happen yet. Now, I thank you for dinner. My compliments to your cook for the sturgeon. Good afternoon to you all."

The old lady's walking stick tapped on the floor as she departed.

"Time will cure the problem of my lacking in years," Aveline said, "just as quickly if I'm a member of the convocation as not."

"True." Sibyl paused near the doors. "But think how much more easily and without chaffing and ill-will the time will flow after the advent of a new matriarch."

Aveline frowned to herself as she watched Sibyl limp out the doors. So, Matriarch Melisande actively sought to block Aveline's nomination and selection. After the chilly reception Aveline had met with from the matriarch at the Quatorum Council, she was surprised not at the intention, but that so staunchly independent and outspoken a mother-naer as Sibyl would bow to that pressure had exceeded her calculation. Perhaps she had underestimated Melisande. Then she would have to try all the harder to bring about the Goddess's wish that Aveline become matriarch.

When Aveline returned her attention to her remaining pair of exalted guests, she saw the reserve she expected.

Mother-Naer Urraca drained her wine cup. "The last woman elected to the convocation so young was the seer Blanche of Astyria. A truly holy woman."

Aveline watched her leave.

"Which leaves just me for you to turn your charm on." Mother-Naer Hildegard signalled for a servant to bring a plate of sweet wafers closer. "You realise that, with Melisande set against you, you're pissing into the wind?"

Aveline poured her large guest a refill of wine. "Actually, I would've thought the matriarch's opposition would be a confirmation of my competency. She'd not fear a fool."

Hildegard laughed and sprayed wafer crumbs across the table. "Sibyl has the right of you. But ambition is not enough. A pity, for your sake, that you've not been blessed with some mystic gifts. Speaking in tongues. Levitation. That would impress many."

"Not least of all myself." Aveline signalled for another dish of wafers.

Hildegard chuckled. "You're honest, I'll give you that. But failing a touch from the finger of the Lady of Destiny, you'll have to bide your time until—"

A bone-deep boom, like thunder from the entrails of earth rather than the distant sky, rolled up over Aveline. She felt it with every sinew. Green sparks showered before her. A gold giant toppled through it and crashed to the ground. Gilded wings quivered with the force of the fall.

The sparks died. The fallen statue stilled. Through the quiet, made more profound by the preceding loudness, a faint buzzing hum rose. Aveline peered hard. Beyond the statue's broken left arm, she saw a body. An armoured man. A big man. A sword lay near him.

Aveline picked her way around the broken statue. The sunlight angling through the windows set the gold dazzling. But the broken elbow showed that the gold was merely a skin. A surface brightness. False and showy with no substance.

Aveline stopped near the sword. It hummed. She recognised it as the Goddess's gift sword. The armoured body was Riannon. Her eyes were closed. She looked crumpled though she lay several feet from the statue. Aveline crouched. Riannon's chest moved with breathing. Aveline reached out. Her hand passed through her cousin's cheek.

"Lady!" Aveline muttered.

Riannon vanished. The sword vanished. The statue disappeared, leaving Aveline crouched in the middle of her hall. Servants and her guest's attendants watched her, wide-eyed. One moved towards her.

"No!" Hildegard whispered vehemently and gestured with podgy hands.

Aveline rose. The chubby mother-naer stood staring back at her with a plate of wafers forgotten in front of her.

"Did you hear it?" Aveline said.

"You're back," Hildegard said. "What did you see?"

"The fall of a dragon-headed god," Aveline said.

Hildegard hissed in breath and put both hands to her elaborate crossed-circle pendant. "By our lady!"

"Just a statue," Aveline said. "But it's a beginning. I believe...I believe it might have been at Marketvale. The city has fallen to us. Riannon—Our paladin, the Vahldomne, toppled the statue of their god. The altar can be cleansed and re-dedicated. The crusade moves from victory to victory."

"All praise," Hildegard said. "You...you said nothing of any claim to visions. You might have persuaded Urraca had you done so."

Aveline's hand trembled as she reached for a wine cup from the table. "I've not known such a thing before. The whisper of the Goddess, yes, but...what did you see? Did you hear anything?"

"Nought but your cry," Hildegard said. "And the aura around you as you moved. You looked elsewhere as if truly seeing what our eyes were blind to. I've witnessed enough fakings of such Seeings to know the real thing."

Aveline took a long drink. Her nerves were raw. That rolling boom had been deep and strong enough to leave her teeth aching still.

"Here." Hildegard passed her the wine jar. "Now, you'd best sit. We have much to talk about."

Aveline should have been delighted, but she felt shaken and unsure whether what she had experienced was good or bad—like the morning after losing her virginity.

"We must dispatch a swift messenger," Hildegard said. "To Namour. This very hour. With changes of horse, he can reach the matriarch in four or five days."

Aveline looked up from sipping her wine. She felt unusually dull-witted.

"How else to prove the trueness of your Seeing?" Hildegard said. "There's no way a rider from Evriat could carry the news so fast.

Our Wise Mother must have had a hand in it. Through you. And we'd not want to delay for a moment breaking the good news to our dear matriarch."

"Good news? Of the fall of the statue, or my being granted a vision?"

Hildegard beamed and knocked her cup against Aveline's. "Exactly. Melisande is going to be delighted. How I'd love to be a flea in the rushes to see her face!"

Aveline smiled.

❖

Eleanor jerked off her gloves and thrust them at a servant. Across the hall, she saw Geoffrey lounging on his padded bench with a wine cup in his hand. He looked happy. That did not sweeten her temper after a hurried two hour ride in the autumnal chill and drizzling rain. She gave her damp skirts an angry shake before striding across the hall.

"Ah, my dear!" Geoffrey clasped her wrist and drew her down beside him. "You find me the happiest of men."

"That is both gratifying and surprising," she said. "The tenor of your summons for me to return with all haste from Forditch, where I'd planned to spend the night, led me to suspect calamity."

"You can gossip with your friends any time, dear." Geoffrey's dismissive gesture ended with him indicating a handsome young man sitting on the facing bench. "This is Sir Simon of Ravan."

Simon rose to bow to Eleanor. His gaze lingered a fraction too long on her bodice and his smile curled into insolence. Eleanor wanted to slap his face.

"He's come from Evriat," Geoffrey said. "From the crusade. He's brought news of Ralph."

Eleanor mouthed a polite greeting. She might have known such a man would be an intimate of Ralph's. She set aside for later her bone of contention with her husband, which did not decrease with the realisation that her plans had been overset because of Ralph.

"He brings us the best tidings," Geoffrey said. "My son comes home soon."

Eleanor counterfeited a smile.

"Ravan has been telling me all about the campaign," Geoffrey said. "I know you're not interested, my dear, in the details of war, but

I'm sure you'll be delighted to know how well Ralph acquitted himself, and how highly every lord thinks of him."

"Indeed," Eleanor said. "I'm sure you have grounds for pride."

"As I was saying to his lordship, my lady," Simon said, "Lord Ralph is honoured by the noblest men of the crusade. I myself witnessed an occasion when Lord Henry, the Earl Marshal, praised Lord Ralph for his gallantry and vigour in pressing an attack."

Geoffrey beamed and patted Eleanor's thigh. "Hubert! More wine! The best. We have much to celebrate."

Eleanor thought better of reminding him that the healer had cautioned him against drinking too much. She did not want another of his peevish scolds on top of everything else.

She accepted a cup of wine and feigned interest as Simon Ravan related an anecdote about Ralph that would have done the most imaginative bard credit. Eleanor could think of no chivalric virtue the tale failed to attribute to Ralph. Geoffrey swallowed it all as eagerly as he did sweetened wine. Eleanor wondered how much of it was true, and what Simon hoped to gain by it.

"Oh, splendid!" Geoffrey clapped his hands. "Exactly so! Tell my lady how—No! I'd almost forgotten. My dear. A letter. Ravan brought it from Ralph. I'd rather you read it to me than my clerk."

Eleanor kept some bitter thoughts to herself at the idea that she had been dragged from her comfortable evening with friends at Forditch to act clerk when any of half a dozen men in the household could perform the role.

She opened the page out. She saw Simon watching her. His gaze aimed below her neckline. Geoffrey gave no sign he noticed his wife being ogled.

Eleanor bent her attention on the letter. The writing was the beautiful, dark script favoured by the scribes of the chapels of Naith.

"Be not alarmed that this comes to you from a place where I have had need of minor healing," Eleanor read. "It was but a scratch, though you would think I needed raising from the dead if you knew of the amount I have been required to donate for these services. I have had recourse to borrow money from a silversmith because of the laggard division of spoils and the unfairness with which it has been carried out. I have pledged you for the debt, father."

"Of course I'll make good his obligations," Geoffrey said.

Eleanor frowned at the letter. Ralph had grown no more wise or discreet in the last months. Not only did he complain and spend money not his own, but he had dictated his criticism to a member of the chapel he found fault with.

"I trust Ravan to answer your questions about what we have done here," Eleanor read. "He rode at my stirrup from the time we crossed the Deander River into northern Iruland. He knows the particulars of all our victories. Those victories would have been speedier and more numerous had it not been for certain commanders. Our valiant Earl Marshal constantly tried to direct the sieges and attacks with boldness and daring. Alas, timidity unmanned the other generals and they overrode our excellent lord. I can scarce believe that any man who claims the name would harken to that unnatural creature—"

Eleanor broke off in surprise. Her heart gave a startled thump.

"My dear?" Geoffrey said. "You arouse in me fear of bad news."

"Nothing is amiss." Eleanor arranged a smile before continuing. "That unnatural creature Riannon of Gast. She has the ear of Oliver of Iruland. That prince has been duped into believing the fable that she is the Vahldomne."

"It passes all understanding," Simon Ravan said, "how men good and true can believe this claim of a woman to be the Vahldomne. Valour, honour. These things are strangers to the weaker sex. Not that Riannon of Gast could be mistaken for a true lady. She—"

"Perhaps my stepson left you in ignorance," Eleanor said, "that you speak of a woman who is my friend."

Simon smiled complacently and glanced at Geoffrey. The men shared a provokingly patronising look. Eleanor would have wagered every last acre, cow, and pound of pepper she owned that Simon of Ravan would not dare repeat his words to Riannon's face.

Eleanor returned her attention to the letter in the expectation of reading more execrations of the woman she loved.

"At Mardush, which is what the infidels in their warped tongue called the city of Marketvale, we came close to being rid of that accursed female and her coxcomb brother, Guy. We almost had an infidel idol to thank, for the statue in their main temple fell when that unnatural creature walked close to it. Sadly, she missed being crushed by inches. Alas, Guy also recovers from his wound. Their deaths would have removed two powerful obstacles to the fair division of the spoils."

Eleanor paused briefly to close her eyes and offer a silent prayer of thanks. She had no idea how much of what she read was true, but it seemed too worryingly plausible that both Riannon and Guy had suffered dangerous brushes with death.

As she finished reading the letter, which was mainly more complaints, Eleanor wondered at Ralph's stupidity. He must know his father would make the contents of his letter known to her. He knew both Riannon and Guy to be her friends. Ralph must not care that his scathing, unguarded opinions of the cousins of the queen would reach her. Either he did it in malice, or he truly did not think her a person of the slightest regard. That should not have been surprising, for he certainly did not treat his own wife as of any importance. Indeed, pregnant Phillipa did not even warrant a mention in the letter.

Eleanor concluded her reading with, "I intend to remain here but a little while longer. I hope to attach myself to the retinue of the Earl Marshal and accompany him when he returns. For the rest, I direct you to Ravan."

"The Earl Marshal." Geoffrey stroked his beard and nodded. "Ralph has sense and ambition. A man could do much worse than stand in the favour of the Earl Marshal."

Eleanor suppressed a pithy comment on the flagrant want of sense in roundly abusing Lord Henry's close blood kin. Having done her duty, she had no stomach for hearing more of this talk. She rose.

"If you'll excuse me," she said.

"Of course, my dear," Geoffrey said. "Be so kind as to have a basket of bread, meat, and wine sent to the local chapel. In thanks for Ralph's healing. And a suitable offering to the temple for his safe passing through these months of fighting."

Eleanor left the two men to their talk of war. She sent a lavishly generous gift to the brethren of the local temple of Atuan, god of war, including a sheep. She had three people for whom she owed thanks to the god. Of those three, Riannon dominated her thoughts.

❖

Eleanor retired early after supper, unwilling to listen to yet more of Simon's fawning lies extolling Ralph as little short of a godlike hero, or to bear the young man's oily looks. He made her feel unclean. She found it difficult to believe that Geoffrey did not notice, but if he did, her husband made no attempt to protect her or restrain their guest.

Eleanor sighed. *Oh, Nonnie. Where are you? Are you well? Will you be coming back to Gast? Will I see you again? Do you ever remember me?*

Eleanor could not recall all of Riannon as a coherent image. Instead, she vividly remembered fragments, like pieces of coloured glass that made up a window picture in a basilica. Riannon's smile. How Riannon looked at her as though she was the only desirable woman in all of creation. The way Riannon's voice could sound as softly intimate as the whisper of sheets. Her beautiful, strong hands so gentle as they wound a lock of Eleanor's unbound hair about her fingers or slid up Eleanor's inner thigh.

Eleanor shifted in the bed. Instead of the linen sheet against her breasts, she wanted to feel Riannon's hand cupping her. Riannon's hot breath. That tantalising flick with the tip of her tongue just before she sucked Eleanor's nipple between moist lips.

Eleanor drew in a deep breath. She grew warm. She closed her eyes and slid her own hand across her belly and up to her breast. She imagined the fingers belonged to Riannon. In a surge of imagination powered by longing, she heard Riannon murmur her name. The fingertips trailing down to tangle in the hair of her groin were her lover's. Eleanor parted her thighs. She ached for the hot, muscular touch of a probing tongue. She pulsed, wet and ready, for fingers or fist. *Oh, Nonnie...*

The door thunked shut. Eleanor snatched her hands from her body. The bed hangings twitched. She blinked from surprise rather than the sudden light of a candle.

"I'm glad I didn't need to wake you, my dear," Geoffrey said.

Eleanor struggled to gather her wits. Geoffrey set the candle down and removed his robe.

"You didn't say you wished to come to me this night," Eleanor said.

She regretted the unusual habit she had adopted of sleeping alone. She would have paid a prince's ransom to have Agnes and Enid snoring beside her.

Geoffrey pulled the bedding down and eased himself into the bed. His breath smelled of wine. Dark dribbles stained the neck of his undershirt.

"Ah, my dear, how could I not end this day of celebration with my lovely wife?"

He put his hand on her belly. Eleanor drew away.

"I'm weary," she said. "That unexpected ride back from Forditch has left me tired."

"I won't trouble you long."

He captured her hand and drew it down to his erection poking from under his shirt. Eleanor recoiled.

"I'm tired," she said.

"I'm almost ready for you."

He forced her hand back down to his penis. She gritted her teeth and let him guide her hand in stroking himself. On the middle finger of her hand she wore the charm ring. She prayed that it would prove as effective in wilting him as it did in preventing him swelling.

"Oh, that's good," he said. "So good. Yes, dear. Yes."

Eleanor felt no softening in his shaft. She tried to disentangle herself but his fingers held her wrist tightly. His free hand grabbed her breast. He squeezed hard enough to make her wince.

"If I were younger, I'd come to you more often," he said.

"Geoffrey—"

"I wish you'd put your mouth around me."

Eleanor wrenched her hand free. "I'm your wife, not a whore!"

"My other wives found nought demeaning in it. It'd give us both much pleasure. But perhaps another time. I regret that I've been unable to be as attentive to you as I'd like. I need to teach you more, my dear."

He slipped his hand between her thighs.

Eleanor flinched and eased away. "Please. Not tonight."

His fingers prodded and probed her. "But your body wants this. You're wet with lust. Now, dear, if you'll spread your legs for me."

"Geoffrey, no." Eleanor braced her hands against his chest to hold him off as he tried to climb on top of her. "I don't—"

"You deny me my rights?"

"I'm tired. I've told you. Please. You've been drinking."

"I must swallow the vilest concoction to enable me to be of use to you," he said. "I must wash the taste from my mouth somehow."

Surprised guilt numbed Eleanor's resistance. She wondered how much it had cost Geoffrey's pride to seek help for his lack of sexual potency. A lack which she deliberately inflicted on him in breach of her marriage vows.

His knee nudged her legs apart. Guilt or not, Eleanor could not prevent her instinctive resistance.

"My dear, stop this." He lowered his weight on her. His penis prodded her. "I want—Shite!"

Eleanor felt his sudden loss of stiffness. He softened as quickly as a candle thrown into a roaring fire.

"Atuan's legs! No!" Geoffrey reached down between his own legs to tug at himself. "No!"

Eleanor lay still. Her conscience squirmed, but it did not overmaster her anger at him. She continued to hold her ring unobtrusively against his arm.

When his ministrations proved futile, he rolled off her and sagged with his back to her. He sounded miserable as he muttered oaths to himself. He pounded the mattress with a fist.

Eleanor lay torn. The part of her that had been schooled from the cradle to obey men and be the submissive and passive vessel of their wants urged her to reach out to him. A memory of her mother's voice commanded her to try to console him and salve his wounded pride. Eleanor did not move.

Geoffrey rose and left without looking back at her or retrieving his candle. The door slammed.

Eleanor scrambled out of bed and snatched her chemise from the wall peg. She stood shivering in it with her arms wrapped around herself, staring back at the bed. She wiped at tears that would not stop.

Was she really the same woman who, less than a year and a half ago, had wept for joy in that bed?

❖

A month later, Eleanor looked from the smiling faces of Geoffrey, Ralph, and Phillipa to the messenger, and wondered. She directed the messenger to retire to claim food and ale. Without doubt, his black and green livery belonged to the Earl of Northmarch, the husband of Riannon's and Guy's sister Joan. The astonishing invitation must be genuine.

"What an honour!" Geoffrey shook his head while beaming. "To hunt with them at Isingtor. My dear, what say you?"

"It's a singular and uncommon invitation," Eleanor said.

"Think who else will be there," Phillipa said. "The Earl Marshal himself, I dare say. Perhaps even the queen. We—"

"You have me to thank for this," Ralph said. "I told you, father, that I'd lift our family to the highest ranks. I have the ambition and skill you lack. I worked hard to gain the Earl Marshal's attention whilst on crusade. And look what has come of it! I'll be the envy of every place-seeker in the realm."

"I hope the roads are not too muddy." Phillipa put a hand to her swollen belly. "I wouldn't like to spend too much time travelling."

"You'll remain here," Ralph said. "I won't have you putting the health of my heir at risk."

Phillipa looked crushed. Instead of saying anything, though, she bit her lip and lapsed into unhappy silence. Eleanor had found her no friend, but if anyone could provoke her to Phillipa's defence, it was Ralph.

"Women have travelled on horseback late into pregnancies with no ill effect to either mother or babe," Eleanor said. "But if it concerns you, there is the litter."

Phillipa shot her a surprised look of gratitude.

"Your knowledge of childbearing must be second hand, madam," Ralph said, "since you haven't successfully borne any yourself. My wife will not risk my son's life for a pleasure jaunt. I'll not be gainsaid on that."

Eleanor seethed but held her tongue betwixt her teeth. She knew better than to look to her husband for support against his son. Geoffrey patted Phillipa's hand.

"Perhaps you can join us next year," Geoffrey said. "I'm sure Ralph's favour will continue high, and this is but the first of many prestigious invitations to join the company of the highest folk in the realm."

Ralph nodded smugly.

Eleanor could not help pointing something out. "The invitation comes from Lord and Lady Northmarch, not the Earl Marshal."

Ralph waved aside her words. "They're kin of his. He has asked them to invite us as a courtesy to himself. That is plain."

Eleanor did not find it so. Indeed, had they received an invitation from the Earl Marshal, she thought it more likely the courtesy due to her being aunt to the Earl Marshal's wife, not Ralph. Lord and Lady Northmarch had more than one close relative to ask them to invite the Howes. Was Guy behind the invitation? Or Riannon?

❖

Riannon squelched across the muddy forecourt at Isingtor and through the noisy press of horses, grooms, dogs, and the other returned hunters. Guy fell into step with her.

"Mayhap tomorrow, little Nonnie, we'll blood our spears and leave those braggarts to be the empty-handed ones."

"Mayhap, then, you'd best leave your brandy behind."

Guy smiled. "It wasn't drink that affected my aim. It was all the yawning from listening to their reliving each siege and skirmish of the crusade. And how much better they could have done in command. It's hard to sight quarry when your eyes are closed in a doze."

Riannon grinned as they stepped into the large hall. Her sister kept logs roaring day and night in the great hearths to combat the draughts and chilly dampness. But it was not the embrace of warmth which stopped her three paces inside the doors. She spied the small group at the hearth with her sister.

"Oh ho!" Guy slapped Riannon's back. "The lovely Eleanor is here. We're in for a merry time now. It's a pity her husband's son is with her. I wish they'd left the useless dog's pizzle in a ditch somewhere."

Riannon stood rooted to the spot. She had lost count of the times she had imagined seeing Eleanor again, and had prayed that she would come to Isingtor, but the reality of being so close to her again jarred every sinew.

"Nonnie?" Guy stopped a few paces away and stared back at her. "Is aught amiss?"

"No. I...I must change my hose."

Riannon strode away from Guy's astonishment. She trotted up the winding stairs to her small chamber. Riannon shut the door and leaned back against the wall.

She did so dearly want to see Eleanor again, but perhaps she had been wrong to arrange this meeting. Nothing good could come of it. Eleanor was accompanied by her husband. Riannon had found it nigh on impossible to be civil to the man before. How could she bear exchanging pleasantries with him knowing that Eleanor had lived with him for a year and a half?

What if Eleanor's fancy had turned to him during that time? She and Eleanor had had so little time together during that fateful summer. Could it have faded for Eleanor? Would Riannon be no more than a pleasant, hazy memory to her?

Riannon's hands trembled. The intensity of her need, her longing, her love for Eleanor formed an ache in her chest. It felt as real as any physical pain. If just a brief glance of the lady could do that, how could she endure several days in close company? Yet, if she still burned so fiercely for Eleanor, did that not mean there was a chance that Eleanor's feelings also remained strong for her? Despite *him*?

But what if their passion did still burn in them both? Eleanor was married. Riannon could neither do nor say anything that might cast any shadow on that compact.

Yet, Riannon could have gone no longer without seeing Eleanor again. A look. A soft smile. The sound of her voice. Riannon had fed on memories for five seasons. She hungered for more. Addiction and torture in one exquisite package. Love was truly an affliction, like a canker eating her away inside. Like the seeds of pain left buried in her flesh from the cursed blade that had disfigured her. There was no cure for her body, merely the sword that kept death at bay. Was there any treatment for love? Seeing Eleanor again—being close enough to touch but forbidden to lay even a heavy glance on her—would be an ecstasy of suffering. Like a spiritual gangrene, love ate at her soul and rotted her wits to madness. Riannon willingly courted it.

She groaned and pressed the back of her head against the wall.

"Oh, gods, help me."

Eleanor completed another look around the hall and felt a cool wave of disappointment. Surely Riannon was amongst this company. *Holy Mother, she must be here. I need to see her. To know that she's safe and well. Please let her be here.*

"For certès, we're pleased that all our men folk have returned from crusade, however temporarily," Cicely said. "Are we not, Aunt Eleanor?"

Eleanor mustered a smile for Cicely on the facing bench. Her niece had grown more mature and more assured than Eleanor had dared dream when she escorted the timid girl to her wedding.

Henry beamed fatuously at his young wife and affectionately patted her hand. "Though I was asked to remain over the winter, and will return in spring, I had to come back to see my wife."

Cicely's smile at him seemed no deeper than her lips. How well she had learned a wife's part in a year and a half of marriage.

"Your husband didn't go, but your stepson did, did he not?" Joan said to Eleanor.

"I'm pleased to say that most of those I know have come safely home again." Eleanor tactfully included the Earl Marshal as well as Guy, sitting beside her, in her smile.

"Nonnie is here somewhere," Guy said.

Eleanor couldn't stop herself turning to him. Every nerve felt as if he'd lit a taper at their ends. Riannon was here.

"Riannon made a strong impression on King Fulk and his son," Henry said.

Eleanor heard pride in his voice.

"You should ask to see her sword," Henry said to Humphrey of Northmarch. "Prince Oliver gave it to her. A finer weapon I've never laid eyes on. She can cut men in two with it. I would've offered to buy it from her, save you cannot put a price to the honour of the gift."

"She saved me with it from being cut in two," Guy said. "Which I think far more important and beyond price."

Eleanor smiled at him. Movement beyond his shoulder drew her gaze to the far end of the hall. Her breath caught in her chest. Riannon stood just inside the doorway.

In a dizzying moment, Eleanor's memories—worn threadbare with use—stretched to fit the reality of Riannon. She was so large. So striking. Her colours were dark and deep with life. Eleanor's gaze devoured her. If anything, Riannon looked too vivid, like an altar candle that brightly tempted with the promise of more than a mundane flame but would scorch just the same. Eleanor clasped her hands in her lap. She wanted to touch.

"There she is." Joan beckoned. "Nonnie!"

Had Eleanor not been watching so closely, she might have missed the hesitation before Riannon strode towards them. Riannon moved without a limp or other sign of past injury. She halted near the end of the bench without casting a glance at Eleanor. After nearly a year and a half, a war, and hundreds of miles, only four feet separated them.

The poor knight errant Eleanor had fallen in love with had prospered in the holy war. The realisation that she stared up at a stranger came as a shock. Clad in new, well-made clothes and an austere expression, which made even her horrible scar martially appropriate, Riannon had become the Vahldomne—the hero befriended by kings and princes, whose valour found its way into song.

"Nonnie, our last guests arrived while you were at the hunt," Joan said. "Lord Howe and his son are at the other hearth there. And Lady Eleanor is with us."

"Yes, I saw them." Riannon nodded to Eleanor without meeting her eyes. "My lady."

Eleanor recognised that flat tone easily enough, and it did nought to salve her unease. Riannon had retreated behind her buttress of stiff formality.

"It pleases me to see you again, and so hale," Eleanor said.

"My thanks." Riannon nodded. "By your leave."

Disappointment ripped Eleanor apart as she watched Riannon walk away. A few meaningless words exchanged without emotion should not have been the sole content of their reunion.

At supper, which Eleanor had no appetite to eat, Guy drew her to a seat between him and Lord Northmarch. Riannon sat at the table with most of her nephews and some of the more important servants. Eleanor didn't catch Riannon looking at her once, though she spent most of the meal glancing at Riannon. She drew thin consolation from Riannon eating little, drinking less, and giving the impression of being oblivious to everyone. Except, at the end of the meal, when people rose to move back to the hearths, Eleanor's husband directed a question at Riannon. The expression she turned on him was all snow-crusted stone walls, which, by their formidable nature, betrayed the emotion they sought to hide. He smiled up at her, clearly unaware that she hated him.

Riannon left the hall.

A raucous burst of laughter cut through Eleanor's unhappy ruminations and made her cringe. Ralph, who had already drunk much, had attached himself to the sons of the Earl Marshal. Eleanor could not hear what passed, and was glad of it, for she could imagine too well

Ralph's embarrassing bragging. Geoffrey looked unconcerned. Cicely kept glancing across the hall, but Eleanor doubted that it was Ralph who drew her niece's furtive attention.

A handsome boy of perhaps ten or eleven years sidled up to Guy. Edmund was Joan's son, now serving as a page in his Uncle Henry's household. Utterly unlike his Uncle Guy, Edmund was a quiet, unobtrusive boy. Eleanor would not have heard his soft-spoken question had she not been sitting beside Guy.

"Aunt Riannon is a knight, isn't she?" Edmund asked.

"Not just any knight," Guy said. "She is one of those lofty beings, a member of the Grand Order of the Star. Ask if you can sharpen her dagger for her. It was given to her at her knighting at Vahl by Prince Roland of Iruland."

Edmund nodded as he digested that. "She is the Vahldomne, isn't she?"

"None other," Guy said. "Though you'll not hear it acknowledged by her own lips. Surely you've heard your Uncle Henry boasting of his blood ties to the Vahldomne?"

"And mine," Edmund said. "For I'm her nephew. But that man over there, sitting with Cousin Richard and Cousin Walter, he's saying that none can be sure Aunt Riannon is the Vahldomne because he died at Vahl."

Eleanor knew Edmund meant Ralph. Guy did, too, for he flashed her a look before crafting a plausible lie.

"There are some who are confused about your aunt being the Vahldomne," Guy said. "Because the bards sing so many tales about her and not all sing the same things."

Eleanor loved him for trying to protect her from Ralph's folly. She would tell him later, when they were private, that she was well aware of the situation. Remembering the look Riannon levelled at Geoffrey, Eleanor could only pray Ralph would not speak so ill-advisedly about the Vahldomne within her hearing.

❖

Eleanor retired early feeling shaken and desolate. Riannon had not returned to the hall.

As she sat for Agnes to brush her hair, Eleanor attempted to untangle her thoughts and feelings. Riannon's distance hurt. That tallied with none of Eleanor's daydreams of their meeting. The strongest emotion Riannon had shown was her dislike of Geoffrey. Perversely, that gave Eleanor hope. Had Riannon's feelings cooled to indifference—had she found another woman to love while away on crusade—surely she would not loathe Geoffrey? His only possible offence against her was that he had married Eleanor.

Eleanor stiffened and gasped when Agnes's comb caught and pulled her hair.

Even if Riannon's passions burned undimmed, it would be wholly unreasonable to expect her to throw herself at Eleanor's feet and declare herself. Eleanor was married. Unrequited love of the style lauded by troubadours might suit flirtatious place-seekers and bored wives, but the Riannon she had known would not play such a part—and the Vahldomne looked as though she wore an even thicker mantle of chivalry.

Agnes divided Eleanor's hair and began to plait it.

All Eleanor's reasoning aimed at one target. She wanted to believe Riannon still thought well of her. For whatever reasons, the gods had fashioned in Riannon of Gast the one person in all of creation who made Eleanor feel truly alive. Mind, body, and soul. Irrespective of Geoffrey and how many willing women Riannon had found to warm her bed, and understanding the constraints that imprisoned them, Eleanor needed Riannon to know she still loved her.

Eleanor knelt before her portable shrine. She closed her eyes and bowed her head, but her thoughts would not clear. She saw Riannon. Dauntingly cold, formal, and remote. A stranger.

I want her to look at me like she used to. Just once. To see her smile and know it is because of me. Surely having her friendship is not wrong? Oh, gods, you would not deprive me of that?

Eleanor cast a despairing look at the shrine candle and reached for her book of prayers. She froze. Her breviary. Eleanor hastily flicked back through the vellum pages to a gorgeous picture illustrating a prayer for a day in summer. A man and a woman with a lute sat together in a garden under a cloudless blue sky. Eleanor moved her bookmark.

"Agnes? I have need of you to deliver this for me."

A hand tapped on the door. Eleanor tried to conceal her annoyance and distaste at the thought that it might be Geoffrey. She would not share a bed with him while she was so close to Riannon.

Agnes opened the door. Cicely slipped in.

"I hope you don't mind," Cicely said. "I was too eager to speak privately with you to wait until an opportunity on the morrow."

Eleanor signalled to Agnes. The waiting woman quietly withdrew and closed the door behind her.

"You're looking well," Eleanor said.

"Not nearly as well as you, aunt." Cicely set her lamp down and cocked her head to the side to study Eleanor. "Are you with child? You have that look about you. That glow."

Eleanor doubted that she looked other than as wretched as she felt, and if she did look different, it was not on account of anything her husband had done to her.

"Not that I think all women carrying a babe look more beautiful," Cicely said. "Or, mayhap, it happens with time. When the babe begins to show."

She looked down at herself and put a hand to her belly.

"Oh!" Eleanor smiled and reached out to take one of her niece's hands. "You're with child?"

"Yes. At least, my woman and I believe so."

"I'm surprised the Earl Marshal said nothing. He is so proud of you and well pleased with your marriage. Indeed, he looks besotted with you."

Cicely frowned. "Yes."

Eleanor watched Cicely wander into the shadows near the bed. She had not been mistaken in interpreting Cicely playing a role as dutiful wife.

"Poor man," Cicely said. "I can feel sorry for him, even if I don't like him. Aunt, I—"

"Oh." Eleanor levelled a frown at Cicely's stomach. "The Earl Marshal returned from crusade how many weeks..."

Cicely looked stricken and flung herself across the chamber to kneel beside Eleanor's stool. She clasped Eleanor's hand between hers.

"You won't tell anyone, will you?" Cicely said. "It was the most foolish thing I've ever done! Not Richard. I don't mean that. Never that. Had I the choice to make a thousand times over, I'd do it again and again."

"Richard?" Eleanor gaped. "Holy Mother, you don't mean—"

"Aunt, please!" Cicely pressed Eleanor's captive hand to her hot cheek. "You know I didn't want to marry. How I feared it. He's so old. I cannot bear it when he touches me. I weep every time he wants to...But Richard is so perfect. Handsome. Strong. His body is so fascinating and not at all repulsive. He loves me!"

"He's married to another. And he's your husband's *son*—or did that slip your mind?"

"I thought you'd understand! You're married to that toothless old man. Surely you feel trapped?"

Private acknowledgement that she tiptoed close to hypocrisy kept Eleanor from an immediate retort. However, her infidelity had been only of thought. Where the gods might hold her accountable, she was guilty of nothing in the eyes of men.

"You're pregnant to your stepson." Eleanor squeezed Cicely's hand. "Sweeting, this is utter madness. Think you that your husband cannot count? Or there'll not be people around him eager to point out the truth about your swelling belly to him?"

Cicely released Eleanor and stood. "I'm glad I'm having Richard's baby. His wife loves him no more than I love Henry. Not that Richard visits her bed. Not since he fell in love with me."

Eleanor stared, astounded.

"I don't worry about Henry." Cicely twisted her wedding ring as if it were a fetter she wished to be rid of. "He loves me. If anyone whispers slanders about me, he won't believe them. I wish he would. Then he might annul me, and I could marry Richard."

"Holy Mother! I can scarce believe what I'm hearing. You don't truly believe that?"

Eleanor rose and crossed to Cicely. She clasped her niece's arms firmly and only just resisted the urge to give her a strong shake.

"Sweeting, you cannot commit adultery and not expect your husband to mind. Especially not *your* husband. Henry has nothing if not a strong sense of family. He has a position to maintain as Earl Marshal. He'll not sit tamely at your feet and let you put cuckold's horns on him!"

Cicely sighed away her defiance to leave glumness. "I know he'll never repudiate me. Or set me aside. Or pay the Patriarch to have our marriage annulled. What a foolish mistake I made. I thought my marriage would be bearable if my husband loved me. What I should have done was ask for a charm that made me fall in love with him, too."

Eleanor frowned. "Charm?"

"I asked Naer Aveline to make me one. It made Henry fall in love with me. I threw it in a moat last year. But the effect hasn't stopped. I was hoping that his being away at the crusade would allow it to fade. You hear about men taking concubines during wars. But Henry didn't. Aunt, what can I do?"

The charm ring on Eleanor's finger seemed heavier and tighter. Whatever she said would be wrong—either for her niece or in the eyes of the gods and men.

"You vowed to be Henry's wife," Eleanor said, "faithful and obedient to him until death parted you. You have no just cause to separate from him. He has not mistreated you or degraded you, has he? Loving another is not enough."

"I know," Cicely said miserably. "But why did the gods make me fall in love with Richard?"

That cry from the heart struck Eleanor silent.

❖

The next morning, after a restless and anxious night, Eleanor joined the others in the shrine chamber for the dawn service. She stood in the second row beside one of Riannon's nieces. A priest of Naith officiated, but Eleanor found it difficult to pay attention to him when Riannon stood so close. During one of the hymns, the intervening people shifted and Eleanor saw the breviary in Riannon's hand. Her hopes soared and she prayed harder.

At the end of the service, Eleanor remained after everyone else departed. Everyone except Riannon. She moved close enough to touch. Eleanor's body remembered what Riannon felt like. But Riannon wore her most tightly guarded expression.

"I thank you for your generous gift." She offered the breviary to Eleanor. "But I have not learned my letters since last we met."

"The message I wished you to read was in the picture," Eleanor said.

Riannon frowned. The prayer book looked small in her big, beautiful hands. She opened it at the marked page. Eleanor held her breath. Would Riannon remember? Would she think it improper? If she had found another lover, would this reminder from their past embarrass her?

Riannon put a finger to the picture. "It's the same. This sky is the exact same shade of blue as the sleeve of the tunic you wore that day we first—"

Riannon's expression bore a strong resemblance to how she had looked on that summer's day when they began their affair. Unsure, cautious, and hopeful—not indifferent. Riannon had promised to return to her. Perhaps, after all, she had. Eleanor could not imagine a greater sense of relief and wonder if one of the gods had reached down to touch her. Mind, body, and soul reeled.

"You don't hunt," Riannon said. "I thought you might not come."

"I didn't come for sport."

Riannon's jaw muscles worked. "Nor I."

Giddy with relief, Eleanor couldn't stop herself from smiling. "I still enjoy riding. With the right company. I can think of no one whose company I'd prefer to yours."

Riannon nodded. "I am at your service."

Eleanor felt her whole body radiated happiness like painted saints glowed with golden auras of holiness. She turned to leave. Riannon caught her sleeve. Eleanor's heart pounded hard as she watched Riannon lift her arm. She anticipated Riannon's kiss on her hand—to feel Riannon's lips on her bare skin. But Riannon merely stared at Eleanor's fingers. Eleanor needed the length of several rapid heartbeats to realise that Riannon looked at the charm ring.

"It has not been off my finger since you put it there," Eleanor said.

Riannon scowled as if Eleanor's words troubled rather than reassured.

"The Goddess continues to bless its efficacy," Eleanor said.

"I'll send instructions to the stables."

Riannon pressed a brief but fervent kiss on Eleanor's fingers, released her hand, and strode out.

Eleanor put her kissed hand against her lips. She should not have doubted. If any mortal deserved her faith, that person was Riannon of Gast.

Eleanor turned to the altar. A sacred flame burned steadily. Belief. Faith. Devotion. Love. She traced the quartered-circle against her chest and kissed her fingers.

"Thank you," Eleanor said.

CHAPTER TWENTY

Eleanor watched her husband's servant lace Geoffrey's boots about his bony ankles.

"The weather is like to turn to rain," she said. "And you're fatigued from our ride yesterday. Perhaps you should rest instead of—"

"Rest?" Geoffrey snapped. "Anyone hearing you would think me ready for my winding sheet. Save your fussing for someone who needs it. I'll not hear it!"

He irritably cuffed his servant out of the way.

"I was invited to hunt," Geoffrey said. "And hunt I shall. You may spend your time cozened by a fire gossiping and sewing and whatever it is you women do. I'll be with the men."

"I'll be taking a ride today," Eleanor said. "For escort, I've—"

"Yes, yes." Geoffrey tugged his hooded mantle about his shoulders. "Do whatever you wish for your pleasure, but hinder me not."

Eleanor swept out of his chamber. If he wished to get cold and wet and overtax himself, then he could. But he need not expect her to have to forgo her evening to sit cosseting him. She bumped into Ralph.

"You'd best watch where you tread, madam," he said.

The hard edge to his voice caused her to pause as she stepped past him.

"That's a fine gown to be wearing while you sew," he said.

"But not too fine for Lady Northmarch's company." Eleanor moved away.

"Nor Lord Guy's," he said.

Eleanor turned. The open door to Geoffrey's room stood just a few feet beyond Ralph. Their voices would easily carry.

"But he hunts today," Ralph said. "Though it is well known that the pretty lordling is no stranger to warming himself at women's hearths."

Eleanor dropped her voice. "You'd be well advised to have a care with your tongue."

"And Lord Guy is none too particular whose women he favours, either," Ralph said.

Eleanor bristled, but kept her voice to a vehement whisper. "I'm your father's wife. That's a disgusting insinuation. You'd best not repeat it within Guy's hearing or your father's. And you might spare a moment from your gutter thoughts to contemplate how slandering his brother will demote you in the favour of the Earl Marshal."

"There'd be nought for me to insinuate, if my father's wife had a care of her own." He grabbed her arm. "Phillipa was right about you. And I have eyes, lady. I'll not let you make a fool out of my father."

"If you wish to accuse me, let's step into your father's chamber where you can do so openly and fairly."

Ralph's eyes narrowed. "Be warned, lady."

"Take your hand off me. If you cannot drag your mind from the midden, remember that any slanders you cast at my honour also taint your father and whomever your disgusting fancy chooses to accuse with me. Don't deceive yourself that any slight regard you believe you enjoy with the Earl Marshal would protect you from his brother's wrath."

Ralph grinned. "I don't fear your wastrel lordling."

"Then you're an even bigger fool that I imagined."

Eleanor strode off. She could feel him watching her. Whatever poisonous lies Phillipa had whispered to him had found fertile ground and festered. Should she caution Guy? No, Ralph was a blusterer and bully, but not even he would be so stupid as to publicly accuse Guy in such company as this—and on the basis of no evidence whatsoever.

❖

Riannon gripped the book hard, just as she might try to cling to a healer's hand as she slipped into a delirium. Eleanor still loved her. She wore the charm ring. Her affections had not drifted to him. With this book, Eleanor had fulfilled all Riannon's wishes. Riannon did not know if she was strong enough to bear them.

She set the book on her bed and turned to retrieve her sword belt. The gold and red enamel hilt of her knife mutely reminded her of sworn oaths. To be true. To be just. To protect the weak. To defend the defenceless. To uphold the word of the gods and the laws of men. Riannon buckled the belt about her waist.

The heavier weight hung at her left hip where, today, she wore the Goddess's blessed sword. The preternaturally sharp blade could cut where it should not. It was a moral dilemma forged of metal, and one she had yet to resolve. Eleanor, on the other hand, should present no difficulties to her conscience. Lord Howe's wife stood inviolable beyond Riannon's reach. As far as Riannon knew, he had done nothing cruel to Eleanor and enacted no heinous neglect—nothing that might justify Riannon stepping in to champion Eleanor. But how could Riannon not touch her? Eleanor loved her.

"Gods, give me strength," Riannon said.

If only she could look at Eleanor and not remember how sweet it was to make love with her. That might have helped.

I can kill men. I can ride into battle. I can face death. I have served contemptible men. I have eaten wormy meat. I have slept in lice-ridden clothes. I've endured cold. And blistering heat. Hunger. Thirst. Fear. I have survived wounds that should have killed me. I can spend an hour or two in her company without disgracing either of us. I can. I must.

Riannon spurred her horse to follow Eleanor's precipitate gallop. When Eleanor slowed to allow Riannon to draw level, she smiled and didn't bother tugging the hood of her fur-lined mantle back into place. With her eyes shining with pleasure, and colour high in her cheeks, she looked as glorious as Riannon's memories. Riannon could not get enough of looking at her. After so long of wishing and imagining, it seemed unreal that the two of them should be alone and riding together. Truly, this was an addiction of the acutest kind.

"You're still reckless," Riannon said.

"I feel free."

"You do not know the ground. You might have broken your neck, or your mare's leg."

"I might have run that risk, had you not chosen a path that you knew would be safe for me to ride at speed. I trust your judgement every bit as much as I do my ability to keep to the saddle. Was I wrong to do so?"

Riannon grinned. "No. I have ridden this way before."

Their horses, winded from the gallop, walked close side by side.

"You knew what I'd do if given my head," Eleanor said. "Instead of seeking to curb me, you aided and abetted me. You do not expect me to pretend to be meek and unadventurous. I need not try to seem less than I am. You're the only person who has ever allowed me to be myself."

"It passes my understanding why anyone would want you other than you are."

"They're the same people who would have you something you are not. Although, you seem to have finally garnered some of the respect you deserve. I've heard nought but praise of you. The Earl Marshal speaks of you with pride. It was he who boasted to me of your favour with Prince Oliver of Iruland. You look as though you've prospered."

"I'm fortunate enough to be on good terms with the prince. The crusade goes well. We suspect the Lion Emperor will counterattack come spring. He has legions uncounted spread through his vast empire to the west. But the crusaders are strong and determined to reclaim Evriat. And we have the right of the gods on our side."

"You'll be returning?"

"Yes. I'm the principal representative of the Order of the Goddess. Aveline wishes me to return," Riannon said. "It's my expectation that Prince Oliver will grant me a generous reward when he's in a position to do so."

"I warrant it'll be no more than you deserve. Any lord who secures your services should count himself fortunate. You intend to make your home there, then?"

"I have not even a blade of grass, yet." Riannon frowned down at the reins in her fingers. "It might be a year or two, and likely more, before I am in a position to be able to settle. And marry."

Eleanor looked sharply at Riannon before quickly turning away. "That will be a good step for you. You won't want to spend all your life moving from war to war. Is there someone—But you have said this might be years hence."

"I'm not the soundest judge of men, but I believe Prince Oliver will not baulk at my taking a wife."

"I didn't imagine you would submit to a husband," Eleanor said. "I suppose since you have much goodwill with members of the Quatorum Council, that will make such an irregular arrangement possible."

Riannon stared at Eleanor's profile and came close to saying what she should give no voice to even though they were alone with only the muddy ground and the dripping trees to hear them. Not even the barking dogs or horn calls of the hunting party carried to this part of the woods.

"Your husband enjoys good health?" Riannon said.

Eleanor was slow to reply. "It was a mistake. I regret marrying him."

"You had no choice."

"You're correct. We did what we had to. Our reasoning was sound. I don't see how either of us could have decided other than we did. But knowing that wormwood is necessary to one's health makes chewing it no less bitter. I haven't been able to stop thinking about what might have been. I have missed you so much."

Riannon let her horse stop. Eleanor halted hers. Their legs were but inches apart.

"Not a single day has passed that I have not thought about you," Eleanor said.

Instead of saying what clamoured for voice, Riannon frowned down at her gloved hands. *I love you. I have not stopped loving you from the moment I saw you.*

"You were always in my prayers," Eleanor said.

"I prayed for your continued good health."

"You shadowed my days and haunted my nights. I couldn't begin to count the hours I've lost in wondering about you, what you did, how you fared, and where you were."

Nor I you. Hating every moment you might have been with him.

"I've relived every moment we shared," Eleanor said. "Times beyond number."

Every day and every night.

"Nonnie?"

"You should not say such things."

"Keeping my words behind my teeth will not make them less true. The gods see directly into our hearts and minds, and can read our souls. They know how much I have missed you and how often I prayed to see you again. I need you to know it, too."

Riannon nodded, even as she continued to frown. *I needed to hear it. I love you.*

"I know that the Riannon I love won't lavish me with sighs and bardic promises or poems. Not even about weeds. Or fish."

Riannon grinned at her horse's neck.

"You haven't changed so very much, I fancy," Eleanor said. "But, Nonnie, is it so very wrong of me to want to be able to hope?"

Riannon lifted her anguished stare to an autumn sky filled with shades of grey.

"You can have no idea," Eleanor said softly, "how much it means to remember what it feels like to be loved."

"Oh, lady, you are wrong. I do know." Riannon turned to see Eleanor looking at her. The Eleanor she remembered. Her Eleanor. "Almighty gods, there is so much I would say to you that I cannot speak to Lord Howe's wife."

"The gods willing, there will be a time when I am myself again."

"When that day comes, I'll ask you if you would consider becoming a wife again."

"Oh." Eleanor put a hand to her face. "Oh, Nonnie."

Riannon offered her hand. Eleanor clasped it. Though they both wore gloves, the contact produced a fierce surge of pleasure through Riannon. She gently squeezed Eleanor's fingers when she wanted to grip her so tightly that nothing would ever be able to pry them apart again.

"You'd not ask in vain," Eleanor said.

Riannon grinned. "In all likelihood, though, I might gain only modest holdings compared to yours. When we considered it before, you could not—"

"Now is not then. The ground has changed. *You* have changed. You're the Vahldomne now, a leader of the victorious crusade who gathers glory for the gods, and who sups with princes. You're not just a poor cousin with a stained name. If we can marry with the sanction of the gods, the queen would be foolish beyond prayer to alienate your wife's lands. Our liege lady might be many things, but her wits are not disordered when it comes to her own gain. I expect we would have to pay dearly to have our own way, but in coin and your services—not with our liberty or land."

Riannon's horse shifted, but she maintained her hold on Eleanor's hand. She wished she held more. Even so, she had hope and a surety to buttress her against more waiting.

Riannon reached inside her collar with her free hand and tugged out a lock of chestnut hair tied to a green ribbon. With Eleanor watching, she lifted the hair to her lips and kissed it. Eleanor's fingers tightened against hers. Eleanor smiled in that special way Riannon remembered and brushed a tear from her cheek.

Riannon dismounted before her mind formulated the impulse to move. As she walked around the horses, she recognised the danger she courted. But she could not stop herself. She could not leave Eleanor to weep uncomforted.

Eleanor slipped willingly from the saddle into Riannon's arms. Whatever else about Riannon had changed, the part that enjoyed the feel of holding Eleanor pulsed as strong as ever. That supple weight against her—the solidity of Eleanor's body in her arms—the feel of Eleanor's hands on her arms.

"Oh, Nonnie, how did I live without you?" Eleanor ran her hands across Riannon's back. "I flattered myself that my imagination was so strong and vivid in conjuring your comforting revenant. But it was, in truth, a feeble ghost that came not close to this reality of you."

Riannon wanted so badly to kiss Eleanor.

"I've imagined this times beyond counting." Eleanor sniffed. "Not once did I believe myself so wretched that I would weep on you again. Do you think it's a case of wishfully overestimating my self-control? Or can I blame you for overpowering my poor, feeble senses? After all, you have a history of doing so. And it's far more comforting to blame someone else for one's weaknesses."

Riannon grinned. "Blame me for aught you wish."

Eleanor reached up to touch Riannon's lips. "Your smile. Your laugh. I tell myself they're mine alone."

"They are."

Riannon felt herself slipping into the most welcome madness as she returned Eleanor's gaze. How had she wanted anything in creation more than this splendid woman?

Riannon drew an unsteady breath and forced herself to let her arms fall from around Eleanor. Not trusting herself to remain close to her, she walked away to gather the reins of their wandering horses. Their time had been, and would be again. But it was not now.

"Nonnie?"

"If thoughts weigh a tenth as much as deeds, I'm already damned.

A crusader's vow and contrition absolves me of any sin. But no matter how many infidels I killed, I'd never attain paradise. Because I could not truly repent if I committed adultery with you."

"Nor I." Eleanor lifted her skirts clear of the muddy ground and damp leaf litter to move closer, but she made no attempt to touch Riannon again. "We have endured a year and a half, beloved. We can continue to wait. Patience is not a virtue I possess in abundance, but I shall think of the rewards. Of you."

Riannon nodded. "I'll do all I can to make myself worthy of you."

"You are already. More. My perfect knight."

"No. I cannot support you, make you happy, or even protect you."

"He doesn't hurt me," Eleanor said. "He's never beaten me. I swear it."

"If he touched you. If he did aught to demean you or dishonour you. If he—"

"He doesn't." Eleanor rested her hand on Riannon's forearm. "And the charm ring works."

Riannon frowned. In giving it to Eleanor, she had sinned, for it contravened Eleanor's marriage vow. Perhaps she had blackened her soul beyond redemption already, as well as condemning three people to unwanted chastity. Though, Riannon had obtained it from Aveline. It was blessed by the Goddess. Surely it would not work if the effect it produced was contrary to the will of the gods?

Sin or not, though, Riannon could not be sorry to think Eleanor's husband incapable of coupling with her.

"Would it be irredeemably wicked of me to ask to hear my name from your lips again?" Eleanor asked. "No one has ever spoken it as you do. I would have that fresh and strong in my ear to cherish."

"Eleanor," Riannon said. "Nell."

Eleanor gently touched Riannon's lips. Riannon wanted to pull her close and kiss her. To taste her. To reclaim her. To hear Eleanor's soft gasps and murmurs. To whisper her name to her in a voice thick with passion. Her body ached for it to the marrow of her bones. What was being damned for eternity compared to being loved now?

"Nonnie?" Eleanor's lips remained softly parted as she stared up at Riannon.

Riannon sharply averted her head from temptation and sucked in deep breaths of chill air to cool her fevered blood.

Eleanor removed her hand from Riannon's arm. "Who would have wagered that I'd ever envy a serving wench?"

Riannon grinned. Eleanor did right to remind her of that first time they kissed, and how they controlled their desire rather than lie together on the ground. How like her, too, to remember her tease.

"Think you it's some divine jest that the charmed ring has no efficacy with me?" Riannon asked.

"Did you not have it made by your cousin, Naer Aveline? Mayhap the jest was hers."

Riannon shook her head. She could not begin to unravel the sinuous turns of Aveline's mind, but she had the strongest impression Aveline had acted truly in blessing the ring.

"I know not how I'll bear waiting for the day you put a different ring on my finger," Eleanor moved away to stand prepared to mount her horse. "But I shall. Because of the promise that we'll have each other along with everything else we hold dear. From that day hence, I'll envy no woman."

Riannon smiled across the safety of the gap between them. Eleanor's return smile developed a wicked, teasing gleam.

"When we have the sanction of men and gods," Eleanor said, "we can tumble to the content of our hearts and bodies, wherever and whenever the fancy takes us."

"I suppose I am at fault for such an unchaste turn of your mind?"

"For certès! This wretched ring has no power over me either. I would not dream of exposing the breadth and depth of the fancies you've spurred in me. Suffice it to say that you would be well advised to husband your strength against the day we wed."

"The prolonged campaigns of war will seem restful by comparison?"

"You will need to be your most heroic."

Riannon laughed. "You are worth waiting for."

"So are you. Let us hope, though, the gods do not make us wait too long."

"A day is too long. But if it takes two years, five, or even ten, I'll come to you as soon as you send me word."

Riannon pressed a courtly kiss on Eleanor's gloved hand, helped her up into the saddle, and escorted her back to Isingtor and her husband.

❖

Eleanor smiled at the wall as Agnes drew the brush in long strokes through her hair. Her mind's eye returned to earlier in the evening. At Joan's request, Eleanor had played her lute and sang. Geoffrey had swelled with pride and beamed as he bestowed his permission for her to continue after her first song. But her performance had not been for his benefit. Riannon had taken a seat beside Guy to listen. How much easier it had been to sing of love when she had only to glance across to see Riannon watching her.

Someone pounded on the door. Eleanor frowned as she nodded to Agnes to open it. The knocking sounded too heavy to be Cicely and too vigorous to be Geoffrey. Agnes cracked the door open.

"I would speak with my father's wife," Ralph said.

"Sir!" Agnes clung to the door. "The lady is prepared for bed."

Ralph shoved her aside. "Out of my way."

Eleanor glared at him. "Something ails your father?"

"Yes, though he knows it not." Ralph turned on Agnes. "Leave us. Now!"

"You've no right to order my women about," Eleanor said. "It's you who should leave. Whatever you wish to speak with me about can wait until the morning."

"No, madam, it cannot. And it isn't something I wish gossiped about, even if you're too wanton to care for my family's reputation."

He grabbed Agnes and shoved her out the door.

Angry, Eleanor stood. "I've warned you about the laxity of your tongue, and your unwisdom in letting it flap without the power of thought behind it. Now, be so good as to leave."

He slammed the door shut and dropped the bar into place. Eleanor felt the first stirring of fear. He stomped back to stand near her. She smelled wine. Her fear grew. She held her dressing robe closed.

"You've been in your cups," she said. "We can talk in the morning, when it will suit us both better. Now, I'd thank you to leave."

"A whole tun of wine would be insufficient to befuddle my wits so that I'd not understand what game you play, madam."

He brushed past Eleanor as he strode to the bed. He yanked the hangings apart.

"Empty," he said. "But for how long?"

"Get out!" she said. "Now. And I'll not say a word of this to your father. You're drunk and know not what you say."

Eleanor started towards the door. He grabbed her forearm hard enough to bruise.

"You've a right nerve talking about my father," he said. "You sang your love songs and simpered and made eyes for all the world to see. All the while, my poor foolish old father sat beside you and smiled and dribbled his wine down himself and did not see your wantonness."

Eleanor tugged her arm, but he held firm. "You dare—"

"He should never have married you. He's too old. Ripe for a woman like you to put horns on. You should've been mine. You were supposed to be. He cheated me. I'd have kept you in hand. You'd not have left my bed wanting to spread your legs for some piss-proud skirt-chaser."

"Let me go!"

"I have eyes!" He shook her. "Even the dogs see how you throw yourself at Lord lick-my-arse Guy! The only poor fool who is blind to your harlotry is my addle-witted father."

Eleanor struggled to free her arms. He gripped her all the harder. She opened her mouth to scream. Ralph punched her in the face. Eleanor's head snapped back as pain exploded in her mouth. She tasted blood and fell on the bed.

"Let's see if your precious lordling will come from behind women's skirts long enough to face a man for the consequences of his wenching with wives. Gods, I've wanted an excuse to wipe the stupid smile off that bastard's face. It's high time you and he both had the lesson that you cannot drag my family's honour in the dirt with impunity. My father might be incapable of teaching you, but I'm not."

Ralph reached under the front of his tunic. Terror lent Eleanor wild strength. She scrambled across the bed. Ralph caught her hair and yanked her back. Eleanor screamed. Ralph hit her face. Agony slammed her cheek. He ripped open her chemise and clutched one of her breasts.

"You should've been mine," he said.

Eleanor spat blood at him and flailed with her nails.

"Bitch." He punched her and smashed most of her consciousness away.

CHAPTER TWENTY-ONE

Riannon dragged her frown around the hall again. From her position standing at the side of the hearth, she could see all the knots of frustrated hunters as they drank or talked or diced. Guy sat across a chessboard from Humphrey. Rain hurled down loud against the roof as if the gods wished to wash Isingtor away.

At the sound of a lute string plucked, she turned. Instead of Eleanor, one of Joan's daughters idly played the instrument.

Riannon turned her frown back to the other side of the hall. Geoffrey's loudmouthed son drank with Henry's sons and their cronies. Something Ralph said made Guy sharply turn to him. Geoffrey was absent. Riannon didn't want to think he might be the reason Eleanor had yet to leave her bedchamber.

Joan halted near Riannon. "This wretched weather. What could be worse than having to entertain a group of men who'd rather be outside slaughtering?"

"Have you seen Eleanor this morn?" Riannon asked.

Joan glanced around. "Now that you ask, I haven't. And though it's highly unmaternal of me, I'd rather she held that instrument than Elizabeth."

"Perhaps she is unwell," Riannon said.

"Or, mayhap, she has the sense to remain abed on such a dreary morning. I'll go and see how she fares."

Riannon knew they would be unable to keep their engagement to ride together, but she did wish to see Eleanor. Sitting across a hearth from her and listening to her spiritedly swapping jests with Guy proved good entertainment. Riannon could have listened to Eleanor's singing and playing all day long, though she would infinitely prefer not to have to watch Geoffrey of Howe sitting beside his wife and pawing her between songs.

❖

Eleanor sat on the chest beneath the window. She couldn't keep warm. She pulled her fur-lined mantle about herself but still shivered. Rain hurled down past her narrow vertical opening on the world. Occasionally the wind blew some of the wetness inside. Trickles, like tears, ran down the limed wall near her skirts. She had had no tears of her own this morning. She felt too numb. Too sore. Her mind jumped erratically between utter blankness and horrifically sharp images of last night. She could control her mind no better than she could her trembling limbs.

The door latch jumped. Eleanor flinched. A hand knocked on the door.

"Eleanor?" Geoffrey said. "This door is barred."

Eleanor gripped the stone window embrasure. Her face hurt as she frowned. She did not want him to come in. She didn't want anyone to see her. She hadn't even had the courage to look at herself. One eye would not open. Her shame would be livid and swollen on her face for all to see.

"Let me in," Geoffrey said.

"My lady?" Agnes whispered. "It's your lord husband."

Eleanor felt the deepest reluctance to tell Geoffrey what his son had done to her. Yet, she had done nothing to invite Ralph's attack. The blame was his, not hers. The shame should be his, though she burned with it. Her husband, of all men, should have protected her against the unwanted attentions of other men.

"My dear, open this door," Geoffrey said. "I grow impatient."

"My lady?" Agnes whispered. "Shall I?"

Eleanor wanted it to be yesterday. When it hadn't rained. When she didn't hurt. Riding with Riannon and glowing with hope and love.

"I know not what game you're playing," he said, "but I tire of it. I demand that you let me in."

"I ought to admit him," Agnes said.

Eleanor put a shaking hand to her forehead. Her thoughts, her nerves, everything had been bashed to tatters.

"Eleanor!" Geoffrey said.

Her husband needed to know. He had a right to. He was her protector. It was his duty to see justice done against her attacker. Even if that man was his son. Eleanor needed to feel safe again—to know that she did not stand alone. She needed to hear someone tell her that she was not to blame.

"My lady?" Agnes said.

Eleanor nodded, though she continued to stare at the rain. How could there be so much wrong in a world created by benevolent gods?

The door opened.

"Really, my dear," Geoffrey said. "I should not be made to wait outside my wife's chamber. What if someone had seen?"

Eleanor tugged her mantle more closely about herself as she heard Geoffrey approach. Part of herself wished to flee.

"I wanted to tell you, my dear," Geoffrey said, "that you should feel free to play and sing in company if our hostess solicits your performance again. You have a voice pleasing to all. Being entertaining is the key to future invitations to gatherings like this. On such a dreary day, we will all have ample opportunity to prove our worth as guests. Now, come, my dear."

Eleanor continued to stare out at the rain. "I...I cannot."

"Have your woman bring your instrument."

"I cannot go downstairs."

"What's this?" Geoffrey said. "If you have some chill or woman's complaint, you're better off beside a hearth, not shivering up here. Come. Let's all play our parts to do our family credit. Ralph feels this is but the beginning of grander things for us. He should know. Come, my dear."

"I cannot." Eleanor swallowed heavily down her bruised throat. "My...my appearance will not do your family credit. Quite the contrary."

"Your appearance? If you have some spot or redness of nose from a cold, no one will notice, my dear. You're being unduly vain. Now, let us tarry no longer than we already have."

Eleanor shook her head. He would understand if she turned around to face him, but she did not want to.

"I know not what ails you this morn," he said, "but this contrariness is unbecoming, my dear. Everyone will have broken their fasts and have gathered in the hall. Come. We'll join them."

Eleanor's eyes stung with tears.

Geoffrey made a grunt of irritation. He moved closer and put a hand on her shoulder. Eleanor twitched away from the contact.

"Really, my dear," he said. "I'm losing my patience. I wish us to go down. Have the goodness to obey me."

"Goodness?" Eleanor turned around. "I have little faith in goodness today."

Geoffrey's eyes widened in shock. Eleanor instantly regretted letting him see and quickly turned away.

"Atuan's toes," Geoffrey said. "What happened?"

Eleanor gripped the edge of the window and wished she had not started this. She didn't want to think about any of it.

"Have you fallen?" he said. "We must ask Lady Northmarch to send a servant to the nearest grove for a healer priestess."

"No," Eleanor said. "I want no one to see me."

"It looks painful, my dear." Geoffrey stepped closer and peered at Eleanor's profile. "Did you fall from your horse? I've warned you about riding so fast. That mare of yours is too spirited. I'll buy you a more placid animal, such as Phillipa rides."

"I came to no harm riding," Eleanor said.

"Who escorted you yesterday? Whoever he was is much at fault for allowing this to happen. Was it Lord Guy? I shall have to protest to him for his laxity in care."

"It wasn't Guy." A bubble of anger rose inside Eleanor and burst. "I had no accident. I didn't look like this at supper, did I?"

Geoffrey frowned. "No. Then what did you do? Was it those back stairs? I've slipped and almost fallen there myself. I've been meaning to speak to Lady Northmarch's steward about them. You need to take more care, my dear."

"Why do you persist in believing I brought this on myself?"

"Well, my dear, you can be headstrong. And you don't always heed my advice on how best to comport yourself."

Eleanor sagged against the cold stone wall. "How do you suggest I should've comported myself when a man shoved his way into my chamber and beat me nearly senseless?"

"A man?" Geoffrey bristled. "You allowed a man into your bedchamber last night?"

Eleanor peered one-eyed at him in disbelief.

"I can scarce credit that my wife has admitted that she allowed a man into her chamber!" Geoffrey hit his hand with a fist. "Ralph warned me there was one in this company who might try to take advantage of his position. I should've listened to him. He's always right. And you should not have let whoever it was do this. You're my wife. My family's honour is at stake."

"*Let?*" Eleanor blinked away tears. "You think I had a choice? He might have killed me. You think I wanted him to—"

Eleanor turned her face to the wall. Gods, this couldn't be happening. She wanted everything to stop and go away. Tears dribbled over her split lip.

"Well," Geoffrey said. "Who is he? I shall have to approach Lord Northmarch about this. Mayhap the Earl Marshal, too. They'll ensure justice is done, though it's unfortunate that this will expose our good name to a stain and cast a pall on this hunt. Still, there's no helping it now. I must have redress. Whether you invited him in or no, he has no right to beat my wife. Who is this man?"

Eleanor wanted to dissolve with the rain and seep away into the earth. Yet, part of her wished she had the courage to go down into that hall and call Ralph to account for what he did in front of all those witnesses. Make him feel his guilt.

"If you had no part in inviting this man to your chamber," Geoffrey said, "you won't try to protect him from the consequences of his actions."

"It was Ralph."

In the ensuing silence, Eleanor heard the rain drumming down outside and Geoffrey's faintly wheezing breath behind her.

"He'd been drinking," Eleanor said. "I asked him to leave. He pushed Agnes out and—he hit me."

"But—" Geoffrey paced away and back. "This is beyond—There must be much you're not telling me. What did you do?"

"I asked him to leave."

"He would not have come here without good reason. Did you invite him?"

"No."

"Why did he come?" Geoffrey grabbed her shoulder. "He's younger than me. Is that it? Because I've been unable—"

"No!" Eleanor pressed her forehead against the hard stone. "Holy Mother, no. Do you honestly believe I would want anyone to do this to me? He was drunk. I thought he would kill me."

"You must've provoked him."

Eleanor turned until she could see him. The whole of creation had stopped making sense. She was surprised not to see the floor littered with broken fragments of reality piled around Geoffrey's feet.

"I know my son. He would not have acted without cause."

"He accused me of dalliance with Lord Guy."

Geoffrey nodded. "I've noticed that you two are always smiling and more than friendly."

"No. Gods, no. I have never lain with Guy. And if I had, how could you think that would justify your son beating me bloody and raping me?"

Geoffrey's expression hardened. "Your language is unseemly. I'll talk with Ralph. We must decide what to do. Lord Guy is the Earl Marshal's brother. This is a heavy accusation indeed."

"It's false. A lie!"

"Now I see how it was. Ralph merely chastised you for wantonness that imperilled our family good name. Yes." Geoffrey nodded. "That is what happened. You will remain here, madam. You are to see no one and communicate with no one through that woman of yours. You will obey me in this. I'll not have you causing scandals that will make my family the meat for gossip and derision. Ralph and I must decide how to proceed. We'll deal with you when we get home. Mayhap, because of you, we might have to curtail our visit. This is not well done."

Eleanor heard the door shut behind him. Beyond disbelief, and beyond despair, she found fear.

❖

Riannon saw Geoffrey appear in the far doorway. He was alone. He sent a servant to his son sitting amongst a noisy group at the other hearth. Ralph looked annoyed but rose and went to join his father. Whatever Geoffrey said made Ralph sneer. He grabbed his father's arm as if he might shake him. Ralph leaned close to his father to speak. Geoffrey nodded several times and looked around the hall. His gaze snagged on Guy and Humphrey. Ralph clapped his father on his shoulders, laughed, and strode back to his drinking companions. Geoffrey, looking worried, departed. Riannon's frown deepened.

Guy strolled across the hall and stopped beside her. "How about you take your turn at the game board with our host?"

"Did you beat him again?" Riannon asked.

"Can you doubt it? That is why you should play. It'd cheer Humphrey considerably to thrash the Vahldomne."

"Perhaps later. I'm in the wrong mood."

"Are you ever in the right mood to lose badly?" he asked.

"I needs must be when I get caught betwixt you and Nell. My wit is no armour against the shafts from your tongues."

Guy laughed. "I told you that she'd make this trip merry. Though I am close to throwing that dog turd stepson of hers into the nearest midden."

Riannon and Guy glanced across to a loud burst of laughter. Ralph returned their gaze with an expression close to an insolent sneer. He said something to his companions which provoked another burst of laughter.

"The whoreson has been doing that to me all morn," Guy said. "I've no notion why he wishes to raise my hackles, but if he persists, I'll forget the courtesy I owe our sister as our hostess and the trouble it'd cause Nell. I've long wanted to ram his teeth down his throat."

"Have patience," she said. "We'll not always be restrained, nor he protected by, our obligations to others."

Guy flashed her a grin.

"What miserable weather, eh?" Henry planted himself in front of the fire to warm his backside. "We'll have to persuade Eleanor to play for us. We—"

He broke off to frown across at the raucous group across the hall. "I could wish that Geoffrey's son was the same worth as his father. He has a fondness for talking about more than he does. And it's not seemly to use such language in company with ladies. He forgets that he's not in an Irulandi brothel. I'll not have my wife exposed to such language."

Henry stomped across the hall. Riannon did not witness the effect of his arrival on the rowdy group because Joan returned.

"How is she?" Riannon said.

"Unwell," Joan said. "And choosing to keep to her bed this day."

"Does she need a healer?" Riannon said. "I can fetch one from the nearest grove."

"I offered her the services of my woman," Joan said. "But she declined. She claims that she suffers merely a light stomach upset and no great malady, but feels it best to remain quiet. Or, rather, her woman did. Eleanor remained in bed and didn't speak with me."

Eleanor was ill enough to remain abed but refused aid? She would admit Riannon to her chamber. And, mayhap, accept her offer to fetch a healer. Riannon strode out of the hall and headed for Eleanor's chamber.

❖

Eleanor watched her hand on the stone embrasure. She could not make it stop trembling. Everything in creation had slipped from her control, even her own body. She was unworthy of being protected. Less than a wife. She had become a shameful thing to be kept hidden.

She hurt. She deserved it. She asked for it. Ralph had been in the right to do it to her.

Or had she always been an object to Geoffrey? A rich, younger wife to show off before other men.

They would deal with her when they got her home.

Eleanor's nails scraped the stone as her hand tightened into a claw. *Holy Mother, what more could they do to her?*

A hand rapped on the door. Eleanor squeezed her eye shut and pressed herself against the wall. *No! Please, no.*

❖

Riannon repeated her knock. Agnes cracked the door open.

"My sister tells me that your lady is unwell," Riannon said. "I wish to speak with her."

"She wishes no visitors, Vahldomne, your honour," Agnes said.

"If she is so stricken, I'll ride to fetch a healer priestess for her. You or she have but to say the word."

Agnes cast an uncertain look back into the chamber behind her.

"Please," Riannon said. "I would help her or see her."

Agnes bit her lip. Something more was amiss than a stomach upset. Eleanor would not have refused her admittance if that mild complaint was truly what she suffered. Riannon wanted to shove the door aside and stride inside to see for herself.

"Please," Riannon said. "Your lady's health is dear to me."

Agnes visibly made a decision. She whispered, "I'll talk with her."

Riannon scowled as the door shut. What, in the name of fiery hell, was wrong?

❖

Eleanor put a hand to her mouth and swallowed with difficulty. That was Riannon's voice.

Agnes's feet scuffed the rushes as she approached. "Lady? I know your lord husband forbade you to receive any visitors, but...it's the Vahldomne."

Eleanor's face hurt as she frowned out at the rain. Riannon could make her feel safe in a world where that illusion of safety had been brutally and bloodily smashed from around her. She craved protection and reassurance as much as she needed her next breath. Her husband had denied it to her. Worse, he blamed her for what Ralph had done. He threatened more.

Riannon loved her. Riannon had never looked on her as a possession to be used. But would Riannon believe she had brought it on herself?

"The Vahldomne has offered to fetch a healer priestess," Agnes said. "Mayhap such services might be helpful."

Eleanor stared through unshed tears at the relentless water pounding the world outside. Geoffrey had forbidden her to admit anyone. She had vowed obedience to him when she married him. But as part of that same ceremony, he had sworn to protect her. What else would he allow Ralph to do to her? Distant thunder rumbled as if the sky broke and collapsed to the earth.

"My lady?" Agnes said.

Eleanor nodded. "Let her in."

Agnes's footsteps hurried away.

Holy Mother, what's happening to me? Help me.

Eleanor knew the approaching footsteps belonged to Riannon, but she could not stop herself gripping the window's edge as if she expected to be pulled from it. Every nerve tightened with fear. Her face hurt where her bruised flesh pressed against the cool, hard stone.

"I missed you in the hall," Riannon said. "My sister said you're unwell. I'll fetch whatever help you need."

At the sound of Riannon's voice, Eleanor bit her split lip and tasted fresh blood. Relief spilled out as tears.

"Eleanor?"

Eleanor desperately wanted to feel safe. She remembered clinging to Riannon and how it felt to have Riannon's arms around her. Riannon would not let anyone touch her—not even if Geoffrey and Ralph both barged into the chamber. Shame held her immobile. Turning to Riannon would mean exposing her injuries and having to explain. Why did she have to think? Why must she face decisions? She wanted everything to stop, and stop hurting.

"Nell? I wish to help. If you'll let me."

Riannon moved closer. She stood just behind Eleanor. Eleanor frowned down at her hand gripping the stone. This was madness. She should never have let Riannon in here. If Riannon saw her, she would want to know what happened. She should have obeyed Geoffrey and kept herself hidden.

"I begin to think the worst," Riannon said.

Riannon stepped to the side of the chest Eleanor sat on. She was so close that her leg brushed against the skirts of Eleanor's overtunic. Eleanor averted her head. Riannon squatted. Eleanor could feel Riannon looking at her.

Riannon gently rested a hand over the one with which Eleanor clutched the bottom of the window. "Love?"

Eleanor snapped. She turned, flung her arms around Riannon's neck, and pushed her face against Riannon's shoulder without caring how much it hurt. "I'm so scared."

"Scared?" Riannon slipped her arms around Eleanor. "What cause have you to fear?"

"I thought he was going to kill me." Unshed tears threatened to choke her. Her body shook. She couldn't control what she was doing. "He believes him. Not me. Nonnie, what am I going to do?'

"Kill you?" Riannon stroked Eleanor's back. "Who are you talking about? Your husband? What has he done?"

Eleanor dug her fingers into Riannon. Solid. Safe. She burst into tears.

"Love?" Riannon said. "What has happened? Why should you fear anyone?"

Eleanor tried to stop her sobs, but couldn't. Riannon held her.

Eventually, Eleanor's weeping subsided and gave way to shivering. She felt winter cold despite her fur-lined mantle and clinging to Riannon's warm body.

"You ought to be abed, love," Riannon said. "This sickness—"

"No!"

"Nell?"

"Not the bed," Eleanor said.

Eleanor felt Riannon stiffen.

"What did he do to you?" Riannon asked. "Nell?"

Eleanor's teeth chattered. The ice gripping her body froze her thoughts.

Riannon turned her head to speak to Agnes. "Bring an extra mantle. Or cloak. Yes, that will do. Wrap it around her."

Riannon and Agnes settled a woollen cloak around Eleanor's shoulders. She didn't feel as though she would ever be warm again, no matter what they wrapped around her.

"You ought to be close to a fire," Riannon said.

"No. I...I can't go anywhere."

Riannon went still and taut. "Let me look at you."

Riannon urged Eleanor to straighten. Eleanor should have locked her arms around Riannon's neck and resisted. But she yielded to Riannon's gentle pressure. Riannon gasped. The shock on her face as she stared at Eleanor swiftly solidified and hardened into implacable anger. Eleanor again looked at a stranger in Riannon.

"Who did this?" Riannon asked. "Your husband?"

Eleanor shook her head.

"Has he gone to call the whoreson to account?" Riannon asked. "But he did wrong to leave you here. I expect this is the last place you wish to be. Let me take you to my chamber. You'll be safe there. Can you walk?"

"No. I can't let anyone see me. Not like this."

"As you wish. But you need healing, love. Let me send Alan to fetch a priestess from the nearest grove." Riannon gave Eleanor's hand a reassuring squeeze, but she went tense again and her thumb touched the charmed ring on Eleanor's finger. Her gaze snapped back up to Eleanor's face. "Did he—?"

Eleanor reflexively averted her face. But why was it her shame that he had done that to her? Riannon did not move away from her in disgust, though. Instead, her fingers clasped Eleanor's hands with reassuring strength.

"Who?" Riannon's voice sounded remote with controlled anger. "If your husband needs help bringing this cur to justice, I will do all I can."

Eleanor shook her head and clung to Riannon's hand as if it were her only lifeline. It might be. What had Geoffrey said? *Ralph and I must decide how to proceed. We'll deal with you when we get home.* He would hit her again. And worse. Geoffrey would do nothing to stop him. He'd see no wrong in whatever Ralph did to her.

"If the offal masquerading as a man who did this is beyond your husband's reach," Riannon said, "he's not above mine. No one is."

Eleanor heard the danger in Riannon's voice as she stared down at their joined hands. Riannon's sword hand. If she spoke Ralph's name, she knew what Riannon would do. She flinched at the memory of Ralph's fist punching her. The look on his face as he'd ripped her chemise. The pain when he rammed himself—

"Has your husband gone to Humphrey to lay charges and ask for an arrest?" Riannon said.

"No." Eleanor felt Riannon's frown in the tightening of the hand she held. This was the only protection she had against it happening again, and again. "Geoffrey will make no complaint."

"But—"

"He holds his son blameless."

"Ralph." Riannon surged to her feet. "I'll return. I won't be long."

Riannon strode away, told Agnes to bar the door and let no one in, and then she was gone.

Eleanor lifted her gaze from her empty hand to the continuing rain.

"The Vahldomne will kill him," Agnes said.

"Yes."

❖

Riannon stalked across her chamber to the chest. Her two swords lay there in their scabbards. She grabbed the sword that had been a gift from Prince Oliver and strode to the stairs. She marched into the hall and paused to locate her quarry. Ralph stood at the far hearth with his back to her. Geoffrey was nowhere to be seen. Riannon strode through the hall. She shouldered one man aside and shoved Ralph in the back.

He turned. "What the—"

Riannon punched him in the face. Ralph staggered, tripped, and dropped to his backside.

Riannon ignored the surprised outbursts of the onlookers. She drew her sword and levelled the point at Ralph's chest. He stared up at her with blood trickling from his nose.

"I'll give you the chance to fight back that you didn't give her," Riannon said.

Ralph's mouth dropped open. "*You?*"

"Riannon?" Henry pushed through the startled spectators. "What's the meaning of this?"

"He knows," Riannon said. "Well? Do you fight or do I butcher you where you lie like the pig you are?"

"Nonnie." Guy put a hand on her arm. "What—"

"Stay out of this." Riannon kept her gaze on Ralph. "Well?"

"Fetch my sword." Ralph eased himself from under her sword point and to his feet.

"This is breaking the queen's peace," Henry said.

"If he committed some offence under my roof," Humphrey of Northmarch said, "the onus is on me to enact justice."

Guy stepped between him and Riannon. "We all heard a challenge issued and accepted."

"Aye." Ralph wiped the blood from his nose on his sleeve, and sneered at Riannon. "I'm more than willing."

Riannon wanted to kill him. To hack him apart. To make him hurt and scream and regret every seen and unseen bruise he had inflicted on Eleanor. Make him feel helplessness and fear. Ralph's squire hurried back with his lord's sword.

Geoffrey elbowed his way through the ring of men. "Ralph! What is this?"

Ralph drew his sword. "It seems that this self-claimed Vahldomne would play the man in the bedchamber as well as on the battlefield. It's past time someone showed her that she's not a man."

Riannon ignored Guy's questioning look as she strode past him towards the doors.

Rain hammered the muddy courtyard. Cold wetness pelted her shoulders and bare head. She took a stance with a two-handed grip on her sword. Ralph swaggered out to meet her. People poured out of the doors to press against the walls under the shelter of the eaves to watch.

"Stop this!" Geoffrey called. "Please. My lords. You cannot let this happen. Neither wears armour. It will be a death!"

Ralph acted as if he had not heard his father. He swung his sword before taking a stance. "You face no soft imperial pig this time."

Mud oozed over Riannon's feet and sucked at her as she tried to move. Ralph suffered the same hindrance. They shifted warily. Ralph smiled.

"She begged me for it," he said.

Riannon's grip tightened on her sword. If he wished to ignite her temper into a reckless strike, he mistook her completely. Her mood cooled and hardened further, like a new-forged blade plunged into a smith's bucket. When he stepped forwards and swung, she met his blade with her own. The clang reverberated around the courtyard. The skies answered with a banging of thunder.

Ralph retreated and shook his head to dislodge rain trickling down his face. Riannon did not want to remember the pulpy face she had left upstairs. Her boots splashed in a puddle as she advanced on him.

"She felt so good around me," he said. "Wet with lust. Tight. Hot for me."

Riannon swung. Ralph's sword smacked against hers in a solid parry. He grinned. Blood from his nose stained his teeth pink.

"She wanted it," he said. "Moaning for me. You wouldn't know what that felt like, would you?"

Riannon swung. Ralph threw his sword up to block the strike at his head.

"She told me how good I felt inside her." He smirked.

She swung again. And again. And again. She drove Ralph back across the muddy ground where men, dogs, and horses had churned the muck. His foot slipped. He parried too slowly. The end of her sword bit into the meat of his upper arm. Ralph lost his sneer as his left hand fell away from his sword hilt. Blood ran down his sodden sleeve.

"Stop!" Geoffrey called. "Ralph! Stop this!"

Ralph flailed a strike at her. Riannon beat it aside and stepped close to him. She thrust her sword low into his belly. The hilt jumped in her hands as his body jerked with the shock of the impact. He grunted and dropped his sword.

"Does that feel good inside you?" she said.

Riannon shoved her blade deeper into him. He gasped. His body sagged. Riannon released her sword and let him fall. He splatted into the mud with his hands clutching at the blade sticking out of him. Riannon grabbed her sword hilt and yanked the weapon free. Ralph screamed. The blade released another gush of blood and a slippery loop of squirming entrail.

"I know I am not a man," she said. "You aren't much of one."

"No! Ralph! My son." Geoffrey splashed across to fling himself down in the mud beside his writhing son. "Help me. Quickly. Send for healers! Get away from him. Would you strike him again now?"

Riannon, soaked to the skin, glared down with contempt at the pair. "I do not hit the defenceless. Nor will I let you do so. Remember that, old man."

Riannon turned to squelch towards the door.

"Arrest her!" Geoffrey called. "My lords, you're all my witnesses. I demand justice!"

CHAPTER TWENTY-TWO

Aveline strolled behind the priestess sprinkling droplets along the path from a green bough and a ewer of blessed water. The noon sun beamed down on the forest of the grove casting short, dark shadows. The singing grew louder as they approached the clearing.

Half a thousand priestesses, from aspirants to naers, stood in the great clearing. No less than four mother-naers, in robes stiff with embroidery and gold thread, stood beside the pool. They flanked the thin, white-haired figure of the matriarch. The old woman's skin looked more grey than brown, but her eyes defied age. They bored into Aveline. How she hated to do this. Aveline smiled. Matriarch Melisande replied with a wintry thinning of lips.

Though the preliminary ceremony, with its prolonged singing and chanting and prayers, lasted nearly two hours, the investiture itself was of short duration. Priestesses removed Aveline's plain green robe and led her to the side of the pool. Another helped her shrug off her chemise. She stood naked before her peers, the woods, the pool, and in the presence of the Lady of Creation.

One of the mother-naers put the questions of piety to Aveline. Matriarch Melisande stepped forwards to perform the purifying immersion. Aveline felt small hands hard against her back give her a strong shove. She hit the pool water face-first and unintentionally swallowed some of the blessed water.

The matriarch's ill-will could not lessen Aveline's triumph. *I shall endeavour to let no mortal obstacles block your wishes.* Aveline was making good her promise to the Lady of Creation. She stood one long step closer to the matriarchy, one step closer to the goal that the Goddess urged her towards.

Aveline waded out to the sound of beautiful singing. Priestesses passed her towels and helped her dry herself. She put on a clean chemise and one of the mother-naers helped her into a new robe that signified her rebirth from the sanctified water as a mother-naer.

The heavy robe about her shoulders felt as natural as if she had been fitted for the dignity from her emergence from her mortal mother's womb. As she led the prayer of thanks, she could all but taste the power thrumming through the clearing. Could that be a divine signal of approval of her success? Mother-Naer Aveline. Member of the convocation of the Order of the Goddess. One of the twenty. When the matriarch died, which could not be more than a dozen years hence, the twenty would elect one of their number to assume the fallen mantle. Aveline could become matriarch before the age of fifty. The youngest ever. The one with the most time to steer the order to ascendant power. One day, she would stand at the edge of the waters in the Cave of the Pool and make the whole world tremble in the name of the Goddess.

The matriarch beckoned to Aveline. Aveline stepped forwards and bowed her head for the kiss of sisterhood. Melisande's eyes were glacial. She signalled for the hymn to start.

Under the cover of the singing, Melisande whispered, "You won this round. But this isn't the end."

Aveline merely smiled, bowed, and took her place with the other mother-naers. She had the Goddess on her side.

Her dreams were coming true—she was making them unfold before her. The crusade had begun well. Part of poor Evriat again breathed free of the infidel yoke. Perhaps, in time, they could smash the whole rotten empire and beat the unbelievers back to the sea. With a matriarch in command of the power of the cave pool and her paladin wielding the blessed sword as no less a person than the Vahldomne, dreams could become reality. With a little effort and planning, there was nothing Aveline could not do to enact the will of the Goddess.

As she walked out of the grove with the other mother-naers following the matriarch, Aveline smiled. How unexpectedly valuable that meeting with her cousin Riannon had been. Who would have predicted their paths so intimately entwined? Perhaps greatness lay ahead for them both. Aveline still sometimes marvelled at how close she had been to losing control of her most valuable asset through that liaison with Eleanor of Barrowmere. She ought to return to Tirand soon, to ensure that nothing untoward happened in her sister's kingdom, and to check Riannon's resolve.

Aveline stepped out of the trees of the grove into the full glare of sun. She had every right to exult in her victories this day, and expect many more such days to come. *Wise Mother, I do your will.*

❖

"Riannon!"

Riannon halted halfway across the hall. Henry spearheaded the group striding in her wake. Impatient as she was to return to Eleanor, she did not want all these men stomping up to Eleanor's chamber behind her.

"By Atuan's beard," Henry said, "what have you done?"

"I need an accounting of this," Humphrey said. "That man is like to die from that belly wound. He was my guest."

"I offered a challenge," Riannon said. "He accepted. It was no murder."

"That might be so," Henry said, "but it was hardly a fair fight."

Riannon's fingers tightened on the hilt of her bloody sword. "Do you accuse me of using dishonourable means?"

"Of course I don't!" Henry said. "But you're the Vahldomne. You could kill better men than Ralph Howe with your arm in a sling."

"He is not dead," she said.

"He will be in two or three days when his belly rots and fills with maggots," Henry said. "Damn it, Riannon, I like him as little as anyone, but you can't just go killing men because they're half-witted braggarts."

A scream caused them all to turn. Men carried Ralph into the hall. His father shouted at them to have care. Joan left them to stride across to stand beside her husband.

"I've dispatched a man to the local grove to fetch a healer priestess," Joan said. "Saving a miracle, though, he'll die under our roof. Nonnie, why did you do it?"

Riannon had no intention of mentioning Eleanor. "It was a matter of honour."

Henry and Humphrey looked unhappy, but both nodded.

"What of my family's reputation?" Joan said. "My sister cannot indiscriminately slaughter our guests."

"Nonnie issued a challenge," Guy said. "We all heard him accept."

Joan threw a hard glare at him. "You're not on a battlefield, you're in my house. Nonnie, you broke the queen's peace. In the name of the gods, why did you do it? Men have been imprisoned or outlawed from the kingdom for less. Did that cross your mind before you drew your sword?"

"My lords!" Geoffrey pushed his way through the guests. "I demand justice for my son. My Lord Earl, I lay a charge against her."

"Be calm," Henry said. "Make no hasty accusations against my sister."

"You saw what she did to him." Geoffrey levelled a shaking finger at Riannon. "He is like to die. You all watched it."

"We saw a challenge issued and answered," Humphrey said. "Have a care before you say aught you might regret. Remember, you speak of the Vahldomne."

Geoffrey clenched his fists. "Pah! My son was right. How can any believe a woman's claim to that name? If you're all unmanned by her, I'm not. Someone give me a sword and I'll have restitution."

"Don't be a fool, man," Humphrey said. "Your wits are disordered."

Riannon was conscious of the weight of her weapon still in her hand. If only Geoffrey had been twenty or thirty years younger, she would make the despicable whoreson pay for Eleanor's injuries. She turned to Alan and handed him her sword. Her conspicuous and casual disarming in the face of his threat incensed Geoffrey even more. His eyes looked wild as if her thrust into his son's belly had cut some of Geoffrey's wits loose.

"I demand justice!" Geoffrey said. "Will you all just stand there and do nought? My son lies in agony because she attacked him!"

"Had you more regard to justice," Riannon said, "I would not have needed to do aught."

Geoffrey stared at her without the faintest glimmer of comprehension. Eleanor and her suffering did not exist for him. He cared only for his worthless son. Riannon's contempt knew no bounds.

"You have a right selective way with invoking law," Riannon said.

"You know what he did. He needed to be held accountable. You did not do it. You blamed the blameless one. He got less than he deserves, and if I could think of a way to make you suffer for your complicity, I would do it."

Geoffrey's white brows drew together as he frowned up at her. "What—"

"If you ever do anything like it again—if you raise your fist—if you raise your voice, remember me."

Confusion gave way to dawning comprehension and anger on Geoffrey's face. "Her. You've talked to—she disobeyed me."

Riannon had much to say on that subject, but where he might have so far forgotten himself as to be unaware of their audience, she was not. She would not drag Eleanor into this, nor expose her suffering to general gossip. While it might be easy to walk away from him, though, how could she leave Eleanor in his power?

"I see how it is, now," Geoffrey said. "She did this. And you—you have no right to interfere in my family affairs."

Riannon stepped closer to stare down at him. She lowered her voice. "Have some sense. Keep her out of this."

"She has always been jealous of Ralph," Geoffrey said. "He warned me. So did Phillipa. I should have listened. Ralph is always right. She has spun some lies to you and—"

Riannon grabbed the front of his tunic. "I've seen her."

Henry clamped a hand on her arm. "Riannon? What is this?"

Riannon released Geoffrey when she really wanted to beat him senseless.

"She has meddled where she had no right," Geoffrey said. "She has incited my wife to disobedience. And my wife has used her to harm my son!"

Riannon turned her back on him and resumed her path to the far doors. The crowd of guests and servants parted to let her through.

"I ask you to support my rights as a father!" Geoffrey said. "And as a husband."

"Riannon!" Henry called. "Have you nought to say? These are heavy matters."

Riannon turned a look of disgust on Geoffrey. She should not have expected the man who condoned the beating and rape of his wife to have even the minimal honour to want to protect his wife's good name.

Well, there was one way to stop this. She signalled to Alan.

"If you wish to detain me," Riannon said, "my sword is there for your taking."

Geoffrey smiled. Neither Henry nor Humphrey moved to relieve her squire of her weapon.

"No," Eleanor said.

Riannon would not have recognised Eleanor with her mantle hood pulled about her face if Agnes had not closely shadowed her. People moved aside to allow her through. The cloth across her face did not hide the ugly livid swelling that closed her left eye.

"You should not be here," Riannon said.

"You didn't return," Eleanor said. "I was worried that you were hurt or—I couldn't have lived with myself if I'd sent you to—"

"I am unharmed," Riannon said. "And you have no cause to fear him again."

Eleanor nodded. "Thank the gods. But I can't let you surrender yourself because of me."

"This is your fault," Geoffrey said to Eleanor. "My son lies with his life in peril. Because you disobeyed me!"

He closed on Eleanor. "You sent her to kill him. By the gods, if my son dies—"

Riannon stepped in his path and pushed him back. "I warned you."

"Get out of my way," he said. "She's my wife."

"It's time you remembered that," Riannon said. "Your duty is to protect her and honour her."

Geoffrey glared up at her. "You seek to teach me a husband's part?"

"You have need of someone telling you what you ought to do," Riannon said. "Your wife should not fear you. Nor your son."

Geoffrey stabbed an angry glare at Eleanor standing behind Riannon, then he finally appeared to remember their audience. "My family. The gossip. My son. Lord of gods, what is happening? What have you done to us?"

Eleanor moved from behind Riannon.

"I trust him not to look to your best care," Riannon said.

"Nor I." Eleanor tugged one of her rings off. "The only part of me he really valued, he has control of."

She dropped her wedding ring. It disappeared amongst the crushed rushes.

Riannon ignored the murmurs as she watched Eleanor walk away. She was unsure she fully understood what she'd just witnessed.

"It's nerves," Geoffrey said. "She—She cannot abide sickness. She's squeamish. Overwrought. My lords, please forget...My son. I must go to my son."

"He is brainsick." Henry shook his head as he watched Geoffrey shoving his way to where his son lay groaning. "Riannon, what is your part in all this?"

Riannon felt as though she stood on the edge of a precipice. She strode off in Eleanor's wake.

Eleanor and her woman sorted clothes. Packing, ready to leave.

"Can you truly sacrifice it all?" Riannon said.

Eleanor straightened. Her mantle fell from her face, exposing the pulpy mess Ralph had made of her.

"I am not thinking as well as I ought," Eleanor said. "I know that. But I cannot live scared. If Ralph dies, Geoffrey will hold me to blame. If he kills me in some rage, or through mistreatment and neglect, what consolation is there to being a wealthy corpse? Will you take me to a grove house? I have enough in my jewellery casket to persuade them to admit me as a dedicant."

"You want a religious life?" Riannon said.

"I'll be safe there."

"You'd be safer with me."

Eleanor averted her face and wandered across the chamber to stare out at the rain. Riannon followed her.

"I can't offer you much," Riannon said. "Not compared to what you leave behind. I know not if I can help you regain any of your possessions from him. But I can protect you. No man will touch you."

Riannon put her hands on Eleanor's shoulders. She felt her tremble. Riannon wished she had twisted her sword before she pulled it out of him. Whatever he suffered was not nearly enough.

"Gast is within four hours ride," Riannon said. "Let me take you there."

"It's raining. You must be soaked." Eleanor turned and put a hand on Riannon's chest. "You are."

"It matters nought." Riannon covered Eleanor's hand with one of her own. "I can borrow a litter from Joan, so you need not ride if it would be uncomfortable."

Eleanor stared at the back of Riannon's hand. Riannon wanted to pull her hard against her chest and never let her go. She wondered if it would hurt Eleanor if she held her. What other bruises had he beaten on her that her clothes concealed?

"Until the day he dies," Eleanor said, "I'm married. I have no right to ask you to sin."

"What is there of right in any of this?"

Eleanor shook her head. "My world has ripped asunder. That does not mean yours must."

"I love you."

"You have your reputation to think of now, Vahldomne. You'd not fare well in company with a runaway wife."

"You will not always be his wife. My reputation is with a sword, love. No one will refuse my service because of my domestic arrangements. Most would be hypocritical if they did." Riannon gently touched Eleanor's undamaged cheek. "Mayhap, too, it's time the Vahldomne gave the bards a verse or two of love for their songs."

"This is no matter for jest. What of your cousin Aveline? And your service to the Goddess?"

Riannon nodded. "We'll winter here, then I must return west to the crusade come spring. I'd like you to accompany me. We can rent somewhere for you to live whilst I'm away with the army. It would be to our benefit if you took the management of our estates in hand yourself, but I'd rather you not be so far from me. Or close to him. Rich men can have long reaches. As for our Wise Mother, I cannot believe she would condone any woman being treated as you have been, love."

Eleanor put her other hand on Riannon's chest. Riannon held that one in place, too.

"You sound as though you've planned this all," Eleanor said.

"No. I've not allowed myself to spin fancies about you this last year and a half, for fear of preferring to live in my daydreams. I speak what is in my heart, and it is the same as what my head tells me makes sense."

Eleanor sighed and slipped both hands free. "If there is one thing I know about you, it's how integrity and rectitude run deeper in you than the marrow of your bones. My perfect knight. Could you live with yourself if you fled with me?"

"I could not live with myself if I left you in danger." Riannon reclaimed one of Eleanor's hands. "There will be those who will look on us askance. Your husband might take a complaint to the queen. Some will find fault with us because we are not a man and a woman. We will face troubles. I am aware of that, love. There is no course of action that does not require our consciences to bend."

Riannon stroked the back of Eleanor's hand. "You once told me things can still function though flawed. Imperfections need not render a thing valueless. The choices we face are all flawed, are they not? But that does not mean whatever we do is wholly wrong."

"You could ride away and leave me in a grove."

"No. You would be vulnerable to him. He could take you away and hold you somewhere and mistreat you, and be within his rights. That I cannot allow. I have served weak and unworthy men, and it did not kill me. I must use a sword that inflicts terrible wounds, yet I wield it in the name of the Lady of Mercy and Healing. I have sworn to protect the weak and defenceless. How could I ensure the safety of some woman whose name I would never learn, yet allow the woman I love to come to harm?"

The expression on Eleanor's ruined face was hard to read, but she offered no more objections.

Riannon kissed Eleanor's fingers. "Will you let me protect you?"

Eleanor lifted her free hand, but a strong rapping on the door arrested her.

"Eleanor? It's Guy. Is Nonnie with you?"

Riannon shared a look with Eleanor.

"Let him in," Eleanor said.

Agnes opened the door. Guy entered and stopped abruptly with a shocked expression. Eleanor belatedly moved behind Riannon.

"Atuan's balls," Guy said. "So that's what the dog turd did. What he said to you when you fought, that wasn't just empty wind and taunts, was it? He—"

"Hold your tongue," Riannon said.

Guy nodded. "He should count himself fortunate you got to him before I did."

"Did you seek me for a reason?" Riannon said.

"You see the family errand boy," he said. "The healer has arrived. She would be better employed in prayers to help the prick in the next life, for he will need every one. Joan wished Eleanor to know. Our sister also said Geoffrey is in need of calming. He rages with one breath and weeps with the next. Humphrey cannot evict him, since his son cannot be moved, so our brother-in-law has asked me to be my most charming to suggest that you make yourself scarce ere the Howes depart. Oh, and he asked me to return this."

Guy held up Riannon's scabbarded sword. Riannon accepted the weapon and the unspoken message it conveyed that neither Humphrey nor Henry had any intention of supporting Geoffrey's charges against her.

"I'll leave within the hour." Riannon turned to Eleanor. "Should I ask for a litter?"

Riannon held her breath as Eleanor lifted her head. At that moment, there was nothing Riannon would not do for this woman. She would face down every angry man in the world, sword in hand. Or forgo every gift from every prince. Slay dragons, even. Take every hurt from Eleanor's body to feel it ten-fold with her own. But Riannon also knew fear. She so desperately wanted to be able to take Eleanor away to safety and look after her that she was afraid she might be denied it.

"Are you sure?" Eleanor said.

"On the surety of my soul," Riannon said.

Eleanor's swollen and split lip made her attempt at a smile into a heart-wrenching travesty. She put her fingers to Riannon's lips. Riannon kissed them.

"I loathe litters," Eleanor said, "but I'm not sure I could ride."

Riannon silently vowed that she would kill Geoffrey rather than let him lay a finger on Eleanor again. "I'll make my peace with my sister and return. Guy will remain here with you in my absence if you'd rather not be alone. Or, mayhap, I could send him to Joan in my stead."

"I am at your disposal," Guy said. "I am at everyone's disposal."

"You had best go," Eleanor said to Riannon. "You must not leave with your sister wroth with you. Change into dry clothes."

"We'll get wet soon enough on the ride."

Riannon strode across the chamber. She wondered if Geoffrey was in possession of sufficient of his wits to understand when she told him that she would be taking his wife away. Not that she cared what he thought of her, her courtesy, or her actions. Nothing he could say or do would change her mind.

Eleanor's "no" halted Riannon just inside the door.

"As you are to take care of me," Eleanor said, "I needs must concern myself with your welfare. Don dry clothes. I have no relish to nurse you through a chill."

Riannon's surprise gave way to a grin. "As you wish, lady."

Riannon escorted Eleanor outside with Guy trailing them. The rain had eased to a drizzle. Congealed blood stained the mud where Ralph had fallen. Riannon helped Eleanor into the litter. One day soon, she would lift Eleanor into a saddle and follow Eleanor's headlong gallop.

"This rain is like to have swollen the Brown River," Guy said. "The ford at Delling should still be passable."

"We go west, not south," Riannon said. "To Gast. I'll not be joining you at Merefield."

Riannon took the reins from her groom and swung up onto her horse. "Come spring, we'll be travelling to Evriat. You'll be welcome at our table."

Guy flicked a frown from Riannon to the curtain of the litter. "We? Our? You mean—? Atuan's legs. What a dullard I've been."

"Yes," Riannon said.

"I'll send word when Ralph dies," Guy said. "What of Howe?"

"He knows Nell goes with me," Riannon said. "He won't follow us. But on the day you hear he's dead, you'd best set out to find us with all speed. I know how laggard you are when it comes to weddings, but I'll not forgive you if you miss this one. I'll need you as best man."

Guy blinked, then threw his head back to laugh. "Ah, Nonnie! You have impeccable taste in women. It's the same as mine!"

Riannon refrained from pointing out that it was she, and not he, who rode away with Eleanor.

The sound of Guy's laughter followed them until drowned by their horses' hooves as they rode away in the drizzle to face whatever the future held, together.

❧

About the Author

L-J Baker grew up in New Zealand and took her wife home there after a stint living in the USA. Her educational background is in the physical sciences. Her particular area of research required her to spend long periods of time operating equipment in darkened rooms or in the dead of night, which proved highly conducive to imagining all sorts of strange and fantastical places, people, and events—especially when the data weren't looking so good. She and her wife are the frequently put-upon slaves of two very spoiled cats.

You can find more information about L-J on her webpage:

http://homepages.ihug.co.nz/~wordchutney/index.html

Books Available From Bold Strokes Books

Lady Knight by L-J Baker. Loyalty and honour clash with love and ambition in a medieval world of magic when female knight Riannon meets Lady Eleanor. (978-1-933110-75-2)

Dark Dreamer by Jennifer Fulton. Best-selling horror author, Rowe Devlin falls under the spell of psychic Phoebe Temple. A Dark Vista romance. (978-1-933110-74-5)

Come and Get Me by Julie Cannon. Elliott Foster isn't used to pursuing women, but alluring attorney Lauren Collier makes her change her mind. (978-1-933110-73-8)

Blind Curves by Diane and Jacob Anderson-Minshall. Private eye Yoshi Yakamota comes to the aid of her ex-lover Velvet Erickson in the first Blind Eye mystery. (978-1-933110-72-1)

Dynasty of Rogues by Jane Fletcher. It's hate at first sight for Ranger Riki Sadiq and her new patrol corporal, Tanya Coppelli—except for their undeniable attraction. (978-1-933110-71-4)

Running With the Wind by Nell Stark. Sailing instructor Corrie Marsten has signed off on love until she meets Quinn Davies—one woman she can't ignore. (978-1-933110-70-7)

More than Paradise by Jennifer Fulton. Two women battle danger, risk all, and find in one another an unexpected ally and an unforgettable love. (978-1-933110-69-1)

Flight Risk by Kim Baldwin. For Blayne Keller, being in the wrong place at the wrong time just might turn out to be the best thing that ever happened to her. (978-1-933110-68-4)

Rebel's Quest, Supreme Constellations Book Two by Gun Brooke. On a world torn by war, two women discover a love that defies all boundaries. (978-1-933110-67-7)

Punk and Zen by JD Glass. Angst, sex, love, rock. Trace, Candace, Francesca...Samantha. Losing control—and finding the truth within. BSB Victory Editions. (1-933110-66-X)

Stellium in Scorpio by Andrews & Austin. The passionate reuniting of two powerful women on the glitzy Las Vegas Strip where everything is an illusion and love is a gamble. (1-933110-65-1)

When Dreams Tremble by Radclyffe. Two women whose lives turned out far differently than they'd once imagined discover that sometimes the shape of the future can only be found in the past. (1-933110-64-3)

The Devil Unleashed by Ali Vali. As the heat of violence rises, so does the passion. A Casey Family crime saga. (1-933110-61-9)

Burning Dreams by Susan Smith. The chronicle of the challenges faced by a young drag king and an older woman who share a love "outside the bounds." (1-933110-62-7)

Fresh Tracks by Georgia Beers. Seven women, seven days. A lot can happen when old friends, lovers, and a new girl in town get together in the mountains. (1-933110-63-5)

The Empress and the Acolyte by Jane Fletcher. Jemeryl and Tevi fight to protect the very fabric of their world: time. Lyremouth Chronicles Book Three. (1-933110-60-0)

First Instinct by JLee Meyer. When high-stakes security fraud leads to murder, one woman flees for her life while another risks her heart to protect her. (1-933110-59-7)

Erotic Interludes 4: Extreme Passions ed. by Radclyffe and Stacia Seaman. Thirty of today's hottest erotica writers set the pages aflame with love, lust, and steamy liaisons. (1-933110-58-9)

Storms of Change by Radclyffe. In the continuing saga of the Provincetown Tales, duty and love are at odds as Reese and Tory face their greatest challenge. (1-933110-57-0)

Unexpected Ties by Gina L. Dartt. With death before dessert, Kate Shannon and Nikki Harris are swept up in another tale of danger and romance. (1-933110-56-2)

Sleep of Reason by Rose Beecham. While Detective Jude Devine searches for a lost boy, her rocky relationship with Dr. Mercy Westmoreland gets a lot harder. (1-933110-53-8)

Passion's Bright Fury by Radclyffe. Passion strikes without warning when a trauma surgeon and a filmmaker become reluctant allies. (1-933110-54-6)

Broken Wings by L-J Baker. When Rye Woods meets beautiful dryad Flora Withe, her libido, as hidden as her wings, reawakens along with her heart. (1-933110-55-4)

Combust the Sun by Andrews & Austin. A Richfield and Rivers mystery set in L.A. Murder among the stars. (1-933110-52-X)

Of Drag Kings and the Wheel of Fate by Susan Smith. A blind date in a drag club leads to an unlikely romance. (1-933110-51-1)

Tristaine Rises by Cate Culpepper. Brenna, Jesstin, and the Amazons of Tristaine face their greatest challenge for survival. (1-933110-50-3)

Too Close to Touch by Georgia Beers. Kylie O'Brien believes in true love and is willing to wait for it, even though Gretchen, her new boss, is off-limits. (1-933110-47-3)

100th Generation by Justine Saracen. Ancient curses, modern-day villains, and an intriguing woman lead archeologist Valerie Foret on the adventure of her life. (1-933110-48-1)

Battle for Tristaine by Cate Culpepper. While Brenna struggles to find her place in the clan, Tristaine is threatened with destruction. Second in the Tristaine series. (1-933110-49-X)

The Traitor and the Chalice by Jane Fletcher. Tevi and Jemeryl risk all in the race to uncover a traitor. The Lyremouth Chronicles Book Two. (1-933110-43-0)

Promising Hearts by Radclyffe. Dr. Vance Phelps arrives in New Hope, Montana, with no hope of happiness—until she meets Mae. (1-933110-44-9)

Carly's Sound by Ali Vali. Poppy Valente and Julia Johnson form a bond of friendship that becomes something far more. A poignant romance about love and renewal. (1-933110-45-7)

Unexpected Sparks by Gina L. Dartt. Kate Shannon's attraction to much younger Nikki Harris is complication enough without a fatal fire that Kate can't ignore. (1-933110-46-5)

Whitewater Rendezvous by Kim Baldwin. Two women on a wilderness kayak adventure discover that true love may be nothing at all like they imagined. (1-933110-38-4)

Erotic Interludes 3: Lessons in Love ed. by Radclyffe and Stacia Seaman. Sign on for a class in love…the best lesbian erotica writers take us to "school." (1-9331100-39-2)

Punk Like Me by JD Glass. Twenty-one-year-old Nina has a way with the girls, and she doesn't always play by the rules. (1-933110-40-6)

Coffee Sonata by Gun Brooke. Four women whose lives unexpectedly intersect in a small town by the sea share one thing in common—they all have secrets. (1-933110-41-4)

The Clinic: Tristaine Book One by Cate Culpepper. Brenna, a prison medic, finds herself drawn to Jesstin, a warrior reputed to be descended from ancient Amazons. (1-933110-42-2)

Forever Found by JLee Meyer. Can time, tragedy, and shattered trust destroy a love that seemed destined? Chance reunites childhood friends separated by tragedy. (1-933110-37-6)

Sword of the Guardian by Merry Shannon. Princess Shasta's bold new bodyguard has a secret that could change both of their lives. *He* is actually a *she*. (1-933110-36-8)

Wild Abandon by Ronica Black. Dr. Chandler Brogan and Officer Sarah Monroe are drawn together by their common obsessions—sex, speed, and danger. (1-933110-35-X)

Turn Back Time by Radclyffe. Pearce Rifkin and Wynter Thompson have nothing in common but a shared passion for surgery—and unexpected attraction. (1-933110-34-1)

Chance by Grace Lennox. A sexy, funny, touching story of two women who, in finding themselves, also find one another. (1-933110-31-7)

The Exile and the Sorcerer by Jane Fletcher. First in the Lyremouth Chronicles. Tevi and a shy young sorcerer face monsters, magic, and the challenge of loving. (1-933110-32-5)

A Matter of Trust by Radclyffe. When what should be just business turns into much more, two women struggle to trust the unexpected. (1-933110-33-3)

Sweet Creek by Lee Lynch. A celebration of the enduring nature of love, friendship, and community in the heart-warming lesbian community of Waterfall Falls. (1-933110-29-5)

The Devil Inside by Ali Vali. The head of a New Orleans crime organization falls for a woman who turns her world upside down. (1-933110-30-9)

Grave Silence by Rose Beecham. Detective Jude Devine's investigation of ritual murders is complicated by her torrid affair with pathologist Dr. Mercy Westmoreland. (1-933110-25-2)

Honor Reclaimed by Radclyffe. Secret Service Agent Cameron Roberts and Blair Powell close ranks to find the would-be assassins who nearly claimed Blair's life. (1-933110-18-X)

Honor Bound by Radclyffe. Secret Service Agent Cameron Roberts and Blair Powell face political intrigue, a clandestine threat to Blair's safety, and the seemingly irreconcilable differences that force them ever farther apart. (1-933110-20-1)

Innocent Hearts by Radclyffe. In a wild and unforgiving land, two women learn about love, passion, and the wonders of the heart. (1-933110-21-X)

The Temple at Landfall by Jane Fletcher. An imprinter, one of Celaeno's most revered servants of the Goddess, is also a prisoner to the faith—until a Ranger frees her by claiming her heart. The Celaeno series. (1-933110-27-9)

Protector of the Realm, Supreme Constellations Book One by Gun Brooke. A space adventure filled with suspense and a daring intergalactic romance. (1-933110-26-0)

Force of Nature by Kim Baldwin. From tornados to forest fires, the forces of nature conspire to bring Gable McCoy and Erin Richards close to danger, and closer to each other. (1-933110-23-6)

In Too Deep by Ronica Black. Undercover homicide cop Erin McKenzie tracks a femme fatale who just might be a real killer…with love and danger hot on her heels. (1-933110-17-1)

Stolen Moments: Erotic Interludes 2 by Stacia Seaman and Radclyffe, eds. Love on the run, in the office, in the shadows…Fast, furious, and almost too hot to handle. (1-933110-16-3)

Course of Action by Gun Brooke. Actress Carolyn Black desperately wants the starring role in an upcoming film produced by Annelie Peterson. Just how far will she go for the dream part of a lifetime? (1-933110-22-8)

Rangers at Roadsend by Jane Fletcher. Sergeant Chip Coppelli has learned to spot trouble coming, and that is exactly what she sees in her new recruit, Katryn Nagata. The Celaeno series. (1-933110-28-7)

Justice Served by Radclyffe. Lieutenant Rebecca Frye and her lover, Dr. Catherine Rawlings, embark on a deadly game of hide-and-seek with an underworld kingpin who traffics in human souls. (1-933110-15-5)

Distant Shores, Silent Thunder by Radclyffe. Dr. Tory King—along with the women who love her—is forced to examine the boundaries of love, friendship, and the ties that transcend time. (1-933110-08-2)

Hunter's Pursuit by Kim Baldwin. A raging blizzard, a mountain hideaway, and a killer-for-hire set a scene for disaster—or desire—when Katarzyna Demetrious rescues a beautiful stranger. (1-933110-09-0)

The Walls of Westernfort by Jane Fletcher. All Temple Guard Natasha Ionadis wants is to serve the Goddess—until she falls in love with one of the rebels she is sworn to destroy. The Celaeno series. (1-933110-24-4)

Change Of Pace: *Erotic Interludes* by Radclyffe. Twenty-five hot-wired encounters guaranteed to spark more than just your imagination. Erotica as you've always dreamed of it. (1-933110-07-4)

Honor Guards by Radclyffe. In a wild flight for their lives, the president's daughter and those who are sworn to protect her wage a desperate struggle for survival. (1-933110-01-5)

Fated Love by Radclyffe. Amidst the chaos and drama of a busy emergency room, two women must contend not only with the fragile nature of life, but also with the irresistible forces of fate. (1-933110-05-8)

Justice in the Shadows by Radclyffe. In a shadow world of secrets and lies, Detective Sergeant Rebecca Frye and her lover, Dr. Catherine Rawlings, join forces in the elusive search for justice. (1-933110-03-1)

shadowland by Radclyffe. In a world on the far edge of desire, two women are drawn together by power, passion, and dark pleasures. An erotic romance. (1-933110-11-2)

Love's Masquerade by Radclyffe. Plunged into the indistinguishable realms of fiction, fantasy, and hidden desires, Auden Frost is forced to question all she believes about the nature of love. (1-933110-14-7)

Love & Honor by Radclyffe. The president's daughter and her lover are faced with difficult choices as they battle a tangled web of Washington intrigue for...love and honor. (1-933110-10-4)

Beyond the Breakwater by Radclyffe. One Provincetown summer, three women learn the true meaning of love, friendship, and family. (1-933110-06-6)

Tomorrow's Promise by Radclyffe. One timeless summer, two very different women discover the power of passion to heal and the promise of hope that only love can bestow. (1-933110-12-0)

Love's Tender Warriors by Radclyffe. Two women who have accepted loneliness as a way of life learn that love is worth fighting for and a battle they cannot afford to lose. (1-933110-02-3)

Love's Melody Lost by Radclyffe. A secretive artist with a haunted past and a young woman escaping a life that has proved to be a lie find their destinies entwined. (1-933110-00-7)

Safe Harbor by Radclyffe. A mysterious newcomer, a reclusive doctor, and a troubled gay teenager learn about love, friendship, and trust during one tumultuous summer in Provincetown. (1-933110-13-9)

Above All, Honor by Radclyffe. Secret Service Agent Cameron Roberts fights her desire for the one woman she can't have—Blair Powell, the daughter of the president of the United States. (1-933110-04-X)